**Praise for
ANNE O'BRIEN**

'O'Brien cleverly intertwines the personal and political
in this enjoyable, gripping tale'
The Times

'An enthralling story of strong women'
Clare Marchant

'One of the best writers around… she outdoes even
Philippa Gregory'
The Sun

'The characters are larger than life… and the author
a compulsive storyteller'
Sunday Express

'A beautifully researched novel told with understanding,
subtlety and a deft touch'
Joanna Courtney

'O'Brien's page-turner vividly brings to life the restriction of
women, and the compassion and strength of this
real-life figure from medieval times'
Woman

'A gripping historical drama'
Bella

'Anne O'Brien gets right inside the heads of her characters!'
Joanna Hickson

Anne O'Brien is a *Sunday Times* bestselling author and has sold close to a million copies of her books globally. Anne gained a BA Honours degree in History at Manchester University and a Master's in Education at Hull, living in East Yorkshire for many years as a teacher of history. Today, she lives with her husband in an eighteenth-century timber-framed cottage in the depths of the Welsh Marches in Herefordshire. Her novels are meticulously researched, spellbinding in their retelling and frequently feature a woman teetering on a knife edge at a pivotal point in our nation's history. *A Court of Betrayal* is her fifteenth novel.

ANNE O'BRIEN

A COURT of BETRAYAL

ORION

First published in Great Britain in 2024 by Orion Fiction,
an imprint of The Orion Publishing Group Ltd.,
Carmelite House, 50 Victoria Embankment
London EC4Y 0DZ

An Hachette UK Company

1 3 5 7 9 10 8 6 4 2

A CIP catalogue record for this book is
available from the British Library.

ISBN (Hardback) 978 1398711198
ISBN (Trade Paperback) 978 1398711204
ISBN (eBook) 978 1398711228

Typeset at The Spartan Press Ltd,
Lymington, Hants

Printed and bound in Great Britain by Clays Ltd,
Elcograf S.p.A.

www.orionbooks.co.uk

To George, as always, with my love.
And with my thanks and appreciation for his endurance,
for the hours listening to me talk about the Mortimers,
and the miles spent walking in Mortimer country and
climbing the walls of Mortimer castles. He now enjoys
them almost as much as I do.

'...the King of Folly...'

Sir Geoffrey Mortimer's assessment of his father
Earl Mortimer September 1329

The
Lusignan Family,
Counts *of* La Marche
and the de Genevilles

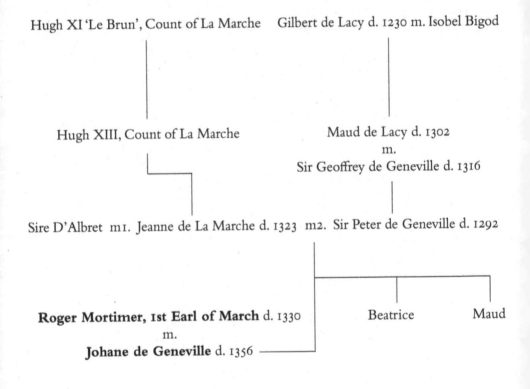

Hugh XI 'Le Brun', Count of La Marche   Gilbert de Lacy d. 1230 m. Isobel Bigod

Hugh XIII, Count of La Marche   Maud de Lacy d. 1302
m.
Sir Geoffrey de Geneville d. 1316

Sire D'Albret m1. Jeanne de La Marche d. 1323 m2. Sir Peter de Geneville d. 1292

Roger Mortimer, 1st Earl of March d. 1330   Beatrice   Maud
m.
Johane de Geneville d. 1356

The

 Family of Roger Mortimer
1st Earl *of* March

Roger, Lord Mortimer d. 1282
m.
Maud de Braose

Edmund Mortimer d. 1304
m.
Margaret de Fiennes

Roger, Lord Mortimer of Chirk
d. 1326

Roger Mortimer 1st Earl of March m. Johane de Geneville
1287–1330   1286–1356

Edmund Mortimer d. 1331
m.
Elizabeth de Badlesmere

*Other children of
Roger and Johane
de Geneville*

Margaret
Roger
Maud
Geoffrey
John
Joan
Isabella
Catherine
Agnes
Beatrice
Blanche

Roger Mortimer d. 1360, 2nd Earl of March
m.
Philippa de Montacute

Edmund Mortimer d. 1381 3rd Earl of March
m.
Philippa of Clarence

Prologue

The Castle of Trim in Ireland, 1299

I shivered. It might have been the dank cold as I stood at the foot of the dais in the cavern of the Great Hall of my grand-father's castle. Instead it was an unpleasant mingling of fear and apprehension. I was thirteen years old, on the cusp of maturity, and I had been summoned. Beside me stood my two younger sisters: Beatrice, a year younger than I, Maud still a child of eight.

'I have been considering the future of the de Geneville family,' announced my grandfather, slapping one jewelled hand against the documents he held in the other. Geoffrey de Geneville, now bowed with age but still thickset, bristling with authority, his hair as grey as a badger pelt, looked beneath his brows at me. 'It is my desire that you, Johane, will wed the heir of one of the English Marcher lords.'

Since Geoffrey de Geneville, Baron de Geneville, Justiciar of Ireland and dominant landowner in the Welsh Marches, decreed that it would be so, there was no doubt in my mind that it would happen. It was my grandfather who ruled my life and my fate.

'Marriage?' my mother, Lady Jeanne de Geneville, queried.

She too had been ordered to hear the pronouncement. 'I did not know. She is still very young…'

'Why should you know?' my grandfather said as if she were a fool to ask. His word was law. Our father, his son, Piers de Geneville, was long dead.

'When will I wed this Marcher heir, my lord?' I asked my grandfather.

'When the negotiations are complete.'

'Will I meet with him?'

'When the financial contracts have been signed.'

'What will…?'

My grandfather cast the documents onto the rough board at his side. 'God's Blood, girl. Do you have any more questions?'

I did not dare.

'What of me, Grandfather?' Beatrice risked his wrath. 'When will I marry?'

His eye slid to the abandoned sheaf of parchments.

'You will not wed. Nor you, Maud. You will both take the veil.'

Silence cut through the air, sharp as my grandfather's battle-sword, harsh as his voice.

'No, my lord. Surely not…' Our mother sounded as horrified as I felt.

'I'll hear no argument.'

'But it is a cruel fate for such young girls.'

Geoffrey de Geneville's eyes blazed with long-suppressed fury, some days, as today, not suppressed at all.

'If you had carried a son, a de Geneville heir, we would not now be in this predicament.'

If the silence was heavy before, now it could be tasted, bitter as unripe fruit on the tongue. I was aware that my mother's fingers had curled into the cloth of her skirts as she wilted under

2

such an attack. I presumed it was not for the first time. The accusation had the air of long usage.

'You will inform your daughters of the need for this,' my grandfather commanded, 'and of their need for obedience. It will be done.'

Scooping up the documents, he marched from the room, leaving behind a chasm of shock. I held out my hand to Beatrice but she knocked it aside and ran to the stairs towards the private chambers. Maud, although not understanding the full weight of this declaration, began to weep in loud ugly sobbing until my mother drew her towards a stone window seat.

I could find nothing pertinent to say. My mother, Jeanne de Lusignan, much sought after as a bride, had given birth only to girls, not one son to inherit the de Geneville name and lands from our father. Thus the man who wed each one of us, the de Geneville daughters, would expect to take a share of the vast de Geneville estates, even a third each. Our grandfather was single-minded in his determination to pass the estates in their entirety, in England and Wales and Ireland, as well as de Lusignan lands in France, into the hands of one man who could protect them.

Oh, I understood the politics of this decision. He chose what he considered to be an obvious solution. Send my sisters as Brides of Christ, unwed and childless for all time, and settle the whole inheritance on my shoulders, offering me as a bride to a powerful family. My sisters would pay the price for my good fortune, incarcerated until the day of their death. My gain had been my sisters' appalling loss.

My mother was speaking.

'You will have an assured future as an influential wife, Johane. You should thank the Blessed Virgin for her grace in this decision.'

But at what expense? I sat on the floor at my mother's feet

and held Maud's hand, weighing my emotions in the scales. On the one side a deep regret and sorrow for my sisters, on the other a tingle of bright expectancy. Which one weighed the heavier, I could not rightly say. I had dared to ask one more question before the door had closed on the back of my grandfather.

'What is the name, sir, of this heir of a Marcher lord whom I will wed?'

Lord Geoffrey looked back over his shoulder, for once willing to pander to my inquisitiveness.

'His name is Roger Mortimer.'

As soon as I could escape I sought out Father Anselm, our priest.

'Do we know when Roger Mortimer was born, sir?' I enquired. Father Anselm was an old man, long in our service, bent and short-sighted with a voice that quavered when he sang the responses in the Mass. If Lord Geoffrey was negotiating a marriage, Father Anselm would know every detail of it.

'We do, child. We know the exact date. If I can find the document...'

He riffled through a pile of parchments taken from a cache in the wall; some new, some dog-eared. I sat on a stool at his side and waited. There was no hurry.

'Here we are.' His finger traced down the list of past Mortimers and their brides. 'The young Mortimer was born on the twenty-fifth day of April in the Year of Our Lord 1287. He is a year younger than you are. I knew that I had it somewhere...'

Father Anselm returned to re-arranging his manuscripts; I left him, but not to return to the solar. My mother being a collector of interesting books and manuscripts, I knew which one I would consult, thus I crossed the inner courtyard to the chamber high in the keep, where my grandfather conducted business. There I discovered the one book that I wanted by that most erudite of scholars Master Michael Scot. It was a book which contained the art of astrology. Sitting in my grandfather's chair with its carved back, shuffling in its wide seat, I simply turned the magical pages with some care.

Some would call this magic, even wizardry, and look askance. I smoothed my fingers over the pages with their bright, perhaps gaudy pictures, to enjoy the mystical depictions of the zodiacs. I loved the artistry, the flamboyant words beneath. Would my mother approve of my interest in what some might call sorcery? I had watched her turn these pages more than once, even though she was never slow in kneeling and offering prayers to the Blessed Virgin.

Now I sought the pages dealing with those born under every heavenly constellation. The one I wanted was Taurus, the masterful bull, dominating the lives of those born in the latter days of April. What would Master Scot have to say about such a man, about Roger Mortimer, who would be my husband? Slowly I read through the words.

Such a man will be a reliable friend, a devoted husband. Once gained, his loyalties are fixed and permanent.

It pleased me. So far so good.

Beware though. Such a man can be stubborn and possessive, an uncompromising adversary once his enmity is gained. He has an arrogance and an ambition to be a man of power. Nothing will stand in his way.

That was good to know too. There was much to think about here.

I stood to return the book to the coffer where it was kept safe from dust and mice, then sat again, turning to the page with the Great Horned Buck. Capricorn. My own sign. I knew the description here by heart.

5

The man under the star of Capricorn is a master of discipline and self-restraint, quick to impose his will on others and efficient in the doing of it. But beware: he can be driven to anger, unforgiving when an enemy is made. An uncomfortable man to live with.

Which I thought to be a fairly accurate summing up of me, for it could apply to a woman as well as to a man. My mother said I had the making of a managing female.

I replaced the book in its safe home, considering this image of a man directed by the stars of Taurus. An interesting meld of conflicting characteristics. Devoted but possessive. Reliable, but uncompromising when alienated. Would this guarantee a happy marriage? It spoke of much conflict to me and yet his loyalty could be strong. I must ensure that I never became his enemy, but then, why would I? I would be his wife. I laughed a little, and with a flutter of excitement. Roger Mortimer would also have much to learn about me.

I returned to Father Anselm's chamber to discover more information that Master Michael Scot could not tell me.

'There is a question I would ask, Father. Two questions in fact.'

'Then ask them, my daughter.'

'Is this young man worthy of me?'

'Indubitably. Your grandfather would not otherwise have chosen him. He will be a powerful Marcher lord in the fullness of time.'

I nodded, accepting this judgement. 'My second question. Is this Roger Mortimer good to look upon? Is he handsome?'

Father Anselm smiled with benign understanding.

'You need have no fears on that matter, my daughter. It is said that he is comely enough to take any maiden's eye.'

6

Chapter One

Pembridge in the Welsh Marches, September 1301

'Is this de Geneville priest ever going to show his face?'

An opinion expressed, not quite sotto voce, by Roger Mortimer at my right-hand side, standing as we were at the church door as was the custom. I glanced across and replied.

'Father Anselm is very old.'

'Then perhaps he has fallen dead in the nave. At this rate we will not be wed before dusk. We should have brought our own Mortimer priest from Wigmore.'

Was the man born under the influence of Taurus the Bull so arrogant? Yes, he was. I had been warned.

'Perhaps you should, if you are incapable of waiting for another few moments. We will be wed soon enough.'

'And this church is very small and plain,' he commented as if on a passing thought. 'Neither carving nor grandeur. This would have been better done in the cathedral in Hereford.'

'Then you can rebuild this small, plain church into one with both carving and grandeur, when it becomes yours,' I replied briskly.

'Perhaps I will.'

The little indented lines at the corner of his mouth spoke of a severe bout of conceit and impatience, worthy of my grandfather. I frowned at him, and although he raised one shoulder in a shrug, he chose not to reply.

As for me, I was wearing my bride-clothes with much enjoyment from the slide of finest French silk, dyed a celestial blue worthy of the Virgin herself. Above my head there was a clamour of rooks in the stand of elms in the churchyard. Those of a nervous disposition, and there might be many in this wind-blown congregation, open to the elements as we were, might say that such raucous cawing could be as much an ill omen as a sign of good fortune. It was early morning on the eve of the feast of Matthew the Apostle, the twentieth day of September. A day chosen for the blessings that St Matthew would bestow on us: health, wealth and fecundity. But then any saint would do to ensure the successful accomplishing of this union.

Although it was barely past the heat of summer, the day was cool, so that I shuddered beneath the layers of tunic and over-tunic, but more from unease than from the blustery wind that threatened to dislodge the pins holding my simple veil in place, although every hearty gust of wind caused it to flap as if it were a bird about to take flight.

This event in my young life would open a window into the unknown, where the outlook was as shadowy as a misty day on the Welsh hills over into the west. All mists and clouds had been blown away today but still I could not see the future. Perhaps it was as well. I inhaled slowly. De Genevilles did not succumb to baseless fears. The sun shone brightly, making the jewels on my bodice sparkle, a brooch set with cabochon rubies, given to me by my grandfather to mark the day.

Roger Mortimer, unconcerned with my jewels, sighed and shuffled from one foot to the other.

I considered, as we still awaited the priest, if the frowning individual at my side was as uncertain of the future as I? It did not appear so. He might be a year younger than I but he was no callow youth. There was no element of clumsy immaturity about him. We were much of a height although I thought he had not yet grown into his full strength. When not shuffling, he was all confidence, his feet planted on the paving, shoulders square, hands clasped around his belt. Had we met before? No, not even when the marriage contract was signed two years ago. I swallowed against a breath of trepidation after my mother's warning as she brushed out my hair. I was not ignorant of what passed between man and wife, for my mother had informed me in bleak terms, but this was yet another unknown. Would my mother's experience of a cool marriage, hedged about with duty and acceptance and childbearing, be mine? All I could say was that my mother had not seemed to regret her widowhood and the passing of my father from this life.

I would like some passion, some love, some adoration, from this marriage, I thought with a youthful dismissal of reality, as we continued to wait for the ceremony to begin. I had read the new stories coming out of Brittany, of Tristram and Iseult, the tragic tale of star-crossed lovers who had been parted for ever, to the grief of both. I would hope that this match with Roger Mortimer might bring me lasting contentment, even joy.

'You must not even consider it,' my mother had warned. 'The Mortimers want you for your inheritance. There is no emotion in the ownership of land, unless it be greed and ambition.'

It was not encouraging, and so far all the heir had done was annoy me with his high-handed censure. I slid another glance at him. What did he make of me? He did not even look in my direction. Attractive features would not matter to him, since my dowry was so weighty. I was Baroness de Geneville in my own right which would offset the most ugly of brides.

Then here was Father Anselm, smoothing his vestments as if they had been hastily donned, straightening his stole. He was about to enjoy the importance of this occasion, bowing his head to my grandfather who was clearly annoyed at the delay.

'At last! My feet are frozen,' my betrothed observed. 'May St Matthew cast his blessings on us all. Let us get on with it.'

Oblivious to such a discourteous command, Father Anselm took charge and there, at the church door, with the continuing rook chorus, we made our vows before the priest and before God. My betrothed's voice was strong as he made his claim on me.

'I, Roger, take thee, Johane, for my wedded wife, to have and to hold, from this day forward...'

I duly repeated the plighting of my troth. When instructed, Roger clasped my hand in his, so that the priest might wrap his stole around them into a neat parcel, while he pronounced the sacred words of commitment.

'*Ego conjungo vos in matrimonium.*'

It was done. Loyalty and obedience and marital duty was to be my lot. The priest handed to me my gift of gold from my husband, in the form of the plain ring which was pushed onto my finger. To Roger was handed the far more costly gift of my dowry, all packaged up in a charter, heavy with de Geneville seals, as well as a small leather bag of coin, the purse of my own stitching with a de Geneville coat of arms, as a promise of future wealth.

Behind us the Mortimer parents and my mother nodded in benign agreement. Of course Sir Edmund de Mortimer would not be displeased with this addition of a daughter-in-law to his family. The previous year Sir Edmund had turned to my grandfather for a substantial loan to help maintain his castles, but my grandfather did not lend money without assurance that he would gain a return, and had driven a hard bargain. My person had been the legal bond in that contract. I knew this and I knew my worth to both families.

My husband and I shared a brisk marital kiss to each cheek, barely a brush of cold lips, after which we all processed into the church, to stand before the altar in the dark interior, bound by solid Norman pillars, to hear Mass.

'My lady.' My husband bowed to me and held out his hand.

'My lord.' I curtsied and placed my hand in his, to a rustle of amusement.

'At least no one turned up to stop our wedding.'

His impatience had been replaced by a rough good humour.

'Would they dare?' I observed. 'There are enough armed men here to mount an invasion of Wales.'

Roger Mortimer led me out of the church to traditional good wishes, to where our marriage feast was to be held in our castle, just beyond the church. The feet of the throng clattered behind us across the drawbridge which had once been mine but now belonged to Roger Mortimer.

He did not look overly admiring of his new property. Although I had never visited Wigmore Castle, I imagined that there was no comparison, for this was little more than a moated manor house, the accommodations meagre. The main hall impressed well enough, with steps along the far wall to give access to my solar and a chapel, but all the accommodations stood separately to the north, with the stables on the south side. The ground was muddy from a recent shower of rain, so much so that I lifted my trailing skirts and walked on my gilded-leather toes. My shoes were new and I would have a care for them. Inside at least the hall had been festooned with de Geneville banners, the tables set out beneath the heraldic lions awarding an air of festivity.

'It does not impress me,' my new husband stated as we stepped into the hall.

'It was once even less impressive,' I replied, eyeing the rough wood and plaster of the walls and screens where new building had taken place in this little manor that was part of my dowry. 'You should be thankful. Six months ago we would have had to sleep with our guests in the hall. A new bedchamber has been constructed for us.'

'Then there is much to be thankful for,' he said.

And for the first time he smiled at me.

We took our seats at the head of the table and so it began.

The celebration continued all day, as such events were like to do, since many of our well-wishers, the great and the good of English and Welsh nobility, had travelled some distance to witness such a crucial marriage to the balance of power in the area, and would not depart until the following morning. We were crammed from wall to wall while their entourages were forced to make shift in the stables and kitchen accommodations. What would I recall of it later? A motley group of minstrels who sang and played, frequently out of tune. An abundance of roast meats, heavy in thick sauce, with fine bread to mop up the juices. The marriage cup, chased around its rim with a wreath of flowers, that my husband gave first to me with grave courtesy.

We danced, with some enthusiasm, so that I could see the extravagance of his shoes that challenged mine in the length of their toes and gilding of the leather over the instep. Oh, he was dressed as a prince even though he would be a mere Marcher lord, yet Marcher lords were powerful enough, and the quality of his fine woollen tunic in deep russet with its heavy fur around the neck could not be doubted. His elegantly hanging over-sleeves were lined with what looked to me like sable. At least someone had taught him to dance. And to join in the banter as the wine flowed, but he did not drink over-much. His eyes remained watchful, aware, taking in the number and quality of our guests.

Dusk gradually became dark, by which time all were suffused with food and wine, and I, weary of it all, was looking to my mother for permission to withdraw, when a shout went up to bring us out into the courtyard in time to see a heavenly body shooting high across the heavens, like a fiery stone loosed from a siege engine. We stood, Roger and I, and watched as its path vanished, its brilliant light faded, and all was once again tranquil, the stars becoming obliterated in cloud.

'What do you suppose it means?' I asked, more for something to say.

'Good fortune,' he replied promptly.

'Or disaster. Sometimes, my grandfather says, such stars denote a battle or a pestilence.'

He shook his head. 'I see only glory for myself in a comet passing over my head on my marriage-day.'

'Only for you?'

I nudged him with a new intimacy, a sudden confidence brought on by more than one cup of de Geneville wine, which made my heart race.

'We will make it good fortune for us.' He drew my hand through his arm and leaned to whisper. 'We will give the Mortimer family a handful of strong heirs for the future.'

'I should remind you,' I whispered back, mildly annoyed at his absolute certainty. 'My mother had little success. She never bore a son. Not with her first husband, nor with her second, my father.' I looked across to where she was conversing with Roger's mother. 'Not one son. Only daughters. My family does not have a good record of strong heirs.'

Roger Mortimer was unperturbed.

'We will do better. I promise you.'

Which was a promise for the immediate future and made my heart race even faster.

Since we were of an age considered to be appropriate for marriage, it had been decided that we would live as man and wife from the first day of our exchange of vows. What point in waiting before consummation? Without too much ceremony, when the feast was nothing but crumbs and the minstrels, dry-throated, retired to recover with copious amounts of ale, we were dispatched to our chamber and left to further our acquaintance once the bed had been blessed by the priest, our outer garments removed, and all sprinkled indiscriminately with holy water.

Still clad in our linen undergarments we sat on either side of the bed, its coverlet embroidered with the de Geneville lion, matching the drapes at the bed-head, and looked at each other, all our finery laid aside in a heap of silk and wool and fur. It was like casting aside my old life for a new one. The silence grew. The candle-shadows flickered over us in the draughts from the window. Momentarily they gave Roger Mortimer a saturnine look.

'What are you doing?' he asked as I allowed my gaze to move over his face, taking in his shoulders and strong arms, his hands loosely linked.

'Looking at you.'

The corners of his mouth curved. 'What do you see?'

'The priest told me that you were good to look at.'

Now he grinned. 'And am I so?'

'Yes.'

His hair was dark and thick but the density was lighted by streaks of old bronze, and it intrigued me that his eyes were of a similar mix of colour. His fair skin was flushed across his high cheekbones; his nose was straight and undoubtedly masterful. His lean face and chin spoke of a wilfulness. As for his hands, they were broad-palmed, long-fingered. I imagined they would manage a rein and a sword admirably. I liked the manner in which his hair curled across his forehead, but then he pushed it back with an impatient gesture which I would soon learn was habitual with him.

'What of me?' I asked, hoping for compliments.

'I prefer fair women.'

I bridled. My hair was the colour of my grandfather's new bay stallion; rich and glossy perhaps, but fair it was not.

'I like blue eyes in a woman.'

Mine were grey-brown.

'And I like courtesy in a man!'

He laughed. 'I like you very well on such short acquaintance.'

'My two sisters are thought to be more comely than I,' I admitted. 'But I have the inheritance. That is the allure.'

'A magnificent allure,' he agreed. 'And I am not discourteous. You are as tall as I, and that attracts me. I like the way your brows are straight, as if you might readily frown, but you will smile anyway to please me.'

Which indeed made me smile. Silence fell again, but it was a more companionable one.

'Well?' I asked, when he showed no sign of breaking it.

'I have a gift for you,' Roger Mortimer said.

'You have given me this.' I held up my hand on which the simple gold circle shone in the candlelight.

'Not that, although it was costly enough, made from Welsh gold. But that was simply necessary. My father had it made over in the Welsh hills, spiced with faerie magic, so they say, to keep a marriage true for all time. This is something you will enjoy. Your mother, Lady Jeanne, says that you will.' His eyes glinted with a minor conspiracy. 'I had my mother talk to your mother. This is the result.'

He had thought of me, beyond the necessity. He had asked my mother. It warmed my heart, my childish pleasure in gifts reborn in an instant.

'What is it? Where is it?'

'Here.'

Bounding off the bed he walked to the coffer where a package lay, bringing it back to present to me with a courteous bow. There was an innate swagger about him, even when wearing only braes.

'To my new wife, who will one day be Lady de Mortimer, to mark the day of our marriage.'

It was a book. A costly book, its leather cover glowing with gold embossing. Opening it at random I was more than admiring of the illuminations of the Court of King Arthur and his Knights. All the stories that I knew well were recounted there. I sighed over it in delight.

'It is the finest book I have ever owned.'

'Look at the first page.'

Opening it as directed I saw what he had written there.

The book of Johane de Mortimer. From her husband Roger Mortimer, on this day of their marriage.

The tales were written in French, probably sent from the home of his mother who was from the powerful de Fiennes family living in Picardy. It touched my heart, but I would not show it yet. I looked up at him beneath my lashes.

'And you can write.'

Spiky, angular, uneven, as if a pen were not his first weapon of choice, but still a firm, strong, confident hand.

'Of course I can write.' There was the hint of temper that I had seen in the church doorway. 'The Mortimers are not peasants.'

'I did not intend to besmirch your birth. The Marcher lords, so my grandfather says, prefer the sword to the pen.'

'I can wield both with equal dexterity. Although,' he admitted after a pause in which he garnered the truth, 'I prefer the sword. It tends to be more effective and quicker to get a result. I doubt I will ever be good at diplomacy and treaty-making. Unless at sword point.'

I laughed at the naivety, the sheer confidence. I thought that he would not always be naive.

'I have a gift for you,' I said, putting aside this most beautiful of books on my pillow.

He looked round at the sparse surfaces where it might be resting. 'It is here?'

'No.'

'Then where is it? Can I see it now?'

His enthusiasm was most endearing. Wrapping a chamber-robe around me to cover my shift, I opened the door, calling for a servant. A brief, low-voiced conversation ensued.

'Now we must wait.' I returned to sit beside him once again, during which we exchanged inconsequential comments, some scurrilous, on our guests. Then a scrabbling of claws at the door.

'Do you have large rats in this place? Before God, it is no palace, Johane.'

I refused to rise to the bait. My manor was lacking luxury but it was not more vermin-ridden than any other castle, I would swear.

'Open it,' I urged.

Leaping up again, he did so, to be almost swept off his feet by two young Irish wolfhounds, held hard on their collars by a page who released them and closed the door behind them. They promptly bounded around the chamber, sniffing in corners, searching for their quarry before coming to stand in the centre of the room as if unsure of what to do next. Then they sank before the fire and sighed at the warmth, as Roger squatted beside them, running his fingers through the dark grey pelt of each, soft without the coarse hair of adulthood. Their noses were still blunt, their jaws short, their ears small. When they grew they would have all the traits of high-bred dogs; the recognisable long noses, long jaws, ears flat to the head, their shoulders high, their legs long for fast running. One day they would reach his waist but now they rolled around his ankles as they snuffled at his hands.

He crowed with laughter.

'Magnificent!'

'My grandfather bred them. They are brought from Trim Castle in Ireland.'

'Do they have names?'

'They are for you to call. They have an illustrious ancestry.'

He thought, flinching as they gnawed on his fingers with their sharp teeth. 'Something Irish, I think.'

'And heroic.'

'They will be Cúchulainn and Lugh, of course. Ouch!' He rolled them over, rubbing their ears, enjoying their lively spirit when they resisted being pushed away. 'They will be good hunting dogs. God's Blood, they have teeth!'

'Perhaps we should send them back, or we'll have no rest. Call for Martin.'

He glanced up at me. 'I was not thinking of rest.'

Pushing himself to his feet, he opened the door and bellowed for the page who had brought them. The hounds were handed over; we could hear Martin pulling them down the stairs with much crude encouragement.

'How did you know that I enjoyed hunting?'

'Who does not in the Marches?'

He went to the bowl of scented water, washed his hands and face with unexpected fastidiousness where the hounds had licked him, applying the blanched length of linen effectively, then returned to me again, and took the book from the pillow, placing it on the floor beside the bed.

'Thank you,' he said.

'It was my pleasure to give you something that would give you pleasure.'

Capturing my hands, he kissed my fingers.

'We have other things to attend to, which may be equally pleasurable.'

'I have no experience of this,' I admitted, watching him douse the candles, moving with an unconscious ease.

'But I have.'

'And where did you acquire that?'

'Do you wish to know?'

I could well imagine dalliance in one Mortimer castle or another. 'No. I do not. But I, Roger Mortimer, am no kitchen wench, to be tumbled without grace.'

'And I would never treat you with such lack of consideration, Lady Johane.'

He bowed with elegant dignity in the shadows, full of humour, at odds with his unclothed state. I remembered again the traits of character of Taurus the Bull. What manner of man would he become? Would it make my life comfortable or balancing on the edge of danger or humiliation? His smile began to fade.

'What are you thinking now?' he asked.

'How important is loyalty to you?'

In an instant his expression became severe, as if it were an issue that had exercised his mind more than once. His lips pressed tightly, I thought that he might not answer, thinking it an impertinence for a new bride to ask. He did anyway.

'More than you can guess at. Loyalty will guide my life. Loyalty to my King. To my rank as a foremost Marcher lord. To my family.' His eyes captured and held mine. 'And to you, my wife. Today we exchanged binding oaths.'

A straight enough answer that touched my heart. As long as those loyalties never found the need to collide. Then any worries over conflicting allegiances vanished when he leaned across the space between us and touched my mouth with his, very gently.

'Have I told you that you have the sweetest lips to kiss?'

Which was romantic enough to startle me. 'From which poet did you learn that?'

'How unflattering!' He laughed. 'It is my own thought.'

'Then you can tell me now.' I frowned at him when he leaned to kiss me again. 'I do not know you.'

'Well, I do not know you either. We will know each other better tomorrow.'

And so we did. I was ignorant but willing to learn since Roger Mortimer had more knowledge of what was required in a marriage bed than did I. It was a breath-taking experience with little skill but much enthusiasm, rumpled bed-linen, and some laughter, after an initial screech of discomfort on my part.

'Do you think that you will quicken straightaway?' he asked after he had claimed his marital rights and now lay with his face buried in his pillow. 'My father and your grandfather are probably wagering on it even now.' He became serious, pushing himself up on his elbows and looking across at me. 'We will do better at this too.'

I stroked my hand down over his shoulder. It pleased me mightily, all my initial irritations with him having fled. I thought that we had done well enough for a first time. It was in my mind that we should try again, and soon. It was in his too.

Chapter Two

Above my head, secured by a hook and chain, a skull was hanging, old enough to have lost most of its flesh and hair but there was still a remnant clinging to the bone. It was a gruesome object. It seemed to me that one of the cheekbones had been shattered by a blow. The jawbone on one side hung loose.

'He died from some violence,' I observed, determined not to be unnerved.

'Indeed he did,' Roger admitted with relish. 'I thought your grandfather would have educated you in the Mortimer history in the Marches. Do you know who he is?'

'I claim all ignorance. I am sure you will tell me.'

We had ridden north from Pembridge to Wigmore, the Mortimer castle overlooking and thus guarding the route along the Marches, a formidable fortress to the south-west of Ludlow. It was a celebratory cavalcade as I remarked to Roger, who was riding beside me, the accompanying minstrels breaking into song with much laughter and ribaldry.

'I expect it is. They are all extortionately pleased to be escaping from Pembridge.'

I bridled. 'No one complained.'

'They would not, of course. It was a wedding and the ale was good.'

I huffed at such a rude comment and kicked my mare on to ride beside my mother. Roger overtook me, saluting both of us with sly grace. I did not see him again, except for his back and felt cap decorated on the brim with a rakish pheasant feather he had picked up on the way, until we arrived in Wigmore. Cúchullainn and Lugh bounded along beside him, disturbing birds which rose up with a clap of wings.

It was a steep ride beyond the church to attain the height, for the castle was sited on a long, narrow ridge, perfect for defence. It dominated the whole area, overlooking the low-lying ground and the old Roman road of Watling Street that crossed it. As well as its height it was protected by deep ditches and a series of strong walls. I looked up at them as we rode beneath the outer gateway.

My first impression of my new home: it was very much a fortress rather than a home for comfortable living. I assessed it as we rode through the outer bailey which housed stables and granaries and other buildings of general storage. Then beneath another gateway under the bulk of a vast gatehouse, we came within the curtain wall with towers to repel all comers. I had been raised to know the value of defence as well as attack and realised that this might not be as formidable as my own castle at Ludlow but was still a fortress of distinction. Once in the inner bailey I slid from my saddle, shaking out the russet-red skirts of my woollen over-tunic. Now I knew why Roger Mortimer had looked askance at my small de Geneville manor. My eye was, of course, taken by the great shell keep ahead of us. It did not promise warm accommodation within the massive structure of the round tower set on its motte. I must look to my garments before winter set in.

Roger handed his reins to a page and appeared at my side.
'Come with me.'

It was quite definitely a command.

'Where?'

'I have something to show you. You said that you did not know me. I will put that right now.'

'I know you better now than I did last week.'

I regarded him, open-eyed, waiting for his reaction. It was what I expected as he laughed, gripped my wrist and pulled me along at his side.

'If we don't hurry they'll find something for us to do or sign or witness. That's the problem of not yet being of age.'

I looked towards my mother who watched me with raised brows, but now I was wed, and as a wife I could make my own decisions. I followed him up the steps and through the arched doorway into the keep, which proved to be as dark and dank as I had expected, then on into a room opening off a spiral stair-case within its walls. It was a small room with narrow windows allowing little light. He lit a lamp and lifted it high so that the shadows leapt back as I stepped across the threshold. Was this an excess of lust to renew his acquaintance with my body, despite his lively efforts at dawn before we had broken our fast? Clearly it was not, for this was no bedchamber.

'What is this place?'

'The Treasury.'

He was silent, hitching a hip on a coffer beside the door, allowing me to look round in my own time. Old pieces of armour and weapons, left for cleaning or wrapped in stout linen. A linen surcoat emblazoned with the gold and azure strips of the Mortimer coat of arms. Coffers that might contain treasures of great value to the family or items that were no longer in use. We had such in our own dwellings. I ran my hand over an ageing suit of chain mail.

'They belonged to my ancestors,' Roger explained as I picked up an enclosed helm and held it high, until he took it from me and placed it on his own head so that his voice echoed strangely from within. 'I think that my father once wore this. It is Italian.'

I tilted my chin.

'It becomes you. I cannot of course see your face.'

With a hoot he slid from the coffer, scooped up another metal helm and dropped it on my own head. It was too large so that I must lift it to be able to look out through the eye slits.

'If there is a spider in here, now crawling down my neck, I will shriek,' I warned.

'Are you such a coward, to fear something so harmless?'

I faced him. 'Do we wage war against each other?' My voice was equally hollow, making me laugh.

'Not today. Tomorrow perhaps.' He removed my helm and his own.

'They are dusty,' I complained, attempting to brush away the cobwebs that had adhered to my veil.

'I have new ones, of course.'

'Do you keep all your family possessions here?' I asked.

'Not all. The important ones, the chronicles and grants and documents of ownership are stored at Wigmore Abbey where my ancestors are buried. We own the Abbey.'

There was the pride of possession.

'Is it close?'

'Just across the valley.' He took my cobwebby hand and led me to the window. 'Lean forward and look over there to the left, through the trees. You can just make out the arches and tower of the church. That is the Abbey.'

I could see the sandstone walls and roofs in the distance, of what would be a building of some significance.

'Will you take me there?'

'Tomorrow, perhaps.' He tucked my veil neatly between us, his expression quite serious as he followed my gaze. 'One day I will be buried there. So probably will you, and all our children in the fullness of time.'

I did not like to think so far ahead. Death was close to us all, but not yet.

'Thank you for showing me the Mortimer Treasury,' I said, on the whole not particularly willing to be impressed by ancient armour. Why had he been so urgent in bringing me here unless it was pure ownership, to boast that he had a Treasury? I did not think so. Roger was not finished with his visit. Lamp now once again in one hand, he led me to the opposite wall.

'This was what I wanted you to see, so that you would understand. Look up.'

I did so. Stepping back with surprise and not a little dismay. This was not what I had expected. Even so I tilted my chin and kept my gaze steady.

'And who is that? Is it a Mortimer?'

'By no means.'

And there it was, above my head. The skull with its scant fringe of decaying hair.

'It is not a custom we employ at my grandfather's castle at Trim. Or at Ludlow,' I said. 'You will not find our enemies keeping company with us as we break our fast.'

I saw his teeth glint in the shadows. 'Yet I imagine you have enough enemies in Ireland to decorate the whole of your Great Hall at Trim. This, my wife, is the head of Simon de Montfort.'

Whose name was of course known to me, and tales of his rebellion, but not that his head resided with me in this castle.

Simon de Montfort, Earl of Leicester, long dead now, had led the barons in war against the third King Henry, seizing authority in the land, until the barons resisted and de Montfort was killed at the Battle of Evesham. What de Montfort's head might be doing here I had no idea.

'And what are those?' I asked, stepping aside so that I might see more clearly since the shadows deepened beneath the roof arches. Attached to the chain was a wizened object.

Roger was watching me, to see my reaction. 'His balls.'

I wrinkled my nose. 'Why are they here? Why are they not buried with the rest of his body?'

'My grandfather, another Roger Mortimer, a famous fighter after whom I am named, fought in the battle at Evesham to safeguard our King Henry and our Prince who now rules as Edward the First. Lord Roger forced his men to march through the night to hold the bridge at Evesham with great bravery. In the battle de Montfort was pulled from his horse and his body hacked until he was dead for raising his sword against his King.' Roger relished the telling of it. 'His head and his balls were given to Lord Roger as a trophy for his victory. Lord Roger sent them here to be presented to his wife Lady Maud as a symbol of his courage in battle at the King's side. They have been here ever since, to mark our martial achievements and our loyalty to the Crown.'

I looked up at the sad memento.

'I can imagine Lady Maud's shock at such a gift arriving at her door. Would she not have preferred a more gracious rendering of her lord's prowess in battle?'

He shrugged his disinterest in what Lady Maud might have preferred. 'Perhaps she would. But she kept them and they have remained here.'

'Then I will have to live with them, I suppose.'

Roger was still afire with the family's glorious past, gripping an old, worn sword, applying the heavy weapon in the air with a cut and thrust. 'We have fought the Welsh. We have fought the English. We have remained loyal to the King. I will do likewise. It will be my honour, my glorious ancestry.' He swung round, dropping the sword with a clang on the cold hearth. 'Do you know what is written on my grandfather's tomb?'

'Of course I do not.'

'Then here it is, engraved on my heart, although he was dead before I was even born.' He stood, fists planted on his hips and declaimed with superb grandeur.

> *Here lies buried, glittering with praise,*
> *Roger the pure, Roger Mortimer the second,*
> *Called Lord of Wigmore by those who held him dear:*
> *While he lived all Wales feared his power,*
> *And given as a gift to him, all Wales remained his.*
> *It knew his campaigns, he subjected it to torment.*

He took a breath. 'I would hope to have a similar epitaph on my tomb to my glory and that of my family.'

'I am sure that you will.'

And in that moment I was certain of it. It would be his life's ambition to emulate the grandeur of his grandfather, a shining example to all future Mortimers. I wondered where I would fit into this Mortimer planning other than to produce the future Mortimers. Meanwhile Roger seized the sword once more, raising the cross of the hilt to his lips as if he made an oath as binding as the one he had made to me.

'You should understand that I am a soldier. Bound by loyalty and duty to the King. I told you that, but it is my ambition to fight as gloriously as one of King Arthur's knights. I will go where my King desires me to go. I will not always be here with you. I will seek glory on the battlefield and in the tourney. You should know that now. I would not wish you to be disappointed when my duty takes me elsewhere.'

It was a warning. A cold one that engaged my thoughts. I would live my life part widow, spending weeks and months alone, anxious that his lifeless body would be brought home across the crupper of his horse, from some distant battlefield or tournament.

'I admire your dedication,' was all I chose to say.

After a lively sortie around the room, a thrust of his sword at the suit of chain mail in one corner, a hacking at the dim figures in the old tapestries against the far wall as if they were a mortal enemy, he abandoned the sword once more with a self-deprecating grimace.

'Now that you have seen our greatest treasure, let me show you your new home.'

He bowed and kissed my hands as if I were a great lady and he my chivalrous knight; my new husband had enough schemes for the future for both of us. Whether I would be satisfied in being abandoned at the beck and call of the King or by the recalcitrance of the turbulent Welsh, I was unsure, but this was the life marked out for me as the future Lady Mortimer.

'I thought I should warn you,' he said as we walked along the wall-walk so that he could point out the Wigmore lands to the north and west where the castle was surrounded by deer parks, and nearby, below us, were fish ponds and a dovecot; over to the brow of the hill a rabbit warren to provide sources of fresh meat. 'These are all Mortimer lands.' He gestured widely with a sweep of his arm. 'These and so much more. One day they will be mine. I will let no man take them from me. If it demands war to keep them, then so be it.' The curve of his lip was more snarl than smile. He had taken hold of my hands, gripping them posses-sively, palm to palm within his own, which caused a light shiver to race along my skin, a delight in such a possession. At that moment I cared nothing for the Mortimer inheritance, but I did for the Mortimer heir. But did he experience the same awareness of me? Of course he did not. His thoughts were centred on his inheritance and his future greatness. I was merely a means to an end, to bring him more land and the hope of an heir.

'There. I have warned you of the worst of me,' he said. 'I am a man of ambition.'

'As if I did not know,' I responded, unable to keep the sharp-ness from my tongue, at his lack of perception. 'If the King calls, you will leave me forthwith. If Mortimer land comes under attack, you will instantly ride out to secure it. I will exist, as I am sure do many wives, with infrequent couriers at best, and no news at all at worst, until the arrival of your lifeless body, to be dropped at my door.'

Of course he refused to leap to the bait, leaning instead to-wards the distant mass of the Abbey, until we were interrupted by Lord Mortimer striding along the wall-walk towards us. Lord Edmund, although slight and in no manner impressive in height, would be recognised anywhere as a Mortimer with the same severe features and dark hair as inherited by his son, and the same confidence and pride as he aimed a paternal punch at Roger's shoulder.

'Here you are. Don't let him burden you with family history, Johane.'

'He does not. Besides, I need to know. Am I not a Mortimer now?'

'So you are. And now you have made the acquaintance of our enemy from the past – don't tell me that Roger has not introduced you to our resident skull – you must come and be made truly welcome in your new home.'

I merely smiled as I wondered what Roger might say if I arranged for a seemly burial for this grizzly memento. But not today. I had a position to make for myself in this household. I frowned a little. There was also a journey I must make where I was not sure of my welcome at the end of it.

But not yet. Not quite yet. First I would enjoy my new status as a Mortimer bride. First I would become more closely acquainted with my new husband. Tomorrow I might grasp the disagreeable nettle that had nothing to do with a skull.

Chapter Three

Aconbury Priory in the Welsh Marches, October 1302

It took me a year to make that journey, and in the end guilt drove me to it. Would my sisters be overjoyed to see me? I did not think that they would, and who could blame them. But to refuse this visit would heap even more remorse upon my head.

I had put it off as long as I could. It was now late autumn, a twelve-month since my marriage, with threat of winter cold when I rode through the rolling countryside, seated decorously pillion behind Ralph, one of Roger's squires, borrowed for the occasion. It was still early in my pregnancy, so no danger in my riding any distance and I had refused the offer of a litter. Because I was protected by a Mortimer escort, the blue and gold heraldic symbols clear for all to see, I felt in no danger. The place where I was going had been established by a de Lacy ancestress of my own almost a hundred years ago. My de Geneville family had a reputation and a loyalty in this part of the Marches, as well as a hard hand against any who might challenge them. So of course did the Mortimers.

'How far now?' I asked, for I had not travelled this way before. It was intended that my mother accompany me, but suffering from a bout of marsh fever she had taken to her bed and I was alone. I had the sense that she was not sorry to step back from this visit.

'Not far, my lady.'

I shuffled a little on my padded cushion, anticipating our arrival, relieved when the light picked out the edges of the red sandstone buildings of Aconbury Priory in the valley. My pregnancy might still be new, but the growing child had a tendency to make me aware of bodily discomforts. My destination would have the promise of a latrine for my use and a welcome from the black-clad Augustinian nuns. Since we were expected, and the Mortimer and de Geneville banners recognisable to all, the gates were instantly opened, allowing me to ride into the courtyard where visitors were permitted to lodge in the gatehouse. Aided by my solicitous squire I dismounted and looked around. I might never have been here before but it was much as I had expected. It would not be my choice to live in such a place. I wondered what my sisters thought of their dwelling, not that they had had any choice in the matter. The regret within my heart deepened a notch or two.

A nun approached and, hands hidden in her sleeves, bowed her head, as I did to her to acknowledge her decision to withdraw from the world, a step that I could never willingly take. For a moment I considered how I could possibly exist for the whole span of my life behind enclosing walls and locked doors. Never to step outside, never to meet visitors and share their experiences. Some found contentment, or a life-calling, but I would not.

'Our Lady Prioress will receive you, my lady.'

'Thank you. I will make use of your guest house first, if it please you.'

She bowed her acquiescence. I was shown into the comfortable rooms where I could remove my cloak, my maid brushing the dust from my skirts and my veil before unpacking the gifts I had brought in the wagon that had travelled with us. The latrine was as I expected and gave much relief, while the gifts disappeared into the recesses where the kitchens and the storerooms might be. Black woollen cloth for their habits. Dried meat to tide them through the coming winter. A barrel of fine Mortimer ale and one of Gascony wine. I grimaced. My sisters would accuse me of buying their favour.

As I was escorted into the inner reaches of the Priory I assessed what I could see, the atmosphere that drew me in: the silence in the cloister, the bulk of the church wall with its plain lights, built along one side of the arched walkway where no one sat to converse or walked at this time of day. A door opened into a refectory where long wooden boards set on trestles could be seen, and next to it the beautifully carved arch into the chapter house where daily orders, commendations and punishments were delivered by the Prioress. I did not know where the cells might be for the holy sisters. All was peaceful, but to me it was the quiet of the grave. No, I would not wish it for myself. It was also cold and could only grow colder as the winter months set in. And how dark the chambers where candles had not been lit. Candles would be considered an unnecessary expense, something I need not consider at Wigmore.

And then the door was opened into the private accommodations of the Lady Prioress. They were spare and to my eye bleak, but the Prioress's chair was occupied by a cushion and on one wall there was a magnificent tapestry of the Blessed Virgin walking in a garden of flowers. A silver cup and ewer gleamed on the lid of a carved coffer. If the sisters lived in poverty, the Prioress was not without acknowledgement of her superiority.

'My Lady de Geneville.'

On her black breast a gold crucifix rose and fell slowly as she breathed, the jewels set in it catching the light from the high window. A sapphire glowed on her left hand to remind her that she was a Bride of Christ.

'I am now Mortimer,' I reminded her.

The lines that marked her features were deeply engraved, a life of deprivation and duty. Yet she was not unkind.

'Forgive me. It is easy to forget when shut away from the world, although we have our sources of knowledge. You have come to visit your sisters.'

'Yes. Is it permitted?'

'Of course. They are too young to have taken their vows.' Then she added as if she regretted it, 'They receive few visitors.'

'Does my mother come here?'

Living at Ludlow as she did, there was no need for her to tell me of her travels or her desire to visit her daughters.

'Not often, my lady. Their grandfather Baron de Geneville not at all.'

Which was no surprise to me. It was his hand that had put them here.

'Are they well-mannered? Do they attend to their studies and their prayers?'

A tight smile. 'They are very young, of course. Maud is the more biddable of the two. We are always pleased to take in those young women with de Lacy blood in their veins, however willing or unwilling they might be to see the value of a monastic life.'

Ringing a small silver bell at her side, she summoned the same nun who had brought me here, who, without a word, conducted me to what I presumed was a parlour, used by the nuns in the cold of the winter months when the cloisters were inhospitable, for the hour of freedom from silence. It was empty, the fireplace cleansed of all ashes. There were two wooden settles along the wall but no other comfort. When the nun bowed her head and departed, I waited. This was not destined to be a comfortable reconciliation. I should indeed feel guilt, for my Mortimer status had been bought at the expense of their freedom and their de Geneville inheritance. If I had been born after Beatrice, she would be Lady Mortimer, and I would be walled up here.

Footsteps returning put me on my mettle. I straightened my shoulders and lifted my chin as the nun ushered in my sisters. Beatrice now almost full grown at fifteen years while Maud was eleven, both clad in black but without the black veil, their hair enclosed in a plain white coif as postulants. Beatrice must be of an age to take her vows. Beatrice took Maud's hand and held it tightly.

'We did not expect to see you, Johane,' she said.

'But now I am here. You must understand that my time is no longer my own to determine how and where it is spent.'

'Three years since your betrothal, before your feet could find the path here to Aconbury,' Beatrice replied.

How clear and judgemental was her voice. How confident her speech, how accusatory her stare. Pale with lack of sun, they seemed far removed from the sisters with whom I had grown up, despite their de Geneville cast of features. It was impossible to see the colour of their hair, so like my own.

'What is it that has brought you here today?' Beatrice demanded in un-nun-like tones. 'I can think of no reason why you should abandon your comfort at Wigmore to enquire after our health. If either of us was to die of illness or neglect, I expect that you would be informed.'

The challenge in her eye was uncomfortable. I could have expected no less.

'Have you come to release us?' Maud asked, a plea in her voice. 'May we return with you?'

'No. That is not possible.'

'Why not?' Beatrice picked up the question. 'We are no threat to you. Are you not wed? The inheritance is disposed of into Mortimer coffers.' Her eye travelled to my waist. 'Are you carrying a Mortimer heir yet? If you are, will your lord not give you anything you ask for?'

'He has given me a mare,' I was surprised into replying, although it would be impossible for my sister to know of my pregnancy other than through clever guesswork.

'Which is more important to you than the release of your sisters from these garments of piety and obedience.' She paused. 'And chastity.'

Chastity. Ah yes. For was not that the important entity? I read the fire of resentment in her face, in her eyes. Maud, who had had so little to say to me, merely looked troubled. I could only be honest.

'I understand your resentment. Chastity is the reason you have been consigned to this life.'

'As gifts to God to end any troublesome de Geneville line from the womb of Maud or Beatrice de Geneville. Why have you come here, if not to release us? Was it worth the journey?' There was no softening in her.

'To see how you fare.'

I recalled the days when we were children, sharing lessons and youthful joy at Trim, but quickly I closed that memory down. It would bring no pleasure to any one of us. What had I expected? A warm welcome? An affectionate embrace? Our childhood was now a bitter memory.

'What can you do for us?'

'Nothing.' I would not say that I would pray for them.

'Then it was a journey to no purpose.'

'I have brought cloth and food. I will leave money as a gift for the convent.'

'That will not make life any better for us. You know nothing of our life here. How could you be so ignorant? You simply do not care.'

'Then all I can do is tell you news of our family. Our grand-father is still hale and our mother is in good spirits.'

'We are grateful for such knowledge. We will remember them in our prayers.'

The bitterness emanating from Beatrice filled the room to overflowing.

'You have my compassion but you must understand.'

'I do not want your compassion.'

'You must understand,' I continued. 'Power. Land. Status. It means everything. I do not agree with what was done but our grandfather has the family name uppermost in his mind. My lord will fight for my name and my lands.'

'Which are now his.'

'Which are now his.' I could only agree.

Beatrice tilted her chin, considering me.

'Do you like him? This man who has wed you for what you can bring him?'

'Is it not the same for every woman in our rank of society?' I thought for a moment. 'And yes, I like him. I like him very well.'

'I wish you well, my lady.'

She dropped a deep curtsey. And pulled Maud into doing likewise. I realised that Maud had still not said one word after her plea that I take her home with me.

'Have you no greeting for your sister?' I asked her gently, walking forward to touch her shoulder, but she flinched away. She shook her head.

'Nor have I anything more to say,' Beatrice said, walking towards the door, pulling Maud with her. 'I think that it is convenient for you to forget both of us. Or you might still do something to alleviate our situation. It would not have been my choice to take vows. I would have a husband and children.' She looked back over her shoulder, despair suddenly come to life in her face. 'Can you do nothing for us?'

'You know that I cannot. Our grandfather is still alive. He would prevent me from taking any step that might give you freedom.'

'Then we are condemned here until death releases us.'

If there were tears in her eyes, she hid them. I stretched out my hand but she stepped away to open the door. At the last, Maud allowed my touch on her arm but in no spirit of friendship, merely because she did not know what else to do.

'I am sorry. I will pray for you.'

'And we of course will pray for you. Is it not our role in life to pray for those outside these walls? We hope that your marriage will prove of value and bring you happiness.'

'I anticipate that it will.'

I stayed overnight but had no further private conversation with my sisters. I saw them at worship, and then in the refectory where they sat at the far end of the room as we ate the meagre diet of thick vegetable soup, coarse bread and a platter of apples. My visit had been just as bad as I had expected. They had been the sacrifice for my advancement in the world. I must make sure that their sacrifice was worth the making.

The uncomfortable thoughts stayed with me on the journey back along the March during which sorrow pressed as hard as the lowering clouds. Most of all I missed the affection that we had shared as children when there was nothing to cast a pebble into the pool of our happiness. But gradually my spirits lifted, as they must, for I was still young and full of optimism. And I was happy. I would seize my life, bequeathed to me by the price that they had been forced to pay, and enjoy it. Roger would be waiting for me at Wigmore. He would welcome me and make me smile with his casually uttered words of endearment. Did he ever speak that dangerous word love? No, he did not, but he did not despise my company.

And then, making my heart beat just a little faster, there he was riding towards me as we neared the environs of Wigmore, a goshawk on his gloved wrist, the now grown wolfhounds running at his horse's feet, his small escort making a bright backcloth to the scene. My squire Ralph pulled his mount to a standstill. It was a picture that would remain with me all my life as Roger lifted a hand to smooth the feathers on the hawk's breast so that it dipped its head and crooned. How the similarities struck home. For here was an image of creatures of dignity, of power, masterly in their separate elements, able to show affection just as easily as they could tear and rend their enemies. A sudden burst of sun at the end of the day struck Roger's hair with fire and the wolfhounds' coats with steel. It caused me to feel an unsettling frisson of desire for Roger Mortimer. At a nudge from me Ralph pushed his mount on, drawing attention to us.

Roger turned his head from his hawk and saw me. Had I been expecting a welcome? By the Virgin, it was not forthcoming. Here was no passionate declaration that he had missed me. Instead, he kicked his horse forward and pulled up beside me, his brow as dark as his hair escaping from beneath his brimmed beaver cap.

'God's Blood, Johane, I've been imagining you dead in a ditch. Where have you been?' he demanded.

'To visit my sisters at Aconbury.'

'I did not know. You did not tell me.' He glared at his squire. 'You should not have taken her.'

Nor was my reply any more amenable, although his anger was not displeasing to me.

'You were not at Wigmore for me to tell. Your mother knew. She found no objection. And it will please me if you do not take Ralph to task. He was under my instruction.'

Roger inhaled, the perfect image of an arrogant Marcher lord at odds with those under his command. His voice gained authority.

'I forbid you to travel such a distance without my permission.'

'Do I need your permission?'

'You are my wife.'

'As I know. And as your wife I will be sure to consider your wishes.'

His brows met above his beak of a nose in an even deeper scowl.

'I have come to look for you.'

'As well as taking the opportunity to enjoy the hawking, I see. You do not look inordinately worried to me.' I smiled with great sweetness. 'Was the hunting good? That is a fine hawk you've been flying.'

'Never mind the hawk and the hunting. You are carrying my heir. I will not allow you to put yourself in danger. You and I, Ralph, will have a conversation about this later.'

My own temper began to simmer.

'Do you announce that I am breeding to the whole of our escort? It may well be a girl.' I nudged Ralph to push my mare on past him. 'Perhaps you would care to escort me home. And in the interest of my health, since you are so keen to ensure my safety, do not stir a quarrel between us.'

We rode together, in shimmering silence, for the final mile into the inner bailey where, his brows still in a heavy bar, he handed over the hawk and helped me to dismount. Keeping a hand around my wrist he pulled me to walk with him into the keep, up the stairs and into our chamber. There, slamming the door, he released me and took my shoulders in a firm grip, fingers digging in through the cloth of my cloak.

'Ow!' I said, watching his reaction. I was in no mood to be taken to task again, but a vigorous reunion would please me mightily.

'I was worried.' He shook me, but not too harshly. He had a care for both my person and the unborn child.

'So you said. But now I am home and your fingers are not gentle. I am not a wolfhound.' I had seen him reduce Lugh to a state of ecstasy by digging his fingers into his pelt.

Instead of releasing me, he said: 'I missed you. I was surprised how much.'

'Which I am not sure is very flattering. I too missed being hailed with angry words across half the width of the March, for the whole of your escort to witness.'

His anger fleeing as fast as it had arrived, Roger huffed a laugh and pulled me closer. 'Welcome back, my own heart's flower.' He kissed me. 'My chamber has been empty without you.'

'You have plenty of company.'

I eyed the hounds that had followed their master and now panted at our feet, and the fledgling gyrfalcon, sulkily moulting, that sat on its perch in the window embrasure.

'Their conversation is not as engaging as yours.' He leaned to whisper in my ear. 'Nor are they quite as kissable.'

And proceeded to prove it, to my delight, folding me into his arms so that I could feel the strong beat of his heart, his mouth undeniably proprietorial, pressed against mine.

He did not ask about my sisters, which hurt a little since all his gains had been at their expense, nor did I embarrass him with my own longing to be back with him, that I had missed his presence in my daily life. I did not yet have the confidence in affairs of the heart, if that is what it was, to speak of love. The word didn't cross his lips, even when he stripped my under-linen from me at night and woke my body to an urgent response to be possessed by him. Sometimes I did not think that he ever would consider that he loved me, even though I might welcome such an admission. To him I was merely a possession which he would enjoy, as he enjoyed my lands.

I was pleased to be home. His annoyance with my absence had been a sop to my self-esteem.

Chapter Four

Wigmore Castle in the Welsh Marches, early 1303

When my belly grew greater with the child so that the seams of my kirtles and over-gowns must be let out, when riding was forbidden me and we waited the birth of the Mortimer heir, Roger read to me. Reluctantly it had to be said, but he did it with commendable dedication, in spite of my having a liking for the delectable romance of the verses in the *Roman de la Rose*.

> *From here to Jerusalem no woman has a more beautiful neck;*
> *It was smooth and soft to the touch.*
> *She had a bosom as white as the snow upon a branch,*
> *When it has just fallen.*

Roger growled to a halt. 'Do I have to read these witless verses?' he asked.

'Only if it pleases you.'

I smiled winningly.

He almost closed the book, keeping only one finger between the precious pages with their fine artistry.

'Can we find nothing more exciting?' He took an apple from the dish and sank his teeth into the firm flesh, before tossing the core to the nearest wolfhound. 'A battle would be more entertaining.'

'I have no wish to hear of war and fighting. This child is turbulent enough in my belly.'

He turned over three pages, abandoning the admirable woman.

'The more a man gazes on what he loves, the more he sets fire to his heart and bastes it with bacon fat.'

Roger closed the book completely and guffawed. 'Bacon fat indeed. Is that romance?' Upon which, growing weary of it, he tumbled me, albeit gently, onto our bed where I had been sitting, enjoying the remnants of sunshine through the high aperture. He stroked a hand over my hair which was braided but free from any covering. 'I think I'll leave you to rest while I take a hawk and the wolfhounds along the river,' he said. 'I can stand no more of these simpering phrases.'

By now I knew what would keep him.

'Then tell me the tales of King Arthur and his knights, and his magnificent sword that would slay all comers and endow him with magic.'

There was no lack of enthusiasm here. Roger's family claimed descent from the Welsh prince Llewellyn the Great, and thus legend said that they could number King Arthur among their ancestors. The sanguinary tales of brave knights and fair ladies were much venerated in the household, but instead of those old tales, Roger settled himself to paint a vivid picture of the event held by his famous grandfather at Kenilworth Castle.

'Kenilworth was the treasure he seized from Simon de Montfort, the vast fortress in the centre of England. What should he do to commemorate such a victory? Hold a great Round Table tournament, as King Arthur would have done.

What a magnificent occasion it must have been, with all of the knights of the realm attending.'

'Did the King attend?'

The child stirred within me and I stroked it back into sleep.

'He did, and Queen Eleanor, and all her ladies. The armour glittered and the women were as bright as flowers in their gowns. Deeds of great renown were carried out although my grandfather was past the age of taking part in the melee. Men spoke about it for years afterwards. The swords might have been blunted but there were some hefty blows traded. Did you know that more than one Mortimer has died in a tourney? I imagine that I might hold such a tournament to honour the Mortimers and King Arthur, perhaps here at Wigmore, or at Ludlow.'

Silence settled around us, the magic remaining.

'Thus I am royal born and worthy of all high office. Perhaps even the Crown.'

His words meant little to me in my somnolent state.

'You are too arrogant for your own good, Roger Mortimer. The Crown will never be yours. Does not King Edward hold it securely in his fist?'

'That cannot be denied. But Merlin prophesied it. King Edward is old and his days are numbered. One of our family could make a claim. Why not me?'

I took the book back into my possession to preserve its leather cover since he was lying on it.

'Ha! My family is as well born as yours!' I declaimed.

'I know. My father would never have agreed to the match otherwise.'

I preened. I was French through and through and enjoyed listing my family achievements. Roger deserved that I repay like for like.

But Roger, as impatient as ever, had had enough of poetry

and history, and sat up. 'Do you perhaps walk in the herbarium to chase away the megrims? My mother tells me that I must keep you in good spirits. You can go and sniff the herbs while I go hunting.'

'Only if you will read me some more verses from the *Roman de la Rose*.'

He groaned but did so in good heart. How young we were. How hopeful for the future. Responsibilities lay in wait for us but these months granted us a little respite. Life would never be easy in the Marches where enemies lurked under every stone, both English and Welsh, but this Mortimer-de Geneville alliance would hold fast. Happiness engulfed me. Contentment stalked me. Roger and I, man and wife, close companions, spent our days together, enjoying hunting and hawking, visiting my mother in Ludlow Castle, as well as learning the pleasures of physical intimacy. Lord Edmund and Lady Marguerite remained at Wigmore, keeping tight hold to the reins, allowing us our freedom for a little while. When Roger gained his majority he would have more influence, greater responsibilities. Longer times of absence, when his presence was demanded elsewhere by duty to Mortimer affairs, would separate us. Our time would no longer be our own.

'What do we do tomorrow?' I asked.

'Whatever your heart desires. As long as I am not called on to read more mummer's nonsense!'

The decision was made for us. An outbreak of revolt across the border into Wales came to Mortimer ears. Roger was already struggling into a mail hauberk, ordering up a well-armed escort, before the hard-riding courier had time to draw breath after gulping down a cup of ale.

'What are you doing?' demanded his father, stepping between his son and the steps down into the courtyard.

'There is imminent rebellion in Powys that needs putting down.'

It had to be said that Lord Edmund was also partially clad in mail, the mittens hanging free from his wrists. Lord Edmund spoke with calm decisiveness.

'You will not go.'

A familiar black cloud descended on Roger's brow.

'Do you order me to remain here?'

'No. You are needed elsewhere. You will go to Lord Roger at Chirk.'

Lord Roger Mortimer of Chirk. Lord Edmund's brother. One of the old warrior lords, quick to fight and slow to forgive past sins inflicted on his lands by the Welsh. A man with an unfortunate reputation in some areas, hounded by the rumours that one way to seize a Welsh inheritance from the Lord of North Powys, was for Mortimer of Chirk to drown his two small heirs in the River Dee. There was no proof, but there were few who would deny that Mortimer of Chirk was of a sufficiently vicious character to do so.

'The Mortimer lands are under threat,' Roger was arguing loudly. 'Or will be by the end of the week if we do not take action. Am I not of an age to lead my own men?'

'I wish he would not shout at his father,' Lady Marguerite observed, standing with me in the Great Hall. Whereas my mother was tall and slender, Lady Marguerite was as small and neat as a field-mouse, her face framed in a spotlessly white wimple and veil, and as lively as such a mouse in her attention to her own household. 'It is not good for the whole castle to hear. He has the voice of Thor the Thunderer. Where does he get that from?' This from a lady who, however gentle in appearance, could make herself heard from one floor of the keep to the next when a bout of de Fiennes temper shook her.

'Not yet.' Lord Edmund was keeping his patience. 'Not into the heart of Welsh resistance. They are savage fighters. You do not yet have enough experience to lead an expedition on your own.'

'You belittle me, Father.'

The cloud was darker yet. I saw the pride, the belief in his own strength, his resistance to any who would dictate his actions against what he saw as his own interest, his right, even when it was his father who issued the orders. For the first time since we were wed I recognised these harsh aspects of his character. Taurus the Bull indeed. I held my breath. So did Lady Marguerite at this clash of will on the steps, for all to see and hear. Surely Roger would not defy his father, and not before an audience of Mortimer men-at-arms. I watched as his lips thinned, his shoulders tightened. He was quite capable of riding out from Wigmore without his father's blessing.

'Well?' Lord Edmund demanded. 'Do you defy me?'

Roger gave a brusque nod as if an unacceptable decision had been forced on him.

'I will go to my uncle.'

There was no general exhale around us, but it could be im-agined. Lord Edmund stepped aside to allow his son to walk down the steps beside him, in visual harmony at least.

'I understand your need to clash swords against the Welsh. Has it not been mine since I was your age? You are a true Mortimer and I respect you for it, but you have so few years be-neath your belt. Go to Chirk. He is a fine soldier but sometimes his sight is not as keen as it might be. A pair of young eyes will benefit him, and you will learn much too in managing crusty magnates.' Which made me smile. It was not just about physical sight. 'When you return, full of glory, you will lead your own knightly band into Wales.'

Roger almost tossed his head like a mettlesome steed, as if he did not quite believe the promise.

'I promise you,' Lord Edmund continued smoothly. 'It is time that you blooded your own sword with Welsh blood. As long as you remember to negotiate first, when it is possible. Your uncle is good at negotiation in spite of his hot blood. Learn from him.' He slid a glance at his son. 'Although not in all aspects of his lifestyle.'

'You don't approve of his morality then.'

'I do not. His sins are deplorable. Be sure to give our regards to his lady wife, Lucia. She has much to put up with.'

They were at one again. Did Chirk need help? It did not matter. It was a clever peace-offering, and the cloud on Roger's brow had lifted. He bowed before Lord Edmund and pressed his lips to his father's hand in formal acknowledgement and farewell.

'Take care of yourself. You are my heir and I need you to return in one piece. So does your wife and the coming child. You are now at the centre of this Mortimer family.'

Roger and I parted formally as was necessary.

'That was well done. To step back. I too honour you.'

'As I honour you, my wife.'

'As long as you don't learn Chirk's habits of adultery.'

'I would not!'

And I believed him, but added a parting shot. 'If you do, you will not find a welcoming wife but a harpy with an axe, intent on evisceration.'

Which made him laugh, and all his temper was smoothed over as he rode out to the massive medieval fortress of Chirk in which Lord Roger kept control over a lawless country, when he was not seducing the wives of his neighbours. I regretted his departure, even more the absence of any declaration of affection on his part, but he had warned me, had he not?

While Roger growled at his own lack of independence, I fulfilled the most important of my duties. The birth pangs struck late in the day. I had not spent weeks in seclusion as any royal woman might. Life in a border fortress was far different, and I continued with my household duties until the eleventh hour although aware that Lady Marguerite took a heavier burden on her own shoulders when it came to supervising the brewing of our beer and interviews with passing merchants.

But as soon as I groaned 'Blessed Virgin!', clutching at my belly, I was ushered into my chamber where all had been made ready for some days. My women joined me, stitching linen for the much-longed-for infant. Roger was summoned back from Chirk.

'How long do I tolerate this?' I asked as the pain waned.

'As long as God wills it,' Lady Marguerite remarked with acid memories. 'It is the lot of womankind. I had five children, and each birth was no better than the last. Sometimes hours, sometimes days.'

Now I groaned in despair but set to my task with stoicism, my fears of my own death assuaged when Lady Marguerite sent to the Abbey to obtain the length of linen that was said to be the girdle of St Anne, the mother of the Blessed Virgin, to wrap around my belly when the pain was at its greatest. By the time that my mother arrived from Ludlow, St Anne had truly blessed me, as the babe was already born in a slither of pain and blood. The child, rapidly wrapped in fine linen, was placed in my arms, my recall of the excruciating agonies receding. I regarded the mat of dark tawny hair and wizened face as if the child had struggled through the fires of hell to draw its first breath.

'Tell me it is a son. It needs to be a son.'

'It is a son. A Mortimer heir.' Lady Marguerite beamed at both of us. 'The first of many, I hope. Our families have been short of male heirs.'

'My thanks to St Anne and her girdle. Roger will be able to rejoice!'

I marvelled at the child, so weak, so tiny, that held so much of the ambition of this family. Until he began to bawl and I laughed at the element of power.

'Take him to Roger.' I would not see my husband until I was churched and returned to the world of men, nor was I sorry, since I was weary and Roger's enthusiasms could have an enervating effect. 'He will wish to tell him all about his ancestry from Llewellyn and King Arthur. He will already have a sword in the making, named Excalibur, ready for his tiny hand. Do you suppose that he will wish to call him Arthur?'

Lady Marguerite smiled in understanding. 'He will be Edmund. After Roger's father. It is a good tradition.'

I was exhausted but elated at my achievement. Roger sent me a book of verses to while away the hours and days until I was churched. They were romantic. He knew my preferences well and, even better for him, he did not have to read them to me since my world was one of women until I knelt in our chapel in thanksgiving.

'What is your ambition, now that you have a son?' I asked him when I was once more restored to life in the castle. Did I not already know?

'To be a great lord in the March. To protect my lands, and yours, to hand them to our son in the fullness of time.' He hesitated, his eyes brightening. Here was something new which he had not spoken of before. 'It is my wish to go to the royal Court. To make my name in the tournaments much loved by the King, and the Prince who will one day replace him.'

The Court held his vision, as did the young Prince Edward of Carnarvon whom he admired. I knew little of him.

'Why do you admire him so? Is he of a martial nature?'

'No, I think not, but that does not mean that he is unwilling to lead men into battle. His royal blood shines in him. He is tall and golden and smiles on those who please him. He is a first-rate horseman. I would serve a man like that. I met him at the siege of Caerlaverock Castle, when we were at war with the Scots, before we were wed. My uncle of Chirk was appointed to watch over the Prince, so he watched over me at the same time. My uncle had a heavy hand when dealing with young lads who did not jump into instant obedience, but the memory has lit a desire in me to experience the glamour of Court life.'

I had not met this Prince who was tall and golden and generous to his friends, who was a good horseman. It would please me to do so, to assess for myself what it was that drew my husband to him. One day I would travel with Roger to the royal Court and watch him flex his muscles and his military skills in the tournament.

Could our halcyon, somewhat carefree, existence last for ever?

Of course it could not. It was only a matter of time. The cause of such an upheaval for all of us was not one that we had expected so soon. Nor would we ever have wished it.

Chapter Five

Wigmore Castle in the Welsh Marches, July 1304

'Open the gates!'

A rider was spurring his horse, galloping up the hill and along the ridge, without care for his mount's safety or his own. A series of shouts reached us, increasingly breathless.

'Open up!'

There was no doubting the urgency. I was down in the inner courtyard, my second newly born baby, a daughter named Margaret, in my arms, before the rider, one of our own with the Mortimer shield on his chest, had dismounted. Such an arrival must herald some disaster.

'Where is Lady Mortimer?' the rider asked, his hands on his thighs, his face coated in dust, as he fought for breath.

'At the Abbey. You will report to me.' Handing the baby to one of my women, I grabbed his arm and hauled him upright. 'You will tell me.' It was my role to deal with any emergency since our menfolk were elsewhere. In truth, I did not know where Roger was, but probably dealing with a difference of opinion between two of our tenants over common-land rights in the manor at Leintwardine. Lord Edmund was much further afield, somewhere in Wales, with a body of Mortimer retainers, keeping the peace.

'A skirmish,' the rider announced. 'At Builth. A skirmish that should have been easily put down.' He shook his head as if still in disbelief, his eyes stretched wide. 'Lord Edmund is wounded.'

A hand closed hard around my heart; yet if it was a skirmish, surely it would not be so dire a wound. The glazed expression on the rider's face would deny that.

'Where is he?' I asked.

'They're bringing him home.' He took a deep breath. 'In a litter. They follow me but sent me on to make preparation. It's bad, my lady. Bad. He'll need good care.'

Leaving him to the attention of our steward, I did not hesitate, but sent a servant riding fast to the Abbey to alert Lady Marguerite and their physicians, another to ride north to discover Roger. They would be needed. Then I sent to make Lord Edmund's bed ready and warn our own physician.

And, on a thought, our priest.

By the time Lord Edmund was carried into our Great Hall the castle physician and the Abbey infirmarian were in attendance, concern etched in their tight features and rigid postures. Although not a man of notable physique or champion in battle and warfare for its own sake, nor even with a love of jousting, for Lord Edmund to agree to ride in a litter was a sign of severe damage. Swathed in his cloak, closely hooded, he was not conscious. Ordering that he be carried immediately to his chamber, since I could do nothing else but ensure that the physicians had the necessary linen and hot water and healing herbs, I was left to note the damage as our physician peeled back the cloak and hood.

It was clear from the start that there was little hope. A blow to his head had shattered his skull above his left temple. Had he removed his helmet? Surely he would have been well protected from such a blow. But there was no doubt of its mortality. We all knew that blows to the head were the most dangerous.

Then Lady Marguerite was come, to stand beside me at the foot of the bed throughout the night, when all possible succour had been given. Her hands were tight clasped, her lips moving in prayer.

'I fear that my lord is nearing his end,' the physician announced, beckoning to the priest who had the holy oil to anoint the dying for the last rites at hand.

'Is there nothing you can do?' Roger asked, his face as pale as the new dawn when he had ridden in and entered the room like a whirlwind. 'He is still young, he is strong.'

'He has more than fifty years to his name. This is the blow that has caused so much damage.' He pointed to where fragments of bone were visible beneath Lord Edmund's hair. 'The bleeding will be within where we cannot see. It is impossible to staunch it. We have made him comfortable, but we can do no more.'

Lady Marguerite was not satisfied. Later I found her kneeling beside the bed, the scent of herbs redolent. She looked up as I entered, as if she would make an excuse, then beckoned to me.

'Will you join me?'

I knelt beside her. There was St John's Wort tucked around Lord Edmund's pillow. Over the door there was tied a pungent bunch of rosemary.

'What are you doing?'

'Keeping demons from this room and from my lord.' She slid a glance at my face, probably to assess my reaction. 'Will you keep watch with me?'

'Is it magic?'

'Of a sort. A charm, certainly. If it works, I'll not decry it.

55

My lady mother swore that she had seen such herbs stop the bleeding of a horse.'

We kept watch beside his bed, on our knees, as the early dawn brightened, when Lord Edmund passed from this life, the priest administering to him the last rites of holy unction to succour him in death and forgive his sins. He had not spoken one word since his return to Wigmore, showing no sign of recognition of those who watched over him, leaving his wife and son without comfort. When Lady Marguerite retired to her own chamber, the priest keeping her company to pray with her, Roger climbed to the highest point on the crenellations of the castle, leaning on them, looking out over the land to the east that was now his. I left him there for a little time, alone, since I could do nothing to alleviate his grief for a father who had been kindly and generous, then I joined him.

I tucked my hand into his arm, all my thoughts unsettled with a sense of foreboding, for did I not know well the difficulties when the heir was not of an age to claim his own inheritance? Roger, at seventeen years, was not of such an age. I knew immediately the trend of his thoughts. These Mortimer lands were not yet his to call his own. It would not sit well with a man of Roger's self-worth. Predictably Roger thumped his fist against the stone coping, released himself from my clutches, and marched off to look in the direction of Powys where his father had been so grievously wounded. Nothing deterred, I followed him, leaning back against the stonework to look up into his face. There was a groove as deep as the channel of the River Wye at Symond's Yat between his brows.

'I grieve with you, my husband.'

'I know.'

'What now?'

'We bury my father with all due dignity and respect. At the Abbey.'

'Of course. And then?'

'Then? You know what will happen, Johane.' He glanced down at me before once more fixing his attention to the distance. 'The Mortimer lands, my lands, will be taken under the control of the Crown since I am a minor. Why could my father not have lived longer, until I came of legal age to inherit?' He bared his teeth. 'That sounds callous. I did not mean that. I regret his death with all my heart. But I cannot see the future with any clarity except that I will not be in control of what is mine.'

I took his hand in mine, lacing my fingers with his, and he did not resist.

'But in the not-too-distant future you will be of age and all will come to you. We must simply wait.'

'How pragmatic you are. And I am too impatient.' I sensed his anger dissipating as he drew me within his arm. 'Do you remember on the day that we were wed? I warned you that we would not always be together. Now I think the time has come when we must part. Whoever is appointed as my guardian might summon me to live under his dominion. Or King Edward might order my attendance at Court.'

'And I do not come with you.'

'Not until all is clearer.' He smiled bleakly down at me. 'I will need you and my mother here at Wigmore. There must be a Mortimer presence.'

'Even though it is only a woman!' It hurt a little that I should be expected to remain and care for the children when Roger stepped out into the world of power and politics, but I would not let it show. 'It will not be for ever,' I assured him. 'Where is the King now?'

'Campaigning in Scotland. We will have to wait to hear his

57

thoughts on me and my inheritance. And meanwhile we give my father a worthy interment at the Abbey. But I have to say...' His grip around my shoulders tightened. 'I do not relish having my land under the hand of any man.'

For the first time I truly heard in Roger the voice of Lord Mortimer of Wigmore. When sent to Chirk, his initial refusal had the element of youthful temper when his will was thwarted. Now he might still not have grown into his full strength, but the lift of the chin, the bracing of the shoulders, the stern visage – they were all present and issued a warning to any who would deny him. He stomped off down the steps, leaving me to follow. I made my way to the nursery where to my surprise Roger soon joined me. I smiled at him in welcome.

'I thought you would be knee-deep in documents and charters by now.'

'And so I should be, but I thought I should give some time to you first. I have seen so little of you in past days. And I have come to pay my respects to the heirs of the Mortimer inheritance.'

It pleased me. I could feel a faint wash of colour in my cheeks that he should offer at least a handful of moments at this difficult time to his young family. He sat on the floor, allowing Edmund, now unsteadily walking, to clamber over his legs and grip the handle of the dagger that he habitually wore in his belt. Margaret sat on my lap, chewing the cuffs of my long sleeves until I dissuaded her with a wolf's tooth mounted in silver which was a gift from Lady Marguerite for the new generation of Mortimers. My mother-in-law's interest in objects of magical protection no longer surprised me.

'What a fearsome child she is,' Roger announced as his daughter gnawed at the tooth and dribbled down her chin onto her linen. 'I knew that we should have called her Guinevere.'

'And I am thankful you did not. Besides, your mother was honoured by our naming our eldest daughter after her.'

Roger's heart was easier now.

'I will miss you when I am summoned to Westminster,' he announced, lifting Edmund above his head so that he squealed with excitement. 'I know that I can leave these two infants safe in your care.'

He was already dreaming of what the name Mortimer would become under his jurisdiction.

'He is his grandfather's heir, not his father's,' said Lady Marguerite in those restless days between death and burial. 'Lord Edmund was a younger son and trained to be a clerk. He enjoyed the demands of education rather than the tournament, but when his elder brother died, the inheritance was his to grasp. He did it well, but sometimes I think his whole heart was not in it. The old Lord Roger was a mettlesome leader and my son follows in his footsteps. Sometimes I fear for him. Roger will seize life by the horns and wrestle it to the ground. Who knows what he will become.'

'Who indeed.' It was a worrisome time. 'I think I will become a half-widow…'

Not that my mind was on any temporary widowhood, rather the arrangements of the burial of Lord Edmund at Wigmore Abbey. A truly sombre occasion, it demanded a vast gathering of Marcher lords, many from across the border into Wales. We processed along the nave behind the coffin carried by our own people and placed before the altar. High Mass was sung. There was no effigy or inscription yet, but a display of cloth of gold to cover the tomb-slab until all could be completed. It was impressive enough with the Mortimer coat of arms displayed in a blaze of blue and gold. Black-clad, black-veiled, Lady Marguerite and I stood beside his earthly memorial while Roger laid Lord

Edmund's sword on the cloth of gold where its honed blade glinted balefully. Lady Marguerite knelt to place his helm there, while I added a pair of gauntlets. One day, before they could tarnish, they would be reproduced in stone. For now, it was a keen memory of Lord Edmund's role in the Welsh Marches, repulsing the Welsh with force of arms.

Others paid their respects with bent heads. Roger's uncle, Lord Roger Mortimer of Chirk, from the depths of his border fortress. Walter de Thornbury, grave and erudite, who had been named Roger's guardian and the executor of Lord Edmund's will. We were also joined, as might have been expected, by a royal courier who handed his missive to Lord Walter, who, with a nod of acceptance, scanned it rapidly and passed it on to Roger. The contents came as no surprise. Roger informed me of King Edward's demand after the final prayers at High Mass in the Abbey, when the mourners were finding their horses.

'You had better tell me, sooner rather than later,' I said.

It would have its effect on both of us. A royal courier was not here by chance. I felt a ripple of anxiety mixed with the sadness of the occasion.

'I am summoned to Court, as we expected. I shall become a royal ward until I am of age to inherit.' The twist of his lips was wry. 'It seems unbalanced, that I should be deemed old enough to be wed to you, with a son and daughter of my own, but not considered of an age to hold my own lands.'

Yet it was indeed nothing more than we had expected. Roger would be too important a landowner in the Marches to allow his inheritance to fall into the hands of any man who would despoil it. Tradition of land-inheritance must be followed for the security of our local dominance.

'When do you go?'

'Tomorrow.'

So soon. If a vast hole of despondency loomed at the centre of my life, I made no mention of it.

'Then all we need to do is to make ready for your departure as soon as our guests have gone,' I said, as if it were commonplace to lose my husband to the royal Court. 'I will set it in motion. Your mother has enough to do.'

How uncertain our future suddenly was, depending on the whim of the King and his arrangements for the Mortimer lands. And, I supposed, Roger's own inclination. Would he, during a lengthy stay, during which he made friends with young men of his own interests, enjoy the luxury and brilliance of Court life better than the constant juggling of relationships in the March? And then there would be the tournaments. The excitement, the blood-stirring joy of victory. They might prove far more appealing than my company, far more exciting than teaching young Edmund to hold a merlin on his wrist and running the wolfhounds in the hunt. I expressed nothing of this. I would not exhibit my fears, my weaknesses. I was now the wife of a Marcher lord and must comport myself as one, waving him off with stoic confidence and self-sufficiency. I dared not show any emotion in case it escaped out of my control and shamed me. To my surprise it was Roger who made the farewell personal.

'I will send you gifts so that you will not forget me. And to show you that I will think about you across all the miles between.'

It was a good thought. 'My thanks. Do you leave the wolf-hounds here?'

'I'll take them. There will be hunting aplenty, wherever we are. Will you stay here? Or will you go to Ludlow to keep company with your mother? I think my own mother might go to her property in Radnor.'

I did not know. Nor would it matter greatly to Roger, taken

up as he was with the immediate future. I could see the anticipation beginning to glow in his eyes. For the first time since the death of his father he had come alive.

'I have nothing to give you now,' I said. He was too busy stowing an assortment of weaponry into a coffer to look disappointed. 'I will keep my gift to you here,' I continued, determined to break his concentration. 'It seems that I carry another child.'

Which captured his interest immediately.

'Then I will offer prayers for you.'

Which I supposed was comforting enough, but since his preoccupation returned, I gave up. I would really have appreciated some words of everlasting love to cushion me against his departure, but I knew the Mortimer lord well enough to recognise a lost cause.

'The question is,' remarked Roger Mortimer of Chirk, emerging at my shoulder from the Mortimer escort when we had all gathered outside to send the heir on his way. 'The question is, to whom will the King grant your land in wardship?'

Mortimer of Chirk was short with a slight stoop, caused from an old wound to one shoulder that had never healed as well as it might. His hair and beard were grizzled with grey, his eyes bracketed in fine lines so that he had always appeared much older than Lord Edmund, who had more claims to be suave and elegant. Mortimer of Chirk, rough and belligerent, laid claims to neither, and would refuse them if offered, yet he had a gift for homing in on the truth.

'We will not know until he tells me,' Roger replied.

'If you want my advice...'

'You will give it, Uncle, whether I wish it or no. Do I not always seek it?'

I hid a smile at Roger's impatience to be gone, even though my heart wept a little.

'No, you do not seek it often enough, my boy. But here it is, for what it's worth. My advice is to buy back your land from whoever holds the wardship as soon as may be. Keep Mortimer lands in Mortimer hands. We want no interference from some decorative, prancing courtier who has never been to the Marches and has no interest in them. As for Ireland, there are many at Westminster who could not even say where it might be...'

'Of course I will,' Roger agreed again with false complacency, with a bite in his reply. 'I'll come to you for the money. I doubt it will be cheap. There will be Johane's lands to recover as well. Have you any further advice on where to raise such vast sums?'

Mortimer of Chirk gave a noncommittal snort. As we all knew, it was all very well to talk of financial remuneration, quite another to do it in the short term. Roger cast an eye around his property, and probably over me.

'When I return, we will set in train much rebuilding here. We will have a palace worthy of Lord Mortimer of Wigmore.'

And then Roger was gone, with his baggage, his weapons and his armour stowed in a wagon, Mortimer banners lifting in the breeze, the hounds bounding at his side with their loping gait, all accompanied by his guardian Lord Walter, as well as a string of horses to enable him to compete in the tourneys, while two of his men carried raptors on their fists. I knew, because I had witnessed the ordering of it, that another wagon contained clothing for hunting and feasting. This would not be a short visit. Young Mortimer of Wigmore intended to make an impression on his elders and betters. After a final embrace with an arm casually around my shoulders, followed by a kiss on my cheek, he did not turn his head even once to look back before he was lost from view. I lifted my hand in farewell, but he did not see it. I wondered how many times that would happen in my life.

'I think that he will enjoy life at Court,' I said a little sadly as we watched the cloud of settling dust as the cavalcade rode south towards Hereford.

'Yes,' Lady Marguerite agreed.

'Will he forget me?'

'I expect that he will.' Here was cynicism born of long experience when men were away from home and their minds taken up with martial arts. 'We shall both be widows one way or another.'

I slid a glance at her. 'I imagine that he will have to stay at Court.'

'Yes. And looking at the carts that accompany him, he intends to indulge in all aspects of courtly life offered. I don't anticipate that we will see him again for some time.'

I thought that she was right and felt a dull ache of loss in my breast.

'Fortunately he has left me with enough to do raising his two children.' Did I feel resentment that I had been left behind? I did, and felt no guilt for it. 'I think that I will indeed go and visit my mother in Ludlow.'

'I wager that you will return here to Wigmore before Roger does!'

'A wager that you would win. I expect I will have given birth to this new child also before his father puts in an appearance again. It might even have celebrated its first birthday.'

Lady Marguerite embraced me with understanding.

'We will both learn what it is to lose a husband. At least yours will return one day.'

I instantly regretted my selfishness.

'Come to Ludlow with me,' I invited. 'We will all mourn together.'

*

Lady Marguerite and I had assessed the situation with impressive accuracy. The Marches saw nothing of Roger in the following months. There were no gifts delivered to me, either to Wigmore or Ludlow, to remind me of his affections. In all justice we received one letter that was more a matter of business than an intimate exchange between husband and wife. The Prince, Edward of Carnarvon, much admired by Roger, had persuaded the King his father to grant the Mortimer wardship to his great friend Piers Gaveston, a knight from Gascony.

'Do we know anything about this knight?' I asked Mortimer of Chirk, who visited us with relative frequency. 'Is he a fair man? Is he important enough to be given custody of our estates? Will he look to their care or strip them bare to his own advantage?'

Mortimer of Chirk considered this.

'An excellent man in a tournament to have on your side. An admirable companion. Nothing to dislike in him. Roger could do much worse than to have the wardship in Gaveston's hands. That's not to say that he's not a man of ambition and will not be bought off lightly. His family from Gascony cannot measure up to the status of a Mortimer, of course. A commoner in fact, but my thought is that it will not always be so. Gaveston seeks lands and titles, and with Prince Edward's friendship I would not wager against him getting all that he wants. A man with whom it is best to be wary, if you are forced to have dealings with him. I would advise against it. What other does my absent nephew have to say?'

I summoned a smile. 'That life at Court is all that Roger expected it to be.'

Another habitual cursory summing up was all I got in return.

'Let us hope that he does not fall into bad habits of spending too much money for no value. Let us hope that he does not beggar us before he even comes of age,' the Chirk uncle growled before riding off into Wales. 'If you want him home, tell him that there is a revolt in Brecon.'

But indeed there was no competition for Roger's attention, no dangerous rumbling of serious insurrection in the March; not even the news I sent to him would bring him to Wigmore.

It pleases me to tell you that you have a new son. He is baptised and it was decided that he would be named Roger. He would be pleased to make the acquaintance of his father. So would I. It would please me to know when you might return. Your children and I are like to forget you.

It brought no return of the Mortimer lord. Prince Edward had doubtless cast his magical mantle over my husband and won him to his side. I recalled Roger's description of Prince Edward. I asked the Chirk uncle before he departed back to his fortress across the border.

'What manner of man is this Prince?'

Sadly the old man's opinion matched that of Roger. 'A golden gosling, generous to a fault.'

That night I looked in my mirror, not dissatisfied with what I saw. A pleasingly oval face, a long nose. My hair, plaited for the night, now held the fairness of summer in its brown waves. My skin was pale and without blemish. Fair enough, but I suspected that I could not compete with the golden beauty and charisma of a Prince who might hold out his hand in friendship to my husband. I was no golden gosling.

Did I miss Roger? Not at all, unless it was like missing the wolfhounds under my feet. Not unless it was like the birds anticipating the dawn to burst into song. Not unless it was like the barn owl that awaited dusk to fly and hunt across the meadows, seeking for the voles that inhabited the banks of the

River Teme. Not unless it was the constant nagging ache of absence that was lodged in my heart. Not unless it was my daily perambulations of the wall-walk to see towards the south the first hint of dust of the heir's return.

No, I did not miss him. I refused to miss him.

My bed was cold at night. My heart grew even colder at my lord's neglect.

Was Prince Edward a threat to my marriage? He certainly kept Roger well away from the Marches. Jealousy was an uncomfortable habit to fall into.

So was fear, that snapped at me with sharp teeth.

Chapter Six

Wigmore Castle in the Welsh Marches, spring 1306

Roger returned in a snow storm, having been absent for more
than a year. I was there to watch him walk up the steps into the
Great Hall, to see what effect the passage of time and the Court
finesse had had on him. The wolfhounds bounded in with him
as he issued orders for the care of his horses and escort.

He had grown, was my first thought. In height, in breadth
of shoulders. In confidence too as he walked into his Great
Hall, and, I suspected, naked ambition beneath the magnificent
fur-lined cloak. His clothing smacked of the Court. I had not
seen his embroidered gauntlets before. So did his manners show
a year's influence of courtly extravagance, as I saw with the same
cynicism as his mother, as he bowed before me with a flourish
of his cap. His fine leather boots shone despite the patches of
damp. The sword at his belt was new to me, with gilding and
gems that sparkled in the cold air. Not a suitable weapon for
war against the Welsh, but perhaps for King Arthur at Camelot
who might also have worn that finely woven tunic with a dagged
hem.

I would have denied the leap of intense awareness within me.
I could not deny it, but I would not admit it to the returning

lord of Wigmore Castle who surveyed his surroundings with a domineering air ownership. I might have longed to run forward and cast myself into his arms but I would not do it.

'Good morrow, my lord.' I curtsied. Warned of his arrival, I had made a hurried improvement in my own appearance, donning an embroidered over-gown, my hair confined with a circlet and a crispinette, my veil draped over all, my sudden magnificence more worthy of a celebration rather than a day spent in household duties.

'How formal, my lady.' He bowed again. His eyes were as direct as ever in their gaze round his Great Hall as if re-familiarising himself with his property. They returned to me.

'Indeed,' I said. 'I barely recognise you. You have a new taste in sable caps.'

I would not make this return easy for him. I was of a mind to be cool if not exactly unfriendly. Would he now be satisfied in remaining here in Wigmore? In spite of the rebuilding he wished to set in motion, it was far from the allure of the royal Court and the grandeur of the Palace of Westminster. For the first time in our marriage I was aware of a frisson of real disquiet. Roger had never left me in any doubt of his ambitions. Now I might have to face them in practical terms if they took him away from me, be it a tournament or a more dangerous battle. With this thought in my mind I became more recalcitrant than perhaps a Marcher wife had the right to be.

Why did love have to be such an agonising emotion?

'Do you welcome me to my own hall, my lady?' he asked, becoming aware of the growing tension.

'Have I not done so? It is yours, my lord. You need no welcome.'

Lady Marguerite, raising her eyes to heaven, and, sensing something of a battle developing, made a fast retreat after patting her son on his arm, while I turned on my heel and walked away from him. I heard his boots on the stone floor, then rustling through the softness of the new rushes, as he followed me. We had not yet touched. We had not yet stood within ten arms' lengths of each other.

'Do you turn your back on me, Lady Mortimer?'

Ah! There was a hint of surprise. He had not expected my welcome to be so crisp.

'I do, until you invite me to sit with you, as a wife might expect when her husband has been absent for so long.'

I heard his footsteps stop.

'The invitation is offered. I presume my chamber is where it was when I left.'

'I have made no changes to your arrangements, my lord. How would I dare?' I too stopped. I turned round. It was like combat in a tourney with the two adversaries circling. 'Do you wish to have conversation with me? Or are there business matters for you to attend to first? Perhaps to send some communication to the Prince who has become so close a friend?'

Roger Mortimer lifted his chin. There was fire in his eye. But then there was in mine.

'I do not offer an invitation that is not seriously considered.' His eyes narrowed a little in a challenge. 'If you can find time from your wifely duties to talk with me.'

'It is accepted. Come to my solar.'

It was warm there, with candles set to give us light. I dispatched my women and poured cups of wine. All without a word being spoken. We sat facing each other on either side of the hearth. The room might look welcoming but there was no warmth between us; the mood in the room was as chilly as the snowflakes still to melt from the edges of Roger's hair.

'Do we make peace?' he asked.

'I was not aware that we were at war.'

'Nor are we,' he replied with a quick assessment of the situation. 'Do you wish to know how I spent my time?' he asked with an innocence that did not fool me for one moment.

'Feasting, drinking, honing your sword skills, hunting, flirting. Perhaps whoring. Does that cover it?'

'More or less.'

'Do I tell you about my time? I have given birth to a son. Edmund wants a sword which I have refused. Margaret is walking and into every nook and cranny so that she must be rescued from dangers of her own making. I have also had numerous conversations with your tenants about manorial problems – you will find the documents for your perusal – as well as receiving frequent lectures from Mortimer of Chirk about keeping an eye on the riotous Welsh since you were not here to do so.'

'A more worthy use of your time than mine has been, many would say.'

'So would I.'

I watched as he took a breath, throwing the sable hat to the floor. Then as if on a decision, leaning forward he stretched out his hand. 'Be friends, Johane. I had no choice but to remain at Court.'

'For such a long time?'

'Be friends, my wife,' he repeated.

I tilted my chin. 'What is it worth?'

'I have brought a gift for you.'

'Do I see it now?'

'Later.'

'I think that I am not in the mood for friendly banter.' I stood. 'I have work to do. So I am sure do you.'

I left him to his own devices.

'You will have to forgive him sometime,' Lady Marguerite

71

observed with a fascinated eye after we had all shared a meal in almost total silence until Roger took himself off about his own affairs.

'I suppose I will. But not quite yet. I am in a mood to be wooed first.'

'Then I pray that it will be soon. Silent meals bring on a headache and disturb my stomach.'

'Then take a draught of Wood Betony. There may be many before we have come to terms in this battle.'

When Mortimer of Chirk visited, he and Roger took over the practice yard to exchange a few sword-blows with much noise and loud encouragement from the household who had immediately been drawn to watch. We had spent a few days of wary hostilities. Roger was not prepared to make excuses for his long absence. I was biding my time. The gift he had promised had made no appearance. Lady Marguerite had taken more than one dose of Wood Betony. So had I, although I had found no need to admit it to anyone.

I kept my distance from the sword play. How easy it was for men to draw attention to themselves. Yet even I could not resist in the end. It was an impressive display of armed talent and the outcome not worthy of a wager. Mortimer of Chirk might be old in years but still knew a trick or two with heel or elbow to put a young opponent on the floor, hard with frost. Roger fell with a thump and an oath while his uncle decried his lack of talent.

'Let's try that once more.' Roger shouted when he had recovered his breath. 'You'll not find it so easy to topple me again.'

Chirk helped him to his feet. 'Enough for today. I need a cup of ale. I'm getting old.' His smile was sly. 'Your wife is here. You might want to mend a few fences with her.'

Roger slumped on a wooden settle in a patch of sun against

the wall, brushing back his hair and smearing more dust on his face. I sat beside him and took his gauntlets from him. He turned his head to look at me.

'Have you decided that we shall be friends, Lady Mortimer?'

'Perhaps. I cannot have you die on my hands and still be at odds.'

'Thank God. I would not want you as an enemy. It has been like living in an icy cellar.'

'I have thawed.' I smiled at him. 'Tell me about your inheritance.'

I could not have asked a better question to build a bridge over the void between us.

'It is done. An agreement has been made to end the wardship. I am to pay the sum of two and a half thousand marks to Piers Gaveston. Then the inheritance will be mine.'

I blinked at him.

'Is it possible?' I was astounded. Such a vast sum of money. Could such an agreement be made? This was the sum of the Mortimer income over at least three years, to be paid out to end a wardship that would end legally anyway, in the foreseeable future when Roger reached the age of maturity. 'Why not wait until you come of age? Surely it is not too long!'

Roger's hands were clasped hard together around his sword hilt, his knuckles white.

'It must be possible. And yes, it is far too long to wait. A month is too long. I will not have my inheritance taken from me. I'll not have my lands in another's hands one minute longer than I can tolerate. Not even to please the Prince or Gaveston.'

Which was much in character. 'But where do we raise the money?'

'There are men I must talk to. About loans. Mortgages and

such. There is no need for you to worry about it. We will not lose one acre of Mortimer land.'

Such confidence. A thought touched my mind. A thought that bloomed red around the edges as anger took hold.

'Make sure that you do not sell any of my lands to achieve it. De Geneville lands must never be sold to secure Mortimer lands.'

'I will not.'

'Or mortgage them.'

'How can you so accuse me?'

'With ease.' Perhaps I had seen a flicker of guilt in his eye before it was veiled. 'I'll not forgive you if you do. My sisters were sent to a convent for the sake of the land I brought to you.' I stood up, all prickly again. 'I will order hot water to be carried up to your chamber. You are covered with dust and sweat.'

I left him to consider my reply, but heard his voice follow me, spiked with impatience.

'It is my land now, Johane, as you well know. I can do with it as I wish.' True enough. I chose to ignore the threat. He was home and under my feet. 'I thought that we had made peace.'

'I think that we have. Now we will prove it.'

I accompanied Roger to his chamber where he bathed, and I stepped out of my surcoat and under-tunic with an eye to making use of his bed in the fullness of time. The array of abrasions, cuts and scrapes on his body was impressive.

'Tournaments?' I enquired, anointing the worst and most recent with a decoction of St John's Wort to draw the bruising and the pain. 'Perhaps the nails of some court whore?'

'God's Blood, Johane. You are no ministering angel!'

'At least it was nothing fatal.'

'Which I hope will please you mightily.' He shrugged into a light linen under-tunic.

'Tell me of life at Court,' I encouraged. Better the enemy I knew, if the courtiers proved to be my enemy.

And he told me. As I expected, all circled around the Prince and his group of young friends. It would be enough to blind any man who saw himself as a descendant of King Arthur.

'Were you accepted into the group of noble friends?' I asked.

'Of course. Why would I not be?'

Well, I would say it. 'But you are only a baron. Not a great lord or an heir to such a one. You live far away on the Welsh border, distant from any Court that the King might hold.'

'Only a baron?' I had nettled him. 'But a rich and powerful one.'

'With my land.'

He emerged from the linen with which he was drying his hair. 'Ambitious barons are cunning. They seek the brides they want and marry well!'

Which put me in my place. 'And doubtless get themselves heirs by the handful,' I retaliated. 'Did you enjoy the tournaments?'

'Of course. I have a talent for jousting. I did my best, to attract attention through skill and victory in combat. Is this not a kingly gift?' Full of pride he walked over to the wall to retrieve the weapon I had noticed on his arrival, and handed the jewelled sword to me. 'An acknowledgement from the Prince when I came to his rescue in the melee, when a knight was belabouring him with a mace. I dispatched him with a blow to the head and the Prince escaped with little more than a tumble to the floor. There is much to be won at the King's side, and I will cultivate his son since it is in my interests.'

I had heard enough of the Court. I would turn his thoughts back to me since I had a need to feel his lips on mine, his hands sliding over my skin.

'You said that you had a gift for me,' I reminded him slyly, as he replaced the sword with care. He delved into a leather purse and retrieved a small wrapped parcel.

'I thought that this would express my thoughts and sentiments to my wife.'

Unwrapped, it revealed a silver heart-shaped brooch, quite simple with its central pin, but with letters hammered in around the edge. There was no glitter of gems to please me, but the sentiment was indeed perfect. It warmed my heart.

'Can you read it?' he asked, sitting down beside me.

I read the words aloud. '*I am a love token. Do not give me away.*'

'I hope that you will not.'

'I will keep it safe.' I regarded him through my lashes. Would he speak of love to me? 'You could pin it on my shift, if you wished.'

'It was in my mind to take your shift off.'

'Now?'

'Why not? Since it was in your mind too. Are we at last reconciled?'

I hid a smile. I could wait no longer and I knew full well that neither could he, with or without a declaration.

'It is beyond time that we were. Kiss me or I will die of desire.'

We had been apart for a year and this was a sweet reunion. Although his hands had become calloused from the use of sword and lance, they were gentle with me, until a surprising passion overtook both of us, to our mutual satisfaction.

'Did you truly miss me?' I asked.

'Of course. You are my wife.'

'Was there no Court lady to claim you in dalliance?'

'None that I would admit to.'

'Then show me again how much you love me and are pleased at our reuniting.'

He needed no encouragement, and he showed me indeed, with fire and passion. And afterwards, since it was not in his mind to overlook my own achievements in his absence, Young Roger was duly visited and admired. I knew that my Roger had been in the nursery on more than one occasion since his return.

'Do you remain here, or return to your gilded hero?' I asked, because I could not simply let the possibility lie that he would be travelling again within the week.

Roger bared his teeth at my gibe, but his arm pulled me close as he looked down at his third child, asleep in his cradle, this miracle of blood and bone and flesh. Although he slept he still managed to curl his fist around Roger's finger and hold tight, making Roger laugh aloud.

'I stay here. There is much for me to do. I have neglected you for too long, and I have neglected Wigmore too. We will start to build so that you and my heirs will live in a palace worthy of a Marcher lord.'

I turned my face into the soft wool of his over-tunic and sighed gently. There was nought for me to worry about after all, until he was summoned to war or to Court once again. Of course I forgave him, even though he would never speak of love. The love token must be enough.

Chapter Seven

The Port of Dover, January 1308

In the last week of January in the new year, Roger and I were found standing in a well-swathed crowd on the foreshore in Dover. It was a day of bitter wind, and the threat of snow showers, but we had chosen to be here. Although still not crowned, our new King Edward had been to France to find a bride as high-born as he was himself. It seemed that he had no difficulty in finding that noble-blooded bride. On the twenty-fifth day of that month he had married Princess Isabella, daughter of King Philip of France, Philip the Fair, in Boulogne. On this day when Edward was bringing home his bride, we were here to welcome her.

We had been busy at Wigmore, where Roger was now officially Lord Mortimer of Wigmore, in full possession of all the estates inherited from my father and from me. We were no longer answerable to any man for our inheritance. Where had Roger raised the money to pay for this? I presumed that it was borrowed, perhaps from Mortimer of Chirk and perhaps my grandfather. Yet although Piers Gaveston no longer had a call on his loyalties, Roger still had to answer the demands of the King.

Thus Roger had presented himself for the Scottish wars,

and I had worried and envisioned the worst through endless nights until he returned without undue harm other than some picturesque bruises and scrapes, to put his abundant energies into creating a palace at Wigmore and crushing the Welsh insurgents. Meanwhile our old King Edward died, leaving his throne to the golden gosling whom I was led to believe intended to become a gilded swan. It was in my mind to see this Prince for myself, as I informed Roger when the opportunity arose. I would not be left behind on this august occasion.

Thus here I was to see two vessels emerging from a bank of cloud which no wind had been able to dispel, both steadily approaching land. On the first, his fair hair shining even in the mist, stood our new King Edward. On the second, the *Margaret of Westminster*, specially commissioned for the journey to carry the bride to her new land, I could see a little knot of well-clad travellers on deck. Royal flags and French ones lifted in the breeze to mark this auspicious occasion.

Immediately after the landfall, without undue fuss, for the sea was complacent, the King leapt ashore onto the quay as we made suitable obeisance. I expected Edward to address the crowd, to lead his bride from the second vessel, introducing her to her new subjects, but Isabella's arrival was clearly not his first priority. His eye was searching the crowd before him. When he found what he sought his face broke into a gleam of a smile and he strode forward to where Piers Gaveston stood, clasping his shoulder and bestowing a salutation on each cheek, exchanging greetings.

He was younger than I expected, this Gascon knight who had once held Roger's lands in his care. He might lay claim to a mere handful of years more than Roger in age, but what a swagger he had in spite of his being a mere Gascon knight. A bright countenance, thick hair the dark russet of an old fox, and blue eyes. Not a tall man but one with a presence, and not just in the sapphires that shone on the upturned brim of his felt cap.

The crowd fell back to allow them a space when Edward indicated that they should.

What of the little Queen?

It was left to her brother, Prince Charles, who had accompanied her, to escort her from the ship. Lifting her trailing skirts in her gloved hands she walked gracefully to set foot on English soil for the first time, releasing her brother's hand so that she stood alone, Queen of England, even if yet uncrowned, meeting her subjects for the first time. I watched with interest to see how she would respond. How long would she have to wait for the King to recall her presence?

Too long, I thought. Too clumsily thoughtless. Edward continued to shower his friend with compliments after their long absence while I looked towards Isabella again. She was watching too but made no movement, merely stood, head raised, waiting, with all the dignity with which she had been raised as a Princess of France. What was she thinking? What were her thoughts at her abandonment on foreign soil? We had grown accustomed to this overt attachment between Edward and Gaveston; it would be new to her. Her thoughts masked by a bland, unsmiling acceptance, Isabella calmly folded back her hood.

'She is as fair as the first light of day,' I murmured to Roger.

Isabella was indeed born with the promise of beauty with hair, neatly plaited and confined within a crispinette, as golden as that of her husband. But what made the greatest impression on me was that she was still so young, younger than I by a good few years, yet even now she possessed a surprising elegance. Her features would firm into true beauty. She also possessed a composure that was unusual in a girl so young.

'Perhaps our King should not have placed his need to be

reunited with Gaveston before the welcoming of his new wife,' I suggested to Roger.

'No,' Roger agreed. 'It was not the wisest of actions. Look at the crowd.'

There was the displeasure, rank, silent criticism of such discourtesy towards a young woman who had set foot on English soil for the first time. Edward, her husband, should have been the one to lead her, not her brother. It would have been courteous on the part of Edward if he had introduced this most puissant French contingent, the royal uncles who also accompanied Isabella. It had not even entered his mind as he continued to exchange comment with Gaveston. Isabella continued to stand alone, her face a perfect pale oval within the frame of her veil, waiting to observe what would happen next.

What other thought did I discover in that critical little moment when Edward neglected his bride? To Edward, the French Princess was merely a means towards an alliance, acquired like a beribboned gift from her royal father. Perhaps one day he would appreciate her but not on this day. Gaveston took his eye to the exclusion of all else. A loud guffaw of laughter between the King and Gaveston made me think that the little Queen might have to wait long, and my compassion was roused. I took a step forward.

'What are you doing?' Roger demanded before I could take another.

'I am going to welcome the Queen,' I replied keeping my voice low. 'She has had a poor reception so far. What will she make of the English? Ill-mannered and obtuse. I will at least try to paint a smile on her face.'

I twitched my sleeve from his grasp, walked forward and curtsied.

'Welcome, my lady. I would welcome you as a fellow

country-woman. I am Johane de Geneville, now Lady Mortimer. I know what it is to come to a new country to wed an Englishman. That is my husband, Lord Mortimer, in the dark green mantle.' I waved vaguely in his direction. 'We hope that you will find happiness in your new realm.'

She blinked. Those beautiful clear grey eyes like winter-ice. She regarded Roger, but her gaze moved quickly over him to where the King was now issuing brisk orders to her uncles for our return to London.

'I am grateful for your reception. It is my intention to be happy here.'

I thought that she would win many hearts.

'Who is the man who holds the King's interest?' she asked.

'That is Sir Piers Gaveston, now Earl of Cornwall, a Gascon lord.' How to explain? I felt a need to lessen the pain of any careless wounding. 'They have been friends of long-standing. The King will be pleased to be reunited. Do you wish to meet with more of the women, summoned here to welcome you?'

'I will wait until the King recalls that I am here. But I thank you for your concern.'

So there we stood, exchanging inconsequential details about the voyage and the weather and where we thought that Isabella would stay that night, my hands growing colder, my thoughts stultifying, with no way forward, until King Edward's royal cousin, the Earl of Lancaster, approached and murmured in his ear. With a final clasp of Gaveston's arm, Edward swung round and strode across to his wife, bowing low before her before taking her hand, towering over her.

'My lords, my ladies, I show you my wife, your Queen. The most beautiful bride in Christendom, whom I have wed in France before bringing her home.' It was well done, at the last, as if there had been no intermission between the landing and the introduction. 'She is the woman I have most desired as my bride,' he continued, raising his voice so that all might hear. 'She has beauty and grace more than any other woman in the realm. I know that you will give her your loyalty and affection. I know that you will welcome her in my name and that of England.'

Perfectly done.

Edward bowed to his wife with effortless grace, as did everyone else. Keeping her hand, he led her forward to exchange courtesies with those who pressed forward. All the previous tension was expelled under the King's benign power.

'Why could he not do that ten minutes earlier?'

Roger's brows rose. 'Edward rarely sees beyond his own desires.'

'Your loyalty to him astonishes me.'

'It should not. He is the King and thus commands us all.'

'If I were Isabella...'

'But fortunately you are not. Now come and let us escape this God-forsaken spot and find some warmth and a cup of wine. The royal couple are returned and we can all go home.'

'And that will not be until the crown and holy oil are placed on Edward's brow,' I remarked, 'so set yourself for a long stay.'

'I have no quarrel with that. It will all be arranged with ceremonial perfection. As is everything that King Edward sets his hand to.'

I gave up. Roger would see no fault in the King. Or if he did, he would not voice it, so I caught Roger's eye and, smiling slightly, mentally promised not to be overly critical. Although I could not resist an obvious observation.

'It is regretful that Gaveston could not be sent on some foreign mission for the next few weeks.'

'I might agree, but Edward will be pleased to have him at his side against the Earls.'

'Then let us hope that he can keep his mouth shut and his manners douce. It should not be beyond him to bring the Queen round his little finger as a friend.'

What did I think of this soon-to-be-crowned King? Yes, I was impressed, even when it was in my mind to be critical of him. The tales I had heard from travellers had not been false. Tall, taller than Roger, he was a leader of men, surely. He had the physique of a soldier with broad shoulders and hands perfectly made to wield a sword. And he was handsome, without any doubt, with fair hair that curled to frame his face with its straight nose and sculptured mouth. His eyes were the clear blue of a summer sky. A gilded prince who had claimed my husband in friendship and loyalty. How could he not win honour and glory? How could any knight not wish to be a friend to this imposing young man? Roger brought me to the new King's attention before we all mounted for the procession to Westminster.

'My wife, my lord. Lady Johane de Geneville, now Lady Mortimer.'

The King took my hand and saluted my fingers with utmost grace, smiling with a show of even teeth. 'You are right welcome. So you are the heiress that Mortimer was fortunate to entrap.'

'Yes, my lord.' I would not argue the point although it rankled that it should be the first comment he might make to me, even if it was exactly what the Mortimers had done.

'We are pleased to see you here.' Turning to Roger, 'Will you hunt with me when we return to London?'

'I will, my lord.'

The King beamed at us in genial bonhomie, then with his arm thrust through that of Lord Gaveston, they walked away, leaving Isabella to her French uncles once more.

'Was it worth the long journey to witness this return?' Roger asked with sharp cynicism.

'Yes. In so many ways. Now take your entrapped heiress to find some food or she will expire of starvation. Then all we have to do is to survive what might prove to be a strained coronation if Gaveston insists on playing a major role.'

'When he should have none at all,' Roger added, leaving me to acknowledge that although he might appear complacent, Roger was not blind to those who sought power at the expense of those who had the right of inheritance.

Chapter Eight

The Royal Palace of Westminster, February 1308

What could go wrong?

'Nothing!' Roger said, scowling at our cramped accommodations.

'Everything!' I replied when I considered the possibilities.

The coronation of King Edward and his bride was planned for the eighteenth day of February. All that Isabella must decide was which garment to wear for the occasion. There she stood in the chamber newly prepared for her, surrounded by all the gifts showered on her as her trousseau by her father; a veritable treasure trove of golden basins, tapestries and more hangings for her bed than I could imagine using in a whole year. Amidst all this French glory she stood in her plain linen shift, her hair neatly braided to encircle her head in a fair crown in its own right, but other than that she was unprepared when I presented myself to see that all was in hand. The King had suggested it.

'What will you wear, my lady?'

'I know not.' Isabella was overwhelmed, allowing me to see her lack of confidence. 'I know not how to go about this.'

'You will have friends there as well as your uncles and your brother.' Her lips curved in a smile, that visibly trembled. 'Do you wear this?'

I draped the gown laid ready for her use over my arm so that the cloth shimmered as the candles flickered in the endless draughts. These were the wedding clothes made for Isabella, brought with her from France and entirely suitable. A robe fashioned in blue and gold, the colours of a daughter of France, superbly matched with a mantle of red lined with yellow sindon. She looked at the ensemble, considering its merits. Her reply surprised me.

'I will not. It has already been seen at my marriage. I will wear a new gown today as Queen.'

'But this is beautiful.'

'Will my lord wear the same garments in which he wed me?' she challenged me.

'No. He will wear the ceremonial coronation robes with an ermine cloak.'

'Then I will not wear the same. Pack it away against the moth, if you will.'

'There is no time to stitch a new garment,' I suggested, wondering how to reason with this young woman who had suddenly acquired a mind of her own, who must be handled with care. I hid a sigh before casting my eye over the coffers and boxes that were still to be unpacked. I could see no alternative unless she chose to attend her husband's coronation in a garment merely fit for the solar. And then...

'What about this?' Placing aside the rejected silk, I lifted the layers of a garment, still as yet unpacked, with pungent rose petals between the folds.

'Show me that,' she demanded.

It was a robe of crimson velvet, with a flowing mulberry over-tunic. Isabella frowned. Before she could reject it I intervened.

'Think how this gown will glow against the dark stones of the Abbey. You will be visible to all if you wear this.'

'That is true,' she replied, beginning to smile. 'I am not very tall yet, but no one will overlook me. And I wish to wear that.' She pointed to a gold circlet studded with jewels that had accompanied her from France. She added quietly: 'I wish my lord to have eyes for me rather than for Gaveston.'

Once again I was impressed by this young woman who had proved herself not slow in reading the depth of friendship between her lord and the man who was so frequently at his side.

'You could not have chosen better,' I replied.

She was still a child in her desire to be noticed, but her view of her place in this new kingdom was not child-like at all.

'I will be seen. Will I not be Queen? No one will then question my right to stand at King Edward's side.'

I wondered if the King knew the quality of this woman he had taken to wife. With smooth complacence, Isabella allowed us to clothe her in the velvet and jewels. Next time there was a ceremonial occasion, I knew that she would choose her own garments and adornment with no help from me or anyone else.

It was the eleventh hour. All should be on the move to the Abbey to take their places in the procession that would guide Edward to the royal throne, to the placing of the crown on his head. It did not happen.

I was in my own chamber, donning my robes, when Roger arrived.

'What's wrong?' I asked him as he stepped over our coffers to find a space. There was no mistaking his black mood, so I waved my woman away since privacy might be useful. The half-laced over-garment slid from my shoulders so that I must hitch it up. 'The invitations were sent out a month ago. The Queen has been ready for the last hour.' I read his face. 'Tell me it is not Gaveston!'

'Gaveston indeed,' he grimaced, casting off a heavy surcoat, flinging his hat on top. 'Or perhaps it is Edward who, in a thoroughly royal temper, is determined to be obeyed. Or perchance the mighty Earls should not have chosen this moment to take issue with Gaveston's role in this ceremony.' He cast his gloves onto the bed with the rest together with the jewelled chain from his shoulders. 'Whoever is at fault, it will not happen today.'

'What has Edward done?'

Roger might apportion the blame around, and rightly so, but surely Edward could remedy the problem to allow his crowning to go ahead. True, the Earls, the greatest magnates in the land, were powerful indeed: the Earl of Lancaster, Edward's cousin, together with the Earls of Hereford, of Lincoln, of Warwick, the warrior Earl of Pembroke. But surely our young King would smooth over the ripples in this particular pond. Pushing aside Roger's sword and belt which he had also dropped onto the bed, I sat down to hear the worst.

'Edward demands that Gaveston carry the crown of St Edward the Confessor before him in the procession. It is a great honour. Unfortunately it is the most important role in the whole ceremony, apart from that of the King. Which is of course exactly why Edward wishes to grant the honour to Gaveston.'

'Ha!' So the ripples were caused by the King himself. I could imagine the scene, Gaveston leading the King, the crown glittering in his hands as if it were his gift to give. 'I can imagine the reaction of the Earls.'

'Indeed. And the French Princes, who have been equally voluble.'

Roger was now stripping off the rest of his finery for his own role in the ceremony which was not to be.

'Then when will he be crowned? What do the Earls intend to do about it?'

Roger stopped unfastening the laces.

'God's Blood, Johane. How would I know?'

I moved to help with defter fingers since he had tied the laces in knots. His expression was grave. 'The Earls have delivered to our King an ultimatum. Banish Gaveston or face the consequences. How can they expect Edward to bow before such a threat to his power, but they are in no mood to be compliant. Those thrice-damned ceremonial tapestries have already caused resentment, with Gaveston's coat of arms stitched side by side with that of the King. Edward is blind to it all.' He ran his hands through his hair in frustration. 'Edward has made it clear that he will not banish his favourite and he will have the tapestries displayed where and when he wishes, however much the Earls demand their removal. Now we await the consequences!'

'And what will those be?'

'If Gaveston stays, Edward must agree to sanction any and all new policies produced in the new parliament. He must take an oath to uphold and defend the laws and customs of the realm.'

'But what if parliament demands that he banish Gaveston? Will Edward accept?'

I could not see it. Nor could Roger.

'No, he won't accept, but he will make any empty promise necessary, to ensure that he is crowned and anointed with Gaveston marching before him, proud as a dunghill cock.' Roger groaned and caught my wrists, planting a brief kiss where my pulse beat. 'I only see further trouble for the future.'

As he prepared to leave, clad once more in serviceable garments of wool and leather, more suitable for hard bargaining than festivity, I decided to ask the one pertinent question.

'Roger.'

He looked back over his shoulder.

'Where do you stand in all this? Are you ranged against Edward, on the side of the Earls? Or will you support Edward, whatever he does?'

Roger shrugged, his hand still on the door latch. 'He is King. He cannot be held to ransom by his subjects. But he might conduct himself with more understanding of the outcome of his wilfulness.'

Which was a two-handed sword thrust, leaving all in doubt.

'Would you consider supporting the Earls against him?' I persisted.

'Only if I was foolish enough to write my name on the list of Edward's enemies. Would I be willing to pay the price for so doing?' His smile was wry. 'You know well my ambitions, Johane.'

With this brief but uncomfortable résumé churning in my thoughts, I went to see the bride, to break the news to her. If she had not heard it already.

She had been told, and I learned for the first time that our little Queen had a voice and a temper.

'Why?' she demanded. 'What could possibly stop it now? Is my husband not King?' She was still clad in her velvet finery but the circlet had been cast aside and she was pacing the floor. A cup of wine was in her hand. 'What can possibly have brought so crucial a ceremony to a halt? Is it as my brother tells me? Some minor dispute over who carries the great crown?' Her lovely face was flushed, but any lack of confidence had vanished. 'Who is this man Gaveston? I hear much talk of him. Did we not all witness the King's reuniting with him?'

'He is Edward's friend.'

'I know of the friendship,' Isabella said. 'A man needs friends. But why has this lord been allowed so much power?'

How to be subtle. It was impossible to be anything but plain. 'Because Edward wishes it. Their friendship is of some years now.'

It would not be easy to explain that who might carry the crown of King Edward the Confessor was not a minor ruffling of feathers, but eventually she must learn the balance of power in this kingdom. I took the cup from the girl and began to help Isabella dispense with the jewels and the heavy gown until she was once more in her shift.

She raised her hands in frustration. 'My lord must be crowned.' Then Isabella looked at me, a sharp glance. 'Is Gaveston my enemy?'

'I think not.' I decided to give advice to this new Queen of England. 'It would be good for you to be aware of the strength of friendship between them. The King sees him as his adoptive brother, his brother-in-arms. He believes that they share the power of government as brothers.'

'How can a crowned and anointed King share any royal power with a mere man, a subject?'

I did not reply, letting the young woman pace once more.

'Can these Earls who have such loud voices stop this coronation?'

'It may be. The Earl of Lancaster is King Edward's cousin.'

'They would not dare to do so if I held the power. I do not like this man Gaveston. That he has so much power over my husband. That Edward puts his desires first.' Once more she looked at me, her eyes narrowed. 'Should I work to get rid of him? Do I support those who would have him banished?'

A question that horrified me as much as it intrigued.

'Perhaps not yet,' I soothed. 'One day, if you are of the same mind. But my answer now is no.'

'Why not?'

I decided on honesty. Isabella must know the truth.

'Because you are still young and untried. Because the King likes Gaveston more than he likes you. It is still early in your marriage and may not always be so, but you must not make him choose between you. Not yet.'

A thought intruded uncomfortably into my mind. As King Edward took control of the realm, would Roger ever have to choose loyalty to me or to Edward? We had years and experience behind us and a quality of deep affection, but there was that powerful streak of ambition that would determine all Roger's loyalties. A disturbing thought. I stretched out my hand and touched Isabella's wrist where it emerged from her linen sleeve, risking a rebuff.

'My advice, if you will take it, my lady. Do not make Edward's friend your enemy. Watch and wait, and show your loyalty to the King above all else. Also smile on Gaveston. If it is possible.'

Isabella stood, frowning down at her clasped hands. How small and seemingly frail they were to be taking on such a burden. Then she looked up, her decision made.

'It is good advice, Lady Mortimer.' She shrugged, a youthful gesture after all, as her woman returned to lace her into a plain kirtle under-tunic more suitable for the day. Her next query, sotto voce, was far from naive. 'Do you suppose that he is my lord's lover?'

It was a question that I could not answer. Nor would I, in a chamber where every servant had ears.

'Such matters are not for me to discuss here, my lady.'

'I cannot like it, if it is so. I cannot be Gaveston's friend after all. But perhaps it will be useful to pretend to be so.'

'I think that you have shown great wisdom today, my lady.'

'And you have shown me that you are my friend, Lady Mortimer.' Her gaze was steady on mine. 'Do you ever question the loyalties of Lord Mortimer? Do you ever fear that your hopes and desires will be disregarded?'

'No, my lady.'

Did I ever question them? I had never had need to do so. His fealty had always been to his King, his family and to me, but was it not a moot point in any family? As before, I pushed the thought aside.

Chapter Nine

Westminster Abbey, February 1308

A royal coronation, with all the panoply and grandeur worthy of the event, tottered on the edge, until all was resolved between King Edward and his truculent Earls. A mere week later than was anticipated, Isabella was once more clothed in her coronation finery. All would proceed as planned, although I think I was not the only member of the vast congregation to experience a slow slide of fear along the spine.

Edward had agreed to the demands of the Earls. No, he would not banish Gaveston, but he would acquiesce in the demands of parliament. The Earls had also compromised, although we all knew that they would have Gaveston's removal in mind for another day. The King would not be allowed free rein in what they saw as a dangerous friendship, allowing Gaveston to garner even more power into his elegantly grasping hands. Had not the King already created him Earl of Cornwall and allowed his marriage to his own cousin, the formidable heiress Margaret de Clare? Yet the Earls were present at the ceremony, clad in cloth of gold as was their right, three of them carrying the great swords of state, so that it seemed that Edward had made his peace with them after all.

My own gratification knew no bounds in seeing Roger among the four nobles who carried the royal robes displayed on a fine cloth. Young he might be, and no earl forsooth, but he enjoyed the King's regard sufficiently to be chosen. Pale and serious, walking with great solemnity, was this not what Roger wanted? To be noticed, to be recognised in the close circle of Edward's friendship. All was as it should be in the ceremonial procession, but then I saw what would cause all the trouble in the world.

Blessed Virgin! King Edward had made no compromise at all.

At first there was no noticeable reaction during this sacred procession, not so much as an intake of breath, but all must be aware. There was Sir Piers Gaveston, the final figure to enter, just before the King himself. Gaveston, Earl of Cornwall, was carrying the crown of St Edward. More regal than the king, clad not in cloth of gold, but in royal purple, enhanced with pearls, taking all eyes as he raised the magnificent crown with all its symbolism, arms outstretched before him.

Would there be a disturbance? Not so. Edward knew his strengths well. The ceremony was laid down by tradition so that nothing might go amiss. There was not one magnate who would intrude upon this sacred bestowing of power, however much he detested it. Thus Edward and Isabella were crowned, the new reign set in train. Edward led Isabella the length of the nave in her chosen crimson velvet and French circlet along a cloth strewn with flowers. Walking barefoot in piety, Isabella was as pale as whey but as composed as a Queen should be, yet she took my attention. In brutal comparison with Gaveston's royal-purple-clad performance, Isabella, small and overshadowed, had hardly been noticed even though she had been crowned. Her smile was brilliant in satisfaction, but I did not think that she would be pleased at the adoration being deflected from her. She had agreed to smile at Gaveston but I thought her smile was falsely luminous; it meant nothing.

All we had to do now was survive the wedding banquet.

It did not bode well from the beginning, held in Westminster Hall beneath the glory of the offending tapestries, where all eyes were on Piers Gaveston, still clad in his detestable purple with the pearls shimmering in a baleful gleam. Nor did it improve for the French lords when they must see that Isabella's coat of arms was entirely absent above their heads. A terrible slight. A public insult, while there was no sign of Gaveston's promised humiliation. After the platters of the first course had been cleared away, King Edward decided that he no longer wished to sit beside his new Queen, choosing a seat next to Gaveston himself where he laughed, ate, joked and paid no attention to anyone else, raising his cup in frequent toasts to his brother-in-arms. What a gloriously dramatic scene the new King orchestrated to show the Earls where they stood in his regard. He had stamped his authority on the event, but at the cost of humiliating his new French wife. There was a set look to Isabella's jaw, but that was nothing compared with the fury on the faces of both the French lords and the English Earls. The tension in the great chamber was as taut as a well-strung bow.

And Roger? I found it impossible to read his face, but certainly the visceral anger that touched the expressions of the Earls and the French lords was absent. It was like watching the preamble to the playing-out of a game of chess. The King supreme in his newly acquired power. The Queen as yet powerless in her youth. Gaveston the valiant and mighty knight at the King's side. Who were the bishops and rooks? The Earls who vied for power around the King but failed in their attempts to bring him to heel. And Roger. He had no role in this game unless it were a mere pawn who as yet had served the King with utmost loyalty. Would he be vying to be a power in the game? No one could depose Gaveston from his position at the King's side. No one could challenge the Gascon's ultimate authority as long as the King smiled on him.

My final impressions of that diabolical banquet. The minstrels silenced, the servants clearing the dishes and the uneaten food to distribute to the poor who hoped for largesse. A shout of laughter from our newly crowned King as he linked his arm with Gaveston to lead the way from the hall. Gaveston's solemn demeanour which entirely failed to disguise the arrogance of his satisfaction. The Earls who followed, stony-faced, no longer voicing their fury but still it hovered like a thundercloud. The French nobles equally silent, faces blank with shock at the treatment of their Princess.

And there was Isabella, still smiling bravely as if there was nothing amiss with the whole terrible disaster where her own potential position had been usurped. I admired her fortitude. I feared that she would need it. It should have been the most satisfying day of her life. Instead, she had learned that it would be impossible to build a relationship with her husband as long as Gaveston was there to curl his little finger and summon Edward to his side. It must all taste like ashes in Isabella's mouth, bitter as gall. And over all the shivering of the outrageous tapestries, vivid with their new stitching, which proclaimed the friendship of a King and his subject, without one mention of the royal wife.

What did I think of the King after that demonstration of royal authority? There was a mantle of self-serving generosity on his shoulders, to win friends, but I did not like him. I would not say it to Roger, but I would not trust him. King Edward would hold out a hand of friendship, but equally discard any such friendship that did not bring advantage.

'Would you accept an outbreak of insurrection?' I eventually asked Roger as, abandoning the hotbed of Westminster, we rode up the hill towards Wigmore. I hoped that this would be the final time that we discussed Court affairs. 'If the King pushes the Earl of Lancaster into raising arms against him, who would you support? Earl or King?'

Roger drew his horse to a halt and, reins held lightly, one fist on hip, he surveyed his castle and the surrounding lands.

'I would pray it will never happen. The Earls have no right to question the King's God-given authority.'

'They may not have the right, but they might have the power.'

The chill of uncertainty hovered over me. All I could hope was that it never came to a question of open warfare, and we could be left in peace. The King and his young wife must come to their own terms in their marriage while the Earls must make their own plans. It was not my affair, and yet it seemed that the coronation had set light to a fire in Roger's eye as he dismounted in the bailey, pushing aside the wolfhounds that rushed to greet him.

'Whatever happens, I will be more than a mere Marcher lord,' he announced, looking across at me. 'I swear it.'

'I don't doubt that you will,' I replied dryly. Roger's ambitions were not new to me.

As he helped me to dismount in the inner bailey, the dust of Wigmore once more on my shoes, I fervently but silently hoped that such ambitions would not take him back to Court too often. It seemed to me that there was a poison brewing there and I would not wish Roger to become engulfed in the noxious fumes.

Chapter Ten

Wigmore Abbey in the Welsh Marches, 1314

Helped down from my luxuriously cushioned travelling litter, I walked into the Abbey where Lauds had just come to an end. With me was Isabella, well swaddled in soft wool and cradled in my arms. I was met by the Abbot who peered at the most recent infant, who slept through the clerical admiration.

'And which Mortimer is this, brought to receive my blessing?' he asked.

'This is Isabella,' I said. 'So named in honour of the Queen.'

'You are indeed blessed in your children, my lady. Will you dedicate her to the church? It would be good for the family to have a daughter in a convent, to pray for your eternal souls.'

I had thought about this. I had thought of my own sisters still in Aconbury, with my continuing guilt that I had not visited them or done more than send money to the endowment. I would never condemn one of my own daughters to such a life of seclusion. They would all wed, raise their own families, enjoy the control of their own households, as did I.

'No. Isabella will never take the veil. She will marry well, as my lord chooses. In fact I have no ambition that any of my daughters will enter a convent, unless it is her wish.'

The Abbot nodded. 'We must add the child's name to the Mortimer Roll. And where is your lord at this moment? I think that he is not at Wigmore.'

'I wish I could give you a clear reply, my lord bishop.'

He took Isabella from me, holding her with some surprising skill, and smiled at me with compassion.

'He will return when he can.'

I sighed a little.

The past years of our marriage had seen much change and movement as we settled into our life as Marcher lord and lady. Roger campaigned in Ireland as well as in Scotland. The death of my grandfather in Ireland in his eighth decade after a day's hunting handed more power to us, and the building progressed at Wigmore to create the palace that Roger dreamed of. Our family increased with healthy sons and daughters. I proved fertile and childbed was no worse for me than for any other woman. Roger made a name for himself both in battle and in negotiation. I travelled with him, to Ireland and back, as the demand took him. So the Mortimers thrived as Roger tackled his lawless tenants in Ireland. Infrequently he had the freedom to enjoy his family or a day's hunting, and I accompanied him as we unleashed the wolfhounds. Cúchulainn and Lugh bounded forward, even though growing stiff in leg and grey in muzzle, against the wildfowl along the water's edge in the land where they had been born. When they ran to the end of their days we buried them in the grounds of Trim Castle, as was only fitting. Then there were new hounds to raise and train.

Roger was summoned back to England at the whim of the King and I perforce travelled with him, like a flea hopping from one warm body to the next, when affairs demanded his presence in the Scottish wars, or in the uprisings in Wales which threatened our hold on the Marches. Roger and his Chirk uncle worked tirelessly to put the insurgency down.

As for Wigmore, it grew around us, the defensive walls raised to repel attack, the towers strengthened, the gatehouse rendered more impressive with an outer barbican. Yet not all of Roger's improvements were military. Within the inner ward we gained a new range of stone-built structures for storage and to house guests. The drainage was improved so that it was possible almost to walk dry-shod. It became the palace of Roger's dreams, although the de Montfort skull still held pride of place in the Treasury.

Lady Marguerite lived her life between Wigmore and her own property at Radnor. My mother soon decided that Ludlow was a more peaceful place.

'I am fond of your small herd of children, but their games make my ears ring.'

'You should give thanks to God that they are healthy.'

'As I do. Frequently. But there are no riotous children at Ludlow.'

I hugged her in compassion and waved her farewell as I considered my own situation. Did Roger and I enjoy the life? I was certain of it. It was his metier, ultimately being rewarded with the title King's Lieutenant in Ireland.

'I could wish that your metier was to remain at home for at least a week.' I was still in a mood to complain after a particularly lengthy absence.

'You have all my attention when I return.'

His arms were strong around me, his lips pleasurably demanding.

'Sometimes I could wish that I had less of it.'

I could not deny it. Our children were born with unnerving regularity during those years. Did his absence worry me?

Whether I lived in Trim or Dublin or Wigmore, I grew used to the perennial anxiety until Roger rode up to the door looking either harassed and none too pleased, or vibrant with triumph. He was not one for sending a letter or a courier, as I soon discovered.

'Greetings, my long-lost husband. You are alive.'

How many times would these be my first words to Roger after weeks alone? Far too many. Meanwhile we made marriage agreements for our children. I saw no dangerous storm-clouds on our horizon as we entered the names of our sons and daughters in the Mortimer Roll kept at Wigmore Abbey.

The Abbot escorted me into his own accommodations, sending for the small coffer that protected the Roll, summoning a scribe with a fair hand while he spread the Roll for me to see. It was a marvellous work, started far back into the past, long before Roger was born, detailing the Mortimer sons and daughters and their heraldic achievements, the colours bright since it was kept with great care. I was not so interested in the distant past, of those I did not know, recorded in the crabbed Latin script of some unknown scribe, although Roger was proud enough of it.

This is what I had come for. The record of the birth of our children and their carefully plotted marriages, all deliberately noted for future generations to know. This was a time of establishing the Mortimers as a power for the future. A time of me chivvying Roger into making provision for our children. Not that he needed it. Roger now had sufficient standing to make impressive contracts. How successful we were in planning alliances. How well we had set them on the path to power and dominance, while I ensured that we had a true record of it here at the Abbey, formal agreements of marriage-bonds which would be fulfilled when our children were of an age to be wed in body as well as in name. There would be no disputes about our achievements or the inheritance of our children.

Edmund, married to Elizabeth, daughter of Bartholomew, Lord Badlesmere.

What an advantageous match that was. Badlesmere had paid two thousand marks for the marriage. In return Roger endowed our son and new daughter-in-law with an impressive array of the Mortimer manors. Then there were the Irish lands to look to.

Roger, wed to Joan, daughter of Sir Edmund Butler.

A marriage agreement, granting to our son Roger all our Irish lands on the occasion of his marriage to Joan, daughter of the mighty Irish magnate Sir Edmund Butler, who paid one thousand pounds for the connection.

The Mortimer star was rising in the heavens. Were we indeed setting up a Mortimer power here in the March, and beyond? My pride was as great as Roger's at our achievements.

Margaret, born at Wigmore Castle, wed to Thomas de Berkeley, son and heir of Maurice, Lord Berkeley.

Maud, born at Wigmore Castle, wed to John Charlton, son and heir of the Lord of Powys.

Such important connections for our daughters, so coldly noted. And then the rest of our children, born at Trim or Wigmore, all still young and so far unwed.

Geoffrey. John. Joan.

I watched as the clerk took his pen and ink pot and inscribed the name of Isabella in the list of Mortimers. My children, the jewels in my Mortimer crown.

Isabella, born at Wigmore...

How fortunate we were that not one of our children had to be marked as departing this life. Would I want more children? I was not averse to it.

It was the most contented time of my life, with no premon-
itions, earthly or heavenly, to disturb it. At Court it was a time
of some satisfaction for all except Edward, since the exile of
Gaveston had at last been forced on the King by the frustrated
Earls in the aftermath of England's defeat in Scotland. All
breathed more easily. And yet was not change inevitable? A
breath of it came to hover over us. It was an occurrence that we
could never have expected, a death to shake the country.

Chapter Eleven

Kings Langley, on the second day of January 1315

Roger and I were standing beside a new grave, as yet empty, at the royal manor of Kings Langley. Piers Gaveston, Earl of Cornwall, was dead. He had been dead and unburied for almost two and a half years while we had been in Ireland. As all here present on this cold winter day knew, the royal favourite had been under a judgement of excommunication, burial in holy ground being forbidden. The King kept the body embalmed and wrapped in cloth of gold at the Dominican Friary in Oxford, surrounded by candles, until the excommunication was lifted. Now it had been. Thus here we were at Kings Langley.

We had joined the lords and clerics at the graveside. I looked round the crowd of mourners, all muffled in cloaks and hoods against the winter blast, most of whom I recognised. Edward himself was looking grim, through grief or a thwarted desire for vengeance on those who had killed Gaveston and still remained alive, rejoicing in his death.

'Will he take revenge on those who murdered him?' I asked.

'Not until he has buried him with as much splendour as he can achieve,' Roger replied. 'Then I expect he will set his mind to it. Happily it is not our affair. We will return to Ireland as soon as this is over.'

How did Gaveston die? Not from fever or some noxious wound experienced in battle in Ireland. Gaveston was done to death by the King's own subjects. Returned from exile he was cruelly murdered with no pretence at legality at the hand of the Earls who feared a return of his influence over the King. Run through with a sword, then beheaded by men employed by the Earl of Lancaster, his body was left to rot. Gaveston might have been welcomed back by Edward who declared all past judgements against him unlawful and thus restored all his lands and titles, but the Earls saw only the extent of Gaveston's power after his reuniting with the King at Knaresborough. Gaveston's greed and his marriage to a royal cousin had pre-empted his death, and his posturing as a glorious god of the ancient world at Edward's coronation had hammered the nails into his coffin. For the King it was a terrible loss, casting him predictably into gloom and despondency.

'Who will it be for Edward's eye to fall on next?' I asked Roger as we still waited for the solemnities to begin. He needed a friend to take Gaveston's place, another confidant, another brother-in-arms. Probably another lover, if rumours were true. 'I see that Isabella is here.' She was standing next to Edward but not within touching distance, circumspectly allowing him to grieve alone. 'With Gaveston buried at last, here is the chance for her to take his place and make a position for herself in Edward's life.'

Roger shrugged under the heavy fur on the shoulders of his cloak that glistened with rain drops.

'I doubt that the Queen will make a successful bid for the King's affections.'

'Why not? I think that we have not yet seen just how head-strong and determined our Queen might be now that the years have blessed her with experience and confidence.'

I imagined Isabella silently rejoicing at the removal of this challenge to her own influence over Edward.

'We have to accept, Johane,' Roger replied with grim stoicism. 'If the past is any measure of him, Edward needs a courtier of some glamour and wit to snatch at his attention.'

'Do you see such a one here?'

'Perhaps.'

I followed his line of sight. There were two I could not name. From their age and similar cast of feature they were father and son.

'Who are they?' I nodded subtly in their direction, knowing that Roger had been watching them.

'Hugh Despenser, father and son. The elder is Earl of Winchester.'

'You do not like them?'

Roger's lip had curled in what was not a smile.

'They have an ambition to build their own power, but the King seems to find them amenable. The younger is wed to Edward's cousin Eleanor, another one of the three de Clare girls.'

A troubling thought. 'Then through that marriage the Despensers have an interest in lands in Wales.'

'Just how much needs to be seen. Come and meet them.'

We made our way to join a group of magnates amongst whom the Despensers were engaged in a discussion of the difficulties of travel in this wintry weather. I was given the opportunity to assess them as they bowed to me and welcomed me into the group. Well presented, perfectly mannered, gently spoken, they shimmered with courtly gloss. Would the younger appeal to Edward's wayward affections? There was nothing to dislike in either unless it was an air of arrogance, but many could make a claim for that, as I well knew from the man at my side.

I sought Roger's opinion pertinent to our earlier conversation, as we moved on and were free to talk. 'The younger is fair of feature.'

Roger saw my direction. 'And will our King see the attraction? He might. We must pray that he does not. It might not be well for any of us if Edward is moved to hand out enough titles and lands to please the Despensers.'

Meanwhile King Edward laid his friend Piers Gaveston to rest in a deluge of rain, the body wrapped in three layers of cloth of gold. The only consolation to the congregation was that Edward had provided twenty-three tuns of wine for the mourners after the event. There was no mention of the bloody murder that brought it about.

'A salutary lesson to us all,' Roger stated as we turned to collect our escort and horses. 'A mere twenty-eight years. He whom the gods love dies young.'

Roger was not one for quoting ancient writers.

'Very true. He whom the King loves can also find his life in danger if he makes the wrong enemies,' I suggested.

Roger had cast a final glance over his shoulder at the Despensers.

'We have enemies there,' he admitted at last. 'I would not wish them to step close to the King and whisper in his ear.'

At last there was a chink in Roger's reserve.

'And will you tell me why?'

'Family history. Nothing for you to worry about.'

So the chink would not be widened. Nothing could have

made me more anxious, yet his reticence resurrected a memory for me, when Roger had told me of his family history so long ago now, that first day in the Treasury at Wigmore. At the Battle of Evesham, Roger's grandfather had dispatched the Despenser lord with his own hands. Did not a simmering campaign of revenge lurk in the Despenser hearts? Would such a campaign still exist after so many years, to be avenged for a Despenser death at Evesham? I had not taken it too much to mind, but now it behoved me to be aware.

'What are your plans?' I asked as he lifted me into my saddle.

'A return to Ireland. I have some over-powerful Irish lords to deal with, and some castles to reclaim. I will not be bested by them.'

Enemies in Ireland were one thing; in England quite another. I needed to know whom I should fear on my own threshold. I had caught a glint in the elder Despenser's eye, which might suggest that he would happily bury a knife between Roger's shoulder-blades.

Considering all I knew of King Edward and of Roger, one more question I asked before we turned for Wigmore and home.

'You would not consider yourself as a future royal favourite, would you? It would bring you land and power.'

For the first time on that dreadful day Roger's smile became genuinely warm.

'I would not. I am too fond of my wife's embraces.' Pushing his horse close to mine, he placed an arm around my waist to draw me close and planted a kiss on my temple. 'Edward needs a man who will cleave to him, with love as well as loyalty. My sworn fealty is his, without question, but all my devotion belongs to my de Geneville heiress.'

I felt my cheeks grow warm, despite the whip of cold winds. Sensibly, I put it down to the excess emotion engendered by the dramatic the interment of the royal favourite.

Chapter Twelve

Dublin Castle in Ireland, mid-September 1320

The day began the same as any other day in the vast stronghold of Dublin Castle, except for the delivery of four letters from England. I took them from the courier, selected two for my own perusal, then sent the other pair on to Roger who was planning his business dealings for the day.

I opened mine, placing them side by side on my knee, deflecting Beatrice's three-year-old inquisitive fingers, kissing her coifed head before pushing her to sit at my feet with the kitten that she had acquired from the kitchens. My other young daughter, four-year-old Agnes, was, reluctantly, practising her stitching in the nursery. Here for my perusal was one letter from Lady Marguerite and one from my mother. The content of the missives was surprisingly similar. Uncomfortably, unsettlingly similar, after the usual family gossip and queries after the children.

The information they imparted caused me to look up from the clerk-written lines, surveying the chamber that I had made my own in this massive stronghold. I had risen and dressed long after Roger had started his day with his clerk, documents and pen in hand, a burden that prevented him from riding out to survey his territory. He had only recently returned from a progress through the distant wilds of Athlone and Kilkenny. Now he was restored to our household. Weary, aching from long days in the saddle, restless again as news of the perennial Irish insurrections arrived, it was a way of life to which he was dedicated.

The mornings were growing darker, signs of autumn tightening its grip once more. Would winter find us in Ireland or back in the Marches? Either would find me content. There was nothing to disturb my peace here or in England as far as information and rumour made me aware. My mother was still in good health in Ludlow. Lady Marguerite travelled from Wigmore to Radnor and back again, no great distance, and was sure to report on any adverse circumstances other than a local bloodletting over the ownership of a dozen cattle. Other than that, I knew nothing of events in England, or Wales, where the Chirk Mortimer was now Justiciar. Ireland had a strong hand of justice at the helm, and Roger, where he continued as Justiciar, was much complimented. Would he not remain here? In truth, I would not be averse to it although I had an occasional yearning to go back to Wigmore and Ludlow and visit my older children.

My attention was drawn back to the letters. Perhaps all was not as peaceful as I had thought, since both these women close to my heart had been moved to write to me. I decided to disturb Roger before the Irish lords descended with their soft voices and hard demands. Taking Beatrice and the kitten, I went to find him. There he sat, legs stretched before him, letters open under his hand and a groove of deep thought between his brow; I had a presentiment that it had not been there a half hour ago. The two wolfhounds, Brigid and Dagda, now well-grown replacements for Lugh and Cúchulainn, pricked their ears at the entry of possible prey, but then sank back with a sigh at Roger's feet. The kitten sensibly fled with a scrabble of claws before I could close the door. As I often did, I went to lean against him and read over his shoulder. I recognised the scrawl immediately; a clerkly hand I knew well for its indecipherability.

How would I, on that placid morning when all was well with my world, have foreseen the intricate weaving of future events that would change my life for ever?

'You namesake from Chirk, I see.'

'Yes.'

A surprisingly brusque reply since their views were usually so well meshed together.

'I see one name there that rouses my suspicions,' I read. 'If they had not already been stirred up. Hugh Despenser. And what might he be doing?'

'The younger of the pair.' Roger cast the letter aside whether I had finished reading or not. 'My uncle is all gloom and doom and I know not what to make of it. He writes – or his clerk – writes in circles.' He looked up at me. 'What has already ruffled your feathers?'

'I should tell you that Despenser has troubled your mother and mine. I have letters from both. Mostly family chatter, but both expressing some concerns.'

'So Chirk might not be quite lost in false rumour.' The frown deepened. 'This letter might clear the matter up.'

He shrugged off my hand as he leaned forward, picked up a second letter and began to read. I gave up trying to read over his shoulder and sat opposite him as if I were a petitioner. Something had troubled him but he would tell me in his own good time.

'Who is the letter from?' I would at least discover that.

'The Earl of Hereford.'

Humphrey de Bohun. One of the powerful Earls, a man of authority in England and one with an interest in the Marches to rival that of Roger. I allowed my thoughts to wander, bringing together the strands of danger that might tie Roger, Hereford and Chirk together, with Despenser, in the same net. Two letters in one day that creased Roger's forehead like a summer-dry Irish bog. Perhaps the Mortimer and de Geneville women had also picked up on accurate worries in England.

'And what is it that moves my lord of Hereford to write to you?'

'Despenser, again.'

'But what is different now? Has he not been building his power-base and land all the time these past years?'

'The difference now is the swath of land called Gower. The critical little matter of Gower in South Wales, and who will take possession of it. Whoever owns it will have a perfect base for launching attacks on the rest of Wales. And on the Marches.'

The shadow hanging over all of us was, of course, the brooding affair of who held the balance of power in the Welsh March. Roger had found an element of friendship for Piers Gaveston as jousting companions and fellow combatants in the Irish wars. This new royal favourite, for that is what Despenser had become over the last years, was a different matter. Despenser had ambition as we all knew, but this ambition had grown to enormous proportions, willingly sanctioned by the King. Moreover, now appointed King's Chamberlain, he controlled, in his own interest, that most desirable route to the King's ear.

'Do I understand that Despenser wants more land in Wales and along the March?'

'You understand it very well. He wants land and power wherever he can get it. He is already lord of Glamorgan through his marriage to Eleanor de Clare. Of course he wants more.' Once again I felt a fleeting sympathy for the de Clare sisters, wed for their inheritance. 'And we know that he will have the earldom of Gloucester in place of the dead Gilbert de Clare, his father-in-law, killed at Bannockburn.'

Roger cast down the letter from the Earl of Hereford, to lie on the much-scarred board, its seal curling.

'Well?' I asked. 'You may as well tell me. I can see it troubles you.'

'Troubles me?' He pushed himself to his feet and strode to the window that gave him a clear view of the courtyard protected by the high curtain walls and massive circular towers at each corner, all built back in the days of King John. He lifted Beatrice to stand on the window seat, pointing out to her the ever-present guards on the wall-walk and a circling buzzard beyond. 'Trouble is not the word. If Despenser is really set on this path to take Gower, he will become a major player in South Wales. And what next? I swear he will destroy me and my uncle and take our lands. What's more he'll take the greatest pleasure in doing so.'

'Has not Gower been legally purchased by John de Mowbray? Was it not his land anyway through his wife's inheritance?'

'It has been purchased by de Mowbray, and with my blessing, even though I made a bid for it myself, since it is large and strategically placed, perfect for us to own. But Despenser has complained to the King that it was bought illegally without royal consent.' Roger slammed his hand hard against the window's stone surround, causing Beatrice to look up at him so that he must stroke her head in reassurance. 'Since when did matters of land ownership in the March need royal consent? We have never needed royal licence. Why would we now? Except Despenser is wishful to claim it for himself, with Edward's gracious support and gratitude for his friendship. Thus he creates some false situation that will tip Gower into his own hands.'

Roger's mouth curled in familiar cynicism. Lifting Beatrice down, returning to fling himself back in his chair, such that it creaked, his fingers tapped against the words on the Hereford document as if they could absorb more wisdom from whatever it was the Earl had suggested.

'Surely Edward will not allow it,' I suggested. 'He must know that it is vital for him to keep the loyalty of his friends in the March, including de Mowbray. To allow this would simply push them into hostilities.'

'Mmm. Edward it seems is more a slave to Despenser's desires with each day that passes.'

'Would the King not feel gratitude to you, for your past loyalties?'

'Do you think?'

But no, I did not think that Edward's gratitude could be relied on. What a fair-weather friend he was proving to be. I wondered how Queen Isabella was faring in the middle of all this, with a new favourite to take Edward's fascination. I did not envy her, but at twenty-five years now, I thought that she could keep Edward from committing too many dangerous manipulations of his power. I hoped that she could.

'Despenser is intent on persuading Edward to confiscate Gower from de Mowbray, and then give it to him – Despenser – as a gift,' Roger growled. 'If the King does this, we are all at risk. Whatever he asks for, Despenser will get, even if it means obliterating the Marcher laws of inheritance. From there he would snatch up any land he could take in the Welsh Marches.'

Which would tread heavily on Mortimer toes. And those of the Earl of Hereford. I was still reluctant to accept that there was any real danger here for us. Then remembered that even our womenfolk were concerned.

'It may interest you to know that your mother and mine are in communication with Eleanor de Clare.'

117

Roger's ears positively pricked, much like those of the hounds with a kitten in view.

'And?'

'Nothing that will surprise you, in the circumstances. Eleanor says that her Despenser husband, in whom she sees no wrong, has in mind to take over the entire Clare inheritance in South Wales. Including the lands of her sister Elizabeth. Which simply confirms what Hereford is telling you.' Roger grimaced at this piece of news. 'What is the Earl of Hereford suggesting?' I asked.

'Insurrection.'

It made me inhale sharply in shock that he would even consider voicing it. I ran my nail over the folds in my two letters. 'To go to war?'

'To challenge the King with force of arms.' He hesitated, scowling again. 'Or at least to challenge Despenser. Hereford is as much under threat as we are.'

'And your uncle? What will he say?'

'I am as yet uncertain.'

'Does he not demand retribution against Despenser?'

'As I said, he writes in circles.'

'And what does Lord Mortimer of Wigmore think?'

Roger hesitated again. This was the cause of the frown. And here was perhaps the answer to my previous question that had been carefully wafted aside.

'Lord Mortimer too is uncertain.'

'Then what will be your reply to the Earl of Hereford?'

'I have yet to decide.'

It was like trying to squeeze water from a dry cloth.

'How grave a threat is he to us, Roger? Despenser, I mean, not the King.'

'A serious one.' Stretching out his hand, he took mine when I made to rise to my feet since this discussion was getting nowhere. He pulled me round the table until I stood next to him again, our fingers entwining. His face was grave, the lines beside his mouth pronounced. 'Hugh Despenser will happily make us pay the price for the death of his grandfather at the Battle of Evesham, with our lands if not our lives. And now that he has the King's ear he might just be able to achieve it. I think nothing will hold him back from it.'

I recalled Gaveston's burial, the ripple of unease and Roger's silence when I thought that he knew more than he was saying.

'I remember the Despensers,' I said. 'They looked at us as if we were vermin beneath their feet.'

'There is no love lost.'

'What do you do?'

He stared down at our joined hands, then up into my face, searching as if for an answer. 'What would you do?'

It surprised me. 'I don't think I recall you ever asking me before.' I considered. 'This is what I think will already be in your mind. You will leave the Irish to their own devices and return to England and test the lie of the land. Nothing will be gained by your remaining here, wondering what Despenser is doing in London or in Wales. We go back to England and, if necessary, make a challenge. We take the Earl of Hereford's warning to heart.'

'Very politic, my wife.'

'I have my uses.'

He stood and we walked to the door together, collecting Beatrice and the hounds who were hoping for a foray into our hunting runs. Then he stopped, his hand on the latch, still clearly troubled.

'All my life I have been loyal to the King. I am a man of appetite for power, as you know. What Mortimer is not? Loyalty to the King is the path to that ambition. Now I fear I can no longer trust him to have my interests at heart.'

'I think that you read the King well.' And on an afterthought, 'Why is your uncle ambiguous in his letter? Will his thoughts not move in the same direction as your own? To attack one Mortimer is to attack both.'

'It is the same problem for both of us.' He opened the door, allowing the hounds to squeeze out before us, lifting Beatrice into his arms. 'Here it is. Dangerous indeed, for all of us, if we raise arms in opposition to the new power in Wales. Will it be against Hugh Despenser? Or will it be against the King? Which is, of course, treason. Edward might well argue that to defy Despenser is to defy his royal person. We know the penalty for treason. I have no intention of bringing the Mortimer inheritance into any form of danger. Beatrice will have her marriage and her dowry worthy of a Mortimer.' He handed her to me with a smile for his daughter. 'There is nought for you to be concerned over.' He kissed my cheek in passing. 'I will not risk my own neck in a careless challenge to royal power.'

It was a statement that I was often to bring to mind in the coming months. One that did not fill me with confidence, but rather an unceasing worry that one day he might just see the need to make that challenge, and where would we be then?

Chapter Thirteen

Wigmore Castle in the Welsh Marches, October 1320

We returned to England with our whole household, first to Wigmore, where I would remain while Roger continued on to where the Court was settled in Westminster. It was clear to both of us that I had no part to play in this. It was clear to Mortimer of Chirk too who, on a rapid visit to us to discuss some matter with Roger, was not slow in informing me of my role in Mortimer affairs.

'Stay out of men's affairs, woman. There's enough for you to do here. Keep your gates locked and your eye on your children.'

Chirk was now sixty-six years old, more cantankerous than ever and with barbed opinions. A sharp reply from me would have no good effect, and indeed, before I could think of one Chirk had pulled his felt cap well down over his ears and departed towards his own lands. Roger grinned as he embraced me in farewell.

'Well done. I did not think you could resist a reply to that.'

'Nor I.'

We exchanged an embrace and a clasp of hands while I had an acute premonition that we would not see Roger again before the end of the year. I watched him go, praying that he would keep his temper if the Mortimer lands came under threat, and that King Edward would see good policy in refusing his favourite everything he demanded. I had little hope for either. In the past I had feared for Roger's safety on a Scottish or Irish battlefield. Never had I thought to be so anxious over a visit to the royal Court. The days when Roger could trust King Edward were long gone. Was Roger now a rebel or still a loyal subject? I did not think that he himself was entirely certain of the answer. As we had feared, King Edward had taken the Gower lands from John de Mowbray into his own hands.

The question was: what would he do with Gower now? It did not take much imagination to hazard a guess that it would become a gift for Hugh Despenser at some time in the very near future. Indeed, it might already have happened. If that were so, the Marches might just erupt in fire, engulfing us all.

I waited for news, all through the weeks of late autumn when the leaves turned bronze and the birds feasted on the berries in the hedgerows. All through Christmas, a cold grey season when no one felt like making merry, although we made a good effort for the sake of the youngest children. Occasional letters found their way to me, none of them encouraging. Despenser continued to reign supreme. No one could approach the King without his permission. No one could petition the King without Despenser giving advice. This was truly taking royal power into Despenser's own hands to an extent that Gaveston had never done.

Edward has an emotional dependence the like of which I have never seen, Roger's scribe wrote to his dictation.

The Earls and Marcher lords are furious at being kept from the King's planning. No good will come of this. Keep your ears open for any rumours. However bad they seem to be, they will most likely be true. Stay safe, for me, your husband.

There was no room for endearments, only formless warnings.

Then uncertainties bloomed into a crisis. When the King's officer tried to take Gower under his authority in the name of the King, he met with de Mowbray's armed resistance. Of course in the end the King's men managed to wrest it from de Mowbray, but it left an unpleasant miasma descending over the heads of all the Marcher lords. News spread through the country like a swarm of wasps.

'Well. Now we know,' my mother sighed as she stretched her feet to the warmth of the fire in my solar and made a surprisingly harsh judgement against her distant blood relative. 'The Earl of Pembroke, whom we could always rely on as the best moderating voice at Court, has decided that there is little to be gained in moderation and has left the country to live on his French lands, from where he can consider King Edward's mistakes in peace. I never thought him to be so weak-minded.'

'Nor I. Did you know? Our neighbours have withdrawn from Court to arm their castles. They see nothing but war on their horizon.'

'What of Roger?'

'Now that is where we need magical divination!'

She did not offer. I did not know. Was his loyalty to the king still paramount?

If you are asking what I will do, my dear Johane, I can hear your voice all the way from Wigmore. I have decided that I will stay at Court to try to achieve some level of compromise. It is a hard task that I have given myself. What do I do? Give my blessing to Despenser's corruption or aid the Marcher lords

*in instigating rebellion? There is no easy road for us here.
Despenser is already taking lands with little compensation given
to their rightful owners. Will ours be the next parcel of prime
land to be gobbled up?*

There is an uneasy atmosphere at Court.

And then the sentence that proved above all else the depth of
Roger's concern.

*Keep our gates closed until I can come to you. I think I will not
remain here long.*

Keep our gates closed? Well, I did and I didn't, not seeing
events at Westminster as an immediate attack on our security
in the Welsh March. I still welcomed travelling minstrels and
merchants alike.

'A costly affair, the Christmas celebrations at Marlborough,'
from a troop of travelling mummers to whom I gave bed and
board on a stormy night, and with whom I willingly gossiped.
'They say the Queen is carrying a child, but she danced as
spritely as the rest of them,' the brightly clad leader of the
quartet informed me. 'Sixty pounds the King is said to have
spent on food and trappings.' He shook his head, looking doleful. 'The Despensers were there of course, father and son, the
son playing the great man, although he was slow to hand out
largesse to such as us, even though he laughed long and heartily
at our best mummings.'

'I am sure. Greedy men are always unwilling to empty their
purses,' I encouraged, signalling to a servant to refresh the cups
of ale. 'Was my Lord Mortimer there?'

'Yes, indeed. With a face as long as a spring eel. Bad doings
in the Marches, my lady. The King in his wisdom has confiscated Gower from de Mowbray whose ownership is without
question. A slap in the face for the other Marcher lords, I'd

say. You need to hang onto your lands, my lady, and guard your gates well.'

I knew all of this. It did not help to have it repeated, or to warn me that I had been too flagrant with my welcomes to passing travellers. The next cloud of dust to herald an arrival from the west caused me to give orders to keep our gates closed. No group of itinerant travellers could expect a welcome in these troubled times.

'No matter how persuasive they are!' I ordered.

The reply came back from my Commander of the Guard.

'You might wish to remedy that, my lady.'

'I will not.'

'It's Lady Marguerite. Mortimer colours flying proud. She'll not thank you for shutting her out of her own castle.'

'Open the gates,' I sighed, stepping down to greet Lady Marguerite, who had brought a formidable entourage of her own to escort her from Radnor.

'I thought you were going to leave me standing outside!' she complained.

'I did think about it. Until I was sure that your name was not Despenser.'

We embraced and laughed a little, then we repaired to my solar where we sat and considered the repercussions of the Gower fiasco. My own mother had departed to Ludlow to enjoy her own quiet household, and I valued Lady Marguerite's acerbic company. Now she frowned when all had been dissected with much ill feeling towards the Despensers.

'What is it? Do you know more than I?' I queried.

Her reply was as dry as old bones in the midden. 'It may be that we must take care in our dealings with Lord Mortimer of Chirk.'

'Why on earth?' I asked in some surprise. 'He and Roger are usually hand in glove. Surely he will not support the King in seizing Gower.'

Lady Marguerite leaned forward as if walls might have ears.

'King Edward is beginning to see that he has stirred up a hornets' nest. What more did he expect? Not that it will make any difference to his showering gifts and powers on Despenser, but Chirk, as Justiciar of Wales, has been ordered to inspect all castles under his jurisdiction, to ensure that they are in good defensive order to support the King.' Her brows rose. 'The irascible Chirk has been selected as a King's man in this present enterprise. And as far as I know he has not refused the task, pinning the royal colours to his sleeve for all to see. Can we trust him?'

I had never thought to have to consider such a problem.

'And if the castles are not in good defensive order to support the King? What does Chirk do then?'

Lady Marguerite raised her hands as well as her brows. 'Who knows?'

'Wigmore castle defends Mortimer interests, and no other!'

'My brother-in-law of Chirk now has considerable powers in the King's name.'

I felt anger and a little fear begin to rumble within me. I had never had to look quite so close to home for possible dangers.

'Has he now. Let him come here and inspect my castle in the King's name! He'll not find me amenable. Roger told me to bar my gates to all comers.'

'Well, you let me in. Eventually.' Lady Marguerite laughed over her wine cup, but it made a hollow sound. 'I will await it with some trepidation and much anticipation. Do you indeed plan to close the gates to your puissant Mortimer uncle?'

'Only if he has the temerity to demand entrance with a royal banner over his head.'

It was suddenly impossible to know whom I could trust.

Before the month of January could depart in numbingly cold winds and a series of blustery snow showers, Lord Mortimer of Chirk in full battle array and an eye-catching escort rode to our gates, a glorious royal banner prominent amongst the Mortimer blue and gold. My gates remained closed, my drawbridge raised. Lady Marguerite and I stood on the gatehouse to look down on our relative through the crenellations, my Commander of the Guard beside us. I was of a mind to be mischievous after his last parting shot to me.

'Good day to you,' Mortimer of Chirk announced in a blare of words. 'Open up, if you please, Lady Mortimer.'

A polite enough request, politely phrased, although Chirk still had a voice that could raise the dead. I nodded to my Commander who replied.

'In whose name do you demand entry?'

'In the name of the Justiciar of Wales and the King.'

My Commander glanced at me. I nodded again.

'Is this a friendly visit, my lord, or is it royal business?'

My voice would not carry well at this distance, but our Commander could match Chirk.

'This is Lord Mortimer of Chirk, who has never been refused entry to a Mortimer Castle.'

There was an edge to the harsh voice. True enough. Was I being petty in refusing admission? I was, but this was my castle in Roger's absence and I was in a mind to thwart King Edward's strategy to impose his will on all Marcher castles. And if that meant ruffling Chirk's feathers then so be it. Did Chirk not tell me to watch my walls and keep my gates closed? His feathers could withstand the ruffling. I found myself hoping that it would snow again and bury him in a drift.

I nodded again to my Commander.

'Times change, my lord Mortimer. You are not welcome here as a King's man.'

'Then let us make this a formal request. Open in the name of the King who has ordered me to inspect the Welsh castles to ensure their loyalties and good defences for the King's authority in this realm.'

I nodded to my Commander. We were well prepared for this.

'Is there any reason for you to suspect the garrison of Wigmore of disloyalty, my lord?'

A pause.

'Where is Lord Mortimer?' A curt demand in what might have been a growl.

'Still at Court, my lord.'

'I see that you continue to defy me. I know you are there, Lady Mortimer. And probably you too, Marguerite. Are you part of this defiance?'

I walked forward and looked down to where Chirk was looking up, his cheeks red with cold and fury.

'No defiance here my lord of Chirk. Only circumspection.'

'In God's name, Johane, let me in! Do I batter down the gates?'

'You would fail. As you well know.'

I stepped back. Lady Marguerite turned to me. 'What are you going to do now?' I leaned over again.

'I will consider my response. It was Lord Mortimer's instruction that I open the gates to no man.'

We left him standing in the bitter wind and repaired to the solar.

'And if nothing else, it will send a clear signal to any other

Marcher or Welsh lord who might consider carrying out the King's wishes against a Mortimer.'

Lady Marguerite looked faintly shocked, but not too much. 'You will of course let him in.'

'Of course, but I thought it worth making a gesture. Roger is aware of the problem for all of them, particularly for Chirk as Justiciar. Will his loyalties lie with the King or with his Mortimer nephew? It is a hard choice to make when treason rears its head. God's Blood! Hugh Despenser causes too much trouble in the realm.'

'I think we must take care that we do not express such calumny aloud, my dear.'

'In my own solar I will damn him to hell!'

When the snow showers came thick and fast, and our visitors remained at our gates, I took pity, sending orders to lower the drawbridge, open the gates and escort Chirk to my solar after providing his men with sustenance against their long and cold wait. There he stood, steaming in the warmth, with his hands on his hips, his dark hair flat against his head, but he had enough sense not to antagonise me.

'You treat your friends in a cavalier fashion, lady.'

'How do I know who my friends are, sir?'

'I'm too old for this,' he growled. 'My joints creak. If I weren't in a lady's solar I'd get my squire to pull my boots off. My feet are numb.'

'I'll be grateful if you keep your boots on, my lord.' But I felt some regret for the task he had been given. I urged him to sit closer to the fire and gave him a cup of heated wine, the herbs scenting the room with comfort.

'My loyalties remain where they have always been. With the Marcher lords and with my nephew.' Chirk sat but glared at both of us as he continued to steam before the fire and drip icy puddles onto the tiles. 'By the Rood, Johane. You are a hard woman to cross. And a meddling one. And you are just as intransigent, Marguerite.'

'It seems that we might have need to be.'

Chapter Fourteen

Wigmore Castle in the Welsh Marches, March 1321

February arrived and Chirk left. The snow had melted at last, but a cold, thick mist filled the valley and shrouded the hills for days and nights. Perfect days for an attack. I had received no more news, from either of the Mortimers. Chirk had resumed his perambulations of marcher castles despite his advancing years, declaring that the day he kept to his own fireside was the day that we could announce his death. Lady Marguerite, in spritely spirit, returned to Radnor in case that too came under scrutiny from the King or Despenser. I was left to guard Wigmore.

'Horsemen approaching, my lady.'

My guards were instantly alert on the wall-walk and the gatehouse crenellations. I joined them there, tugging my cloak around me, struggling to see, but the valley was obscured.

'Any sign of livery?' I asked my Commander.

'Too thick, my lady.'

Would Despenser actually dare to attack us, knowing that Roger was absent? I feared that he might. Wigmore would prove to be an admirable jewel in the Despenser crown. My fingers closed over the stones before me, my knuckles whitening. Perhaps I should have sent the children to safety in the chapel, under the Blessed Virgin's loving hand. I had not thought. But here were horsemen, in a considerable number, by the reverberation of hooves climbing the hill. They loomed out of the mist at last.

'Lord Mortimer.'

My Commander's laconic comment as the banners became recognisable. My heart steadied and I began to breathe evenly again. He sat below me and looked up at the bristle of men-at-arms.

'It pleases me to see you well prepared against attack, but if you would kindly let us in, my wife. I hear that you refused my uncle. In a fit of malice, he says.'

'No malice here, my lord,' I replied, keeping my voice steady. 'Open the gates.'

I ran down the steps issuing orders for food and ale for the retinue, and I was there in the Great Hall before Roger strode in, handing cloak and gloves and cap to his squire who disappeared with his burden, leaving us alone. He stood before the fire and steamed much as his uncle had done. His expression was equally one of irritation.

'Well?' I asked. 'Are we at peace or at war?'

His voice was more intemperate than I had ever heard it.

'You see before you the makings of a foresworn rebel.'

It had come at last. It was really no surprise, merely the relief that he was alive and at liberty to return to tell me. I took his arm and drew him into my solar.

'I must see to the needs of my men,' he said. 'It has been a hard, fast ride.'

'They will be given all they need,' I soothed. 'I have seen to it. Sit down. Drink this and tell me all. Such as why am I now the wife of a rebel.'

I really did not know whether to be anxious or simply grateful to see him returned. How obedient he was to my urging, groaning as his limbs stretched in the heat from the fire, as the spiced wine warmed his belly. His head fell back against the carved wood and he began to tell me of recent events. It was worse than I had imagined. It was, in his mind, a betrayal. The King had rejected all claims of past service and thrown the Mortimers to the dogs.

'And to a Despenser dog, by God!'

I smoothed his hair as I walked behind his chair, then sat on the other side of the fire, prepared to listen.

'God's Blood, Johane! This is the depth of royal generosity for all I have done! I am no longer Justiciar of Ireland. That office resides in the lap of one of Despenser's henchmen. The news followed me home as I left Westminster. The King did not even have the courtesy to tell me himself. I heard of it when I reached Stratfield Mortimer. What choice does it leave for me? Support the corruption of Despenser, accept the stripping of my powers, or join the lords in instigating rebellion? I now find myself aligned with the Earls of Hereford, Arundel and Surrey and a large contingent of barons who despise Despenser and would raise arms against him. Can you see the result if they – if we – declare war on the royal favourite? Despenser will bring disaster and ruin to the King himself unless he is stopped, but that eventuality requires the King to be willing to take action against him. And that he will not do.'

And then:

'I wish Pembroke would return. His mediation is sorely missed.'

And here was the crux of the matter for Roger.

'I still think you are not a rebel at heart,' I said, 'even when you are under threat.'

'No. I do not oppose the King. None of us do. But we will

fight to the death to prevent Despenser causing havoc in the west. We must not allow him to build up a block of power which would make us all dance at his command.'

I had not been best pleased at being left without news for so long, helpless in ignorance, but his spirits were low and he had found the decision hard without my adding to it.

'What now?'

'A night's sleep and then some decisions to make.' At last he managed to smile although it was an apology for one. 'What did Chirk say when you closed our gates to him?'

'That I was a meddling female. I did not hear the profanities at a distance.' I smirked a little. 'Your mother enjoyed it. He damned her as a meddler too.'

'How right he was. Like me, he is no rebel. I think there is no doubt of where he stands on this.'

'I know that well enough. We let him in, fed him, gave him wine and a bed for the night and soothed his feelings. I was vulnerable for the lack of news. It pleased me to stir up the locality.' I stood and walked to him to take his hand. 'I can offer you more than a bed and a night's sleep. It would please me to comfort you.' I tightened my hand and raised it to my cheek. 'I have missed you, and feared for you.'

'No more than I have regretted your loss in present days. Let us assuage fear in our reuniting.'

We retired to our chamber where I helped him to strip off his well-worn travelling garments, even kneeling to help him pull off his mud-caked boots. This was no time for summoning his squire.

'Do I tell you often enough how much I love you?' he asked as I knelt at his feet, one boot in my hands, scowling at the mud that had transferred itself to my fingers.

It was as if my heart stopped, shuddered, then resumed its

beat, but with a new urgency. Slowly, I looked up, indeed more in shock than surprise, my throat dry as I sought words at this astonishing admission. I had thought his mind on mightier things, such as being besieged by a Despenser force. This took my breath. *Do I tell you often enough how much I love you?* I had waited to hear those words for so long, fearing that I never would, and the depth of my own love would continue unrequited and unexpressed. Affection and care, yes. Fondness and liking. I could not doubt it. But love? Yet here he had dropped that invaluable word into a speech as if it were of little importance. Did he mean it? Allowing the boot to fall with a clunk on the floor, I regarded him, trying to read his expression. I could read nothing but what was indubitably a keen desire in his eyes.

'You don't tell me at all,' I said. 'Except now, when it seems to be by chance.'

'I suppose that I expect you to know it.'

'How could I? When did you discover that love existed?'

He took my hands, regardless of the mud, and leaned closer.

'When I miss you every day that we are apart. Do not you love me? Do you not miss me in the same fashion?' So there it was, the momentous declaration uttered so bluntly, yet still it had been said. He stretched to loose my hair from its pins, dropping the pins into his empty cup. 'Do you doubt it? We have enough results of our occupying the same bed.'

'Which does not necessarily indicate love, merely an ambition to spread the family name. Besides, a woman likes to hear it said.' I found myself smiling at him. 'Have I told you that love exists for me too?'

'Not that I recall.' He grinned. 'Neither of us leans towards the romantic, unless you are reading the exploits of Sir Galahad. Do I ever call you my dear heart's gleam?'

'Not to my knowledge. Please do. It is very poetic, I suppose, after being at Court.'

Standing, he lifted me to my feet, his hands gentle on my arms, leading me to the bed.

'I can quote love verses too. *Love is soft and love is sweet, and speaks in accents fair. Love is mighty agony, and love is mighty care…* Come here to me, Johane, and I will prove my worth to you, before I fall asleep.'

Garments removed, it was a long, slow loving. We knew how to awaken desire, our knowledge of each other as familiar as the chamber in which we lay, until all my world, and his too, was encapsulated within the confines of that bed, within the circle of our arms. This time it was enhanced with a depth of sensation that I had never known. Nor I think had he. We did not speak but our heightened breathing and sweat-slicked flesh was evidence of our need for each other. Roger Mortimer loved me with skill and a marvellous tenacity.

Afterwards, breathless, I pressed my face against his chest to feel his heart beating there, as I hugged the glorious emotion closely, unable to believe my good fortune that, at last, the man with whom I had inordinately fallen into love had decided that he loved me too. Or at least had remembered to tell me before he fell into exhausted sleep. I held him in my arms, his head on my shoulder, and let him rest, all my thoughts too resting, settled and content, because what woman could not be so, with such an unexpected confession of love. Sleep was far from me as in my mind I repeated to myself the following lines of that love poem that he had begun.

Love is utmost ecstasy and love is keen to dare,
Love is wretched misery, to live with, it's despair.

Tomorrow would bring troubles enough for him, and for me. Love was fervent desire, but it held within its glory its own hurts and wounds. Tomorrow would be soon enough to experience them. Tomorrow would be soon enough. I pressed my lips against his hair, praying that misery and despair would not strike too harshly. For now I was loved and my heart sang with joy.

Morning brought counsel and action.

'How much danger are we in?' I asked as we broke our fast.

'Impossible to say, but enough that we should take precautions. If Despenser attacks we can expect no succour from Edward.'

'Does he have the soldiers sufficient to do it?'

'Yes, if he is of a mind to march against us.'

Before dawn we had already discussed the precautions to be taken. I had gathered parchment and pens and a clerk; the bread and meat pushed aside, Roger began to dictate, his clerk began to write, I added anything omitted. All the Irish estates that I had brought into the Mortimer family must be protected in our absence in England. They were vulnerable to attack unless protected in law. Even without this protection they were open to infiltration, but we would do all we could to get the law on our side.

Our morning's work settled all our Irish estates on our second son, fifteen-year-old Young Roger. They could only be taken from him outside the letter of the law. Roger signed the final document. So did I. It might not prevent Despenser if he chose to take his troops into Ireland, but it was the best that we could do. Here would be an independent line of Mortimers for the future with the marriage between Roger's namesake second son and the daughter of the powerful Irish Butler family. It would happen soon now that the two young people were of an age. A most advantageous match to protect all Mortimer possessions in Ireland.

ANNE O'BRIEN

Then Roger ordered a spate of letters to be written and sent out.

Roger was collecting an army, whether against Despenser or against the King even he was unsure. In the end would it matter? The King would do all in his power to protect his favourite; thus Roger was proclaiming himself a rebel against both. Treason filled the room from floor to ceiling timbers. A tremor ran through my heart.

All I knew was that I would be left at Wigmore.

It may be that I must prepare for a siege.

'What would you do, in my place?' he asked as he prepared to leave once more with a formidable escort of Mortimer soldiery. A question that surprised me, showing how uncertain he still was.

'Everything I could to protect the Mortimer lands.' I replied. 'If it means war, then so be it. I will stand with you. Meanwhile I will bring my mother and yours to stay at Wigmore. Better that we are all together if it comes to a siege.'

I stepped close, placed my hands on either side of his beautiful face and pressed my lips against his. It was all so familiar on the occasion of his leave-taking, yet all so different since I spoke the words that had escaped us for so long.

'I love you.'

'And my love is yours,' he replied. 'It will always be so. But now, dear heart, we must prepare ourselves for a time of turmoil.'

We could never have imagined the magnitude of the threat that would eventually emerge against us. And yet at first there seemed to be no threat at all. The Welsh March, and the Mortimers in particular, heaved a sigh of relief. There was no siege at Wigmore. There was no Despenser attack. The great magnates of the realm forced King Edward into capitulation, so that he must agree, albeit with bared teeth, to exile the Despensers. Roger and his uncle of Chirk were for the moment innocent of any treasonous crimes against the King, while King Edward and Isabella, full of religious sanctity, travelled on pilgrimage to Canterbury to give thanks at the shrine of St Thomas for the birth of their little daughter Joan. Perhaps we had worried for nothing. Perhaps with Despenser in exile King Edward would accept his absence, the great magnates would rejoice, and the country would settle into peace. Some might say that we were deliberately blind to the depth of King Edward's malice. Did we not know that the day would come when the King would take revenge for the dismissal of the Despensers?

We knew very well.

It would only be a matter of time.

Chapter Fifteen

Wigmore Abbey in the Welsh Marches, January 1322

The days of King Edward's vengeance came about, driving me in Roger's absence to the Abbey.

Ave, Maria, gratia plena, Dominus tecum.

Hail Mary, full of grace,

The Lord is with thee.

I knelt before the high altar in Wigmore Abbey, my fingers moving over the beads of my rosary. Five little girls knelt beside me: Isabella, Catherine, Agnes, Beatrice and Blanche, muffled in hoods and cloaks against the dank heaviness that hemmed us in and coated the pillars on this January day. It was so cold that I could see my breath hanging in the air every time I spoke the responses. I noticed that Blanche had secreted one of the everlasting Wigmore kittens under her cloak. I relieved her of it and gave it to Catherine who would be a pair of reliable hands.

'Why are we here?' Agnes whispered.

'To pray,' I whispered back with a warning stare.

It seemed to be all I could do. Our fate, the future of the Mortimer family, could not be determined by anything within my power. As so many women before me, I must resort to prayer, and why should I not? If the Blessed Virgin would dispense holy justice, then Roger had a good cause. But Edward was God's Chosen King, anointed with holy oil. Without doubt Queen Isabella would be praying for her lord as I prayed for mine. To whom would God and the Blessed Virgin listen? All would hang in the balance.

'Who do we pray for?' Beatrice's sharp voice claimed my attention.

'For the King and Queen.'

Because it was our duty to do so even though Edward would regard us as the enemy and might not hold back from spilling Mortimer blood. My fingers continued to trip over my rosary beads as I concentrated hard on the words, speaking them aloud.

Blessed Virgin, endow our King with the spirit of compromise, that he might see whom his friends are if he treats them with justice. Mortimers have always been his friends until he allowed the Despenser to become a marauding thief. Send your grace to Queen Isabella, to give her strength in these trying times. May she be a woman of grace. May she appeal to her husband the King in the name of honour and fair-mindedness.

I had no idea what Isabella thought of Edward's malevolent turn of mind, although I imagined she would be relieved at Despenser's continuing exile.

The girls shifted restlessly and sniffed in the damp, but knew well that this was a solemn time.

'Who now?' whispered Isabella as the silence continued.

'You father. He needs our most fervent prayers.'

Blessed Virgin...

My prayer dried on my lips.

All would rest on what happened north of Wigmore at

Shrewsbury. There was no definite news from Roger, who would simply expect me to keep the faith and hold the garrison at Wigmore in a strong hand. At the end of the year we had heard that a royal army of some size was mustering at Cirencester, which for me re-drew the whole of the coming campaign. This was outright war. I could never have believed that Roger would throw in his lot with those who would raise their banners and swords against the King, but to attack our lands was anathema. Roger would fight to the death to keep them safe.

To the death! Fear shivered through me, enough to deflect my prayers.

I knew what Roger and the Marcher lords would do: they must retreat to the west, behind the River Severn, and hold the bridges against the King. The rebels, as the King now saw them, had taken control of the crossing at Worcester, that I knew, but could they hold Shrewsbury against the royal army? The rebels were woefully outnumbered.

All was in a muddle of uncertainty, an entity with sharp talons. Would the Earl of Lancaster come to their aid? Would the rebel lords be willing to negotiate for mercy rather than fight it out? And more importantly, would the King listen? King Edward was out for blood, driven by his loss of Despenser, and I feared that it would be Mortimer blood he would readily spill. The only good news had been that Roger was still alive and fighting for his cause. So was Mortimer of Chirk, undeterred by his accumulation of years.

Blessed Virgin. Look kindly on those of Mortimer blood who are driven to raise arms against their King by the actions of Despenser. Grant them courage and a willingness to come to terms, if good terms can be reached. Keep them safe in battle if war is the only way out of this struggle for land.

And then in an unnecessary afterthought:

I would like Lord Mortimer to return to me in one piece.

What more could I ask? It was a petition that truly came from the heart.

The priest swinging the censor passed close before me leaving clouds of incense, enough to make the girls giggle behind their hands. Far away there came to me a murmur of voices, but there was nothing to fear. They were not raised in anger. I and my daughters would be safe here at the Abbey, although anxiety was never far away.

Blessed Virgin, grant your love and everlasting kindness to our children . . .

There were footsteps on the flags, well shod and hurried, not the monkish sandals with their soft flutter of soles against tiles. The children turned their heads as children would. Beatrice leaned into me.

'It's Father!'

I turned my head sharply. Roger. Indeed it was. And there in the distance by the door was Chirk, genuflecting and making the sign of the cross. Roger marched up, patted the girls on their coifed heads, hushed Blanche who was intent on a loud welcome, and stepped to sink to his knees beside me.

'What are you doing here?' I asked, sotto voce. This was no place or time for loud conversation or cross-questioning.

'Is that a welcome, dear heart? It would be a warmer greeting from King Edward.'

'I doubt it. I have been praying for you.'

His tone became grim, his mouth twisted into a soft grimace.

'Then don't stop now. We need all the prayers that we can muster.'

'The last I heard you were petitioning the King for mercy.'

'Without much success.'

ANNE O'BRIEN

I turned my head to look at him. His voice was the same, instantly recognisable, firm in his determination to resist, but his face was etched with lines of weariness. He had dispensed with armour, exchanging it for wool and leather suitable for travel.

'We will pray together,' I said.

And we did. Roger might have taken up a sword against his King, but the depth of his faith in God's grace was unquestionable. Our prayers complete, the blessing administered by the Abbot himself, we stood and withdrew into the lady chapel, sending the girls to join their uncle by the door. As soon as we had some privacy Roger took me by the shoulders and kissed me. His lips were cold, as I suppose were mine.

'Is this sacrilege?' I asked, holding hard to his sleeves.

'I trust the Blessed Virgin will forgive my lack of respect for her. I have missed you, and I fear my actions have put you and my family in danger.'

'Have we not always been at one in our thoughts and actions?'

'Yes. And I regret nothing that I have done since our lands have come under threat, but our situation is become perilous.'

'Then tell me. The Virgin will understand. No doubt she will listen and make her own judgement.'

Standing hand in hand before the smoothly carved image of the azure-clad Virgin, he told me all that I had not known.

'We could have fought at Shrewsbury, but our men would be slaughtered to no purpose. Lancaster won't commit himself to fighting against his royal cousin. Hereford has taken his men north to join Lancaster, so that's another ally we have lost here in the field. To make things worse some Welsh lords have decided to take advantage of our weakness by supporting the King and attacking our lands from the west. My uncle of Chirk is suffering devastation in the north of Wales.' He shook his head in disbelief. 'Would you believe that Chirk Castle has

144

fallen? I have just lost Clun. We are being squeezed from all sides and there is no way out.'

It sounded desperate indeed. No wonder he looked so careworn with the hard decisions he had been forced to make. I tightened my hands around his as his words continued in spate as if they had been pent up for weeks of failed negotiation, surrounded by enemies as well as allies on whom he could not rely.

'We are just too lacking in numbers, strung out along the Severn. We may have kept the bridge at Worcester and at Bridgnorth, but the King has us on a knife-point at Shrewsbury. When we saw that all was lost, we sent a petition to the King for clemency, asking to meet with him on the thirteenth day of January, reminding him that our quarrel is not with the King but with Despenser. Yes, we burned the town at Bridgnorth, but I would argue that it is not a hanging offence. It does not merit our imprisonment or further punishment. So we asked for negotiation. Edward agreed safe conduct to come and treat with the Earls who now stand with him. They are keen enough for a settlement, and honest men on whom I would rely. Richmond, Arundel, Warenne. Norfolk and Kent who supported my request for safe conduct. And Pembroke, your cousin, who will always argue for restraint. It all seemed possible. We were full of hope.'

'Did you then achieve nothing?'

He frowned abstractedly at the Blessed Virgin as if it were all her fault.

'No. We could not come to an agreement to safeguard our lands. All I could get was another safe conduct until the twentieth day of January.'

'Will you go back?' I was already mentally counting the days. 'Are you not already too late to get there within the safe conduct?'

'Yes. Too late, and I dare not, as things stand. Edward is

demanding total and complete surrender without terms on my part. He will punish me as he wishes. All the years I have fought for him, supported him, shed blood for him in Ireland and Wales, but he will turn on me like a rabid dog.'

'Because he was forced to abandon Despenser. He feels the humiliation.'

'There is that. Anyway, I refused. How could we trust so virulent a hatred?'

I could see no way forward. Now I understood his fears for me and the children.

'What will you do? Petition again?'

'To what purpose? He will see me beggared, if not dead.'

We were without hope as we rode home to Wigmore Castle. As if he had no fears for the future Roger picked up the threads he had abandoned, as any lord of his manor and castle. He hid his fears and restlessness well, speaking with the farrier and the smith, the commander of his garrison, even taking time to speak with his daughters who followed him round until sent back to their daily lessons. I continued to follow Roger. It seemed to be important to know what he was saying, what his thoughts were. What he was thinking was beyond my comprehension. All seemed to be lost for the Mortimers.

One morning we were hailed from the gatehouse.

'Visitors, my lord.'

'Who?'

I resisted clutching at Roger's arm, fearing the worst.

'The Earl of Pembroke, my lord.'

'Let him enter.'

Roger strolled across to greet him, while I kept company with him.

'Is this good or bad?' I asked.

'He is acknowledged by all as a man of good sense. You know

that. He'll not stand by and see me killed or stripped of all I own, now that he is newly returned from self exile. We'll hear him.'

Aymer de Valence, the Earl of Pembroke, a man of repute, a distant cousin within my own Lusignan family. Pembroke was known as a man who valued leniency, a man who would meet another halfway and hammer out an agreement as our black-smith was loudly hammering out new shoes for Roger's horse. We welcomed him, angular and weathered, as tall and lean as a stork as he strode across to speak with us. His voice was harsh, but I thought that beneath it there was an element of com-passion for our predicament. Had he come to speak for Edward, or was this a warning of what was to come? Was Edward already leading his royal troops south from Shrewsbury against us?

Pembroke groaned as we invited him into the hall.

'The roads get no better, and my horse has an uneven gait.'

'Tell me the worst,' Roger invited as our guest stripped off his cap and ruffled his hands through his greying hair, then scratched at his beard. Pembroke's smile was spare.

'It's not the best of news, but neither is it beyond redemption. I am here to encourage you to go to the King once more and ask for clemency.'

Roger looked across at his uncle who had joined us and now stood just within the door. The look they exchanged spoke their refusal.

'Is that before Edward orders an axe to our necks?' Roger asked. 'We achieved nothing last time. Does he know that we have lost the castles at Chirk and Clun to the Welsh? I doubt he will even give us safe conduct, much less a sympathetic ear. If the Welsh cut us down on the way north, Edward would probably order a feast in celebration.'

Pembroke shook his head, accepting a cup of ale. 'He will

not do that. If you show true remorse, you will be spared and pardoned. You will get your safe conduct, that I swear. If you will present yourselves at Shrewsbury on the twenty-second day of this month and submit, all will go well with you.'

Roger's gaze narrowed with suspicion. 'Has the King told you this?'

'You can be assured.'

'Which does not answer my question, Pembroke. I am never assured that what Edward promises is what we will get in the end. Does he know what you are telling me?'

'I can guarantee his generosity. He has had enough of rebellion and warfare, and is willing to listen, but if you sit here like a cock on your dunghill you will achieve nothing other than his hatred and his lack of respect for a Marcher lord who once ruled these lands to great renown.'

'Great renown! It would be a miracle if Edward acknowledged it. Do you know what he has done, apart from removing me as Justiciar? Ordered all those men I appointed in Ireland, all reliable men who would keep the country at peace, to be removed and replaced with those who would lick the royal boots. If that is not spite, what is? He will throw Ireland to the wolves, as well as throwing me. And I have no answer to it.' Roger huffed a breath. He rubbed his hands hard over his cheeks. 'Then all I can do is go and meet with him.'

'That's it. And now that I have delivered my message, I must ride on.' Pembroke stood, finishing his ale in a hearty gulp. 'My thanks, Lady Mortimer. I hope all goes well with you in the future. This is a promise from the King that it would be unwise to refuse.' From the breast of his tunic he pulled a sealed document. 'Here is my safe conduct, in my name and with my seal. It will get you safely to Shrewsbury.' His mouth twisted. 'And home again, of course.'

While Roger accompanied Pembroke to collect his horse and escort, I was left to ponder the content of the last half hour of talk. Hope. Promise. Unwise. Not words to suggest assurance, but Pembroke seemed certain enough. We had nothing to lose and much to gain. Surely Edward would not break promises given so publicly, with all the power of Pembroke's seal. The question of course in my mind was: what would Roger do with this offer? Slowly I followed and we watched Pembroke ride away, colours shimmering in the frosty air. We watched until he disappeared from view.

'What do you say, Johane?'

'The decision is yours.'

Don't go! That was the only thought in my mind, but it would be wrong of me to influence so momentous a decision.

'Tell me,' he encouraged when I did not reply. So I did.

'Don't go. I don't trust the King.'

'Neither do I. But we have not the power of allies to stand against him.' He drew in a deep breath as if to fortify himself against a step he feared would take him into the abyss. 'I trust Pembroke. We will go to Shrewsbury and negotiate, for better or worse.'

I could not speak of my anguish at what might await him; it would merely add to his burden. We spent the night sharing words of love, sharing caresses, both soft and fervent in passion; exchanging memories, as we might after a long marriage and much tenderness between us, but we were held in a net of tension, both fearing that it might be many weeks before we were together again, afraid of what would await Roger at Shrewsbury. We did not speak of it, and although it lingered in the room, a malign entity that lurked in every corner, a warmth of love and care enfolded us. The touch of his hands, the slide of his skin against mine, the heat of his mouth, roused in me the passions

I recalled from my youth before we were weighed down with responsibilities and the demands of our enemies. Nor was there any doubt that he took possession of me with an urgency that made me gasp.

'My dearest love, I must leave you, but never doubt my loyalty to you,' he said at the end.

'I do not doubt it. I will never doubt it.'

We slept little, Roger being restless and I not willing to pass these final hours together in sleep. Overwhelmed as I might be by the lingering splendour of this time together, all I could see were the bitter pangs of future pain and loss, none of which I could speak of. It was still dark when he rose and lit a candle. His garments were already laid out for him.

'Don't forget me,' he said with a final embrace. 'You are indeed the love of my life.'

In that moment I felt a thrust of love so keen that it seemed that it must wound us both. How could I forget him, when I knew intimately every inch of his body, every wound and scar, the springy texture of his hair, the firm play of muscle beneath his skin. I knew his mind too, for did it not run side by side with mine? We were strangely emotional, as if we both feared for the future, yet why should we? Roger had been promised safe conduct. Even so, the unease shivered between us like a frosty wind as he dressed in silence.

'Take care of the girls. Take care of yourself, my dear one.'

'You will be the one in danger.'

His embrace was fierce, and then, to meet the agreed day, holding the document of safe conduct signed by Pembroke, Roger and his uncle rode north. I watched them ride away to their fate, Roger's familiar broad-shouldered outline, Mortimer of Chirk's lop-sided slouch, while I stood on the wall-walk, clinging to my courage, to my knowledge of events as they should play out. Roger's meeting with the King, when Pembroke had promised a satisfactory outcome for all, was to be held on the twenty-second day. The safe conduct was sealed. King Edward would listen and Roger would assure him of his loyalty, particularly with the continuing absence of Despenser. The Mortimers would once more be the most loyal of England's magnates and King Edward would be grateful and magnanimous.

The best solution for all.

On that final moment before he left, there was an addition to the heraldic Mortimer display, of my own making. I offered it on one knee in due wifely courtesy when they had gathered in the outer bailey, a quite deliberate gesture, to create a chivalric image to live in their imaginations as they rode north. Here were the combined Mortimer and de Geneville heraldic symbols, stitched some months ago when awaiting little Blanche's birth. The colours were vibrant, the banner still stiff with the newness of it and the golden fringing that I had added. I held it up on the palms of my two hands, a folded offering, every stitch placed there with the love that I felt for him.

'So that Mortimer and de Geneville will be displayed together when you face the King.'

He unfolded it with care, running his gloved fingers over the stitching. There was the blue and gold of the Mortimers together with the red lion of the de Genevilles in rampant display. It was the best work I had ever completed. I too could use the drama of this occasion to my own advantage.

'It is magnificent.'

'It will proclaim your cause and remind the King that you are a man of consequence. And it will remind you of your centre of power.' I placed my hand on my breast where the little silver love-brooch picked up the rays of the morning sun.

'Dear heart, I will need no reminding.'

He raised me to my feet, saluting me on both cheeks and finally on my lips. There were cheers from the mustered men. Did I not plan on this drama?

'Take care, Roger, when you travel and when you arrive.'

'I will. All will be well,' he assured me.

So why, in my imagination, should I experience a terrible premonition of royal banners emerged from the frosty gloom on the approach to Wigmore Castle? Was it perhaps the King riding with Roger to be given hospitality at Wigmore on his journey south, all past differences put to rest? We would give him bed and board, entertain him and all would be well. It seemed an unlikely outcome, but I clung to it with all my will, that I would see the blue and gold stripes set with a silver shield to herald the Mortimers, mingling in restored friendship with the royal lions of England. Roger would be a rebel no longer. Treason would be wiped from our escutcheon. Pembroke would assuredly save him.

Will he have the power to do so? How do you know that you will ever see the two Mortimers again?

I felt a tug of a strange sadness in my heart, as if a precious gift was about to be rent in two. A chilling finger scrawled a terror-riven path from top to bottom of my spine as I sent couriers out with two messages: one to my mother at Ludlow, that it might be politic for her to arrange a visit to her de Lusignan family in France. The other to Lady Marguerite, to stay quietly at Radnor but watch the roads, keep her gates closed and trust no one. As for me, I would live every hour, every day, in dread of what Roger might be called on to face at the hands of his King.

Chapter Sixteen

Wigmore Castle in the Welsh Marches, 23rd day of January 1322

The royal Commander's expression was as cold as the January morn although, to do him justice, he bowed in utmost respect, his gauntleted hand flat against his chain-mailed heart. He was clad for war, the whole force behind him bristling with weapons as if expecting trouble. Any trouble would emanate from me. I stood beside Roger's castellan and waited, commanding my voice and my composure. This was what I had feared.

'Lady Mortimer.'

'And you are, sir?'

'Alan de Charlton, royal envoy.'

'What do you want of me?'

From the breast of his heavy cloak he pulled out a fistful of letters and handed them to our castellan, who opened the largest with the royal seal, then passed it to me.

'A royal warrant, my lady, by the look of it.'

I had initially looked down at the array of troops below me on the approach to Wigmore Castle. Alarm had held me motionless for a moment, debate running through my head, but I would not discover the ill news by shouting from behind my crenellations.

Nor could I forbid entry when the royal lions dominated the scene below. I could not afford to be outrageously defiant.

Where were the Mortimer colours? Where was Roger? It might be possible that some compromise had been reached. It would do no good for me to play the rebel and destroy any good-will Roger had earned. Good-will? I doubted that there was any good-will here in this bellicose array of weaponry.

I had walked down, slowly, graciously, collecting my thoughts, as if to welcome honoured guests, ordered my gates open and walked out. No one would ever know the depth of fear that raged within me, like a whirlpool sucking in all clear thought. By the time I had set foot outside my gates the Commander of the troop had dismounted; he walked towards me so that we had met in the middle of my drawbridge, my castellan at my side.

Now I took the document and let my eye scan rapidly down. My heart was beating so hard the parchment trembled and I had to grip it hard and swallow before I could speak again.

'I can read that you are here on the King's business, Sir Alan, with royal authority. Why are you here specifically?'

My voice to my relief remained without expression. The document was motionless. Wigmore, in the absence of my husband, was firmly under my command.

He did not hesitate over his reply.

'I am here to take possession of the castle for the King, my lady. Wigmore is forfeit due to Lord Mortimer's treasonous behaviour. His rebellion against the King will be punished with a heavy hand. This land and castle and all that it contains is forfeit. All Mortimer possessions throughout England are now under terms of confiscation.'

I inhaled slowly, my senses frozen at this ruthless announcement. But pushing all else aside, the one question I needed to ask was of course:

'Where is Lord Mortimer? In his absence I have the authority to forbid you entry. Nor will I allow you to cross this drawbridge until I have my lord's permission.'

'And that you will not get, my lady.'

'Why not? Where is Lord Mortimer?'

I dared not imagine the crude and vicious detail of his reply. Was Roger dead? Was he executed without trial by a furiously vindictive King? I was finding it more and more difficult to draw in a breath. When dark shadows began to draw in around me, threatening to overwhelm me, I felt the castellan's hand close about my arm, and was grateful for it.

'At this moment Lord Mortimer is on his way in shackles to reside in the Tower of London at the King's pleasure. Lord Mortimer of Chirk is with him.'

The words rattled in my head so that I could barely make sense of them. My heart clanged like a mourning bell, picking out the intimidating words. Could it be worse? Could Edward have already ordered his execution?

'Then Lord Mortimer is not dead.'

It was the main hurdle in my mind that I could not step over.

'Not yet.' He must have seen my face pale as all the blood had drained away. 'I would not lie to you, my lady. Without doubt he will face trial in London. If he is found guilty of treason, he will assuredly be sentenced to death. Since he has been in arms against the King, I see no hope for him.'

As bleak a judgement as I could imagine. I took another slow inhalation, glancing my thanks to my castellan who still saw the need to support me.

'Lord Mortimer was promised a pardon,' I stated. 'He was promised safe conduct to Shrewsbury. He had it in writing from the Earl of Pembroke.'

Sir Alan changed his weight from one foot to the other, restless at such inaction.

'So I understand, my lady. But the Earl of Pembroke did not speak for the King, my lady. Treason does not allow safe conduct or a pardon. Mortimer met with the King early yesterday morn in Shrewsbury. I am here today to carry out royal orders.'

Still I could not accept it.

'Was Lord Mortimer not willing to submit? Was there no offer of compromise?'

Had Pembroke deliberately lied to us? Had he come here under false pretences to lure Roger to Shrewsbury and into the King's hands? I could not believe it.

'The King does not accept submission from a traitor who was once a friend but turned against him. It was a short meeting, my lady.'

I was colder than the ice under my feet on the boards.

'What happens now?'

What will you do with me? I could not ask it. Whatever was in store for me, there was nothing I could do to prevent it; it would be whatever the King decided. And what of my children? The girls who were not already wed were here at Wigmore with me, and my youngest son. I thanked the Blessed Virgin that the older boys were sent to other households for their knightly education; in friendly households where I prayed the King could not get his hands on them.

'What do you ask of me?'

'You will wait while my clerks make an inventory of the castle and take all of value for the King.'

Helplessly, all I could do was walk back into my castle and allow the occupation of a hostile force, for that is what it was. Surely I could not watch, taking bitter heed of everything of value that was plundered for the use of the King, but I knew that I must watch. I must bear witness to this wanton and wilful despoiling of my home. One day when Roger and I were reunited, for I could not believe that we would not be, I must tell him of what was done in Edward's name. What was taken.

Thus I stood at de Charlton's side while he directed his men, while every inch of my home was searched, from the smallest chambers to the cellars and then to the chambers in the high keep and the new buildings in the inner bailey. Clerks scribbled hurried lists. All was loaded onto carts to be transported away, covered with coarse cloth to secure them against the sleety rain that had begun to fall. At my side I kept my children, the girls. They needed no warning to remain quiet and still. There was shock on their faces that silenced their usual childish babble. Except for John, who could not stand still and tugged on my cloak.

'What is happening?'

'The King is taking all we own.'

'Does Father know?'

'Yes.'

'Can he not stop it?'

'No.' I put my hand on his shoulder, holding tight when he twitched to get free of any restriction. 'All we can do is be brave and obey the King.'

The outrageous thieving went on before my eyes. Our horses were led away, and then the rest of our livestock, our hunting birds from the mews, the geese and chickens stuffed into crates for easy handling. Then tunics that I had last seen Roger wearing, of velvet and wool with fur edgings, and a fur hat, the colours vibrant in the grey landscape. Bedcovers and tapestries followed, one that I had spent hours stitching for the Great Hall with popinjays and griffons. My most favoured green bedcover embroidered with owls. All gone. Even Roger's most prized chessmen and their board.

Even though they worked fast and efficiently, it took the whole morning to denude my home of its furnishings, finally manoeuvring my wooden bath with its decorated bronze hoops from my own chamber. Only then did Sir Alan return to me.

'Is that the sum total of it, my lady?'

'Yes.'

I was certain that they had missed nothing, so determined had they been that even the contents of the kitchen, even down to the basins and spoons, had been taken, but he was not satisfied. De Charlton stood before me as items of armour were carried past us; he fired questions at me, anger tightening the skin over his cheekbones.

'This armour is old. These are not the weapons expected of a Marcher lord. There are insufficient clothes for Lord Mortimer here. Where is the rest? Where will they be found? Where are the wall hangings suitable to a great lord? Where is the Mortimer treasure?'

I replied clearly, without hesitation, determined to give no hint of where most of our valuables might be.

'Lord Mortimer had his clothes and armour with him. It must be already in the hands of the King.'

I would not weep as our wolfhounds were led away on their leashes.

'Not all of it, I swear. Where is the rest? It is not here.' When I did not immediately answer: 'I would never use physical force against a woman of your high blood, lady, but I cannot say the same for my men if you are found to hinder their work here. Where are the rest of the Mortimer possessions in which the King would see value? Tell me now.'

It was a threat. Dare I risk it being an empty one?

I remained unhelpful. 'Does the King really wish to take pos-session of the pans and platters from my kitchen?'

'There's always Wigmore Abbey, Sir Alan,' one of his men suggested. 'I wager it will be worth a visit there.'

Sir Alan swung round to me. 'Where is that? Where is the Abbey?'

When I did not reply, the soldier added the information. 'Two miles or so north-east of us, sir.'

'Then we will go and take stock. And you, my lady, will come with us to ensure our peaceable entry. I would not wish to have to use violence against the Abbot and his clerics.'

'I need to know that my children will be safe here.'

'We do not wage war on children.'

He stamped off and I perforce had to follow to where they had found me a horse.

I knew the wealth of the Mortimer possessions in the Abbey. Hiding my horror of what was being done, riding there through the increasingly heavy rain, I looked back at Wigmore Castle. Although it looked the same from without the walls, it was empty, little more than a shell, my vision compromised by the rain, unless it was the tears that I could not prevent. The Mortimer colours had been taken down from the keep. It was no longer a Mortimer castle but a royal one, although I would wager that King Edward had no intention of occupying it. These were savage reprisals. I wiped my face with my wrist. I could look no more.

We were admitted to the Abbey without question and for a second time I was forced to watch while all that we owned was carried out and loaded onto carts to be transported to the royal treasury. Carpets and bedcovers and bed-linen, our mattresses and bed-hangings, tunics of my own. But nothing hurt as much as seeing my personal property: a little chest that held my ivory mirror and a belt with enamel and precious jewels, silver basins and dishes, an image of the Blessed Virgin. And then there were my books, my precious books, and a cherished set of ivory chess figures.

I closed my eyes against the pain.

'Why do you confiscate my property?' I must fight to retain something for the future. 'I am no traitor. It is my own, from my de Geneville family.'

'You are a traitor in the King's eyes, as wife of one. When you wed your husband, you and your property became his. All must be confiscated, even your possessions, Lady Mortimer.'

I could no longer stand beside de Charlton, watching the wilful destruction, but found myself in conversation with the Abbot, who was all but wringing his hands in helplessness as the altars were stripped bare of their treasures. They were Mortimer altars too.

'It breaks my heart,' I said.

'Stay strong, my lady. All is not yet lost.' From his sleeve he slid a small book, one of mine full of stories of chivalry and bright illustrations. A gift from Roger early in our marriage. 'I managed to secrete this, my lady. And this, too.' He produced a leather-bound Psalter. 'It may give you succour in future months.'

'Thank you. Thank you.' I hid them in the folds of my cloak where there were deep pockets. But it seemed to me that all was lost. How could two books make up for all the rest? Then one small item carried past me made me step forward.

'Stop!' De Charlton turned his head in my direction. I had seen a chest being carried out. 'That is of no value to any man but a Mortimer.'

'What is it?'

He swung over and lifted the lid to see the documents neatly filed there. He lifted one and studied the contents.

'They relate to Mortimer ownership of Wigmore and the Priory,' I said. 'They are of no value to the King.'

'The King would say that they are of extreme value.' He replaced the roll, dropped the lid, and signalled for his men to continue to carry it to the carts. 'The Mortimers will have no need of their records now.'

I could have wept at the terrible pillage of all that we held dear. All the legal proof of our ownership would be in the hands of the King. Would he destroy it? Would he burn it? It was clearly his strategy to destroy all evidence of Mortimer existence.

The Abbot bent towards me, to touch my cheek, as if to offer comfort or administer a blessing. And there was the faintest whisper, his lips barely moving.

'The Mortimer Heraldry. The roll is safe, my lady.'

That was all. I dared not ask where, I merely nodded in deep gratitude. Whatever became of us, there would be the evidence of the lives of past and present Mortimers.

All was done, the carts beginning their long journey towards London. All we possessed. But now my mind had abandoned that, filled with dread at what the future held in store for Roger and his uncle; my thoughts raged, fully as black and bleak as the weather, rain dripping from the edge of my hood. De Charlton remained standing before me.

'What of me?' I demanded. 'What of my children? And I need to know what will become of my household.'

'There are instructions for you, for your future,' he answered brusquely.

Nothing had been said of this. There had been no violence shown to my men, no indiscriminate hangings, but then there had been no siege, no refusal on my part that would have demanded punishment. I had presumed that I would be allowed to remain here in my denuded castle, or at least take refuge in

ANNE O'BRIEN

Ludlow. Had Ludlow been so desecrated too? Was my mother being subjected to this terrible humiliation? Or at least would they allow me to stay at the Abbey? And what of the children, the little girls and my son John, who were still at Wigmore?

'Am I to be imprisoned?' I asked, meeting his eye.

'You will be kept under surveillance, my lady, as I understand it.'

'What does that mean?'

'You will be sent to live under the jurisdiction of a royal official.'

I took the document held out to me. Here was my future, written in a clerkly hand. I was not to remain here at Wigmore, castle or abbey, nor at Ludlow. I was to be taken under guard south into Hampshire where I would be kept under close surveillance, for I was indeed deemed to be as guilty as Roger. I was allowed my choice of ladies and six men of my household: a knight, men-at-arms, a chaplain for the good of my soul and two clerks.

'It could be worse, my lady,' de Charlton remarked, reading my set expression as I read the curtailment of my household. Never had I, a Geneville, lived with so few to my comfort. 'This is a close observation of your actions and those you consort with, rather than a prison cell. You will be allowed a small income to pay for your daily needs and that of your household. It will be far better than a cell in the Tower with your husband. The King does not yet consider you to be too great a danger to him, with your husband so effectively confined. Arrangements have been made for your children.'

The King had no conscience when taking revenge. I forced my mind to continue working, considering what I knew and did not know.

'One more question, if you please, Sir Alan.'

He nodded, with a slight wash of colour to his weathered cheeks.

'Does the King intend to execute Lord Mortimer?'

There was compassion in his gaze.

'I know not. I would tell you if I could. I am an envoy, not a counsellor.'

'Who gives him counsel? Pembroke assured us that a pardon would be the outcome.'

'The King is his own man, my lady.'

I could not hide the intense bitterness that flooded me like the torrent of the River Teme in winter. It seemed that we were all without friends. All trace of the Mortimer lordship of Wigmore had been despoiled. As I walked along the Abbey nave, I could see the only remnants, the painted effigies of the dead warriors lying on their graves in the Abbey church and the family arms in the stained glass shining down on them. All the rest was gone. One worry toppled over the next, my mind awash with horrors over which I had no control. No prisoner ever escaped from the Tower of London. No man walked out from the gates unless it was to his execution.

Despair was the heaviest weight on my heart. Oh, Roger. Were you lost to me for ever? What would become of you? What would become of all of us?

Chapter Seventeen

The Manor of Wickham in Hampshire, February 1322

Close surveillance. It had a more comfortable ring to it than imprisonment, but I was under no illusions. I knew that I was at the mercy of the King as much as Roger and Chirk were in the Tower of London as I was escorted south under duress, to the home of Sir John de Scures, Lord of Wickham, newly come to the position of High Sheriff of Hampshire, who was considered a suitable guard to imprison my treasonable person. He was Warden of Winchester Castle, but my incarceration was to be in his more comfortable manor house in the valley of the River Meon, some small distance from Winchester. I would be watched and reported on. I would be allowed no true freedom. I would receive no visitors or correspondence. I knew what it would mean; I would be spied on at every turn.

Where my children were, I had no knowledge. It kept me anxious company in my litter with its drawn curtains, which not even Sir Alan's assurances could alleviate. Once arrived after days of lonely anxiety, Sir Alan helped me to climb down in the manorial courtyard. I was aware of the care he had taken over me in the days of travel, even if I chafed at the guard around me at all times. Was it guilt on his part? Compassion? I knew not, but was grateful. I looked round at the manor house that would be my home for as long as the King willed it, too anxiety-stricken to take it in.

'There is something here to cheer you, my lady,' Sir Alan said.

'Nothing would cheer me.'

I had misjudged the man. There awaiting me beside the stable door were my younger daughters. Catherine, Agnes, Beatrice and Blanche, as well as my youngest son John. For a moment I could not believe it, then strode across to touch them, hug them, reassure them. There was a slide of fear in their eyes but they were brave enough, willing to smile at my arrival. Questions were fired at me.

'Do we live here now?'

'Where is our father?'

'When do we go back to Wigmore?'

Tears slipped silently down little Blanche's cheeks even as she scrubbed them away, while I tried to reassure with empty, meaningless replies. Where were the rest of them? I did the best I could to hide my fears before my attention was summoned by Dame Scures, who had been put in place of authority over me and my family. Of little more than middling height and spare in frame, her tongue proved to be as sharp as her nose and her shoulder-blades. Dressed in good-quality cloth, her face almost enveloped in veil and wimple, she had no thought to what might be fashionable at Court, but still created a powerful presence in her own home.

'Lady Mortimer. I trust that you will be comfortable here.'

'Dame Scures. I must be thankful that you are willing to receive me.'

I curtsied before her and she was courteous enough to bow her head in acknowledgement of my status. It was clearly not a welcome task that she had been given, although I was treated with no overt hostility. During the hours that followed on that day I was given my own chamber, accommodations for my household, as well as a list of rules by which I must live. I was free to walk in the gardens when it was clement enough, but since it was February I was more often confined to the house. I must be grateful, although the restrictions on the rooms for my use was painful for me, and the children became fractious and quarrelsome, lacking the freedom of home. They soon knew by heart all the chivalric tales in the book that the Abbot had saved for me. We could not complain of the furnishings but they were meagre and well-worn, having seen better days. I was sure that the bed-hangings had been banished by Dame Scures from her personal chambers. There was evidence of the work of moths, but although there was no luxury, at least we were to live in relative comfort and there was food on the table. As prisoners of the King, could we expect any more? This was a punishment after all.

In those winter days we lived in a cool and distant communication from those who imprisoned us. The Lord of Wickham was frequently from home but it was soon clear that there was no opportunity for my escape. The fortifications of the little manor were considerable, with its formidable walls, outer ditch and gatehouse, and where would I go? I could not abandon my young children, nor could I drag them across the length and breadth of the country without a true plan. That would be cruel indeed.

'We could go to Ireland,' John suggested, seeing adventure in some unplanned escape. 'We would be welcome there and Father could join us when he is set free.'

I could not tell him. There was no chance that I would ever reach Ireland. There was even less chance that Roger would climb undetected over the walls of the Tower of London. Would he ever be set free? His fate was a constant fear that lodged as a weight in my chest.

What I did not know was one major concern. Where were my older sons and daughters? Were they, like Roger, imprisoned? Or in a softer exile like mine?

'In the name of the Blessed Virgin,' I had begged Dame Scures when she first stood before me, as if considering whether to invite me into her home or send me to sleep in the loft over the stables. 'Discover for me if you can. Are they safe? I ask nothing more of you, but find out for me if you have any compassion. You have a son and a daughter. You must know my heartache until I know that they are safe. And where is my mother? Is she still allowed to live in Ludlow Castle? In your generosity, I beg of you.'

It went against the grain to beg, but I must know.

It took longer than a se'nnight before I was summoned to Dame Scures' solar. I could not but note the magnificent tapestries and cushioned stools that were denied me, before she invited me to sit with a brusque indication of her hand.

'I have news. I doubt you will think it good, but I suggest it is the best you could hope for. Your older children are all under restraint. Your two eldest sons, Edmund and Roger, are taken to Windsor and imprisoned there with the children of the Earl of Hereford, who proved to be as much a traitor as Lord Mortimer.'

Imprisonment, but not in the Tower. Would not Windsor be less intimidating for them? There was the slightest lessening of tension.

'But John is to remain with me here,' I said. 'He is too young to be locked up.'

Dame Scures lifted her shoulders in the briefest shrug, denying all involvement. 'I imagine when he is older he too will be moved to captivity in Windsor. You see that the King is not without compassion for your youngest children.'

'I see that the King has no compassion. When John is deemed old enough to become dangerous, he will be taken away from me. He is twelve years old.' She shook her head in denial of any such knowledge. 'My only relief is that the King cannot arrest my son Geoffrey,' I said.

'No. The King regrets it.'

Geoffrey, to his good fortune, was in France in the household of the de Fiennes, Lady Marguerite's family. There he would stay as the only Mortimer not under restraint. There he would fight for justice and our freedom. It was a good thought, if I could believe it, but he was only fourteen, without either the power or the experience to help his father.

'As for your daughters, I am told this,' she continued. 'The three older girls are to be sent to convents where they will be kept safe from any who might decide to rescue them and use them against the King.'

'Where? Will they remain together?'

'No.' She consulted the document at her side. Clearly she had been well informed. 'Margaret will be sent to Shouldham Priory. Joan to Sempringham Priory. Isabella to Chicksands Priory.'

I knew nothing of them: small establishments, poor establishments, I presumed, far from London. They would indeed be safely constrained there.

I frowned. 'What of Maud?'

'I know nothing of Maud.'

I thought that I did. Maud had wed John de Charlton, a man who had made his peace with the King. Maud had been spared. It was all I could hope for. One of my daughters was free, but it was little recompense for the rest of the bad news.

'What of Lady Marguerite de Mortimer? And my mother, Lady Jeanne de Geneville?'

She shook her head. What a powerful weapon was silence. Then added with a malicious little smile. 'It will interest you to know. The silver cups and bowls confiscated from Wigmore have been presented to the King. He was most appreciative.'

'He is welcome to them.' I hoped that every bite of food he ate from one of my silver platters would poison him. 'It is of no importance to me now.'

She bowed her head. 'Also, you should know... the Despenser Earl of Cornwall has returned from exile. He is once more at the King's side giving good counsel.'

I drew in a breath, knowing immediately that the King would give the Mortimer estates to his despicable favourite.

I stood. 'My thanks for your efforts to set my mind at rest.'

'I have further news, Lady Mortimer.'

My fingers cramped around each other, anticipating the worst.

'Lord Mortimer arrived at the Tower of London on the thirteenth day of February. He and Mortimer of Chirk have been separated. They are each locked in a cell where they will spend the days until their trial. From there they will be taken for execution. If you were hoping for royal mercy, there will be none.'

I kept my face expressionless, grateful that the children were not here with us. Making my apologies, I stood and left the room. I told the girls and John that their father was safe in the Tower. I said nothing about cells and rats and lack of light and food. I said nothing of possible ill-treatment. It did not need Dame Scures to describe the conditions there. There was no way of escape for him and certainly not with Despenser's return. Any hope would lie with the Earl of Lancaster and his allies in the north, but was that not a hopeless cause? Would there be a battle? I would pray for Lancaster's victory. Only he could save

Roger now. I could do nothing at all. Even my prayers seemed hopeless.

'Blessed Virgin. If it be your will, may there be a miracle of justice and victory in battle for those who will hold the King to account.'

John, at my side, added: 'Or simply a holy miracle would help, for my father and uncle to scale the walls of the Tower without being seen.'

All I could add was: 'Amen.'

My only source of information in those terrible months was my gaoler. How she enjoyed making my imprisonment even harder to bear than it might have been. I waited daily for her next astonishingly gentle onslaught. How clever she was at offering information in a quiet voice when the words pierced my soul like a needle into fine linen, but I absorbed every word of what was happening outside the walls of the manor.

There had been a battle, between King Edward and his enemies, who might just save Roger, fought far to the north in Yorkshire at Boroughbridge, in March, when winter was fast retreating into spring. It was good weather for battles. If Edward was beaten, the Earls would hold him to ransom until he came to terms with their demands. It was all I had hoped for, although I knew nothing of it until it was too late, so that it was not a matter of any hopes being realised. Instead they were dashed into pieces as if I had thrown one of Dame Scures' slip-ware platters at the wall of my chamber.

It was a disaster for the rebels. All opposition to the Despensers was dead or imprisoned. The Earl of Lancaster was beheaded in the King's presence.

How tragic was this terrible tale of woe, for the men killed, for their families, for us and the power of the Marcher lords.

Now all would be open to Despenser's grasping hands. King Edward had had his revenge on the Earls who had stood against him and enforced the exile of his favourite. I suffered silently in that pretty garden over the news of death for so many men that I knew.

Next it would be Roger's turn to face the royal retribution. Mortimer would simply be another name to be wiped out in a final reckoning of those who dared to raise a sword against God's anointed King. I wondered why Roger had not already been done to death, silently in his cell. How easy it would have been, and with no one to question it; a judicial murder that I could not even contemplate.

All I could do was wait and hope. Helplessly.

On the final day of October of that year, on All Hallows' Eve when the veil between the living and the dead was at its most diminished, the sky never lightened. Instead, it remained as red as blood, the hazy sun engulfed in cloud casting this terrible hue over us for the whole of that day. What reckoning did it demand from us on earth? I watched the dense colour tighten its hold on us from the wall-walk, alone except for John who shadowed me, and two bored Scures' guards, following at my heels to prevent any attempt at escape or rescue. Here was no blessing. In the end I could tolerate it no longer. I returned to my chamber and closed the shutters on my windows to keep out the eerie light.

I learned soon enough from Dame Scures what this freak of nature might foretell.

'There is ill news for you, my lady. Lord Mortimer has been taken to Westminster Hall for trial.'

I stood as still as one of the grotesque images crudely carved on the door of the chapel. I would give her no pleasure. I would not ask about the outcome.

'He has been found guilty of treason and condemned to death.'

I would have to live with this all my days, the never-ending uncertainty of when this punishment would be inflicted.

'Will you tell me? If he is dead? When he is dead?'

'I am sure that I will.'

John was waiting for me in my chamber as if he had picked up the tenor of our conversation.

'Is Father still alive?'

'Yes.'

It was all I could say. My heart was breaking, although my authority over it so far held firm. If released, my heart would shatter into irretrievable pieces.

Chapter Eighteen

The Manor of Wickham in Hampshire, August 1323

Late summer into autumn, then winter. Then the turn of the year, and here we were in late summer again when the trees hung heavy in the heat, the glowing green of spring grown dark with just the hint of autumn colour. There was one blessing in my life. Roger was still alive. While there was life, was there not hope? I came to dread another summons from Dame Scures. Then one night in August:

'I hear that your husband is suspected of making plans to escape from the Tower.'

In the absence of her husband, she had invited me to sit with her in the garden, with the purpose of disturbing any comfort or ease of mind that I might have had. The soft evening air would not be permitted to soothe my worries. Regardless of her motives, I was eager to glean as much information as I could. Her news had been meagre of late, but this was the perfect comment to awake my interest. It was too dark now to set stitches, so that my hands lay unoccupied in my lap. My reply was deliberately as bland as a dish of whey.

'Would that be possible?' I asked. I refused to be encouraged.

I had become adept at deflecting such barbed comments. Lady Scures' lips twisted in relish.

'Mortimer was always full of foolish ambitions. Perhaps he will find a way to circumvent the guards in the Tower. What has he to lose, now that he knows that he will be imprisoned for life?' She smiled. 'It is said that he has written letters to win friends to aid his release.'

I did not return the smile, but asked: 'Imprisoned for life?'

Imprisoned, not condemned to death. I felt a wash of intense relief sweep over me. Yet how would he withstand incarceration, decade after decade, until the day of his death?

'He was fortunate. The King decided to make him a permanent inhabitant of the Tower. There is little change in your situation, Lady Mortimer. The Mortimer possessions remain forfeit. Your children will remain incarcerated, but your lives are spared. Particularly your sons. King Edward no longer has anything to fear from them. The King and the Despenser Earl of Cornwall are in complete control of the kingdom.'

'What has the King done with our lands?'

'They are made over to Despenser, including some of Chirk's manors. What you should know is this. It is said that Despenser plots to have Mortimer murdered. If Mortimer is dead, who can threaten Despenser? You, Lady Mortimer, could be a widow, even now.'

All the relief seeped away. Roger might have escaped with his life, but imprisoned in the Tower, how would he escape an assassination if both the King and Despenser were in league to achieve it? I thought about Despenser, imagining him lording it over our castles and manors, sleeping in our chamber at Wigmore, dining in our Great Hall. I despised him for it, but anger would achieve nothing. I struggled to keep a tight rein on it, as moths flitted around us, their wings magically lit under a rising moon.

'There is news about Lady Marguerite de Mortimer in Radnor,' the soft voice continued. 'King Edward intends to send her to a convent too for the remainder of her days. Shall I tell you more?'

I stood, furious at my weakness, despairing at her animosity. How many times had I walked away from her to still that implacable voice echoing in my head. I would not ask about my mother. I would not give my gaoler the opportunity to turn the knife in my wounds.

'Where are you going?' she asked, about to be robbed of her prey.

'To my chamber. I trust there is no need for you to accompany me, for I know that there is no escape for me either.'

I folded my embroidered length of linen with extreme care, placing it on my stool, afraid that if it remained in my hands I would tear it to pieces. She made no move to follow me, for which I was relieved. My control over my tongue was wearing thin. Her voice pursued me with soft malice.

'We will meet at Matins tomorrow, when you can pray again for your husband's safety. God might even listen.'

I marched through the inner bailey towards the outer staircase, intent on discovering my daughters, who would always be for me some source of happiness. Barely had I set one foot on the bottom step than my attention was claimed.

'My lady.'

Walter, one of my Mortimer men-at-arms, brought with me from Wigmore, a man whose loyalty was without question but who had few demands on his time in this situation. He was all but hidden in the deep shadow of one of the buttresses.

'Lady Mortimer!'

175

I stood still, every sense alert, yet I said nothing, always aware of watchful eyes and ears.

'Come with me.' A hiss of a whisper.

I looked back over my shoulder, but since Dame Scures had remained in the garden, I followed Walter, intrigued;, but where was he taking me?

'Wait here, my lady. Don't move. Don't speak. All is at risk and I like it not, but a message came and perforce I must obey.'

'What is this?'

'You are needed.'

My breathing became shallow with apprehension and I shivered. The soft hoot of an owl sounded close by as my shoes settled into the thick grass on the floor of the defensive ditch. The shadows were darker here beneath the high wall with the unlit windows of Dame Scures' solar above. A little breeze ruffled the leaves of a tree beyond the ditch and fluttered the edge of my veil. Taking a step back against the cold stones, I felt invisible as I waited, my heart a steady thump in my chest, my mouth dry so that I could barely swallow. Minutes seemed like hours. I knew that Walter had left me. I was alone here, and was suddenly afraid after all the talk of death.

Then a darker shadow formed to my right where the ditch led down to the fish ponds, and there was the faintest movement of air that had nothing to do with the breeze. An almost-heard footstep, a whisper of an order, a rustle of grass. In the end it was sense rather than sight. Who else could it be?

'Roger...'

Barely a breath as I whispered his name. The shadow acquired a harder edge, and then he was beside me. He touched my hand with his, enclosing my fingers within his.

'Johane. Are you alone?'

'Yes.'

'It is as dark as the depths of Hell!'

I felt the touch of his lips against my fingers. A bolt of pure delight mingled with fear, but fear had the victory.

'It is too dangerous,' I breathed. 'If you are caught here they will kill you without a second thought.' But then I needed to know. How could I send him away when he had risked all to see me? 'How did you escape? Where will you go? Will it be to Ireland?' The questions, barely a whisper, followed one after the other. 'I cannot believe that you are here. How did you get in?'

I felt the shake of his head in denial to all my demands.

'I had to come,' he said simply.

His arms folded around me, while I brushed my hand through his hair which was roughly hacked close to his head. The cloth on his shoulders was coarse and badly stitched beneath my fingers. Of course he would travel in disguise, a mere travelling man who would arouse no suspicion. Here was Lord Mortimer, breaking into the home of the custodian of Winchester Castle. I could almost laugh at the incongruity of it, if I were not so disbelieving.

'I have been so afraid for you.' His lips brushed mine. 'How long have we got?' I asked.

'A matter of minutes.'

'Where are you going?'

'To Portchester. From there a vessel is arranged to take me to the Isle of Wight and then across to Normandy. I dare not stay in England.'

'So not Ireland. Will you go to Geoffrey? To your de Fiennes family in Picardy?'

'Yes.'

A sigh, shared between us, as I rested my forehead against his shoulder.

'This was too big a risk. To come here to me.'

'But not far from my route. I had to see you. Do they treat you well? I heard that you were being ill-treated.'

'Not so. Unless to be locked up is ill-treatment.' I felt the frown, as if he disbelieved me. 'There is no menace here. All is as well as I could hope for,' I added.

'What of the children? It has been hard to discover news other than that the boys are locked up in Windsor.'

'The younger girls are here with me, and also John; they are all in health. I know nothing of those sent to convents. Would we not have been told if they were ill or punished further, to make our own imprisonment worse?'

Even in a whisper his voice scraped against me with a hard edge.

'I must believe that they will survive the King's spite. They all have a strong Mortimer spirit. But it has been a heavy burden on all of them. And on you. I must bear the burden of guilt for all of this.'

I could not see him, but the self-blame struck home. Anguished that it was impossible to make out his beloved features, I allowed my fingers to trace over his jaw, his cheekbones, the dominant nose. It was eighteen months since I had last seen him. I could not see him now, even though every sense was awake to his nearness. I tried to visualise his face through the pressure of my fingertips.

'I do not blame you. How could you not take on the challenge of Despenser when he threatened Mortimer lands? How did you escape?'

I felt him smile. 'Too complex to tell you now. Thanks to many friends who helped to smuggle letters out and then put my plan into action. It will be a story to tell to our children.'

'How long will you stay in France?'

'I know not.'

All was so uncertain. Although I knew it was useless, there were questions I must ask.

'Will you make your base in Picardy? Will I be able to join you there one day? Will you return to England? Or will it for ever be barred to you?'

I felt him step back, although he kept hold of my hands, as energy flooded through him.

'In God's name, I will return. When I have the power to make things different, I will help England be rid of this atrocious tyranny. I will see Despenser on his knees begging for mercy before I order his death.'

Never had I heard him so bitter with fury, so willing to shed blood.

'And Edward? What of the King?'

'He too will be under my dominion. He will pay for what he has done to you. And to the Mortimers. I will take back my lands and my birthright.'

'I cannot see it, Roger. This is all empty words. You have neither money nor troops to achieve such an overthrow of power.'

'No, not yet. I have no power and insufficient support. I have no money or troops. I would be taken prisoner on sight if I returned without, and this time there would be no escape. I need to build a force to overcome Edward. How long will that take? I know not, but I must work for it and you, dear heart, must have patience until I can come again and put to right all the wrongs. The battle at Boroughbridge was a bleak day for me, for us. So many friends and allies met their deaths. Lancaster, Hereford, Damory. My heart weeps for their loss at the hands of a vengeful King who gives his allegiance to a man who has no thought for the good of the realm. It will be difficult to build up another spider's web of allies, but I swear that I will do it and come back to England. I will reclaim my lands. I will reclaim you, wherever you might be. I will reclaim my children. Never doubt me.'

Closing the gap between us again, I ran my palms flatly over his face again, as if to create a memory.

'Take me with you. By the Virgin, Roger, do not leave me here alone to face the King's wrath. Take me with you, for I am in fear. And I am in love. How can I be parted from you for what might be a lifetime?'

Did I say that? Did I beg that he would take me from this soft prison into exile with him in France? Or was it only spoken in my mind, on a breath of desire to be rescued and reunited with him, even in Picardy. No, I did not say it, for I knew the answer before the question could even be asked. I could not leave the girls and John to whatever scheme would be devised for them. All I desired in my heart must be put aside. I must of necessity accept his absence and my continued isolation, however long it took, holding onto every ounce of courage in my heart.

'Hear me, Johane. This alone I regret. I cannot take you with me.' As if he had read my thoughts, and here was the answer. 'It is too dangerous.'

'I would risk it. If you asked me.'

'And I would risk it if it were only the two of us. But I think you must remain. It is the hardest decision I have ever made. Even more than my turning against my King. I cannot guarantee to get you out of here in safety. And what of the girls? We can't leave them.'

How well I knew what his answer must be, even though we both feared the repercussions for those of us who were left behind.

'You know what will happen, if we remain here, and you escape.'

'Yes.'

'They will punish me in your place. They will make my incarceration even harder.'

'I know it.'

I leaned against him in my weakness.

'I will not ask you. Forgive me. I know that I must remain, for the girls. And our captive sons.' A thought came to me. 'Where is Chirk? Is he not with you?'

I felt him shake his head, his clipped hair harsh against my temple. 'Still in the Tower. It was impossible to release him. He no longer has the strength to follow the route that I was forced to take. He is hale enough, but unable to climb walls. I must pray that he remains stalwart until I can come back and release him so that he can walk out through the door of his cell, a proud Mortimer once more.'

Silence surrounded us again, but time was passing.

'I am afraid,' I murmured.

'Look at me!'

'It's too dark!'

'You look at me, Johane! I will do all I can to see that you come to no harm.'

I would not deny that he had any power to safeguard me. Instead:

'I need a weapon.'

For the first time I felt a smile curve the corner of his mouth against my hair as he slid a short, slim knife from the scabbard at his belt. He pressed it into my hand, a plain blade without decoration or jewels but with a serviceable hilt.

'Can you use it?'

'I can learn fast enough. I know how to disembowel a chicken.'

'Your enemies are far more dangerous than chickens, dear heart.' But he handed it to me and I slid it into the safety of my tight sleeve. 'Hold it firm and stab. It will do the trick in an emergency and no one will expect it of you. Pray God you don't have to use it in anger.'

I pressed a kiss of gratitude against his mouth.

'Now you must go.'

'I will come for you as soon as I can.'

'But how long, Roger? How long? Who will care for me if you are dead?'

A heart-wrenching plea, of dependence on his continuing existence.

'How can I say? You know that I cannot. Be strong, Johane. They will not harm you, I swear it. To wreak vengeance on a woman is not what Edward would do.'

It was what his father had done after his victory in Scotland, ill-treating the women of the royal family by confining them in a cage, to be humiliated as an example to others who would rebel, nor was I sure about Despenser's chivalry towards women. What use in planting that seed in his mind, to grow and fester? I knew that he was aware of my worry, but he would not speak it. He would trust to my strength of mind and will.

'The Queen will plead for you.'

'Did you ask her to do so?'

'Yes. I got a message to her, for your kindness in the past. There is an antagonism between Isabella and Edward because of Despenser's power. She tried to move the King to clemency, and I believe that she will try again, for your sake.'

I did not reply. It had had little success last time but at least she had a voice at her husband's Court and he thought highly of her. How strange that my one hope of succour was in the hands of Queen Isabella. She had spirit to persist, but I feared that she would soon forget about my situation. While my hopes plummeted, Roger pressed his lips to the ring that he had on his finger on the day of our marriage.

'I vow to return. I have vowed that I will build a chapel at Wigmore if I am able to escape. I will return to do that. I will return to restore you to my side as Lady Mortimer. Remember my promise, when all is dark around you and you have heard nothing about me, for I doubt I can send you written word. Keep my words in your mind, and remember that I love you and will not leave you alone here for longer than you can tolerate.'

But how would he know? I thought of my sisters behind the walls of their convent, locked away for a lifetime. I too was about to learn that lack of freedom.

'I will remember. Never doubt me.'

'I don't doubt you.'

I felt him draw in a ragged breath, which should have given me warning.

'Here is one piece of news that it is not my wish to deliver. It will merely compound your grief, but you need to know. It is your mother.' His arms drew me close to give me support. 'She returned to France from Ludlow, fearing for her own freedom. I think you advised her to go. She has died there and is buried in the Abbaye de Valence.'

I could think of nothing to say, merely held onto him because he was the only source of strength I had.

'I will make a pilgrimage there in your name when I am safely across the sea.'

'Yes. Pray for her soul at rest.'

'As you pray for mine in the coming struggle. I am so sorry, Johane. You did not need this with all your other travails.' For a moment we stood together, drawing strength from each other, then a final kiss, a brush of his hand over my hair, my veil. 'Send me away with your blessing, and your love. Will you keep this safe for me?' From the breast of his tunic he pulled the well-folded bulk of the Mortimer-de Geneville banner that I had stitched for him, to accompany him to Shrewsbury. I did not ask how it had survived or how he had kept possession of it during his imprisonment. 'Keep it for me until I return.'

'I will.' I pressed his hand hard to the neck of my tunic. 'Can you feel it?'

'Yes.' I sensed him smile in the dark. 'You still wear it.'

'I saved it from the wreck of Wigmore when the King stole everything. I wear it next to my skin, every day.' It was the brooch given to me so long ago but with words that still meant as much as they did then, perhaps even more now that I was losing the giver. *I am a love token. Do not give me away.* 'My blessing and my love go with you, always. And my prayers to the Blessed Virgin,' I said.

'Amen.' Then the softest of replies, a whisper. 'I vow that I will return and take you home.'

In the next instant he was gone.

I knew not when I would see him again. Alone, I wept most bitterly. For my mother who had ended her life without her family. For Roger in the precariousness of his future. And for me, who would have to live with the results of his treason and his escape.

Chapter Nineteen

The Manor of Wickham in Hampshire, April 1324

'Where am I to go?' I asked, allowing Sir John Scures a brief bend of my knee.

Cool and calm on the surface, my blood had begun to race.

'It is not for you to know, my lady.'

It was not until blossom was beginning to glimmer on the blackthorn in the hedges, and with it the arrival of Sir John Scures on one of his infrequent visits from Winchester, that I was summoned. I had already taken cognizance of the two substantial travelling litters in the courtyard. I was already warned. All through that winter I had waited, for my own fate to overtake me, for the fate of my sons and daughters who were still at the King's mercy, and for news of Roger. Skeins of geese had flown over Wickham from France, their call plaintive, as if they would carry a message for me.

Had Roger reached the de Fiennes family estates in Picardy? I knew he must be alive. If he were dead Edward would be rejoicing and I would surely be informed of it. But I knew the difficulty Roger would have to raise sufficient force to return to claim his birthright. His inheritance had been stolen from him. He had neither money nor power to make promises to aid his return. He had been betrayed by a King who had once held all his loyalty, his sworn allegiance. He had been stripped of his lands and his sources of income; after the disaster at Boroughbridge, he lacked powerful allies. Poor and landless, he might be condemned to a life in exile, and I in doleful imprisonment, to prevent me from aiding his return.

I clung to those few moments Roger and I had shared. They were all I had. Now I must face my future.

'Clothe yourself warmly, Lady Mortimer, and the children. It will be a long journey.'

Sir John, slight and lacking in height, but large in authority even though he was dwarfed in a heavy cloak and brimmed felt hat, bowed with some courtesy. His face was pale and pinched with the cold, his features austere, giving nothing away.

I regarded my daughters who would ride in one of the litters. And then again I took in the scene. It was as I might fear. Had I not been waiting for this moment as the months passed and my son John approached his fourteenth year? He was standing on the bottom step, not yet garbed for travel. I tried to read his expression, but his face was inscrutable, increasing the range of my emotions. How sad, how tragic, that he had learned to govern his feelings before he was fourteen years old. And how well he had learned the lesson, not to give power to his enemies. It was as if he did not care, but I knew better.

I addressed Sir John as Lady Mortimer would, chin raised, not as an abject prisoner.

'Why does my son not accompany me?'

'He will no longer be one of your household.'

How could I bear to allow another one of mine to be taken from me? Sir John took me aside and I read compassion in his eye, an emotion that I resented and resisted when he took my arm in a firm grip.

'The boy is of an age to become a danger to the King. He might attract support and there might be an attempt to rescue him. He will be sent to a place where he can be well guarded.'

'Is it to be Windsor? With his brothers?'

'No. It is the King's wish that he be sent to Odiham Castle.'

'He will be alone there,' I remarked. 'What sort of existence is that for a young boy?'

I was helpless, unable to negotiate. All I could do was accept the loss of the last of my sons on English soil.

'Do you give your permission for me to say my farewells?'

'Of course. I am no monster, Lady Mortimer.'

It was the longest discussion I had ever had with the man, yet it had told me so little. I nodded my thanks and walked towards John, who was still not as tall as I, even standing on the step. Memories of Roger in his youth flooded back. I had forgotten how alike they were, the strong features and dark hair, until now when I would lose him.

'You are to go to Odiham.'

'Yes. I know.'

He seemed calmer than I.

'I am sure that you understand why. As a Mortimer son you are now seen as a danger to the King. You should accept that as a mark of esteem.' I took hold of his shoulders and saluted him on each cheek in brisk fashion to prevent any show of grief. Here was no time for maternal emotions even though my hands trembled. 'God keep you. I know you will be brave. One day I hope that they will send you to be with your brothers in Windsor.'

'One day I hope that I will escape and join Geoffrey and my father,' he replied, his voice cracking on the harsh declaration. 'We will rescue you and restore the Mortimer lands.'

'And so you shall, John. I look forward to the day. I know the time will come,' I whispered as I kissed his cheek again. 'There is a knife in the fall of my over-tunic sleeve. Take it. Use it if you have to. Your father gave it to me, but your need is greater. Now it is yours if you can take it without being seen.'

I felt the slide of his hand, the investigation of clever fingers, and then the blade was gone, secreted somewhere on his person, freeing me to stand back. No tears. No lingering farewells. Mortimers must stand on their own strong feet. I regretted the loss of the knife but thought it well done to give it to John. Roger would have approved.

I left my son, ensured that my daughters were tucked into the litter, and rode away from Wickham, solitary in my own litter, without looking back, but with bitter grief in my heart. It had been my home for more than two years and I had no wish to imprint it on my memory any more than it already was.

It was a long journey over endless days. At last we arrived at our destination as night was falling, riding through the street and market place of a small town before drawing rein at a gatehouse. I could see little of my future home as evening shadows fell; a strong fortification with its great walls and towers looming before us, an imposing and intimidating gatehouse, protected by the two massive round towers of the barbican. Other than that I had no idea of its size. The gates were opened when the royal banner was illuminated by a torch carried by one of our escort. We were led into the bailey and I was helped to dismount by my page.

I was cold, my limbs stiff from travel, but I looked around at this place that would be my home for as long as King Edward wished it.

'You will be shown to your chambers, Lady Mortimer. There

will be food waiting for you and your daughters. We will talk tomorrow. It has been a long day.'

'I suppose I should thank you for my safe arrival.'

Sir John Scures bowed. 'I wish you well in your incarceration. You are a brave woman.'

'Is it brave merely to follow orders?' I drew in a breath. 'Where is this place?' I asked.

'This is Skipton Castle, far to the north, in Yorkshire. You will remain here at the King's pleasure.'

Chapter Twenty

Skipton Castle in Yorkshire, April 1324

I was quick to discover the terrible length and breadth of my fate. I was to be punished for Roger's transgressions by being shut away in the fortress of Skipton Castle. There would be no hope for my release. The Commander of the castle was a man of few words and fewer sympathies, under whose authority I was left to live my life alone with my daughters. Vast and imposing the castle might be to keep out invaders, but the massive drum towers of the castle, six of them altogether, were overpowering in their royal might. There would be no escape. Nor were there visitors, enforcing on us a solitary existence. In a deluge of fury at Edward for his callous treatment of us, I thought that I might even regret Dame Scures' acerbic conversations.

'Who holds this castle in the King's name?' I asked the Commander. 'I swear it was never a royal castle for the King's own use.' It did not have enough luxury for Edward's taste in opulence. 'Who has lived here since the death of Simon de Montfort?'

For once the Commander, an elderly knight named Sir Robert de Wressle, was free with his information.

'The Clifford family owned it. Roger de Clifford held it, but proved to be another rebel against the King and Despenser, like your own lord. He fought and received severe wounds at the Battle of Boroughbridge.' The man smiled in relish of the outcome. 'They hanged him in York for his sins. His estates were forfeit so now this place is under my control as a King's man. If Mortimer is misguided enough to set foot on English soil again, I expect he will join de Clifford with a noose around his neck. Pray that he does not attempt to come and rescue you, my lady.'

'Are my daughters and I free to make use of the whole of this place?'

'No, my lady. You will keep yourselves to the tower in the north-east of the range. There are bedchambers and a hall which you will find of use. You and your children may walk outside in the inner ward with one of my guards in attendance. You may make use of the chapel early every morning. There is a kitchen attached to the tower that is for your use. Now unless you have any more questions...'

Which ended the conversation on a depressing note.

What a sad and neglected place it was, this fortress that had once belonged to the great magnate Simon de Montfort. I walked through the kitchen allotted to us, the domestic chambers and hall, the bedchambers where the windows were no more than narrow slits so that views to the nearby hills were limited and the light meagre. Roger de Clifford had made some improvements, but his death had put an end to that. The northern winds blew cold through the inner ward where we could take exercise. There were few of the comforts of Roger's new building at Wigmore or at Ludlow. The walls were dank and cold with no tapestries; the floors lacked sweet rushes and needed sweeping; the beds were adequate but their hangings old and well-worn. All the chambers suffered from lack of use apart from spiders and vermin.

Wickham Manor had been a place of remarkable comfort in comparison. With clenched jaw I was forced to admit that my sisters' existence in Aconbury was one of luxury compared with our imprisonment.

The issues with my incarceration began immediately when Sir John conducted his final interview before leaving. We stood in my hall, both shivering from the damp cold, I resentfully silent, while my erstwhile custodian handed a small leather purse into my keeping. From the weight of it, it contained coin, but not many of them. When I opened the strings and peered in, it was easy to see that they were of small weight and silver, too. No great value here.

'What is this?' I asked, tipping the bag, emptying the coins into my palm. They did not overflow.

'The money allotted to you during your stay here. The coins will be renewed every year.'

Every year! I shivered even more.

'How much am I allotted, Sir John?'

'One mark every week.'

'Which will cover what exactly?'

'To keep and feed yourself, my lady. Also your daughters and your household.'

I could not take in what he had said.

'On our journey here, it was a mark per day to pay for our food and necessities.'

'It is the King's decision. One mark of silver every week.'

There was no room for negotiation, so nothing I could do to remedy it, even though my heart fell. I had no money of my own, and nothing that I could sell. Even so I could not simply accept this decision without some response.

'Could you keep and feed your family and household on a mere mark weight of silver for each week, Sir John?' I asked.

He did not deign to reply. I thought there was a flush to his lean cheeks.

'You will receive a further ten marks at Easter and Michaelmas, for new clothes. Your household is further reduced, so I expect that you will manage well enough.'

'Then I must be grateful. I have a need to speak with the person who rules the kitchen here, to discover what we might eat for one mark.'

'I will send him to speak with you, my lady.'

'Are there any servants here at my disposal? There is much need of cleaning in this tower.'

'I expect Commander de Wressle can accommodate you, my lady. Otherwise you must make use of those allowed in your household. And now I must begin my journey south, Lady Mortimer.'

'I find it difficult to wish you well, Sir John.'

'I merely carry out orders, Lady Mortimer.'

And yet I regretted his leaving. He was my only connection with the outside world.

I interviewed the resident in my kitchen, an elderly man who might once have been a soldier and who rejoiced in the name of Gilbert. I suspected that he was more used to wielding a sword than applying a ladle. I never saw him smile or express any interest in the tasks allotted to him. It crossed my mind that it was he who interviewed me.

'It is not what you will be used to, my lady. Plain fare on the money you have. I trust you'll not complain.' He tossed the coins I had given him into the air and caught then, engulfing them in his large, calloused hand. 'Bread, of the coarse variety. Mutton stews. We have plenty of sheep on the hills here. Some eggs and cheese. Fruit when the apple trees bear. There is a plum tree also, although it cannot be relied on for good fruit.'

'If we are still here in the autumn.'

In my heart I knew that we would be.

'Some fish of course, which will be cheap enough,' Gilbert continued.

'Then we will do what we can. I will need wood for fires. And candles.'

'Tallow only, my lady.'

'And hot water. I have a laundress so there will be no burden on you.'

His expression suggested that he would make sure that nothing would be a burden on him.

'Ale? Wine?' I asked, pursuing our miserable lives to the bitter end.

'I'll do what I can with the money you have left. It will not be of a quality to grace the royal Court. I doubt you will thrive on what I can give you.'

There was no means that I could employ to get news of our circumstances to Roger. And of what benefit would that be? Roger must not return until he had the might to fend off his enemies. Of Roger's present situation I knew nothing. Who would tell me? Was he not able to get letters out of the Tower when plotting his escape? I knew that he had. I must hope that he could send word from Picardy. But there was nothing. Anxiety and weariness weighed heavily and time dragged its feet like an old crone. What would my daughters and I do with our time, our lives so restricted as the King had ordered? All the possessions I had lost from Wigmore Abbey filled me with regret. My books; how I yearned for my books. I missed the wolfhounds and the horses and the hawks. Everything I had taken for granted in my life had been taken from me.

My daughters were my treasure. And my memories of Roger. I would hold them close. I would hold them dear.

Skipton Castle in Yorkshire, later in 1324

A visitor. Here was a small, smart escort, so a visitor of some importance. My daughters alerted me but my spirits, instantly raised, sank back when I peered down into the inner ward through the only window which gave us a view of that area. I did not recognise the heraldic banners. Not a visitor for me. Not royal. Not Roger. It was a woman who alighted from the litter.

'She has dogs!'

Small white ones that scampered round the courtyard. No comparison with the wolfhounds that my daughters knew from Wigmore or Trim where we kept no lap dogs.

'And look!' A squeak from Blanche. 'She has brought a popinjay!'

Indeed there was a green parrot on a perch, being unloaded by one of the pages.

I would have retreated, allowing this business that did not affect me to continue on its course, but I was attracted by the raised voices, those of the woman and de Wressle. How could I not return to the window and open the shutters as far as they would go? There was a difference of opinion developing with strident accents, over whether the lady should stay. Clad in her fur-lined cloak, she did not flinch, nor did she retreat before the crisp instructions to be gone. I admired her even at a distance. Then it seemed that she and her maidservant were being invited in, to be shown to a chamber while orders were given that the horses of her escort were stabled.

The usual heavy silence of the castle returned.

'Who is it?' Beatrice murmured, obviously pleased at the change in the order of our days.

'I know not.'

'Do you think that she will eat with us?' Beatrice persisted.

'Not if she sees the quality of the food that we can afford.'

'She is very rich, I suppose. Perhaps she will provide her own,' Catherine said. 'Perhaps she will bring sugared plums and share them with us.'

'Perhaps she will bring the little dogs to visit us.'

I hugged Agnes. I hoped for her sake that the unknown lady would do just that.

'Perhaps she will. We will wait and see.'

I spent my life waiting. This woman would be of no importance to me unless she could open the gates of Skipton Castle and set me free. We saw nothing more of her that day. The guest dined in her own chambers as did we. I expect that her dishes were more appetising. My allowance was running out, so that it was much the fare of a convent day of fast, and there were no sugar plums. I had renewed compassion for my sisters in Aconbury, enclosed as they were for the term of their life, with no hope of release, destined to exist for ever on the meagre offerings of fast days. My experience now no better than theirs, I regretted my sometimes callous indifference to their plight. Was this perhaps retribution for my sin of neglect, that my life should mirror their sufferings?

Next morning, as we had become accustomed, my daughters and I went early to the dark chapel of St John the Evangelist in the inner ward. We would not neglect God, no matter what restrictions were placed on our freedom. And there was the guest, neatly garbed, her veils seemly, yet still the cloak was wrapped around her, since the chapel was as chill as a cave. She remained on her knees, her head bent. The priest continued to pray as we knelt behind her, until, blessings finally pronounced, we stood. The lady and I faced each other. She assessed me as I assessed her.

'Lady Mortimer.'

I did not know her. I could not name her. Was there perhaps some familiarity in her face with someone I had met at Court?

'Forgive me ...'

'There is no reason why you should know me. I am Baroness de Welles.'

'No, I do not. Forgive me for the lack of courtesy, since you know me.'

'You will know my family better, if I tell you that I am by birth Maud de Clare.'

'The Irish de Clares. Of course.'

I found myself smiling for the first time for some days. That was why she seemed at least faintly familiar. The round shape of her face, the pale skin with a sprinkling of freckles. Beneath her veil her hair would be true Irish red. Here was Maud de Clare, sister to Margaret de Clare, or Meg Badlesmere as she was to me, whose young daughter Elizabeth was wed to my eldest son Edmund. My grandfather would have known the Irish de Clare family intimately. Yet my paths had never crossed those of Maud, Baroness de Welles.

'I know your sister very well. But why are you here?' I asked.

'A close marriage connection,' she explained, waving aside with easy authority the guard who might wish to terminate our exchange of news. 'My first husband was Baron de Clifford, killed at Boroughbridge, as were so many good men.'

The pieces began to fall into place. 'Of course. This was once your home.'

'It was. Stripped from us because my husband raised his sword against the King. My sons are disinherited. You will know how I feel about that!'

'But why are you here?' I was still not sure.

'To keep an interest in the place. It is my wish that one day it will be restored to my eldest son Robert and he will be once more Baron Clifford. One day the King will see where his real friends should be. On the day that he abandons Hugh Despenser, there will be a Clifford at his side. And probably a Mortimer too.'

'I doubt that will be in my lifetime,' I said.

'If your husband could arrange a rebellion against our grasping monarch, there is every chance. I hope that you prayed that God will guide him back to England.'

There were ten years between us but never had I welcomed a woman into my company as I did this one. I grasped her hands when she held them out to me. I had not realised how much comfort I had needed in the warmth of another woman who might share my views, my sympathies. Here was no Mortimer or de Geneville enemy.

The guard, running short of patience, intervened again, approaching me as if he would drag me away.

'It is time you returned to your chamber, my lady.'

I had learned the limits of my freedom but Baroness de Welles, once Clifford, was willing to exert any power she still might have in what had been her own home.

'Go away. I will have conversation with Lady Mortimer. I will tell you when we have finished.'

For a moment he hesitated, when I thought that she would fail, but not so. Maud de Welles flapped her hands. The children were led away but we remained. She still had authority here which I did not.

'In fact, let us leave this cold place and repair to your chamber, or mine.'

'Yours. We cannot afford a fire until the evening.'

'So the King is being as venomous as I had been led to believe. Come with me, then for I am in need of warmth.'

We made our way out of the chapel with the priest fussing behind us, dousing the candles except for two that illuminated the altar. Could I trust her? Her hands might be warm and strong, but would she be a spy to take any words I might say back to King Edward? I must be circumspect, giving no indication of what Roger might be doing. Not that I knew enough to interest anyone.

Lady Maud pulled up two cushioned stools before the fire and sat down with a sigh. 'How this place has been neglected! I'll soon have it put to rights if Robert ever gets it back.' She regarded me with a stern expression. 'I fear that you may be here for some time. Sadly, you have no man to stand bond for you. No one who would dare show any support for a Mortimer. Thus it is unlikely that our King will show you any compassion. A purse full of gold might have won him over, but without it your imprisonment has no end in sight.'

'No,' I admitted, accepting the truth of it, however much I might struggle to envisage a key to open the lock to my door. It was impossible. 'I may remain here for ever, until the day of my death.'

'Let us be hopeful.' Lady Maud's glance was keen. 'And how much has our luxury-loving ruler allowed you for your maintenance here?'

'I am sure that you can guess. It is very little, not enough to keep us in heat and good light.' My tone was all cynicism.

'Unfortunately for King Edward, Lord Mortimer is well and truly alive and a real threat to him. My imprisonment is the King's true revenge. It will be impossible for me to be used as a weapon against the King, to work for Roger's return. I will stay here until I die unless someone comes to my rescue.'

So much for being circumspect. My bitterness poured out. My opinions would be of no surprise to the King if Maud ever saw fit to inform him. I had lost nothing in their saying.

'How long do you stay here?' I asked.

'Not long. I must not overstay my welcome. But I will return.'

'Any news you can bring me ...' For a moment I hesitated, unwilling to put myself completely into her hands. She had after all a strong de Clare blood tie with the King.

She turned to me, her gaze direct, her lips firm.

'If you were wondering, Lady Mortimer, if I am to be trusted, then I would reassure you that I am. We are not in good relations with the King. We have no reason to trust him, as well as his taking the Clifford inheritance for his own. I married Lord Welles without royal permission, and Edward does not like to be disobeyed. My husband and I live under a cloud of royal disapproval so there will be no carrying of tales from me to him.'

'Edward's approval is paramount. As we discovered to our cost.'

'Indeed. Anything you say to me will not be heard beyond this door. Is there anything I can do for you?'

'Information. Discover for me the fate of my older daughters and my sons, if you will. I do not trust the King with their care.'

She sighed. 'Nor would I.'

'And my mother-in-law, Lady Marguerite de Mortimer. The King was hunting her down at Radnor when last I heard.'

'I will do what I can.'

'Do you know anything of my lord?'

'No. Only that he is still across the sea. To return would not be good policy. As you said, your sojourn here is likely to be a long one. I will ask that you dine with me, and we will talk more. It must be difficult for your young girls with so little to occupy them.'

'It is a burden indeed. They are good girls but the days are long.'

We parted company, by which time I was Johane to her, and she was Maud to me. Her request that we dine together was of course refused. It was not Edward's wish to make this imprisonment comfortable for me. I expect the Commander had satisfaction in his brusque refusal. If the lady had brought sugar plums, we would not see them.

She left next morning, after taking inspection of what was once her home. Who would be taking care of Wigmore? Of Ludlow? Just another layer of sadness for me. But there was joy left behind by Maud de Clare who, by some miraculous means, had persuaded the Commander to be amenable.

'Look at what she has left for us!'

Agnes's voice rang out in the inhospitable dankness of our hall.

There in the arms of one of the guards was a small white dog and a cumbersome perch on which tottered a squawking parrot. The dog wore a blue velvet collar trimmed with silver, the most valuable item that we now owned. With our new additions to our family there was a letter.

'What does the lady say?' Beatrice demanded. 'Are they now ours? Do we have to give them back when she returns?'

It would be too cruel and I did not think so, blessing Maud for the joy on my girls' faces. I opened the single sheet on which Lady Maud's clerk had written, obviously to her dictation, for I could hear her voice loud and clear.

My dearest Johane,

Forgive me if it is not to your liking but I thought the girls would find much pleasure in my gifts. The dog is called Roseau. You will find him a nuisance, but the girls will like him. The parrot is Pierre. I wish your girls well of them. And you can teach the bird to curse Despenser. It has a very strident voice. You will enjoy that.

Your close friend by marriage,
Maud

Two more mouths to be fed. I did not have the heart to refuse them, and I doubted they would cost much. Thus my household increased.

I wished that she had been able to send me a book.

Chapter Twenty-One

Skipton Castle in Yorkshire, winter 1325

Lady Maud had said that she would return. What an empty promise it might turn out to be. Anticipation of an event that might never happen merely added to my restlessness. She had no duty to come to my assistance, even to tell me what might be afoot in the country. She had her own life to lead. In the end I stopped looking for her. She would not travel in winter when the roads were awash with rain and mud.

Our chambers grew colder and damper, our breath visible. Meanwhile the girls grew pale and even my tales lost their magic. I blessed Maud for the gift of the dog and the parrot, although there were only so many phrases we could expect the bird to repeat, and the lap dog was no hound to run up and down the steps with the girls. Beatrice suffered from a cough which refused to succumb to syrup of black bilberries which Gilbert brought us from the moors beyond our walls. We all had chilblains from sitting too close to the poor fire that we achieved.

These were the darkest, the coldest, the most lowering days of my life. Our candles were limited and of poor-quality tallow since I could not afford better. The windows were narrow, more use for defence than soft living, and let in little light. Even the solar lacked what we needed. All was dominated by the six drum towers, and the cliff against which the castle was built, so that the damp infiltrated my flesh, my bones. The loneliness bit even deeper in me. And fear. Fear for my own health and for the girls. And my children of whom I had no news. As for Roger, I had to trust that he was safe and could look after himself.

There was no hope, no lightness, no joy. It was the terrible monotony of it all. Even worse was the desperation that lived within me, a constant companion that robbed me of any emotion other than the anguish that this might be my future until the day of my death. And that Roger too had no future if the King decided to demand the ultimate penalty for treason. I rose with the torment in the morning, and took it to my bed at night, a visceral suffering.

More immediately, what would we do with our time? No books. No music. No visitors. Was it Edward's intent that we die of boredom? Every day the same, every hour, every minute. The only alteration in the pattern of the day when we prayed in the chapel.

This would not do. We could not live like this. But I had no remedy for it.

And then, when April arrived and signs of spring, so did Lady Maud, much as she did before, with an altercation over whether she should be allowed to stay. She got her own way with the Commander, who was willing to be charmed, and more than willing to accept the small bag of coin. We met in the chapel where we knelt side by side.

Blessed Virgin, forgive me if my thoughts are elsewhere.

'You look thin and pale,' she observed.

'I have no appetite and feel the weight of my years, Maud, and the effect of feeding my family on the money I have,' I admitted.

'The damp makes my joints ache like those of an old crone. But we are still alive. What can you tell me about my family?'

'First your daughters. They continued to reside in the convents to which they were originally sent. It is not good news, except that they are surviving the punishment that the King sees to inflict on them, simply because they are of an age to be wed and their husbands might work for the Mortimer cause.'

'Has he not arranged marriages into the families that remain loyal to him?'

It had been one of my worst fears.

'No. He seems to have forgotten them, which is to your advantage. They are stalwart girls as far as I can ascertain. Margaret is still in Shouldham Priory where she has a weekly allowance, although I have it on good authority that it is smaller than that of a criminal in the Tower. What if she had need of a new robe? She would be allowed one mark a year, as would Joan at Sempringham and Isabella at Chicksands, but they have even less allowance to feed themselves. I asked about sending gifts to them but I was refused. There is nothing that can be done about it.'

My heart had leapt with some relief that they still lived, but then had dropped into yet another black chasm of helpless heartache. My precious daughters were far from my care. A thought came to me. 'Have they been forced to take the veil?'

'No.'

The only relief in this sorry tale of deprivation and humiliation for a Mortimer daughter.

'And my sons?'

'They are still in Windsor and John in Odiham Castle. As far as I can tell they are in good heart.'

I covered my face with my hands.

'Thank you, Maud.'

I would not weep. They were safe, they were alive. The anger within my heart burned brightly against the man who would take his revenge on young children. We walked from the chapel into fitful sunshine that might have raised my spirits, but I could not be hopeful. Maud tugged me into the patch of sun and we sat on the steps regardless of the cold. Her eyes sparkled with gossip.

'Now here's an interesting rumour to claim your curiosity in what is happening in the royal love nest. Isabella has been at the French Court where she is negotiating in King Edward's name for the lordship of Gascony.'

'Is all well between them?'

'Not so. It was expected that this month Queen Isabella would return to England, her task complete. Instead, she has chosen not to return from Paris. In fact she is joined there by her son Prince Edward, to do homage for Gascony in his father's place.'

I wrinkled my nose; I could see little interest in this, until Maud continued.

'It is thought to be a marital declaration of war by the Queen against Despenser. Edward is as smitten with Despenser as ever.'

'We cannot blame her. I had hoped that Isabella was strong enough to wean King Edward away from his favourite. It seems she has failed. When does she plan to return?'

'Who's to guess? She has said, in the presence of the whole French Court, that she will not return until Despenser is removed. Until that time she will be wed no longer, but wear the robes of a widow and mourning. And she will stay in France if she must.' Maud smiled. 'Isabella always did lean towards the dramatic.'

'And what does the King of France say to his sister?'

'That she may come or go as she wishes. It is thought that he hopes for an alliance with her against England.'

Once it would have interested me, but now there were more urgent concerns. Lady Maud had not mentioned Roger's name amongst the gossip. Did she carry bad news?

'Where is he?' I asked. Better to know sooner rather than later.

Her reply was smooth enough. 'I do not know for certain. It is thought that he is now in France, travelling there from Hainault. Perhaps to petition the Queen for aid in returning. Perhaps next time I will know more.'

There was nothing here to concern me, nor to raise my hopes, although when Roger had asked Isabella to beg for my release, she had been willing to do so. It was the fault of neither Roger nor Isabella that they had been unsuccessful.

'It may be that Isabella and her brother will make an alliance, and Lord Mortimer may become part of it,' Maud encouraged me. 'It is something he would hope for.'

And so did I, as the girls ran across the courtyard towards us.

'They are growing fast,' Lady Maud observed, 'despite the dull fare. They grow out of their tunics.'

All four of my daughters had grown beyond the sleeves and hems of their over-gowns. We had already done what we could to lengthen and mend. I cast a glance over them, suddenly noticing in the short time that we had been at Skipton that their ankles were visible, their wrists pale and angular from their sleeves. The food might be of poor quality, insufficient in quantity but they were growing as girls should. Catherine's cotehardie was straining at the stitches. We did not have the money to remedy it with new lengths of cloth until Easter.

'Can I help?' Lady Maud asked as she prepared to leave.

'Send us books. At least we can read and tell stories. Anything to ward off the darkness of these days.'

And until she did, there was one story to tell, when the nights were dark and the silence of the castle pressed down on us.

'Tell us how our father escaped from the Tower of London,' Agnes demanded, casting aside her stitching of a new girdle made from an old one of mine.

A never-ending enchantment in our cold captivity for my girls who were fast growing up. Catherine was eleven, Beatrice nine, Agnes eight years and Blanche still a child at six, while I had just reached my thirty-ninth year. When the draughts whistled round our chamber, we could do nought but wrap ourselves in the bedcovers, huddling together in the large bed that was officially mine; the little dog curled in our midst and snored, the parrot dozed on its perch by the dying fire, one candle shedding a poor light. My stories of King Arthur and his gallant knights, of the tragic but ill-conceived love of Lancelot for Queen Guinevere, were rivalled by the exploits of Lord Mortimer in the Tower of London. It kept them close to their father in spirit when we had no knowledge of where he was or what he was doing. I could not bear that they might forget him. I was not certain how much was honest truth and how much make-believe in the detail of the telling, but it was a fine tale that would be recorded in the Mortimer annals when we were finally released. When we were released. There were days when I feared that it would never be, for who would come to our rescue?

'This is how it came about.'

We settled into the story while I took a comb to Catherine's hair and plaited it into tidiness, and so I told them about Roger, unjustly locked up simply for opposing the royal favourite Despenser, yet discovering ways of getting letters out of the Tower to powerful friends on the outside who might help him to freedom. When some of these letters were intercepted and the plots to rescue him became known, the King and Despenser decided that they would never be safe as long as Roger was alive to plot his escape. They would murder him, with no recourse to justice.

But Roger had friends to come to his aid. At the Feast of St Peter ad Vincula there was to be a celebration at the evening meal for the garrison. So much wine and ale was consumed, until all the men who should have guarded him lay in a drunken sleep, the wine being drugged. Stones were levered out of the cell wall so that eventually the hole was large enough for a man to squeeze through. Down the stairs he ran, and into the vast kitchen, where he climbed up through the rotting wood of a poorly maintained roof, while the cook pretended not to see and continued to baste a pan of eels. Out onto the roof, he was still not yet free. From there he used a rope ladder to climb down into the outer ward, then over the curtain walls, to drop into the marshy waters of the Thames. A small boat was waiting there to ferry him across the river to Greenwich where four Mortimer men-at-arms were waiting with horses. Roger disappeared into the night, finally crossing the sea to France.

Which brought the usual litany of pride from my daughters.

'Father is very brave...'

'And very clever...'

'Was he not followed?'

'The King sought for him but did not find him,' I said because this I did know.

'And now he is safe.'

'Yes, with our de Fiennes family in Picardy. The King and Despenser cannot get their hands on him there.'

'Will he be building support, to come back and rescue us?' Catherine as the eldest had the appropriate turn of phrase.

'I think so.' I hoped so.

'But when will he come home?'

There was no answer that I could give. I did not know. Nor

did I care to guess. The main fear was that it might be never. And what would become of us then? Any man who opposed the King would create in Roger a powerful symbol of freedom against tyranny. A sop to Mortimer pride, but dangerous all in all. The children and I were Roger's weak links. We were being held to ransom for his continued absence. If he dared to return with insufficient power, I knew that we might all face an unpleasant death.

I told the girls none of this.

Instead I painted him as a chivalrous knight from the old tales who had escaped against all the odds and would come to our rescue. He would restore us to the life we loved in Wigmore. Thus I had created a hero for them. Sometimes it worried me. Pray God that he could live up to such an image. I made of him a hero for me too.

A log dropped in the hearth in a cloud of ash. The little dog woke with a yap. The parrot stirred and stretched its wings with much flapping and an answering squawk.

'We will fly away from here, like the parrot,' Agnes said.

'You are growing feathers already,' I said, picking up a small green one that had floated down to land in her hair.

They laughed, much cheered, their hair neat for the moment. I had done my job well, to lift their spirits and remind them that Roger was a man of great ingenuity and courage. Of course he would return and release us.

Were they the darkest days, the grimmest days for me? When all was without hope? Afterwards I thought that they were not. At least in those days I had a knowledge of love to warm my heart, and a strong spirit of revenge to feed my desire for the future. I stitched a tapestry for which Lady Maud had sent me the linen and the rich woollen threads. Was this what I would do for ever, creating a tapestry in which there were scenes of freedom? And what would I create? Lovers in a glade? It made me weep. Better to weave a scene of battle with a distant castle about to be captured and the inhabitants released from their imprisonment.

And yet I chose to stitch a lord and his lady in a garden. Around them were trees festooned with blossoms, their feet brushing through a meadow of flowers which shone in the grass as bright as stars. In one of the trees a small green parrot sat, looking down at them. Above all was a sky of ethereal blue with scudding white clouds. I took such care with it. If the lord in all his stately tunic and velvet cap bore any resemblance to Roger Mortimer, then who could blame me. And if the lady was a more beautiful rendition of myself, more comely than I had ever laid claim to being, in her flowing blue gown, then what lady would not so stitch herself into a tapestry? It helped to ward off the darkness as my thoughts remained with my absent lord. He would not leave me for ever: he would not fade; he would not die. I would not allow it. One day I would walk with Roger in a garden just like this.

Skipton Castle in Yorkshire, spring 1326

'She's here.'

Lady Maud. No longer was there the habitual altercation over whether she might stay, which chambers she would make her own, whether she would be allowed conversation with me. She was permitted to take up residence and we met on the wall-walk, the dogs as usual around her feet.

'My thanks for the linen and tapestry wools. I have enjoyed them.'

'You must show me the result. I have brought you a packet

of sugared plums. Smuggled in, of course. I am becoming most proficient. Who would have once thought that I would be so willing to break the King's rules?'

'The girls will welcome them.'

Although her tone was light, her face brightened by a shaft of spring sunshine, I thought that her smile was tight-lipped and her expression severe when she turned away from me to loosen her hem from the depredations of one of her dogs. Her regard had not quite met mine, even when she had smiled at her unauthorised gift.

'And there is news,' she said.

'Which I will welcome even more.'

We walked slowly along the wall, to look out over the little town where the inhabitants were gathering for market. It was a busy scene that made my incarceration so much more bitter.

'First some news of your mother-in-law, Lady Marguerite. Edward has accused her of holding seditious meetings in the name of her son.' Maud laughed softly at some memory, so that I thought I must have been mistaken in her inner troubles. 'Royal soldiers were sent to Radnor to take her into custody and deliver her to Elstow Priory, where she would remain at her own cost for the rest of her life. At least, that was the King's plan.'

It was terrible news. I doubted that Lady Marguerite would survive, enclosed in a nunnery. I could not imagine her acceptance of such shackles on her freedom, but then we all had this burden to bear.

'Did they take her?'

'Not so. She fled, where I know not, but she was not to be found in Radnor or Worcester, or anywhere else that the King sought for her. It may be that she escaped to the de Fiennes family across the sea. Wherever it is, she remains a Mortimer at large. Edward is furious but can do nothing.'

Enough to make me smile too at courageous Marguerite forestalling the royal troops. Once again, when Maud did not respond, I thought that she was hiding something from me. There was a distinct shadow over her usual lively features.

'Is Isabella still in France, with her son?' I asked. 'At the French Court?'

'Yes.'

'So she keeps the heir near her.'

'Indeed.'

'When does she plan to return?'

'No one speaks of that.' She bent down once more to pat the head of one of the dogs that bounded up for attention. My suspicions deepened.

'Tell me what you know about Roger.'

She answered readily enough, but her eyes once more did not quite meet mine.

'He is in France too. You should be told this, of course. It is said that he arranged an exchange of opinion with Queen Isabella. What's more, it is in general acceptance that they are working together to form a scheme to invade England. To remove Despenser. The plan is to betroth Young Edward to Philippa of Hainault, then gather what troops and money they can.' She paused. 'It is said that the invasion will be before the end of the year. They will return with a force strong enough to force the King into an agreement with them. Isabella will only return if Despenser's power is brought to an end. The King will never agree unless he is forced into it.'

But my initial interest was not in Despenser or Isabella's desires. A leap of hope caught in my throat. Before the end of the year. If that were so, if they could raise the troops with the support of Isabella and her French relatives, then our release would be imminent. Roger was returning. My days of isolation and imprisonment would be ended and we would all be free. Roger and I could return to Wigmore, to Ludlow. My days in this dark fortress were numbered.

My joy for that moment was difficult to contain. I would see Roger again. We would sit and talk. He would hold me in his arms.

'Thank God for such news!' Still doubts assailed and my fingers curled into the worn cloth of my over-robe. 'Can King Edward not prevent such a stratagem? Will not the Earls stand by him and prevent an invading force from landing, in spite of their hatred of Despenser?'

'I think not. Our King has made too many enemies. He still cannot shrug off Despenser's advice and power.' A longer pause. She turned her face away from me. 'You should know. There are rumours. More than rumours. There is a scandalous truth that we have heard, even here in England.'

Here was a terrible bleakness.

'What is it? What is it that worries you?' I did not think that her expression, when she turned back to me from her attention to her lap dog, reflected good news. 'Is there something to impede their return after all?'

'No. None that I know of.'

'Yet something is of a concern to you.'

'No. No.' She stood from where she had been sitting between two of the crenellations and shook out her skirts. 'The Queen will assuredly return, and Lord Mortimer with her. Enjoy the joyful prospect that one day soon you might ride out of here with your daughters and be reunited with the rest of your family. It is beyond what you could ever dream of.'

'But what is it that you fear?'

'Nothing that need be a burden on your soul, my dear friend.'

What a strange comment. If she had been about to tell me,

she had changed her mind and instead stalked off towards her own chamber.

'Maud...'

'I must see to the state of this castle.'

She raised her hand in farewell, leaving me with a sour taste that something had been hidden from me. I could not imagine what she would have to say. If Roger were returning, all would be well for me. What was it that could provoke disaster? Debating the possibilities through the night gave me no clear answers but there was undoubtedly something keeping Maud silent. For the first time she had not even invited me to sup with her, even if it was always met with a refusal from my guards. Rising early, I could not consider her leaving the next day without knowing. I asked permission to be in the inner bailey when she prepared for her departure.

It was allowed. She was standing beside her litter, the rich blue curtains looped up for her to enter, her dogs already ensconced, her escort around her. I thought that given a choice she would have pulled the drapes across and departed, to leave me standing at the gate. But she did not. Instead, she walked forward so that she faced me. I held her eyes with mine.

'You know what I will ask,' I said.

'Yes. I do.'

Her eyes were strained, her usually gentle features marred with worry, as if she had slept as little as I, but I, riven with menacing doubts, was without mercy.

'And you will tell me. You will tell me what it is that you hid from me yesterday.'

'You will not thank me for it, Johane.'

All my married life I had been issuing orders and commands. I did so now.

'Tell me! If there is anything that you know appertaining to my future, you will tell me. In the name of the Blessed Virgin, Maud. You owe me the truth in this abominable situation in which I find myself.'

'Then I must, although it hurts me to do so.'

There, standing beside her litter in the outer ward, Lady Maud told me what she knew. It was callous, but she had the truth of it. I needed to know. In her mercy she omitted no details.

'Is it the truth? Or is it mere rumour, which can be disproved?' I asked, helplessly clinging to some small vestige of hope.

'It is the truth.'

And, accepting, I received the news that struck me with the force of a sword blade, creating a terrible mix of grief and fury within me, emotions that I could barely contain. I could find nothing to say in reply to her, but climbed the stairs to the wall-walk to look out with blind eyes, a fierce anger holding me in check when I would have shrieked my denial to the distant moors. I did not even question the news that she brought me. To hope that it was false would be to make of me a fool.

I said nothing to the girls, yet did not forget the needs of my children. Before Maud's litter passed through the barbican I had run down the stairs and stopped her.

'A favour, if you will. When you see your sister Meg and her daughter Elizabeth, tell them that I have not forgotten them. Tell Elizabeth that when Edmund is released from the Tower he will come and claim her.' I swallowed the thick emotion that might render me speechless with tears. Elizabeth was still little more than a young girl and must not be allowed to think that she had been abandoned. 'Tell her that she will be well loved as a Mortimer wife.'

Back in my much-hated chamber, I completed the tapestry. I detested every stitch that I set in that fine linen but I would not allow it to be unfinished. I had stitched the Mortimer banner with similar care, with every hope of love. Now I stitched with despair. Every stitch, every stab of my needle was made with a boiling emotion, all the more powerful because it was kept under keen and speechless control. The lord and the lady would walk together in their garden of romantic happiness for ever.

Chapter Twenty-Two

Skipton Castle in Yorkshire, September 1326

I had anticipated leaving captivity with a fanfare of trumpets and a riot of Mortimer banners, all the anticipation of freedom and a reuniting with those I loved singing in my heart. I had not expected this deadly morass of horror and fury.

The popinjay had died from damp and probably boredom, to be buried in the neglected herb garden at Skipton Castle with some ceremony by my daughters. I had been imprisoned, one way or another, for almost five years when my husband, Lord Mortimer, together with Queen Isabella and a small band of mercenaries, landed in Suffolk on the north bank of the Orwell on the twenty-fourth day of September in the year 1326. I had been robbed of my dower, my de Geneville inheritance and my freedom; deprived of the company of my older sons and daughters. I could neither forget nor forgive.

Nor was everything immediately put to rights as I might have hoped. My sons were still under threat from King Edward, causing me further anxieties. On Lord Mortimer's return my sons were dispatched from Windsor to the Tower of London, and John from Odiham; surely a more onerous captivity for them. My daughters were still behind their convent walls. Only

Geoffrey remained free in France. I too remained behind locked doors with my four daughters. It was only when King Edward fled from the revenge of his wife and heir into Wales that change came about.

When that momentous event occurred, I was informed of my husband's whereabouts. I was also informed that I was to be freed from my imprisoning when my rescue arrived, a neat escort with Mortimer colours and two capacious and cushioned litters for our comfort. Lord Mortimer was not one of the escorting party.

I did not know what to think, what to do. For the first time within those five years my choices were my own of where to go, who to see. How ridiculous that my strength to make my own decisions, now that I had the power to do so, had wilted like a rose when the first frosts struck. It seemed that I had an escort worthy of my rank. A chest of clothes of quality and some nod to fashion was delivered to me. Someone had been thoughtful on my behalf. I hoped that it had not been Isabella, but I feared that it had her mark on it. The scent of rose petals wafted from the chest as soon as I lifted the lid, almost choking in its pungency, taking me back to the young girl's coronation. The thought made me consider tearing the costly garments into shreds, but beggars could not choose and at least the girls would be well-clad.

And there on top of the fine wool and silk and linen in the coffer, a looking-glass set in an ivory frame. I picked it up while the girls squabbled over ownership of the garments. The reverse of the frame was beautifully created with the image of a man and a woman playing chess together, the figures carved with such precision that their expressions of pleasure were quite clear. A lovely thing, but dared I use it to see the ravages created by the years? Had the months of captivity treated me ill? Was there grey in my hair, lines on my face that I had not seen before? I was forty years old.

Summoning all my courage, I lifted the mirror and I looked.

Not uncomely, not too many signs of impossible age depredations, certainly not as ravaged as I had feared, but my youth had faded in this northern fastness, with the restrictions on my life and a poor diet. Care-worn, a little weary, I decided. Any beauty I had in my younger days, and not that I laid claim to much, had been worn away. The fine lines that marred my skin at the corners of my eyes and my mouth heralded the approach of old age.

Then it was as if the image of Isabella was superimposed on mine. Isabella had been beautiful as a child. I imagined the golden perfection had remained with her. She would only just have reached her thirty-first year.

Look closely, Johane. It is time to face up to the truth.

Had the mirror been Isabella's decision? Was this a deliberate ploy to hurt, to harm?

I put it aside and clad myself and my daughters for a journey. The worn garments of our captivity were abandoned. I would take no reminiscence with me. I should feel victorious that I could leave this place at last. Strangely I felt little emotion. Neither relief nor happiness. Instead, a frozen lack of feeling engulfed me as if I stood in the centre of a snow storm.

Where do I go?

I stood beside one of the litters, the children, already tucked in and waiting with the dog, noisy with excitement in the other, considering where to direct the commander of my escort. I did not know him. Perhaps all those employed by Lord Mortimer were new to their positions. He bowed.

'My lord said that you should go to Wigmore, my lady.'

Well he would, wouldn't he. Was it not the obvious destination? It had been our home together until all went awry.

No. I would not. Not Wigmore. My reaction astonished me,
for it was a place of comfort and security where I had spent
many happy years, enjoying the spacious new buildings. I would
tread the familiar rooms, take possession of my chambers once
more, put to rights what had been destroyed or despoiled during
my absence. Would I not enjoy that?

No. And no. I had no wish to live under Wigmore's roof,
to have memories of happiness and contentment breathed into
bright life at each turn of the stair, in every step of the wall-
walk. In every chamber and corner of the courtyard. In every
view from the towers. I would not. Another image came into
my mind, emerging strongly with scenes I knew well: my own
castle, in need of a castellan since my mother's death. I needed
the presence of my own walls around me. Here is where I would
raise my daughters after their incarcerations with me, and welcome the return of those from convent restriction. They would
live at Ludlow until they wed. I would live there too.

'My lady?'

I blinked, still torn with indecision. I had no wish to live
alone. I regretted the loss of my mother, but what about Roger's
mother, Lady Marguerite? I would invite her to join me. I felt
my lips twist with cynicism. We could exchange opinions on the
morals of her son.

'Not Wigmore,' I said, now certain of what I wanted. 'I will
go to Ludlow. And if you will discover for me where Lady
Marguerite de Mortimer resides, I would be grateful. Perhaps
you could invite her to Ludlow in my name. You may find her
in Radnor. Send a courier if you will. She may be there before
I arrive.'

Thus I travelled to freedom and Ludlow. I discovered there

might be some element of joy in my heart after all as my litter passed beneath the arch of the outer gatehouse and into the vast outer bailey of my own castle. I should have informed Lord Mortimer of my change of plan, but I did not. He would find me when he had the time to seek me out. When he was not preoccupied with other demands on his life. Yet the cloud that pressed down on me every day would not be completely dislodged. When would I meet him? What would I say to him? Would I receive him with dignity as if nothing were amiss, or rant as a wife betrayed? I could only hope that he did not bring Isabella with him. I could not guarantee to offer as courteous a welcome as a castellan should.

I had already decided. One of my first orders on arrival, trivial as it seemed, but urgent in my mind, would be to hang in the Great Hall my new tapestry of the lovers in the garden. It would hang there, a banner, a memento of the past years. A mockery of the present.

Chapter Twenty-Three

Ludlow Castle in the Welsh Marches, October 1326

Lady Marguerite was there waiting for me in the inner bailey, standing on the steps that led into the Great Hall. The girls, leaping from their litter, swarmed around her, accepting her kisses before they vanished inside. How strong were their memories, of their grandmother and of the castle? It was five years since they had set foot here. Catherine would have the clearest, but Agnes and Beatrice would remember very little. Blanche would have no memories at all. As for me, I continued to stand at the foot of the steps as Roseau raced after the girls. Lady Marguerite had aged, as had I, her wimple framing a face imprinted with long days of worry. The smile for the girls had faded, leaving her face cruelly austere. Her fingers were close-linked at her girdle.

'Johane, my dear girl.'

My reply was regrettably sharp. 'I am no longer a girl. I can barely recall my girlhood. And I have to say this. If you are compassionate towards me, I will weep.'

'Then I will not be. But welcome back. This is where you should be.'

We embraced, the strength in her arms showing me that although nearer sixty years than fifty, she was as stalwart as ever.

Her conversation was mildly innocuous, deliberately so in spite of the severe grooves beside her lips, calming my emotions as she took my arm and encouraged me inside, into the Great Hall that I remembered so well. My daughters' voices echoed in the distance, touching my heart that they should enjoy their freedom. I was beyond enjoyment. This was my home, a de Geneville fortress where I should be safe, yet I felt no pleasure in it. It was as if all gentle responses had been drained away leaving only a cruel-edged bitterness and regret, and a boundless wild anger.

Even so I stood patiently and listened with the appearance of attentiveness to my mother-in-law.

'I escaped the King's revenge. Which is more than you did. But then I had news of his coming. He accused me of holding treasonous meetings. How would he know? My family came to visit me, so I presume that was seditious enough for Edward. And Chirk was often on my doorstep when he was not campaigning. Before his arrest, of course.'

'How did you escape?' I forced myself to ask.

'They arrived at Radnor and told me I must be taken to Elstow Priory, as punishment for my supporting the enemies of the King, and remain there for the rest of my life, at my own cost. I was most accommodating. They did not know me well! I arranged to be ready at the crack of dawn – being a woman of some years I would need a final good night's sleep in my own bed. As soon as it was grey-dawn I escaped to friends in Wales. I suppose they did not think an old woman capable of such ingenuity to make an escape. My household was loyal and useful, garbing me as a servant girl to accompany a delivery of cloth down to Hereford. It pleased me and them to thwart Edward. The royal escort made a desultory search, not worth the doing. When they departed, not best pleased, I returned to Radnor,

where I have been ever since, with a good look-out on my gates.'
I felt her gaze touch on my face. 'You did not fare so well.'

'No. Not well at all. There was no punishment, but it was not
the lap of luxury, living on an allowance hardly fit for a mouse.
I saw Roger before he took ship to France. I knew where he
was and what he intended.' I regarded her, wondering what she
would think of the present situation with her son. 'Unfortunately
the outcome was not what I had hoped for. I had lived in hope,
only to have it dashed into pieces.'

She paused, then said: 'It is good to see you, Johane. And the
girls. You all look in need of a good meal.' Her fingers closed
around my wrist which felt fragile in the clasp. 'But before you
wallow in your own sorrows, I should tell you and get over all
the bad news first. Mortimer of Chirk is dead.'

It was another cruel blow. Was it true that I had become
so intolerably self-centred? I knew that I had. I had not really
considered Lady Marguerite's emotions in all of this, not to any
degree, and here was a death that I had not envisaged. I took a
deep breath and tried to make amends.

'He did not live long enough to be rescued by my son,' Lady
Marguerite said.

'Forgive me. I have been unforgivably selfish. When?'

'At the beginning of August. In his cell in the Tower.'

I had certainly become unconscionably cynical. 'Was it
murder?'

'It was said that the corpse had no wounds or obvious cause
of harm.' She shrugged. 'So old age, we are left to presume.'

'I don't think I believe it.'

'Nor do I. He has been buried at Wigmore Abbey. What my
son says of his death I know not. I think Despenser might have
had more than a hand in it. And I regret being the bearer of
more bad news for you.'

It was impossible to believe that Roger Mortimer of Chirk was dead. Such a fractious figure, but with the skill to negotiate when the need arose. I wished he had lived to breathe the clean air of the Marches once again. What my husband would feel for this loss I had no idea.

I shook my head. 'Thank you for coming, and for telling me. Strangely, I did not wish to be here alone. One thing I will say – which will be a relief to you – I do not intend to wallow in self-pity.'

'If you do, we will wallow together. You can say nothing that can hurt me.'

She clasped my hands. At last we had stepped across the divide caused by Roger Mortimer, although the words could still not be uttered.

'You are remarkably well furnished with clothing after your imprisonment,' Lady Marguerite observed.

The bitterness rose once again to all but choke me. My wallowing was not over by any means. 'The clothes were sent to me. It has a royal touch, I think. I reek of the Queen's favourite rose perfume.'

The vibrant green and strong blue, embroidered at neck and hem, were not what I would have chosen to wear, nor could I lay claim to the gold-linked girdle. They were not mine. A longer pause as she summoned a servant and requested that he bring us wine. I must of course return to the habit of ordering my own servants.

'It is so long since I drank wine,' I observed. 'We had not the money for it. Ale was all we could manage, and poor stuff at that.'

Standing on the dais, I looked around my Great Hall, bare and rather grim. Not damaged in any way, but lacking a woman's touch. Everywhere had a layer of grime and dust; my mother would have been horrified at such lack of housekeeping. Lady Marguerite handed me a cup of wine while I sank down on one of the bare window seats. Cold and uncomfortable it might be, but it was mine. I must keep telling myself that I was free and could order my life as I chose. No one could question my right to be here.

'It was a long journey and the litter not created for comfort,' I said.

Once I would have smiled at the sound of the youthful voices and the sharp yapping from the private chambers. My face felt stiff and unresponsive to any feeling other than rancour.

'The girls had a parrot for a short time,' I said inconsequentially. 'It died.'

'Johane.'

I dragged myself back into the present. Lady Marguerite looked at me, and I looked at her. As she stepped into the shaft of sunlight it struck me that Lady Marguerite had indeed aged even more than I had first thought. Her face was thinner, her lips narrow, a ready frown creased her brow. I thought much of her humour had drained from her.

'Do you wish to speak of my son?'

I turned my head away. 'No.'

'But one day we must.'

'Not today. I am too full of anger. He has hurt me mortally, and today I would simply rejoice at your presence and being here in my own home. I cannot be certain that I would not walk away from you and curse you if we broached that unspeakable matter.'

'There is a letter awaiting you in your chamber,' she said.

'A letter! Ha! Should I rush to open it? Do you suppose that he sent one to Wigmore, too, so that I should not live in ignorance, wherever I chose to go?'

The acidity dripped from me. My last conversation with

Maud, in the courtyard at Skipton as she prepared to depart, all flooded back. Word after terrible word, when all had been made as clear to me as a reflection in a sorcerer's scrying mirror. It all came back to me now to fill Ludlow's Great Hall with the stench of despair and fury. It was as if Maud stood here with me now, the purveyor of such terrible news.

Suddenly I was back at Skipton Castle, standing beside her litter as Maud prepared to depart.

'You will tell me. What is it that you would not tell me last night? What is it that you fear to tell me now?' I had demanded of Lady Maud. 'Would you depart and leave me floundering in uncertainty and ignorance?'

'I would say that it will do you no good to know. It is best that you look forward to your freedom, not back to the past.' Maud frowned at her thoughts. 'Or even to the present. I am not intending to be deliberately unkind.'

I would not be deflected.

'Tell me the truth, Maud. It is Roger, I presume. Is it his health? Is he injured?'

Her brief laugh was harsh. 'He is well enough.'

'Then what?'

Still I could not have believed what she would tell me. I saw her drag in a breath and launch the wounding words.

'Here it is, if you insist. You will discover soon enough when you leave this place. It is Lord Mortimer and the Queen. They have committed an act of monstrous adultery.'

My heart gave a single heavy beat, taking my breath away; my throat was as dry as the dust beneath my feet as I sought for a reply.

Maud took advantage of my silence. 'They say that they are lovers.'

'Lovers...'

'The story of it is strong. So strong that I think that it must be true.'

I shook my head. 'No. That cannot be.'

'Why not?'

I sought for reasons, for arguments why this must be a lie. 'I am his wife. He loves me. He has always loved me.'

'I expect that he has said so...'

I was struggling against a storm of disbelief. Suddenly it was impossible to put together all the reasons why it could not be true. Roger could never have committed adultery with the Queen.

'I trusted him!'

'And perhaps he did have a deep regard for you. But circumstances change. You have been separate for so long, Johane. Is it not five years? Who knows what might occur at the French Court to draw an attractive man and woman together, despite their marriage vows? Lust is a powerful emotion.'

They were lovers. I would not accept it. He had promised to return to me and rescue me. He had given me a brooch proclaiming his love. I had borne his children. This was all wrong; my rejections of the news tumbled over each other like pebbles in a storm-flooded stream, as a cold hand squeezed around my heart in what seemed to be a physical pain, of such magnitude that it almost drove me to my knees.

'He is a man of honour, of loyalty,' I said, straightening my spine, but even I heard the plea in my voice.

'He is a man. A virile one. And in the company of a beautiful woman. It seems that their fates lie together.'

The truth stared me in the face, even though I would still deny it.

'Is this plain enough for you?' Lady Maud continued with

brutal frankness. 'He found a need for her to realise his ambition to return. Separately they are weaker than they are in an
alliance together. He needs her royal authority, both in France
and in England. He needs her wealth. She needs his leadership
to garner an army and bring it to England.'

'I can accept that.'

'It seems that they also discovered a need for each other of a
carnal nature. He has taken her to his bed.'

I drew in a slow breath. 'I will not believe it.'

But belief had already crept up on me with stealthy footsteps.

'Would he do that? Would he betray me in so public a fashion,
with the Queen of England?' I all but spat it out.

'Isabella is a young and beautiful woman.'

'And I am not? He needed her. He needed the power of her
name if he was to restore the Mortimer lands, and she needed
him to remove Despenser. Her son is still too young. Of course
they are close.'

How logical it all sounded. And how false.

Maud's voice was uncompromisingly gentle. 'Perhaps he now
needs her glamour, and she finds him more potent than her
husband. They share the same bed, Johane.'

Must I accept this calumny?

'So they are lovers,' I whispered in an agony of acceptance.

'Yes. The Blessed Virgin give you strength to accept it,' Maud
said, her final stitch in the terrible tapestry that she had stitched
for me.

'Johane...Johane!'

· It was Lady Marguerite's voice. It brought me back to the
present, in my Great Hall at Ludlow where Lady Marguerite
was regarding me with concern. I needed the Blessed Virgin's
strength. I still needed it, when I must accept that Maud's

warning was undeniably true if Roger's mother was convinced of it. And then there would be my reunion with my husband. No longer living with his lover in exile but here in England with her at his side. Apart from the state of my own wounded heart, what would I tell the girls? I wondered what they would think of their father's blatant immorality.

It was a lowering thought that they might accept it as a necessity more readily than I could.

'What do you wish to do first?' Lady Marguerite asked.

I lifted my silk skirts in my fingertips and shook my head so that my sinuous veils fluttered around my neck. 'Change my garments for those of my own choosing. These have Isabella's fingerprints all over them.'

'As does your husband, it seems!'

I stared at her. Rarely was Lady Marguerite so crude.

'You cannot deny it any longer, Johane. No one in this realm is denying it.'

'I suppose Isabella is still beautiful.'

'I suppose that she is. Such a depth of golden beauty does not easily fade.'

'Whereas I can offer no similar allurement to any man.'

I stood and left the wine untasted on the window seat. 'Forgive me.' My face felt stiff with the acceptance of what I did not wish to accept. 'I will go and read the missive from my once-loving husband. I promise that I will don my usual courtesy with my own garments.'

I kissed her cheek and made to depart to discover my own chamber, then remembering what I would not find there.

'I have no garments,' I said, unable to hide my horror at that loss, when all my possessions had been carried out by King Edward's orders. 'What do I wear?'

'I have arranged clothing for you,' Lady Marguerite said

gently. 'I was aware of your lack and so put it right. I trust the clothes will be to your liking. And take this,' she said, aware of the emotion threatening to overcome me at such consideration. She held out a small coffer. Immediately I knew what was in it. 'The Abbot kept it from the marauders.'

I wept as I climbed the stairs, the Mortimer Roll tucked under my arm.

In my chamber, ignoring the familiarity of it that should have brought me so much satisfaction, I sought out the letter. A letter from Roger himself, not normally a great writer of letters but perhaps on this occasion he thought I was worthy of some communication. Only a fool would think me ignorant of events across the sea, in Roger Mortimer's bed. Thus a letter in Roger's own hand, not that of a clerk.

For some time the letter lay before me on the pillows of my bed where it had been placed for me. It was well-travelled and dog-eared. I touched it with one finger, then retreated. I had what suddenly seemed to me to be a more urgent task.

I changed my garments, folding away the rich silks and the expensive taffeta of the fashionable side-less surcoat, all miniver-trimmed, as well as the fine wool of the under-kirtle. The gold chain of the belt too was rejected. Would Roger have been so insensitive as to allow his mistress to send garments to his wife? I did not suppose that it even crossed his mind, when the restoration of the Mortimer lands took priority. It was in my mind to dispose of them, but the cloth was too beautiful and would cut to fit my youngest daughters. They would enjoy the deep blue and the flower-embroidered hems. I admitted the small yapping dog who curled on the floor beside the cold hearth as, my veil removed, I combed and re-braided my hair under a new veil of fine linen secured by a simple silk filet, once more aware of the silvering of grey in the brown before it was covered in seemly fashion. I washed my hands and face with rosemary-scented water from my own jug and ewer. I would rid myself of those detested rose petals. I was home and I would be dressed as I wished to be dressed, thanks to Roger's mother. I had no need of the ministration of one of my women.

At last, when I could put it off no longer, I read the letter.

To Johane, Lady Mortimer,
  When you read this, you will have achieved your freedom.

No overt affection. There it was: cool, formal, apologetic for my punishment in his name, regretful for the harsh incarceration and lack of news. Hopes for my comfort on my travel from Skipton to the south-west. The need for him to take political action to secure his own safety before he was free to travel to the Marches when he would come to me. Until King Edward's person was secured, the state of the realm was uncertain.

You know that one of my main objectives will be to reclaim the Mortimer lands and my own position as a Marcher lord. When this is done, and when I come to you, we will talk of the events of the past months that will not have escaped your notice. I am sure that many have enjoyed repeating the rumours to you. All I can ask is that you defer judgement on me until I can speak with you.

I blew out a breath between pursed lips. Not one mention of Queen Isabella in person. Had she written to King Edward, I wondered? Was she just as cool and contained after what was in effect an invasion? I thought that she had not.

I wondered, my mind making haphazard leaps, how much

support Roger and Isabella would have and what would be King Edward's fate. Everything was happening so rapidly after the years of my life being encased within stone walls, like a fly in amber. Yet what did it matter to me in that moment? All I needed to know was how Roger Mortimer would converse with me when he crossed my threshold here at Ludlow. For of a surety I would not travel to see him.

It was an event that I dreaded.

Or did I? Now that I was once more in my own castle, I felt strangely calm about the whole series of events, as if there was nothing left to hurt me. Even the pain was blanketed in a lack of involvement. Nothing I could do would change what had been done, or what would be done in the future. Roger had made a fatal choice, and I was helpless in its grip. Hanging over me like a black storm-cloud, I could not shake free of it, which I accepted since I had lived with it now for some weeks.

All I can ask is that you defer judgement on me until I can speak with you.

It was an impossibility. I had made my judgements in the wake of Maud's warning.

I burned the letter since there was nothing in it for me to keep, either information or sentiments. It was as worthless as the ash that fell formlessly in the hearth.

Searching through my new clothes, I discovered what I wanted and I dressed myself in black, an embroidered over-gown upon a black kirtle. A rich and funereal black. The colour of death. Of loss and of night. Of betrayal. Then I stepped out of my chamber to survey my home, once more Lady of Ludlow. There was much work for me to do here.

Chapter Twenty-Four

Ludlow Castle in the Welsh Marches, October 1326

I settled back into my home, my daughters gradually joining me, travelling from their distant convents. I wondered if they were much changed; all were so well grown and adult, they were resilient certainly, quieter perhaps. Had it any lasting effect on them? It seemed not, when they took up their old lives as easily as they donned clothes more suitable for Mortimer daughters. I noted their growing maturity. Marriages would have to be arranged for them, the old alliances taken up once more.

They did not speak to me of Roger. Had they entered into a pact of silence to spare me pain? Nor did I speak to them, for I did not know what to say. Did I still hope that all would be as it was in the past? No. I could not be so naive. I felt the compassion of my girls as they returned my affectionate greetings. Better than outspoken pity. I would never forgive him for imposing that on me.

There was one question that I asked them when they were once more in my household, before Margaret travelled on to be united with her husband, Lord Berkeley's heir. Isabella and Joan would remain with me until provision could be made for them.

'Were you ill-treated?'

The three young women, as now they were, exchanged glances.

'No. Unless it was a surfeit of prayers in the chapel when the mornings were dark and the days cold,' said Margaret.

'Or the fast days when the sides of your belly clapped together,' Isabella added.

'Or the punishment for breaking the great silence.' Joan had always been a child who asked questions.

The not knowing was the worst of it, they all agreed, but now they were free and of a mind to celebrate. How resilient they were. No, they had not been punished over-much.

'You have withstood all the trials with great fortitude.'

'Because we had no intention of taking the veil.'

They looked at each other again.

'Do we expect Father to come here to Ludlow?' Isabella asked.

'I have no news of it,' I replied.

'Do we welcome him?'

'Of course. Is it not his home?'

'It is yours before it was ever his,' Isabella said, and brushed her lips against my cheek. 'We would, of course, understand if you closed the gates and refused him entry.'

Not one more word was said about their father's return and his present companion. I might wish that Isabella had not been named after the Queen, but her words had strengthened me and I loved her dearly.

Days turned, one into another in that unsettled month of October. Still Lady Marguerite and I did not discuss the state of my marriage, I through a sheer dogged refusal to put into words my turbulent emotions; Lady Marguerite through a sensitive fear of treading on my painful toes. We had enough to fill any spaces in our conversation, for news was easy to come by. The power in the land was in the hands of Queen Isabella and Lord

Mortimer, that much was clear. When I could free my mind of my own mourning for what I had lost, I began to consider the consequences, as did every other man and woman of a political mind in England. What would they do with Hugh Despenser? Even more crucial; what would they do with King Edward?

I might not be willing to discuss the state of my marriage, but I listened avidly to the news of the royal Court, ready to discuss its repercussions with Lady Marguerite. Fearing the worst, when the support that they hoped for did not come to save them, King Edward and Despenser decided to take ship from Chepstow and make for safety in Ireland. An empty gesture. The weather turned against them in spite of a friar praying with them that the wind would change, and after five days they had no choice but to make for port in Cardiff. From there the King and his favourite made his way to Caerphilly castle which should have offered some safety, but in the face of the Queen's wrath his household deserted him.

'So now our King is taken prisoner to Kenilworth Castle. And in his place, the young Prince Edward has charge of the realm, as custodian, at fourteen years old,' Lady Marguerite said after a number of passing travellers had unburdened themselves to us.

'With a goodly number of earls signing the document in support of the Prince. Not that he has any power to wield. We both know who has the country firmly under control.'

'Lord Mortimer and Queen Isabella.'

I was in a mind to be more forthright.

'Who would have ever guessed it? Roger and his lover are rulers of England.'

'May the Blessed Virgin protect us from what will happen next! Do you suppose that King Edward will be allowed to live?' Lady Marguerite queried. 'Or will he be locked in Kenilworth until his natural death? He is still a young man. It could be years, and he will always be a danger, for those with even a hand-span of loyalty towards him will plot his release and restoration.'

'Or those who trust the Queen less than they trust King Edward.'

She eyed me, considering this aspect.

'There is that, of course. She will have made enemies for herself, seizing power that is not hers by right. I would still fear for the King's life. My son might have an interest in seeing it as permanent removal.'

'I don't know about that,' I said, quickly deflecting any discussion of her son, 'but I would not wager that Despenser has a long life ahead of him.'

'I despise the man.'

'As do many. I think the Queen will not allow him to live.' I took a breath. 'Nor will Lord Mortimer. He will never trust Despenser after all the past history between them.'

Lady Marguerite did not pursue the matter. Roger Mortimer continued to remain absent from my company, if not from my thoughts. The light had gone from my life. All that was left to me were cruel shadows of what had once been.

That situation could not last for ever. November brought a change.

'My son is in Pembridge,' Lady Marguerite announced, walking into my chamber one morning without even a knock. A mere two-day ride away. Even one, for a man with a fast horse and a determination to get here.

'How do you know?'

'The travelling merchant. The chatty one with the furs, that you are now perusing.'

My heart thumped uncomfortably, anxiety building in a knot in my belly. I had known it would happen, but as time had passed it had been easy to pretend that I would never have to face him. Here he was on the very threshold of my castle.

'Presumably he has estate business there.' A response that impressed me although I could not meet Lady Marguerite's eyes.

'You could go and meet with him.'

I raised my brows. Still running my hand over the good-quality miniver I had considered purchasing, I did not deign to reply, but neither did the soft fur make any impression on me. My mind was in Pembridge, where we had wed as little more than children so many years ago now.

'Why not go?' Lady Marguerite asked after waiting for my assent, coming to sit beside me, enjoying the luxurious miniver, even though her eyes were on my face.

'Why would I? He will know where I am by now, here at Ludlow. He will know that I am not at Wigmore. He can come here if he wishes to see me.'

'Oh, Johane!'

'I will not seek him out. If he bears any guilt, he must come to me.'

After five years of separation, would he not wish to at least converse with me? Did I not deserve an apology – and how weak a word that was! – for making me a figure of gossip and pity throughout the realm? Did he not bear the guilt in this betrayal, for which I deserved that he should express some regrets? I thought for a moment, noting that my fingers had dug themselves into the innocent pelt of the fur.

'Is the Queen with him?'

Was she perhaps at this moment in Pembridge, ensconced in the little manor where we spent our wedding night and toasted each other in the bridal cup? Did she sit in my chair in my hall? Had she knelt before the altar in my church? Nausea gripped my throat.

'I think not.'

'So he may, or he may not, come here,' I stated. 'It will be his choice.'

'Very well. Do you wish to buy that fur?'

'No.' I was thoroughly unsettled.

'Then I will. And I'll leave you to decide what you will say to my son when he rides up to your door.'

'I already know!' And yet, I did not. I cast the fur aside. 'Choose what you wish and we will return the rest to the merchant. We have enough for winter cloaks.'

I would not go to Pembridge.

I could not help but wonder what he was doing there.

And then Lord Mortimer was not my first priority. My sons had stepped out of the Tower into a new political existence and had joined Roger at Court. Edmund claimed Elizabeth de Badlesmere as his wife, John was with his father, but here, beneath the Court gloss of a short, high-collared, embroidered jacket and sleek hose, was Young Roger. I looked up at my second son after five years of absence. He was a man, twenty years old, and taller than I, the Mortimer feature now firm and well defined in maturity. His hair was dark and glossy, cut fashionably below his ears.

'I see that you have been at Court,' I observed.

'How did you know?' he asked with a delightful naivety.

'You did not get that fine ensemble in captivity in Windsor or the Tower. The points on those shoes are fine enough to spear a rabbit, and those enamelled buttons did not come cheap.' I slid my fingers over the hanging over-sleeve. 'That fine cloth is better than any brought to our door here by a hopeful merchant. I suppose that your father paid for it.'

'Well, I could not!'

It did not take long for our conversation to return to what his father was doing. After he fended off my embrace with the easy laughter I recalled, Young Roger told us why Lord Mortimer had been dealing with manorial matters in Pembridge.

'He has been in Hereford.'

'And what was his business there?'

I could not help but be interested.

'To wreak his revenge on Hugh Despenser, sentenced by a tribunal assembled by my father in true legal style, to be hanged, drawn and quartered at his own castle in Hereford. It was one of the gifts given to him from a besotted King. There was not one of the Earls prepared to speak up for Despenser or make the sentence an easier one.'

He went on to describe the crowds, the trumpets and drums, the demand for blood. And then the terrible detail of the execution. A cruel end for a man who had caused such pain and havoc in the realm.

'Was Lord Mortimer present?' Lady Marguerite asked.

'Yes.'

'And the Queen?'

'Yes.'

Brief replies, as if he was unsure how much to say. There was a wash of colour across his cheekbones.

'So we would have expected,' I said, to put him at ease.

'To see vengeance done, mother. His sins against the Mortimers have been many. You would never have been imprisoned if it were not for him.'

'Very true.' I could not deny it. 'And the King? Does he still live?'

'Still ensconced in Kenilworth.'

What a strange conversation, with none of the underlying pertinent facts being voiced. Mortimer and the Queen: all muffled in thick mist.

'What does Lord Mortimer do now?' I asked.

'I know not. He does not take me into his confidence, even if he pays for my clothes until I have disposable money of my own. I expect that only the Queen can tell you.'

'I doubt that she will give me the benefit of her knowledge. Nor will I ask her.'

A flush of colour once again touched Young Roger's cheek-bones. The subject was dropped.

'By the bye, Mother. John said to thank you for the knife. He said he has had no cause to use it, but he will keep it with him for emergencies.' Young Roger laughed. 'It was very brave of you. He is more a danger to himself than to those round him. I've never met a clumsier lad. He said that he did not think that you would have need of it.'

'It seemed a good thought at the time,' I replied, remembering my distress at John being taken from me. I managed a tight smile. 'As for my needing it, I can think of good use I could make of it just at this moment.'

I uncurled my hand, imagining the fine blade lying across my palm. Whether I would wish to use it against my absent husband or the Queen, I was unsure. Whichever it was, it put another end to the conversation and my family drifted away, leaving me to my own thoughts. Would Roger come to Ludlow? I remembered Isabella's words in France at her brother's Court, if Maud had spoken them true, and there was no reason why she should not. That there were three people in her marriage, she had said. Until Despenser was removed she would be wed no longer, but wear the robes of a widow in mourning.

Were there not three in mine? I would dress as a widow if Roger Mortimer ever found the time to come visiting me. But would I? Would I keep the black garments that I had so far donned daily? I discovered that I was smiling. No, I would not!

Those days were gone. Opening my coffers, I pulled out a rich over-gown woven in the finest indigo silk with gold-stitched borders, with a skirt that rippled on the floor around me, another offering from Lady Marguerite, much like one I had lost, with miniver at neck and sleeve.

'Ah, the robe more suitable for a Court banquet that I brought for you. Are you planning on making a statement here, dear Johane?' Lady Marguerite enquired with more than a sparkle in her eye when we ate dinner together. 'Are we celebrating?'

'No, but I am alive.' I raised my cup in a toast. 'I will no longer play the widow for your son.'

She tilted her chin, eyes squinting at me. 'Do you want an amulet, to ward off the power of a sorceress?'

'Do you have such?'

'It is possible. My de Fiennes ancestors probably found use for one.'

I actually thought about it for a moment. To destroy Isabella's hold on my husband and return him to me. Then I shrugged.

'I think we are past that. Lord Mortimer needs it more than I.' Then on a thought, since Lady Marguerite continued to surprise me: 'Could you make me one?'

'Of course. Amethyst and silver are a powerful combination to renew a love that has died. Such an amulet might return Roger to you.'

'But do I want him if his mind and body lust after the Queen?'

'There is no answer to that.'

'As for this gown, the Queen has cast off her husband and has taken mine, but I have decided that there is no need for me to be a widow. I think that we might expect him here any day.'

Chapter Twenty-Five

Ludlow Castle in the Welsh Marches, in the first week of December 1326

Despenser was dead. Lord Mortimer was very much alive as he rode up to my gatehouse at Ludlow in the first week of the celebration of Advent.

'Does he not look every inch a Marcher lord?' Young Roger, still with us, observed. At twenty years of age he was bound to be impressed by the sight.

'A snake in the grass was more in my mind.'

I was aware of my son and my daughters exchanging glances; they wielded formidable composure to say no more. What I had quite deliberately not told my daughters had been spoken of by Lady Marguerite, and then expanded by Young Roger. It was as if the whole castle held its breath in anticipation of this meeting.

I had known that he was coming. It had been reported to me, since I would not be taken by surprise, giving time for me to clothe myself in a rich red surcoat patterned with tiny lions as befitted the de Geneville heiress, mother of the Mortimer heirs. I would remind him of who I was, and if I was the only one to know that the gilded net, depending from a narrow filet, hid the greying hair of my imprisonment, I was satisfied. The grooves beside my mouth and between my brows I could do nothing to hide, but I would mask them in a cloak of utter self-possession and dignity, as I wore a barbette to disguise the evidence of years on throat and neck. I fastened a de Geneville collar around my neck, the de Geneville lion snarling at its centre, while rings adorned my fingers. I would be no petitioner for Mortimer attention, or for pity. I was Castellan of Ludlow.

I watched his approach through the outer bailey to the Great Tower Gatehouse, a hardness settling in my heart as the gates were opened to allow him access into the inner bailey. I would be there before he had even dismounted. My first thought: no Isabella. He was alone except for his smart escort with Mortimer colours, the bold blue and gold agleam in the bright winter sunshine. The brooch that fastened his cloak was large and glittered with cabochon-cut gems. I did not recognise it. I had never given it to him. A royal jewel, forsooth. It pleased me that I wore no Mortimer jewels as I stood immobile on the bottom step leading from the Great Hall and waited, full of dread, full of anticipation, even a strange excitement. What would he do? What would I do? Certainly not cast myself into his arms after all the years of painful separation.

My heart hurt.

'Give him time to speak,' Lady Marguerite had advised, nervously I thought, as she anticipated the impending clash of temperament.

'To say what? That he prefers the Queen's company, her conversations, and the delights of her body to mine? That his vows of loyalty to me are as empty as an ale keg after a drunken celebration?'

She had frowned at me, but not without some level of fellow feeling. 'I cannot see this meeting having a compatible outcome.'

'I have never expected one.'

She raised her hands in despair at the rift that had been created in our family.

'These things happen, Johane. Before God, Roger is no saint. I'll not make excuses for him, but...'

'I thought I had wed a man of loyalty,' I interrupted. 'Before we were wed I consulted the stars of a man born under the sign of the great horned bull. A man of utter loyalty, I was led to believe. It was a lie. Would you excuse his betrayal?' I stared at her with not one hint of compromise. 'Was your lord disloyal to you? Were you betrayed in your marriage bed? Did he cheat on you with a servant girl or the well-born wife of one of your neighbours?'

It was not a question that she had ever expected me to ask, or that she would have to answer. She blinked before she chose to reply.

'Not to my knowledge.'

'Would you have forgiven him, if he had?'

'If I thought it valuable.' She shook her head. 'But perhaps not in my heart. All I will say is – don't put yourself in the wrong.'

'How would that be possible? I am not the one to break my vows.'

'I know. His behaviour is unforgivable. All I would advise is this. Play the great lady. Don't lose your temper.'

'I never lose my temper. I have kept it for all these weeks since I was told of his perfidy. I will not lose it now.'

'Don't shriek at him so that all the castle can hear.'

'Ha!'

The faces of my household who watched Lord Mortimer's return to Ludlow and his abandoned wife were remarkably expression-less, while I had had time to consider Lady Marguerite's remarks. I perfected a polite smile of welcome and regal posture, as well as a determination to control my fury. What could be gained by venting my anger on a man who would not care and was beyond my powers? It was done, and nothing I could say would undo it. Would he return to me, like some errant knight in the tales of King Arthur, kneeling at my feet in abject penitence? I did not think so, not in my wildest dreams. Nor did I think that I wished him to do so. Could I welcome him back and forget all that had gone before?

I would not.

Dismounted, Roger Mortimer bowed low with a flourish of his cap and gauntlets, the palm of his other hand on his heart, which I considered a travesty of what must pass between us. The brooch, which I could now see was a mass of costly rubies, continued to glitter. I curtsied as if to the King himself. As he surely was in power, if not in name.

'My lady.'

I raised my chin but I would not hold out my hand in greeting. My mother-in-law and my children had wisely made themselves scarce.

'My lord. We have waited long to see you here since your landing in England in September. Doubtless you have been much occupied.'

'Affairs of state that required my presence. I knew you would understand.'

And affairs of Isabella. I had too much self-regard to reply in this public space, but the desire to do so bubbled within me as I turned and walked before him into the Great Hall, to the dais where platters of bread and braised meats, of cheese and the remains of the apple harvest had been prepared and ale was waiting in a jewelled ewer with two matching cups. I dismissed the servants and poured the autumn brewing myself. I knew it was the best quality I could find as I presented the cup of ale to him with my palm below the foot, careful that his fingers should not brush against mine in its taking.

'I expected you to be at Wigmore,' he observed. If he was put out at my refusal to follow orders there was no evidence of it as he raised the cup to me in a silent toast. Which I ignored, leaving my own ale-cup on the board, untasted.

He wore a sapphire ring set in a gold mount, another gem that I did not recognise.

'Then I regret any inconvenience that I am here instead.' I curved my lips into a smile of apparent regret. 'Why would I go to Wigmore?'

Not a whisper of a hesitation. 'Because it is your home.'

'It was once my home, and one where I was content.' I would never again use the word happy. 'I do not envisage ever being content there again. Besides, Ludlow is a de Geneville castle. It is mine. I am comfortable here. You were in Pembridge some weeks ago, to my knowledge. Many might think that you would take the opportunity to visit me then, a mere two days' ride away, if you considered it to be an urgent matter for you to speak with your wife. Doubtless you had other affairs of far greater importance on your mind.'

The muscles in his jaw tightened as if he must withstand an onslaught which he did not want, even though he must have expected it. I would not give way. I was astonished at my level of control.

'I returned to Hereford,' he said brusquely. 'There was the Despenser affair to deal with.'

'So I understand.' I turned away, an essay in grace, to sit in my favourite cushioned window seat, my hands loose in my lap. 'Your mother is here.'

'I did not know.'

'We find good company together. She too suffered in your

absence. It was only the presence of good friends that allowed her to escape King Edward's searching for her.'

'I will speak with her before I leave.'

All as if we were strangers with nothing known, one of the other, and nothing of any import to say. I waited.

'I know that the imprisonment was difficult for you, Johane.'

'Difficult?' He had used my name but I would not use his. 'Yes. Five years of lack of freedom. Difficult is not the word I would have chosen.'

'You look to be in good health.'

He had not touched me, but then I had not touched him. The closest we had been was when I handed him the cup of ale which he had placed down on a coffer by the wall, after I refused the toast. His expression was suddenly harsh, as if he would rather not be here. I should perhaps have admired him for stepping into the lion's den.

'I have had time to remedy some of the remnants of my years in Skipton. Your exile and adventures in Europe seem to have been most fruitful,' I observed.

'Yes, I returned with an army and royal support to take back the Mortimer possessions.'

'For which I must be grateful. But at what cost? It was clearly a cost worth the paying in your eyes.'

'I see what is in your mind.'

'I imagine that you do. Are you surprised? Every wagging tongue in the country knows that your return and your victory rests on the Queen's favour.' And I almost lost my temper, as I had promised not to do. 'Are you her lover? They say that you are. Do they lie? Is there truth in the rumours that reach me every day, whispered behind hands?' I recalled Maud's announcement. 'Have you indeed committed a monstrous adultery?' There, it had been said between us.

His reply was immediate, without regret. 'Yes. I am guilty of all of that, if it is guilt that you wish to apportion.'

I inhaled slowly.

'Is that it? Is that all you have to say? Do you tell me that you took her to your bed for some altruistic motive, to save the Mortimer estates from confiscation and your name from the taint of treason? Was it worth having the aura of treason replaced with that of a cruel infidelity?'

The anger rippled over my skin, but so, for the first time, it did in him, with a savage twist of his lips as he replied.

'What do you wish me to say? I have no excuses. Isabella and I lived together at the French Court and planned together to bring about our return. She is a remarkable woman. Put yourself in this position, Johane, rather than condemning me. Would you take a handsome man to your bed if he was a man who could safeguard all you held dear?'

'A cheap jibe! Is that all the excuse that you can make? Do not put your guilt on my shoulders. I would honour the vows I made. I would not take a paramour to my bed at the first opportunity.'

'Sometimes politics demand that vows be broken.'

'Which you did very willingly. Do you love her? Is it love? Or is it merely lust for the body of a woman who should be forbidden to you, by vows and by status?'

The light in his eyes flared with brilliant anger.

'Does it matter how and why? I love her.'

He had said it. I stood, for I could no longer merely sit, and I looked at him, this man whom I had loved, admired, enjoyed. The five years had barely touched him. Spare, fit with action, smooth with power, hair still dark, longer than I recalled, falling in waves over his brow. Would Isabella touch his hair in love? Would she know the strength of those arms around her? Except for a hardness in his eyes, a sardonic set to his mouth, he was still all I had loved and admired. Would Isabella see the same male attraction that I had seen?

Of course she would.

What would he see in me after five years of an existence that had robbed me of comfort and sustenance? It was irrelevant. I would not contemplate it. I lost control of my fury at last, aware of the brilliant quality of my voice even though I did not raise it.

'How dare you. How dare you come here as if there was no barrier to our reuniting. I spent five years incarcerated, either under an unpleasant surveillance or deep in Skipton Castle, all for you. I spent five years in increasing deprivation, lack of food, lack of sleep, lack of comforts. Did you even realise how bad it was for me and your younger daughters? While you cavorted in Europe and found yourself a royal lover, the most stringent of regimes was inflicted on us. Did you even think of your daughters enclosed in convents, or your sons imprisoned in Windsor? I hope you are proud of it. You cannot expect me to welcome you with open arms. You have rejected me, and you have done it so publicly that I am become an object of pity.'

'I did not choose it, Johane.'

'You did nothing to avoid the lust. Are you telling me that it was all her fault? That she lured you against your better judgement? I doubt it very much.'

For a moment he simply stood and surveyed me as if in indecision.

'No. I am as guilty as she.'

'So much for honesty! And that will make me feel better, that you share the guilt.'

'No. You wanted the truth.'

'The truth cannot hurt me more than your wounding.' I turned and walked away from him to put some distance between us. When I reached the wall with my tapestry of lovers in the garden, I stopped. Turned. 'Why are you here?'

For the first time he looked uncomfortable. He picked up the cup and drank the contents in one gulp.

'Is it that you wish for an annulment?' I demanded.

That caught his attention.

'No. How can that be? The fruits of our loins are numerous. There was no impediment to our marriage.'

'The Pope might see reason, if you grease his palm with sufficient gold.'

'I will not drag us both through such mire. We have been man and wife for more years than I can count, since we stood together at the door of that draughty little church of yours at Pembridge.'

'Which you have entirely rebuilt.'

'Which is of no consequence to this matter.'

I still resented it. All that he touched must be improved, reconstructed. Including his marriage.

'You are my wife and the mother of my children,' he stated.

I would not be won over.

'I should be thankful that you recognise so obvious a fact. What do you intend to do? Lock me up so that I will not be a burden on you? Strip me of my powers as Baroness de Geneville? Prevent me from travelling or associating with those who were once our friends? Do you ban me from Court? Perhaps a convent would be the answer, where I will be faceless and voiceless. Perhaps I should join my sisters in Aconbury. You rejected my love. You betrayed me. You paid for my imprisonment in false coin. I spent all those dreary years incarcerated for you, and you turned away. I made a hero of you for your daughters. You have become a traitor for me.'

'Johane.' This time he replaced the cup with a snap of temper as great as mine. 'This is all foolishness.'

'Foolishness? By the Blessed Virgin, that is not the word I would use! You have hurt me beyond bearing.'

'Then hear me. You will remain my wife, until death separates us, in the eyes of the world.'

'So we comport ourselves as if there was no betrayal between us.'

'I think it will be for the best.'

'But any intimacy will be in the lap of that adulterous Queen, who, since she still has a husband, has as few morals as you.'

A dread silence descended. The vast hall echoed with it. It was I who broke it.

'Why did you do it? Did I deserve such ignominy for my name to be on everyone's lips at Court and throughout the country? If you had wanted her, could you not have used some discretion? Instead, you have emblazoned your affair in every corner of the realm, and as far as I know in France, too. It may be easier for you, but before God, it is an humiliation to me.'

'If you will listen, I will tell you ...'

'Do you wish me to call your mother?' I interrupted. 'I am sure that she too will wish to know how you will vindicate your decisions.'

Oh, I was coated in bitterness. And Roger? He now reacted in brutal honesty, stepping up on the dais, his hands clamped on his sword-belt, the very image of a Marcher lord who now held the power of kingship in his own hand. There were no regrets, no apologies. He had taken the authority and it was his to enjoy. I watched. I listened with fascination. Yes, he had always been ambitious but here was the will, the confidence, the achievement. His brow might have been wearing a crown as he launched his attack, for that is what it was.

'Before you castigate me for my selfishness, listen to me.' It was spoken in a white blaze of anger. 'Here it is, Johane, for you to accept or reject. You want to know what I did and why I did it. I was robbed of my freedom, my title, my lands. My status as a Marcher lord. I was threatened with death, a hole-in-the-corner murder in the Tower. I had to flee for my life into exile, with no hope of return, my proud name blackened. Yes, I admit to pride. It is what you have always known of me. And you were condemned to imprisonment. For my sake. Oh, I acknowledge that. It is a stain of culpability on my soul. As is the death of my uncle of Chirk, for I doubt it was a mere passage of time into old age that ordered his exit from this world. It was murder, I would swear it. And I will have revenge for what was inflicted on me and mine.

'What would you have me do? Accept? Sit quietly in France and accept? Before God, I could not. It was not in my character. I needed to return and take back all that was mine, to put all the wrongs to right. To punish those who had taken my Mortimer inheritance from me.

'Was there no other road I could take to return and restore what was rightfully mine, and yours? There was one route. At the side of a Queen who also found herself in exile from a man who did not love her, did not appreciate what she could bring to his rule. Who squandered his affections and power on those who would not serve him well, only themselves. Together the Queen and I could achieve what could not be achieved alone. Yes, I have shared her bed. Yes, we are beyond division now. I am sorry that you have suffered for it, but it could not be any other way.'

When he at last drew a breath I interposed:

'So it was a means to an end, to take her to your bed, to slake her sexual needs and yours, since you were both estranged from your legitimate spouses. It was just a piece of clever plotting to achieve the right to whisper a conspiracy to undermine the King and Despenser in Isabella's royal ear.'

'Yes, it was a means to an end, but it would be ungracious of me to say that it was a mere conspiracy. That I had no love or affection for her. I did not choose it, but neither do I regret what we have done. Nor, now that we have returned, will I repudiate her. My star has risen with that of the Queen and will continue to do so. My future will stride side by side with hers. I have ambitions. I will see them fulfilled. You will not lose by them, Johane, and nor will our children. The Mortimers will be acknowledged with all the distinction due to them, and you will live in comfort and with rightful recognition.'

'As long as I block my ears to the gossip.'

'I think you can do that. What do you care about gossip?'

'Unlike you, *I* have no choice.'

'I did not deliberately choose this.'

'But choice it was. Do not tell me that it was the Queen who opened the door to her bedchamber and enticed you into this affair. Does she please you, or did she buy your attentions?' I caught the glitter on his breast as he breathed. 'Is that brooch a gift from her? I did not give it to you, and all your treasures from Wigmore Abbey were confiscated by the King. Mine too. That sapphire on your hand is doubtless another gift. Was your body bought with royal jewels? What have you given her, now that your wealth is restored to you?'

'Nothing but my loyalty and my support in winning this kingdom back from a man who does not deserve it.'

'Nevertheless, a man who is anointed and blessed by God as King,' I snapped back. 'I trust that you have not brought me a gift to mark your return. I would fling it at your head!'

'I cannot repudiate her.'

'But you will repudiate me.' My thoughts suddenly swung back to Roger's escape from the Tower, when I had lauded him in chivalric stories for our daughters. 'Did the Queen help you to escape from the Tower? Were you already, even then before you came to me at Wickham Manor, exchanging fervent embraces with her?'

'Before God, Johane! No, we were not.' Perhaps in an effort to soften his reply he marched over with a swing of his cloak to stare into the ashy embers in the great fireplace; then he looked back over his shoulder, his anger no longer hot but as icy-cold as my welcome to him. 'Perhaps you should not be so vindictive in your judgements. Did you not know that the Queen wrote personally to the Treasurer, to ensure that you received the funds due to you for your sustenance when a prisoner?'

Without pause I retaliated. 'It had little effect. We were all but starved.'

'She was concerned with your comfort.'

I would not accept it. 'A guilty conscience, some would say. Lust after the husband and ensure that the wife has enough to eat!'

'Such accusations do not become you, Johane.'

'They become me very well, in the circumstances.'

He returned to join me on the dais where he bowed in acceptance of my disdain. There was nothing more to say between us, for now at least, but I would probably think of more accusations to assuage the hurt within me.

'Do you stay the night? It will give you time to make a re-acquaintance with your daughters. Young Roger is here too. At least they will be relieved to see you alive and well. What they will make of your morals I cannot say. Your mother also awaits you.'

'Yes. I will stay. I have business here.'

'More executions to plan?'

'Despenser could not be allowed to live. You know that.'

'I suppose it was inevitable. Beware that your enemies do not start plotting yours.' I walked towards the stair that led up to the private rooms. 'There are sufficient chambers here for your comfort. I will arrange for some to be put at your disposal.' If he intended to woo my wounded pride, he would not be acceptable in mine. 'You will not be welcome to visit in mine.'

The food lay untouched, the meats congealing in their sauces. No one had been interested in the dishes. Who in my kitchens had ever thought that we would sit down amicably and eat together? With my foot on the bottom step, his voice halted me so that I turned back although there was no more that could be said.

'Johane. Wait. I vowed that if I survived Despenser's determination to kill me, I would build and dedicate a chapel here. I wish to put it in train. I trust that it will not incommode you.'

'I am astonished that you should consider my wishes in the circumstances. You will of course do as you please. After all, the castle, through your marriage to me, in law belongs to you.'

There was no softening in me. I turned when I realised that his footsteps had stopped, noticing that his gaze was on my tapestry. Had I intended him to see it? Of course I had. Why else would I hang it in my Great Hall? I had wanted him to see the work of my own hands and design, the lovers walking hand in hand in perfect amity, in the garden surrounded by flowers and birds. I wanted him to see what we had lost.

'An impressive piece. Not one that I have seen before.'

'A product of my imprisonment.'

Moving closer, he inspected it with care. 'Why did you stitch a popinjay?'

'It is a long story.'

'It is a fine conceit.'

'When I began the stitching of it, it was not a conceit. When I stitched it I had a gleaming future with you to look forward to. I completed it in a deluge of ire.'

His expression was cold, forbidding, resenting that I had made him respond to the situation he had created through my direct challenge.

'You still have a gleaming future. As Lady Mortimer you can demand all respect and honour. Forgive me that I can give you no more.'

'Is that all you have to say?'

'I wish it could be different, but times move on and fate draws us into directions that we would never have dreamed of.'

In that moment I loathed him, and what he had knowingly done to me. I could no longer tolerate his presence and was thankful when he walked away from me, his steps fading as he left the hall. What he would say to his mother I did not know. I regarded the debris on the table. What a waste. The household would eat well in the aftermath of our reunion. Finally I stood before my tapestry, taking in the intricate stitches, the features that I had tried so hard to replicate from the originals. The love ingrained in every inch of it as I looked forward to his return and our reconciliation.

I turned away and did not look back.

'I did not shriek,' I informed Lady Marguerite later in the day when we knelt side by side in the chapel.

'I think that I would have done, in your shoes.'

What I had done was order the tapestry taken down from the wall and carried to the kitchens. I accompanied it, while my rage blistered me from within.

'Burn it,' I said.

'My lady?' The shock on my steward's face was a pleasure to my eye.

'Burn it. There is nothing there that I wish to see.'

I did not watch it burn. I did not watch Lord Mortimer leave, although I noted that Young Roger rode with him. It was what I would expect. He had not touched me once in the length of the visit. But then I had not given him the opportunity.

Don't you wish you had?

I swatted away the treasonous little voice as I regarded the silver brooch, heart-shaped with words hammered around the edge. *I am a love token. Do not give me away.* I held it in the palm of my hand, considering. A sad memento from the past. There would be no forgiveness between us this time.

'What are you going to do with that?' Lady Marguerite asked.

'I am tempted to drop it in the well.'

But I did not.

Chapter Twenty-Six

Westminster Abbey on the first day of February 1327

I stood in Westminster Abbey, swathed in wool and heavy fur, my feet icy within my soft leather shoes, all to celebrate this most important occasion. When had my feet ever been anything but frozen in this place, even in happier times?

This was different. Now my heart was frozen too.

The boy at the centre of everyone's interest was dwarfed by the panoply and magnificence, yet all eyes were fixed on him. Prince Edward, to be crowned King Edward the Third, on this auspicious day. I had determined, as a de Geneville and wife of a Marcher lord, albeit abandoned, to be here to stand witness to this astonishing event where a son replaced his still-living father.

It had been, until the eleventh hour, uncertain that this coronation would ever happen. His father the late King might be kept in captivity in perpetuity. Parliament might have concurred that he be deposed and the crown passed to his son. A new crowning, it was decided, must take place as soon as may be. Thus all was in hand – Lord Mortimer's hand and that of Queen Isabella – except that this young boy, no more than fourteen years old, refused the throne. Nor was a handful of the bishops in agreement with this rapid change in ruler. The Prince would not sanction his father's deposition by his mother and Lord Mortimer to take the crown for himself.

All Roger's plans thus cast into the abyss by a boy who had barely stepped into the shoes of his maturity. Only if his father would personally abdicate would his son agree to take the throne. It had seemed that my journey to London was one that I need never have made, my cramped accommodations in Westminster need never have been taken. I would have been more content at Ludlow without the difficult relationships to manoeuvre around at this centre of the royal Court.

Yet here we were, Lady Marguerite and I. The Prince's face was pale, his lips tight pressed as he was led to the dais, all covered in quilted gold cloth, before the high altar. I stood close enough that I could witness his acceptance of this highest of positions, ordained by God. The golden throne, the gold cushions beneath his feet, the gold canopy above his head, the purple cords. There was no expression on his face that had yet to grow a beard, neither of pleasure nor dismay.

How had he changed his mind?

Roger had been restless, even fidgety, with the imminent failure of his plans when his mother and I had arrived, yet he had found the time to greet me – briefly, with chilly formality – and show us to our chamber. I would not embrace him, even for form's sake, nor did he demand it of me. All was impersonal although in public display he raised my gloved hand to his lips in due courtesy. There was no meeting of actual flesh involved.

'What are you going to do?' I asked, since the Prince's obstinacy was common knowledge. Perhaps I should not even remove my travelling cloak and hood. What value would it be to linger here in this crowded palace if there was no result but the reinstatement of King Edward the Second? I could see temper building in Roger like the approach of a February storm over the Black Mountains. It surprised me that he was prepared to be honest, but then I would be no spy against him. He slapped his gloves into the palm of his hand and frowned.

'At this moment I know not. He must abdicate. In favour of his son.'

'And how will you persuade him to do that?'

The result was a feral grin. 'I'll threaten to take the throne for myself. I have no qualms about threatening to take the crown from him.'

'Which will surely persuade him,' Lady Marguerite replied as I inspected the room for any trace of vermin.

'So I think.'

'Who would have thought my son to be so self-seeking as to aspire to a crown? I had not believed myself to have raised you to such high thoughts.'

Which ended our conversation.

'He is a man of some temper. Nothing has changed,' observed lady Marguerite.

'He is of your breeding, remember,' I grumbled as I sat on the bed, still wrapped in my cloak. I considered wrapping the coverlet, apparently flea-less, around me.

'At least my son remains courteous to his wife.'

'Should I be grateful? And he a man who spent last Christmas in Wallingford Castle with a married woman who is not his wife. Do you suppose that it was a mere meeting of friends? Or minds? I think not.' I showed my teeth in a smile. 'As for remaining courteous, with the eyes of the Court on him. Of course he will. He will do what is best for himself.'

'I cannot argue with you. Would you care to share that quilt? It is as cold as unrequited love in here.'

And so it came to pass much as Roger had predicted while we sat and gossiped and idled our time at Westminster. On the twenty-first day of January in the hall at Kenilworth castle, dressed in black and weeping for his great loss, although whether that was the Queen, Hugh Despenser or the Crown, no one would speculate, the second King Edward abdicated his throne in favour of his young son. The delegation returned to Westminster by the end of the week with the good tidings. The young Prince Edward accepted the news. He would take the crown. We allowed a sigh of relief. A new reign could begin.

'What did I tell you?' Roger asked in passing between one task and the next in getting the young King safely to the Abbey.

'You are as cunning as a bag of cats,' I said.

The coronation was thus held on the first day of February.

'Tell me that you have had this date long fixed, even before Edward abdicated,' I said as we made our way to the vast space of the Abbey, for I had become cynical in past months.

'Of course. You know me better than anyone here. I could not allow it not to happen.'

It worried me, even when I despised him for what he had done. Would the young King, yet to be crowned, see himself as being manipulated, the strings being pulled by a master puppeteer? Therein might lie danger for that puppeteer as the puppet grew in confidence and the desire to dismantle those strings. Why should it worry me? I had no answer to that question.

'Beware,' I warned him. 'You flaunt your power outrageously.'

But already his time and presence were demanded elsewhere.

'I will flaunt it even more before I have finished. Enjoy the benefits of my restoration to power that our sons can now enjoy, Johane.'

My sons, whom I met at the great door before the ceremony, uncomfortably impressed at what they were wearing. Not for them the garments of a knight; my calculating husband had decided that they should wear the costly raiment suitable for an earl. Thus they were magnificent in the scarlet, green and brown fine-spun wool with the notable addition of miniver and squirrel furs, and even a touch of gold tissue on the shoulders of the knee-length over-tunic and mantle. My three eldest sons, Edmund, Roger and also Geoffrey, newly returned from France, looked every inch young men of power.

'Before God, you will take every eye,' I said, astonished at what Roger had done.

I embraced them, their grandeur rich under my hands.

'I think that is what Father wants.'

Assuredly he did. This too would win few friends. Were my sons at ease with their clothing, more resplendent than any man there but the King? I could see no unwillingness in their pride, to make a show of authority with their father.

Thus I was now standing in the Abbey to enjoy the occasion, escorted in by Roger who had not abandoned me as he had abandoned our marriage. He had an eye to civility and to appearances, for there was some ceremonial due to me as Lady Mortimer and to his mother Lady Marguerite. Elizabeth, young Edmund's wife, stood with us to observe the knighting of her husband and his brothers. Her excitement was palpable; I envied her the naivety that she could not see beyond the ceremonial magnificence.

Lord Mortimer's own appearance was as worthy of note as that of our sons, but by now I was anticipating the worst. Almost worthy of that worn by Gaveston, it was not exactly cloth of purple, but he had not dressed with casual unconcern. I wondered if he had been advised by the Queen.

'You are dressed fit for a king.'

'No, but an earl perhaps.'

'Or a royal favourite?'

Briefly his face set in a scowl. 'I am dressed due to the rank that I will one day have.'

'Being a royal lover has it benefits,' I observed, deliberately to shake his lordly and objectionable sangfroid.

He chose not to reply.

The events that followed swept over me. I had no part to play, no role demanded of me, no influence to exert on this most important of ceremonies and the celebrations that followed. Any connection with Roger was fleeting and of no value to either of us, as I presume he intended. He was at the centre of affairs and I was not. All I could do was watch and anticipate. Some moments were full of enjoyment, of sheer pride; some roused in me a mortal fear. They left me with tiny images, as might have been painted in ink in one of my books sadly lost to me. Bright and detailed, to rouse emotions, I would recall them when I was returned to Ludlow, some to enjoy, some to tremble over.

Primarily there was the grandeur of it all. I had thought that exile had not changed Roger over-much. Older of course, a touch harder, driven to restore his Mortimer lands and possessions. I had not realised the half of it. Now during this ceremony I saw the reality, that his ambitions outstripped those of every man present. As did his clothing; like my sons, dressed as an earl but with an eye-catching superfluity of fur and gold tissue. All too much. Too much. Who was King here? To what purpose in my saying anything? I had warned him, but he would go his own way. Gaveston had dressed in rich purple at the second Edward's crowning, and look what had happened to him.

No one could doubt Roger's ability to wield power. Had it always been there? Perhaps it had, but now Isabella made it possible. He might not wear a crown but it patently hovered over his brow. His confidence, his superb economy of movement, his control of every step in that ceremony, proclaimed his position to every man present. There would be many moved by jealousy and hatred. All eyes might have been on the young King, but the atmosphere was created by the master creator, Lord Mortimer.

I barely recognised him as the man I had lived with and loved. He had polished this giving of power and his participation in it to perfection. I could not but be impressed, even when I was determined to watch it through critical eyes.

And my sons, my dear sons. If they had suffered for their father's treachery, they hid it well. I would never forgive the now-deposed King Edward, but I thanked the Blessed Virgin that she, as the Holy Mother, had cared for them in their captivity. They knelt to receive their knighthoods with all the grace and confidence I could have wished for them. Roger had given them their future with an open hand.

Briefly, as the crown was held over the boy's head, because it was too heavy for his young shoulders, I wondered what Roger had received in payment for his allegiance to this young man. Were the Mortimers in control of even more castles, of manors in areas where we had never held sway? Lord Mortimer would not have brought the young King to the crown without due reward.

I stood with the rest of the congregation to acclaim our new ruler. I prayed that he would enjoy a more worthy and successful reign than his father had. As soon as he took power for himself of course. A worrying thought.

In the celebrating after the crowning, we feasted and then we danced. Would my husband dance with me, to draw attention to me as the estranged wife, or would it be worse if he ignored me and invited Isabella to join him in the processional formal dance?

Lady Marguerite read well enough what was in my mind.

'He was raised to behave well in public. He will not humiliate you, Johane.' Roger was walking in my direction. 'Of course he will not ignore your presence here.' She nudged my arm. We looked across to where the Queen had taken her son by the hand to lead him to the head of the procession, and Lady Marguerite pursed her lips. 'She has left my son with little choice.'

'And I will do exactly as I ought to do.'

I fixed a smile on my face and prepared to do my Mortimer duty, however vicious my resentment.

Thus it was that I danced with Roger because for this formal occasion it must seem right to him that we were in unity, if not just for the sake of our sons. There was no room for embarrassment. There was little intimacy in a line dance. His hand touched mine, brushed against it, the first time, flesh to flesh, since he had fled England. I kept the smile on my lips as I stepped and curtsied, all grace and dignity and false enjoyment. Did I enjoy it, when dancing had always been a great pleasure for me? The tension was too strong in that vast chamber at Westminster. Too many eyes upon me. It was like a mouse living under the eyes of the raptors in a mews when they had not been fed.

I had misjudged it of course. The eyes were on Roger.

What of his relationship with the Queen during the whole of this feast? One of circumspection. One of discretion. It was astonishing, and perhaps disappointing for those looking for the juicy meat of gossip; they would not discover it on this occasion. Roger and the Queen were formal, distant, polite; no exchanged glances as far as I noticed, and I looked. He did not sit beside her at the feast. He never once danced with Isabella. I knew the truth of what they were to each other, because he had told me, but for those who still knew only the rumours, it might remain in doubt. How clever he was. How politically aware she was.

The events unfolded as smooth and seemly as the silk of the Queen's over-tunic.

There was only one occasion, one small conversation, probably innocuous, which was not intended for my hearing as we parted from the dance, but which disturbed the tenor of the celebration and painted the possible future in virulent colours. A young knight – newly knighted with my sons – approached Roger to engage him in an exchange of words. I recognised the livery as one of the foremost families in the realm. Sir William Montagu, short and stocky, still growing into his strength, but with the potent shoulders of a jouster; a friend of the young King. His face was an angry one; Roger was calm, as if in discussion of the sale of a horse. How could I not listen?

'I will tell you this, Lord Mortimer. I see what is in your mind, but I tell you this. You will never usurp royal power.'

Roger smiled indulgently at the young man.

'You are not in a position to prevent me, Sir William, if that is my intention.'

'But one day I might be. And so might the Prince who is now crowned and anointed King. Beware what you do, sir. There are those here who will call you to account if royal power is stolen from the one who should wield it. The crown does not belong to you despite the gold tissue that flatters you so well.'

The blandness vanished in an instant and Roger's voice acquired a harsh edge. 'Are you foolish beyond words to threaten me, sir? I have removed a King. Can I not remove a Montagu?'

The young man flushed brightly across his round cheekbones and pugnacious jaw but he did not retreat.

'You can, of course. But I think not even you would be so foolhardy as to disturb the auspicious start to this reign. You returned by the sword. There are many here who would use their weapons against you in loyalty to our new King Edward.'

Sir William strode away. Here indeed were enemies for Roger Mortimer with their eyes fixed on any abuse of power. Roger turned to face me, his voice cold but calm enough.

'You heard. It is an empty threat from a young man who has drunk too much wine.'

'Are you not afraid, that someone will wield the assassin's knife?' I asked. 'Someone might be tempted, in the new King's name, even though I expect that you will deny it. I will say my farewell now. Tomorrow I return to Ludlow.'

'I will prepare an escort.'

'I can arrange my own. You will have enough to do in this new role you have carved out for yourself.' I was exhausted.

'Thank you for caring enough to warn me. It was not needed.'

'I need no thanks. You are the father of my children. That is the only reason I have any care for your life. You have destroyed the rest.'

I remembered my desperate call when he had said his farewells to go into exile.

Who will care for me if you are dead?

What an empty plea that had been. It almost brought me to tears, but I curtsied low and walked away as if unmoved by the whole affair. And at the centre of every image, every toast, every delight, there was the young boy, isolated, looking to a future that he could not envisage. Clothed in red as was tradition, a light gold filet circling his brow, he smiled at Roger. He conversed with him. Was it skin deep, his willingness to allow Roger to call the tune? It was general knowledge that Roger was appointing his own friends and allies to the great offices of state. The young King was old enough to see what was happening, to know that he had no power to dictate his own desires, all of it resting in the hands of his mother and her lover. The crown might have been held over his head by the mighty clerics, but then it had passed into the hands of Lord Mortimer. The young boy was King in name only.

I caught a flash of some emotion, one that I could not name, on the boy's face. Disapproval? Anger? Or was it merely a trick of the light? Probably it was, but still I wondered how long it would be before the new King resisted the hold that had been placed on him and his power. When it came, as I believed in that moment that it would, Lord Mortimer would be in mortal danger.

Was it required that I meet with the Queen? No, to my relief Isabella was far too occupied with the triumph of this occasion to be concerned with the slighted wife of her lover. She had achieved a spectacular victory, leading an invasion and removing her husband into captivity, and not least overseeing the death of her hated rival Despenser. Now her son was King. What would be her interest in me? Would she notice if I spoke with her or not? That is not to say that I did not watch her performance, for that is what it assuredly was, clad as she was in her favourite cloth of gold and scarlet silk tissue woven with gold fleurs-de-lys, her hair caught up in a jewelled net. Did she weep at the ceremony, from pride or some other over-calculated emotion? I was not aware of it. If she did, I would say that they were false tears.

All I could see was that in the years since I had last seen her she had grown into full maturity, into her full beauty. She would be thirty years of age now; her hair encased in its jewelled net would be as gilded as the cloth of gold that covered the throne and the stool on which her son placed his foot. It was an instructive moment. How would Roger look at me when the Queen demanded his notice, his adoration? She had the youth and the authority that I lacked. The power to achieve for him all he hoped for in life.

I should thank her for pleading for my release, despite her failure. I should thank her for restoring my husband to his rightful inheritance. But not today. Not today. Too many conflicting emotions existed to allow me to seek out the Queen and kneel before her in gratitude. I was swamped with a strange multitude of impressions, of pride and grief. Lord Mortimer could make my thanks for me.

I doubted that I would be a subject of conversation between them.

Chapter Twenty-Seven

Between Westminster and Ludlow Castle, February 1327

Next day Lady Marguerite and I were prepared to depart on a crisp winter morning, where all was cast in strong relief by frost and a chilly sun hanging low on the horizon. The horses' breath clouded the air as they waited for us. We had said our farewells to Elizabeth, who was once more in the care of my son Edmund, and also to her aunt Maud, Baroness de Welles, whom I had been delighted to see at Court although my memories of our past meeting were not all happy ones. We embraced, our friendship spiked with the treachery of those around us.

'I need not tell you how pleased I am to see you here,' Maud said, low-voiced. 'I imagine it has not been the easiest of times for you. I often think how clumsily I told you about all of this. It was unforgivable.'

'But necessary. I was bitterly hurt, but at least I was warned, and by a friend.' I turned the conversation away from that terrible moment of revelation, that had destroyed all I had believed in. 'Do you still visit Skipton?'

Her face lit up and her sorrow was gone. 'Yes. And now I have free run of the place without the Commander spying on my every move. He is no longer in residence. My son Robert

Clifford has been restored this very year. And since my sister is now free, I have hope for the future. You must come and visit.'

'A kind invitation, but I will not. Not to Skipton at least. I have no fond reminiscences.'

'Make better ones for yourself at Ludlow. I doubt you will see much of your husband. You will be free to establish your household to your own liking.'

I had not thought of that in quite those terms. At least it was something I could plan for. To my relief, Roger was not in evidence; I need not consider suitable words of farewell, for I could think of none. As we rode from Westminster, there was a hunting party of young men approaching from the river where they had been flying their noble raptors at the heron in the rushes. They were full of laughter and the success of the hunt, falcons still on their wrists. My three newly knighted sons in their midst. And there was Prince Edward. No longer Prince but King Edward. I ordered the litter to halt as the King urged his horse towards us. It was easy to see that, away from the intense emotion of the ceremony, he was full of youthful vigour, his eyes as brilliant as those of his hounds.

'My lord.' I inclined my head.

'Do you go home, Lady Mortimer?'

'I do.'

'Your sons will stay at Court, of course. They keep me good company.' He gestured with a hand to where the young Mortimers rode together, still revelling in their new freedom and their courtly status.

'Yes. It pleases me,' I said, smiling across at them.

'I expect Lord Mortimer will remain at Court also. With the Queen,' Edward added.

'I expect that he will.'

What an uncomfortable conversation this had become after

the initial greeting. There was nothing I could say. For once Lady Marguerite was also struck dumb as the King turned his head to look again at my sons, the sudden gleam of sunlight gilding his hair where it curled from beneath his brimmed hat of sable fur.

'I trust they will serve me well,' he said, as if there might be any doubt.

I took a breath and replied as I read the situation. 'My sons have been raised to value loyalty to the Crown above all else.'

'It is a relief to know that some who carry the name Mortimer can earn my trust.'

It was a forthright comment and put me on my guard. Was it not exactly as I had feared? The new King did not give his full trust to Lord Mortimer, or his family.

'I was a de Geneville before I was a Mortimer,' I remarked.

'But marriage carries its own demands of loyalty and duty, does it not, Lady Mortimer.'

I felt colour tinge my cheeks at this sharp comment. How could I reply to that? But then I did not have to do so. The King took the matter in hand with a lightness that impressed me for so young a boy.

'I accept the friendship of a de Geneville, my lady. Will you return to Court to attend my wedding? To the most illustrious Lady Philippa of Hainault? And you too, Lady Marguerite, will be most welcome.'

'It will be my honour, my lord.'

'You too have daughters to be wed.'

'They are of an age now,' I agreed.

'I hope to have the opportunity to visit you in Ludlow. Perhaps we may celebrate together.'

'It will be my honour, my lord,' I repeated, 'to welcome you there.'

I seemed to have become much like our late, lamented

popinjay in my repetition. What an astonishing maturity this young man possessed at fourteen years, no doubt honed under the hardship of the imprisonment of his father. King Edward continued:

'I will accompany Lord Mortimer to Ludlow.' I saw as he drew in a breath. 'You have, I presume, a sound relationship still, with your husband.'

'Yes, my lord. It is necessary.'

'Loyalties are difficult beasts.' His eyes rested on mine in forthright fashion. 'They can be strained in so many ways. It does not make life easy, when trust is a heavy burden to bear on my shoulders.'

Without waiting for a reply, for which once again I could find none, the King rode on, his smile replaced by an uncomfortably bleak expression, leaving my sons to bid their farewells. But that conversation remained with me. Whom could Edward trust? He would say little to me other than platitudes. He would never express any true confidences to the wife of the man who held such power over him. I decided that in spite of his invitation to attend his marriage, the King's meeting with me had effectively demolished his pleasure in his morning's hunting. I had spoilt his insouciant mood.

'He does not trust me,' I observed to Lady Marguerite as we continued our journey. 'I regret it.'

'You could not blame him.'

'No. The sins of the husband visited on the wife.'

My spirits were low, wallowing in a pit of loneliness, as I travelled home. I could see no bright moments in the future. And then I recalled the knighting of my sons and I was not so despairing. They would carry the Mortimer name well; I prayed that they would not commit the sins of their father.

Chapter Twenty-Eight

Ludlow Castle in the Welsh Marches, autumn 1327

The old King, yet not so very old in years, the once-crowned King Edward the Second, was dead at Berkeley Castle. It was unexpected. He was forty-three years old.

The news from any number of travellers took Lady Marguerite and me into close conversation in my solar, since any affairs at Court would appear to have Roger's imprint on them. At the beginning of April the old King had been removed from Kenilworth by Roger and taken to the royal castle south of us, at Berkeley in Gloucestershire. There he lived, so we were given to understand, with five pounds a day to spend on his food and comforts. I knew the value of that to a prisoner.

'He cannot complain too much, apart from his lack of freedom,' I had said with more than a hint of bitterness.

'But he was a King. While you,' for Lady Marguerite recognised the source of my harshness, 'were merely Lady Mortimer and wife of a traitor.'

'An innocent wife though.'

I regretted my lack of compassion, but who knew better than I how difficult it was to live with few resources. My threadbare gowns had hung on my hollowed shoulders after sparse rations in Skipton. The old King would reside in some luxury while his son ruled the country.

But now he was dead.

'I see that Roger did not inform us.' Lady Marguerite dropped the thought between us over a cup of ale and a platter of bread and cheese and dried fruit as we broke our fast on a day that heralded the onset of autumn. It was time to shake out our winter gowns from the coffers where they had been stored during the summer, layered with lavender and rosemary to keep the moth at bay. Never, after my time at Skipton, would I take for granted the state of my over-gowns and mantles.

'Roger would not see any need to inform us about anything,' I replied. 'Why would he have a need to do so? Affairs of state are no concern of ours.'

My husband's absence and silence, not to mention his adultery, still stoked my fury more often than was good for me, but the wounds had had little time to heal. It had been a bare twelve months since he had returned with Queen Isabella's hand warmly in his.

'He is quite young to die,' Lady Marguerite mused, pushing away her platter after picking up the cheese-crumbs on her finger.

'To die of natural causes.' I followed her line of thought. 'Are we told why he is dead?'

'No.'

'Is there any rumour of ill-intent?'

'None that I have heard.'

I considered his death. It might be a well-reasoned political gesture to remove a King for whom the country had no more need. Not that I would suspect the new young King of so outrageous an act. But a Mortimer-Isabella alliance might see an advantage in judicial murder. I shrugged away the thought. How would we ever know? Would Roger be so callous? He might well, if his authority was at stake.

'Where will they bury him?' Lady Marguerite nudged my hand as if she had asked for the second time, which she probably had.

'In Gloucester. In the great Priory Church of St Peter.'

'Do we attend?'

It was not so far to travel down the length of the Marches. First a coronation. Now a death. I felt compelled to go.

'Yes, I think that we should.'

She slid a glance across to me.

'Do you take the girls?'

I considered this at some length. My youngest daughters, all still unwed and living under my aegis. I had deliberately shielded them from events at Court after imprisonment in a convent or with me in Skipton; I could not shield them for ever. They had not accompanied me to Westminster for the coronation, but perhaps I should shield them no longer. There was much that they must learn about their family.

'Yes,' I said. 'They will travel with us.'

'Do you tell them?'

I knew to what she referred.

'They will know already. There is enough gossip around this place to drown a cat, and what they would not hear in gossip, Young Roger will have told them. I think there is no need for me to say anything more.'

'They might wish to hear it from your own lips. Or are you too much of a coward?'

'Certainly not.' I took a breath, hurt that she would think so, before I admitted: 'Probably, yes. I will speak with them so that not one of us will live under an illusion that all is well in this family.'

I called the girls to my solar, informed them of our journey and gave instructions for some necessary sewing to clothe us all in seemly mourning.

'Why do we go?' asked Agnes.

'To recognise the life and death of a man who was King.'

'But he is dead.'

'And we will honour him.' I had no fond memories of the golden youth who became the malicious King, yet still it seemed to me that there should be a Mortimer presence, and not just Lord Mortimer attending beside his lover the Dowager Queen. 'It will show the world that Lady Mortimer and her daughters are bound by loyalty. There is no treason in us. I expect that your brothers will be there too.'

'And Father?' Catherine asked.

'Yes. He will be there.' Now I must consider my words. Why should it be so very hard? 'I need to tell you about your father.' I looked at their young faces. In the year since our release they had matured, skin tightening over cheek and jaw. They were handsome girls, and I saw no trace of the strains of imprisonment. They were old enough to know and accept, and I would never again be accused of cowardice. 'Your father will be there with the young King Edward. And with Edward's mother, the Dowager Queen. You need to know...'

'We do know, Mother.' It was Catherine who spoke, her voice gentle as if I needed to be treated with care.

I looked at her, raised my brows.

'We know that the Dowager Queen is our father's lover. He is devoted to her. He shares her bed and they work together to rule England. Which is why he does not come to Ludlow or Wigmore. Unless he must. He has broken his marital vows to you but there is nothing we can do about it. It is probably as much his fault as that of the Queen, although she is most likely a harpy. I suppose that Father wanted a restoration of Mortimer power more than he wanted family life with us. With you. The Queen has given him that authority.'

'And I expect that he enjoys possessing her body, too. She is very beautiful, like a lady from the old romances, so our brother Roger said,' Joan added before Catherine's elbow was driven into her ribs to silence her.

There it was. A masterful summing up of the bare truth. Everything I knew and had been forced to accept. All I had tried not to tell them. It all but took my breath away.

'Yes,' I said, gathering together my habitual self-possession. 'The rumour and gossip you have heard is no more than the truth. All that your brother Roger told you is the truth. We may not like it but we must accept it.'

There was nothing more to say about it. I would not sully their understanding by talking about his continuing care and concern for them. It was all a matter of priorities.

'We are sorry,' said Beatrice. 'We thought that he loved you. And that he loved us, too.'

'So did I.' I leaned forward and pulled her into an embrace. 'We cannot choose or determine our fate. But there is no doubt that he still has a care for you, his children. You will never be allowed to suffer for his infidelity to me.'

Isabella looked at her sisters, then back to me.

'Do you still love him, Mother? Your eyes would light up when he walked into a room.'

Now there was an unexpectedly mature question, and an unexpected observation from long ago.

'Adultery has a habit of dealing a quick death-blow to love,' I said. 'I hope that not one of you ever has to learn that. But don't forget. He is your father. He will not forget that when we must make decisions about your futures. You will never suffer for our differences.'

I left them to consider this. I needed some silence and solitude. How my daughters could turn a knife in a wound, and so unknowingly.

Chapter Twenty-Nine

The Priory of St Peter in Gloucester, December 1327

It was full winter before King Edward the Second was laid to rest in St Peter's in Gloucester. The twentieth day of December. A difficult journey for us of ice and hard roads which perhaps I regretted, but it was not to be cavilled at. I ordered three litters to accommodate all of us with our women and an escort and Mortimer banners prominent, a very female procession.

'Why not Westminster?' Lady Marguerite asked. 'Not that I regret it. At least Gloucester is within easier reach of us.'

I had already considered this and could think of no definite answer, not that it mattered greatly to me.

'Lord Mortimer probably wants this interment distant from the Court at Westminster. No centre for a martyr's cult to upset him or the Queen Dowager. Gloucester is far enough away that the old King can be gently forgotten. Out of sight and out of mind, if anyone sees fit to question why he should die so quickly after being brought to Berkeley.'

By the time we arrived, the corpse had been lying in state for some weeks, since October. We had missed all the processions with the magnificent hearse, richly decorated and sent from London to do honour to the dead King. However cynical I might be over my husband's desire to banish the man to the distance of the west, I understood that he had spared no expense on his body's removal from Berkeley and arrival through the streets of Gloucester. I was not sorry to miss it. I had no wish to join with the populace in applauding Lord Mortimer's achievements.

Now we were here, and the once-royal remains of the second King Edward lay in the Priory, before the altar, surrounded by a collection of gilded lions, angels and saints when we approached to bow in recognition of his earthly state. His body was not visible, wrapped in cerecloth, embalmed in wax to seal the corpse to prevent corruption. Instead a carved image of the King dressed in his coronation robes lay majestically on top of the coffin. Not even his face was visible; only an image created by a master craftsman who had done Edward proud.

Was it normal not to lie in state with the features uncovered, even if the body was embalmed? Should the subjects not be able to see and venerate their late King? For whatever reason his face was not visible, perhaps because death had disfigured it. I considered it but cast it aside as a matter of little importance as we withdrew until the burial would take place, finding accommodation with friends in Gloucester.

'My son has made a good effort for his enemy. How much do you suppose he spent on this spectacle for a man he despised?' Lady Marguerite was cold and inclined to be tetchy.

'Your son need no longer fear him now that he is dead. He can afford to be generous. Would it cost so much? All he had to do was employ a good carpenter and unearth the coronation robes.'

Lady Marguerite sniffed her disapproval, but I would not be drawn into an argument. This was going to be difficult enough.

*

The funeral, in retrospect, was a strange affair, even though it followed the usual pattern. Mass was sung, incense filled the vast space as the voices of the choir soared. A plain black slab was evident to cover the vault, until a permanent image could be created. All was seemly and heavy with due reverence. Nothing to catch at my thoughts, and yet I felt a tension there. The mourners were in goodly numbers, the respect was acceptable for a King who had been forced into abdication. There was no outcry and yet... The coronation of the young King had held a nervousness, an agitation all of its own, but this was a sharp affair, as if waiting for some happening. The sensation rippled over my skin within my kirtle and over-gown.

As I paid my respects, surrounded by my daughters and mother-in-law, my gaze was on the royal party. The young King Edward, pale and severe, as he bowed before the body of his father. Isabella, Dowager Queen, swathed in black veils, her face hidden, supporting her son. She laid a flower beside the coffin.

And there was Roger Mortimer, Lord Mortimer, King in all but name. Of course Roger was present, clad in deepest black, as if he truly mourned. I could not take my eyes from his raiment of black patterned silk, all overlaid with a black fur-lined cloak, as if he were truly one of the royal family. Costly, magnificent, eye-catching, doubtless stitched for this occasion. He would be noticed.

And yet there too was the sense of waiting, in his face where his eyes were watchful, anticipatory, the lines deep beside his mouth. He might appear at ease but I knew him well enough to know that he was not. The rigidity of his shoulders and straightness of spine, the angle of his head as if listening, spoke loud and clear. He was waiting for something.

I turned my gaze away, my thoughts become very inappropriate for an interment. What was Roger expecting? This was a very convenient death for him. There would now be no chance of a rescue, to depose the young King and Roger with one blow and restore King Edward the Second. Was I imagining it all? Did it lack the sombre magnificence of a royal funeral where all thoughts were on the man who now lay dead in our midst? I felt that we were all playing our parts in the event, like mummers in the coming Christmas festivities, all following the steps laid down for us.

I looked across towards where my daughters stood in their black veils, unsure of what they were thinking, until Beatrice looked across to me and gave a small nod of her head. I liked to think that it was in some silent support. How they had grown into a strong, political maturity where power and adultery became the norm.

At last all was over. The choir fell silent, the incense began to dissipate like a thick mist in the chill air, the clergy processed out, leaving the congregation and the royal group. We had done what we came to do. The Mortimer women had made a state-ment of loyalty to the new King in recognition of his dead father. Yet still Lady Marguerite and I hovered for a moment. What to do? Should I speak with them, offer my condolences? I thought not. I was not close enough to the King to do so. I had no wish to exchange conversation with Isabella. As for Roger, what would I say?

'Let us go home,' I murmured to the children.

Bowing once more before the graven image of the dead King, turning to leave, suddenly there we were, face to face with the Dowager Queen. It had to happen, and why not in the presence of such loss and death? There would be no cowardice in Johane de Geneville on this day, nor would there be any acceptance of what had been done to me. I nodded to Lady Marguerite to escort my daughters from the Priory Church. Then I, all formality, curtsied deeply, head bent in fealty to my Queen. I would not be found wanting.

As I rose, Dowager Queen Isabella inclined her head, and I knew that this confrontation was quite deliberate on her part. She had sought me out. But why? Why would she force a meeting between wife and mistress when the mistress wore the crown of victory? Unless it were to humiliate me further.

'It pleased me to see you here with your daughters. We value the loyalty of those who live in the Marches,' Isabella said.

Well, that was an innocuous start. Was that all she had to say?

'There is no question of our loyalty, my lady,' I replied. 'I am surprised that you see a need to comment on it.'

'No need at all. I did not think to see you here today.'

'Of course I would be here.' I did not wait for her to begin some meaningless exchange of words. 'I know what it is to lose a husband, even if not to the tragedy of death. There are more depths of tragedy than that final one. You have my compassion for the death of your husband, my lady,' I said, my voice firm, almost conversational, when in reality it threatened to vibrate with fury at her deliberate challenge, to which I had responded in like mind.

'My thanks, Lady Mortimer. I respect you for it.'

Isabella clasped a deeply engraved silver vase against her bosom.

'You hold a fine memento of the late King,' I remarked.

'Yes. A precious reminder of the shortness of life,' she replied, her hand tightening so that her fingers whitened around the costly metal and its contents.

I knew what the vase would contain. The eviscerated heart of her husband. I wondered where she would keep it, in plain sight to remind her of her betrayal of him, or shut away in a coffer to forget. She turned back her veils and I could see her beauty, unclouded; the fine texture of her skin without blemish, the purity of her arched brows and curved lips. How could any man resist her? There was no sense of loss or grief on those finely moulded features. I spoke before I even weighed my words.

'I regret that you see the need to own two hearts. And one of them offered to me in holy matrimony.'

I saw her take a breath. She had not expected me to broach such a forbidden subject.

'In days long past it is possible that you owned Lord Mortimer's heart,' she stated eventually, slowly. 'Now it is willingly given elsewhere. If I understand your complaint correctly.'

'Your understanding is as keen as it has always been. I wish you well of that once-priceless possession. I have given up all claim to it and have no wish for its return, even were it offered. I trust that you will preserve it with as much care as you do the one in its silver case.' I curtsied again. 'Good day, my lady.'

I caught up with Lady Marguerite, astonished at my brazen comments to the Dowager Queen.

'What did she have to say?' Lady Marguerite asked with a sly glance as our litters, readied for departure, came into view.

'Nothing of value.'

'You were marvellously courteous, if your posture was anything to measure it by.'

'If you mean that I did not raise my voice, then I was, although my words were far from dignified.' At last I smiled and it seemed that it was the first time for some days. 'It was my desire to tear her veils and apply my nails to her beautiful cheeks.'

'I admire your self-control. It means that we will not be locked up for damage to a Dowager Queen.'

'Did your son speak with you?'

'No.' She slipped her cold hand in mine in an unusual show of overt affection. 'It has been a trying time. Let us go home.'

My husband had made no effort to seek me out or speak to me, or to the girls as far as I knew. We were no longer important to him. I could have approached him; I chose not to. What was there to say? I returned to Ludlow in a lowness of spirits for the celebration of the birth of the Christ child. It was a joyless Christmas. Death and adultery did not make for celebration.

Chapter Thirty

Ludlow Castle in the Welsh Marches, February 1328

Marriages! There was a family matter to be considered; more than one, in fact a plethora of alliances. Roger's absence in person, by courier, or by letter forced me to acknowledge that he had given it no thought even though it should have been uppermost in his mind. Probably with the events around the old King's death I could not expect him to put his family before politics.

Despite this death, marriage was in the air, so Lord Mortimer's thoughts should have been close to home. In the month of January 1328 in York Minster, young King Edward had wed Philippa of Hainault as had been long planned. I presumed that Roger and the Queen were in attendance. I did not go, even though I had accepted Edward's casual invitation. What would be there for me? I had had enough of royal events, funerals, coronations and now marriages, with no part to play other than onlooker. I had no wish to travel so far to witness the joys of Edward and Philippa at the same time as Roger and Isabella flaunted their adultery. They had been circumspect during the celebrations at King Edward's coronation. I did not know if they still hid their sins from the public. I had no wish to see it.

Now, the Mortimers had marriages of their own to consider.

When the weeks continued to slide past, and since it was mooted that my husband was taken up with hostilities in Scotland, I wrote to him at Westminster, for surely it would eventually find him there. Formal and precise, it was once again written by my clerk Walter to my dictation.

To my Lord Mortimer.

We have between us a number of unmarried daughters. The years are moving past and they should be wed. I trust that you, in your position of power, have the rights to a number of marriages of young men of importance. I know that you have wardships at your disposal. Perhaps you will bend your mind to it. I am considering the girls Joan and Catherine who are of an age and more to be wed. Joan is now fifteen years and Catherine fourteen, if it has slipped your mind in the present demands on your time and planning for the future. I would be grateful if you could find the opportunity to communicate with me over these issues.

Your wife Johane, Lady Mortimer

I did not sign it.

The reply came sooner than I had expected. The courier had been turned round at Westminster and sent back forthwith. It was equally formal and precise, for which I was sorry. I would have enjoyed an outburst of temper, but then this letter too was written by one of his clerks.

To my Lady Mortimer,

I am well aware of the ages of my daughters. I will be with you at the end of the month to discuss the matter, the

continuing winter weather permitting and the state of the
roads. I hope to have your agreement to the young men I have
chosen.

I trust you are in good health. Perhaps you are of a more
forgiving nature than when we last met. I hope that our
daughters will be with you at Ludlow when I arrive.

Then a scrawl of a signature.

Roger

Perhaps a little less formal than I, since he had asked after my
health, whereas I had not deigned to consider his, but equally
acerbic. Forgiving nature? There was no forgiveness rooted in my
heart. Clearly, I should expect a visit. And there he was, before
the end of February, riding through the streets of Ludlow in full
panoply with our son John at his side.

I had thought long and carefully about this, my approach to a
man who had dragged our private concerns into the public gaze.
As it was some months since we had last exchanged any opinion,
not since the coronation of the King, there had been time for
my anger to reduce from conflagration to a simmer. I welcomed
him with calm assurance. I had had much time to practise as, in
the background, the stone masons hammered the slabs of stone
into suitable shapes for the building of Roger's chapel.

'I was not sure that you would welcome me.'

Richly clad, suavely at ease, he actually smiled and formally
kissed my hand. My son stepped into my embrace readily enough.

'Nor was I certain of it, since you ignored me at the Gloucester
funeral.'

'I had critical affairs of state on my mind, as you would have
been aware.'

'I did consider barring the gates to you and ordering my men to shoot on sight.' I gently removed my hand from his, returned his smile with one of icy quality, and turned to climb the steps. 'How could I? I did invite you. I see that you have come alone.'

He was even now looking across to where the building of his chapel was going on apace at the far side of the outer bailey. If he noted my oblique reference to the absent Queen Dowager, he said nothing but turned to greet our daughters. We ate and talked of general estate matters, before repairing to my solar that was redolent of memories of better times, all of which I mentally consigned to the midden. I dismissed my servants. The girls absented themselves too with their brother in their midst to entertain them, doubtless with tales of Court intrigue.

'You still have the knife!' I murmured to John before he left.

'I do.' He grinned with a glance at his father, who was entertaining Agnes and Beatrice with some innocent exchange. 'Do you want it back?'

'Too dangerous for you to return it to me. I might use it.'

John laughed aloud.

'What's that?' Roger asked, looking up.

'Merely a moment of memories of our days in Hampshire,' I said smoothly. 'You have plans for the marriages, I hope.' I broached the subject immediately, to fill the terrible space left by previous intimacies that were now dead and gone.

'Yes. And most worthy ones.' He flung himself into a cushioned chair and stretched his legs to the fire, an ultimate statement of relaxation while I was straight-spined with tension. 'You have no wolfhounds.'

'No. Those days are long gone. I'll not keep more. Tell Isabella to buy a pair for you. Now tell me about your plans and then you can be on your way.'

'I would not wish to take up your valuable time. This is what I think. If you are in agreement, of course. Joan will wed my ward James Audley, Lord of Heleigh. They are of the same age and should do well together. Catherine is betrothed to another of my wards, Thomas de Beauchamp, heir to the Warwick inheritance. Does that fit with your approval? They are both young men of substance and good family. I can think of no better alliances for Mortimer daughters.'

Notable families, the Audleys and the Beauchamps, higher than we might have aimed at when I first wed Roger. This was better than I had thought. He had not neglected family matters after all. I felt slightly warmer towards his planning, if not to him.

'I know of both families. They are good matches,' I replied coolly. 'Did the wedding at York go to plan?'

'Yes. The weather was atrocious and the Minster roof leaked but they were joined together in the sight of God and will make a good pairing. Philippa has a strong character despite her quiet demeanour. Edward is much taken with her.'

'She might need to be strong-willed with a mother-in-law so close at hand and determined to keep hold of her son's reins.'

My intention not to delve into sensitive matters had fallen at the first hurdle.

'Perhaps. The Dowager Queen will be no danger to the young Queen's position.'

'Yet I swear that the authority of both Edward and Philippa will continue to be curbed.'

'They are still both very young,' he replied as if he had no concern in the matter, yet I was certain that the power in the land lay at the forefront of his mind, just as I knew whose hand would tighten that rein if he saw fit. 'Time will put all such matters right. You look well, Johane.'

He was regarding me lightly.

'I have recovered from my incarcerations, if that is your meaning.'

Indeed I knew that I had, having made use of my mirror. Returned to an unrestricted diet, I knew that my complexion was less grey, my face less drawn, my hair once more shiny and lustrous with unguents. I turned the conversation back to the arrangements. There were no dangers in practicalities.

'You have arranged the betrothals. And when will these marriages happen? Will it be a double celebration?'

He gave the slightest of shrugs as if the Scottish hostilities would take precedence over our daughters. 'The date is not yet fixed because of my commitments in Scotland, but it will be at Hereford Cathedral. We have a parliament called in Northampton in May. Perhaps then would be the best time, at the end of that month when the parliament is dispersed. May is a good month for weddings. We will travel on from Northampton. The Bishop of Hereford has indicated to us that he will be pleased to officiate.'

I did not care who performed the ceremony. My ear was well attuned to any possible slights. *We* have a parliament. *We* will travel on. The Bishop has informed *us*... I stiffened beneath the flowing lines of my surcoat, but kept my face in a perfectly amenable expression. I would not foresee problems before they arrived fully formed in my velvet lap. But did that presume that Isabella would be part of the ceremony at Hereford?

I would not ask. Not yet.

'And where is it to be, that the guests for this marriage celebration will stay? I presume that it will be a momentous event for so pre-eminent a family as we have become in the months since your exile and my imprisonment.'

He had anticipated all eventualities. Was not all in hand? Why would I possibly object to any of his planning?

'The guests, and there will be many, will travel here to Ludlow. There will be feasting and entertainment. We will be most willing to impress. I expect that you will enjoy it.'

So innocuous a reply. A creeping horror was cooling my blood as the possibilities were laid bare, until I took myself to task. There was no need for any disturbance of my hard-won equilibrium.

'Of course. I will set all in preparation here.'

He had not once mentioned the Queen. She would go back to London after the Bishop's blessing of the two young couples at the cathedral door. I had been too ready to see the horrors, which in fact did not exist. We ended on an amicable note, Roger telling me of John's growing attraction to the tournaments while I painted an image of Agnes's lack of skill when plying a needle, and we both mourned Beatrice's un-tuneful application to her lute. A domestic interlude where politics and the Dowager Queen did not intrude.

'Will John make a jouster?' I asked.

'More than Beatrice will ever be invited to play and sing if the company wishes to avoid an onslaught to their ears.'

We laughed a little and shared cups of wine.

He occupied his own private chamber as if he were a mere visitor.

If any tears were shed by me, he was not to know.

Perhaps I was beyond tears by now. Was that not a good thing?

Next morning – how short a visit this had been – he was heading to Wigmore to inspect the defences before returning to Westminster. First a visit to the chapel at the far side of the bailey that was nearing completion. I watched him at a distance walking round the construction, no doubt delivering orders to the stone masons who were finely carving heads with which to adorn the windows. I considered walking across to join them but did not, simply awaiting his return, spending the time in a difficult conversation with my son.

'Has Father told you?'

'Told me what?'

I had no suspicions, pulling my hood over my ears, for the day was full of February chill and a persistent drizzle.

'About the preparations for the marriage.'

'Your father says he has it all in hand.'

'You could say!'

'Tell me!'

'Not for me to say!'

I looked sharply at him when he guffawed, then Roger was walking quickly towards us, a swagger in his step, energy radiating around him.

'Are you satisfied with it?' I asked.

'Yes. It will be a worthy memorial to my release and my safety.' He was now mounted and ready to ride out, his escort awaiting the office to leave. Why did I feel that there was still an issue hanging between us, like a cloud that would bring a downpour to drench us both? A storm from which there was no hope of my taking cover.

'Travel well,' I said.

I will.' He hesitated, reins held hard in his gauntleted hand, as if at last he must broach the issue that had been in his mind. Of course he had been aware of it from the beginning. Roger Mortimer was no fool. Roger Mortimer knew me very well. His stare was unequivocal.

'You should know, Johane. I have invited the Queen to attend the wedding.'

I knew it was an issue to be confronted, and confront it I must. There were implications here that should have kept me from sleep if I had allowed myself to be cynical of my husband's arrangements. If I had not foolishly persuaded myself that I could trust him.

'And will she accept? Will she come?' I asked lightly.

'She has expressed her intention to do so. It will bestow great esteem on our family.'

'Of course. I hope that my reputation and dignity can withstand the notoriety.' And here was the crux of it. 'Will she grace our celebrations after the wedding with her presence?'

'Yes.'

'Here at Ludlow?'

'Yes.'

I held his gaze. I puffed out a breath into the cold air.

'I can imagine the tawdry gossip in every chamber and corridor, from the garderobe to the kitchens.'

'You would do well not to listen to tawdry gossip.'

'How can I not? You have put me at the centre of it.'

My mind was racing, grasping at practicalities, wallowing in the shame of what I had become. Did I cause a scene or accept all that was cast at my feet, while the Queen Dowager was stepping gracefully on the ashes of my marriage, in my own home?

'Will the Queen expect to have accommodation here at Ludlow?' I enquired, giving no indication of the raging turmoil.

'Yes, she will. As well as the young King and Queen. They will stay at least overnight before continuing their journeys.'

I did not care where Edward and Philippa might stay. I would give them my best bed and my chamber most willingly, the pre-eminent place on my dais, all the courtesy required from a

Marcher lady to the King and Queen visiting her home. Isabella was quite another matter. The image leapt full-blown: my Great Hall, my solar, my bedchamber, all designated to be inhabited by Dowager Queen Isabella for the duration of the visit. She would occupy my own property in all her regal beauty that had not faded one iota with the passage of time while I had aged, grown sere and unattractive, or so it seemed to me. She would demand the best hangings for the bed. She would sit at my board, on my dais, and welcome my guests. She would rearrange the seats in my solar to achieve the best light. She would sleep in my bedchamber whether I wished it or not, while I must of necessity step back into the shadows. The betrayed wife. A secondary figure in my own household.

The ghost at the feast.

And where would Roger Mortimer sleep during this upheaval?

I smiled up into his face with consummate resolve. How I could be so controlled I did not know.

'And will I be expected to retreat from my position of lady of this castle? Will I be expected to step back, to offer Isabella my chamber and my seat at my own board?'

I saw his hand clench even harder round his rein, but he did not hesitate.

'It is customary when royalty visits to give them pre-eminence.'

My mind swam with a succession of furious and rapid deliberations. Had he given this no thought? This was man's planning with no consideration for me. Had it even entered his mind when he issued his invitation, for I was sure that his had been the hand that brought them to Ludlow. What a position to put me in. To defer to my husband's lover in my own home, my own castle. I straightened my spine, raised my chin, and looked up at him, uncaring of who might hear my denunciation.

'I will not do it. I will not step back to accommodate your lover under the terrible illumination of my daughters' weddings.'

He had not expected me to refuse. I watched the flash of surprise tighten his lips, arch his brows.

'I will not,' I repeated, so that there would be no misunderstanding. 'Curtsey to her I will, because she is Dowager Queen. Feed her and give her a bed for the night, I will do this because I must, and as you say it is customary. Give up my rights to her, my husband's lover, the cause of my shame, in my own castle, I will not. She will not supersede me in my chamber or at my board. Nor can you expect it of me. I am astonished that you should have been so thoughtless of my position here at Ludlow. And do not make the excuse that through marriage this castle is yours to manage as you see fit. I am Castellan here, and I will not accommodate your mistress to my detriment. How can you be so heedless of my dignity to ask it of me? Why bring her to Ludlow? Why not send her to Wigmore, where she can rule as she chooses?'

His hand clenched harder still, causing his mount to toss its head, to snort and sidestep.

'Because Ludlow is more reflective of my power. The Dowager Queen will come here because it is my wish. Have you become so discourteous, Johane? I would never have thought that even being locked in Skipton Castle your good manners should have gone begging.'

'Gone begging? This is not a matter of good manners but of my humiliation. I have never before been asked to accept my husband's mistress beneath my roof. I will not do it. If you do not wish to have further scandal on your hands at a family wedding, then you must make other plans.'

Now he was equally dismissive of any listening ears. The timbre of his voice sharpened.

'You do not dictate to me, my wife. I will not refuse to accommodate the royal party. This castle is indeed mine through our marriage. I will dictate who comes and goes here...'

'A marriage that you have wilfully betrayed. I will not give up my authority to a woman who has usurped my place in it. And if you think to persuade me, you have learned nothing of me over the years of our acquaintance. I will not do it.'

I became aware that my son John had silently removed himself from this confrontation. I admired him for leaving the field to the two of us, yet regretted that I might have embarrassed him. The escort too had withdrawn after a hasty gesture from Roger. No one else was near. There was no need for me to lower my voice. Or for Roger to lower his.

'You will obey me, Johane.'

His voice had acquired an edge as of shattered glass.

My reply matched his. 'Are you so certain? I will sleep in my own chamber, inhabit my own solar, and sit at my own board. Having stated my intent, you are now free to go your own way.'

Before he could reply, I stalked off towards the gate into the inner bailey, yet he manoeuvred his horse between me and my retreat. I stepped to one side, but my husband once more angled his mount in front of me.

'You will welcome her.'

'I will not.'

'This matter is not finished. I will deal with this.'

'I await with interest. No doubt you will inform me when you have decided. But give precedence to the Queen in my own Great Hall I will not. You will not claim obedience from me in this matter.'

'And you will not be allowed to thwart my wishes.' His brow was as black as the storm-cloud overhead. 'I advise you not to try my patience.'

'Patience? It is I who must command patience.'

I had the last word. Lord Mortimer drove in his spurs and cantered to the outer gate, his escort rapidly following, John hastily mounting with an admiring flourish of farewell. I had aroused him to threats and given myself a headache and a sense of trepidation. Would I carry out my statement of intent? I most certainly would. Pride and dignity ruled. No woman could be expected to welcome an immoral queen with a gracious open hand. And if any mythical woman was willing, it was not Johane de Geneville.

What would Roger do? He would not retreat from such determined resistance, that I knew. I had to admit to a frisson of excitement. Or was it fear, beneath the fury, that he had ever put me in this position? My steward, coming to stand at my side, cleared his throat.

'Lord Mortimer has left this for you, my lady.'

He carried a small leather-bound box which, when he lifted the lid, revealed four books. I lifted one, turning the pages, instantly delighting in the beautifully illustrated content. Did I not know these stories well? These were the romances I had lost when my possessions from Wigmore had been confiscated, where chivalrous knights proclaimed their love for their ladies. The quality of these books in their gilded leather far outstripped my original well-used ones.

'Lord Mortimer said to tell you they are a gift from him.'

'Did he indeed?'

These were a sop to his guilty conscience. He knew my taste, knew that I would not be able to resist reading the tales of knights who behaved with utter respect and loyalty to their beloved. The knights whose oaths of love and loyalty could not be broken except on pain of death.

Furious at what he had done to buy my compliance, I closed

the book, replacing it in the coffer with the other three, tempted to dispatch them back to Westminster. To Isabella, who would no doubt enjoy them. I could, if I was in the mood to do so, even burn them.

'Take them to the Abbey, for their safety,' I ordered.

I regretted sending them, but I would not weaken. Of course I would never destroy them. Perhaps one day I would read them, when memories had faded and the pain lessened. It would not be today. It would not be tomorrow, or in the weeks to come.

Chapter Thirty-One

Ludlow Castle in the Welsh Marches, late February 1328

Two weeks later a cavalcade of men, horses and well-loaded wagons approached my gatehouse. Mortimer livery being evident, I ordered the gates to be opened, and the visitors occupied our outer bailey. I could have sent my steward to discover their intent but curiosity got the better of me. Of course I knew what it was all about. Any woman of wit could have read the signs after she had issued a challenge to her husband, a man who could never resist a challenge and answered it with considerable aplomb, or even with a mailed fist.

Here were stone masons, carpenters, blacksmiths, far more in number than our own skilled Mortimer men. Here was the planning for a mighty operation. The carts were loaded with newly cut stone. I recognised the cheerful master craftsman who had supervised the building operations at Wigmore.

'Good morning, Master Gilbert.'

'We have been sent by Lord Mortimer, my lady.'

'To what purpose?'

Of course I could guess, yet surely he would not. So vast an operation to remedy one small invitation to a Dowager Queen and a challenge from an abandoned wife. But it was just what he would do.

'We are to begin building works, if it please you.'

'Indeed?'

He eyed me carefully, warily, unsure of my reactions since the orders had not come from me.

'We are to extend the living accommodations of the castle, my lady. And here is the first delivery of stone, from Whitcliffe Common across the River Teme.' He gestured widely with his arm towards the west. 'No problem in finding stone. We'll have this put together in no time. Before May, were my instructions. It will be more impressive than Wigmore, I promise you.'

He smiled. How courteous, how uncertain he was of my response, even though his minions were already unloading their tools and implements as well as the massive roof timbers.

'If it please me...' I gestured to encourage him to walk and talk. 'Show me what it is that you will do here, Master Gilbert. That Lord Mortimer has ordered you to do.'

Confident now in his own world, he produced a sheet of parchment with writings and lines and coloured inks. When it flapped in the wind as we stood in a corner of the outer bailey, I reached out to take hold of one side of it.

'If you will walk further with me, my lady, I will show you. It will be all that you could wish for.'

Once in the inner bailey, he pointed and explained while I listened in silence.

Cunning. Crafty. This was Lord Mortimer's disgraceful plan. The Dowager Queen would come to Ludlow whether I wished it or not. It was a plan of outrageous proportions to allow me to keep my domestic hegemony and the Dowager Queen to visit in royal comfort. I almost laughed aloud at the sheer challenge Lord Mortimer had presented to his workmen in so short a time.

*

The building began. The ferrying of stone, the mixing of mortar, the scurrying of masons and labourers from dawn to dusk. The chiselling and the hammering. The carving of finials and decorative arches. The erection of scaffolding. Amidst much noise and dust, I watched it grow before my eyes. My solar had acquired another set of rooms above it, which I could make use of and could not fault in the planning. Also, another good move, the kitchens and storerooms were reconstructed on the far side of the bailey to allow more space. But what astonished me was the massive structure of rooms that were being built on the opposite side of the Great Hall. A new solar, new bedchambers and, most luxurious of all, a new tower containing internal garderobes.

I walked through my new home, the dust coating my shoes and my hems, discolouring my veils. Such thorough building, such attention to detail and luxury, money spent with no curtailment on the Mortimer purse; all for the visit of Dowager Queen Isabella, for King Edward and Queen Philippa. But principally for Isabella. Her own chamber with a garderobe and a solar for her comfort. Her own entrance into the Great Hall. All because I had refused to sit back in my own castle and give precedence to the woman who had taken my place between my husband's sheets.

What a magnificent gesture it was. I could not but be impressed. Did I resent the changes to my castle? Yes, because of the reason for their creation. But by the Blessed Virgin it would make life more comfortable, with the extensive accommodations and the garderobe tower. I was not so churlish that I could not admire Roger's extensive vision of what Ludlow could become, as he had re-created Wigmore. Every morning I walked round, getting in the way. Wigmore had been transformed into a veritable palace; Ludlow was becoming a palace of monumental proportions.

I also found my way to the Chapel of St Peter in the outer bailey that was now almost completed. Roger clearly had an eye to his immortal soul as well as to the Queen's physical comforts. It was not vast in size, very much a personal chapel, but the quality of the arching and roof timbering was eye-catching. I talked to the craftsmen there who told me of Roger's intentions. Two priests paid to sing Masses daily to celebrate for eternity the miracle of the Mortimer escape from the most daunting prison in the country.

How impressive it all was. How damnably impressive!

Of course I had to be thankful that he had escaped death, but the consequences for me had been heart-breaking. The man I had loved and cherished had given his heart and adoration to another woman and would build a palace for her. I returned to my solar to help my women and daughters stitch bridal clothes for Catherine and Joan. My heart was light for them, but heavy for me for the future.

'Will it all be finished in time?' Catherine asked as we pinned an open-sided over-tunic to her slight figure, to the cacophony of hammers and chisels and workmen's bellowing of orders.

'That is the least of my worries,' I said. 'Now do stand still.'

Yet I did worry. This marriage celebration could all be a disaster. I was not looking forward to it, under the eye of the whole realm, when I should have been rejoicing at the marital success of my daughters in their alliances with two great magnate families. Yet since it clearly would happen, with or without my co-operation, I had already made some plans of my own. I had sent for two of my sons, Roger and Geoffrey.

'When you send for us, why should it raise suspicions?' Young

Roger asked after he had suffered the habitual embrace from his mother.

'No reason to be suspicious.' I smiled in benign concern that covered a multitude of scheming. 'I merely wish you to travel to France, to your de Fiennes relatives.'

The young men looked at each other, and then at me.

'Of course.' I could see him thinking about this. 'Will our father approve?'

'There is absolutely no reason why he should not.'

'Why have we to go to France?'

'I have a mission for you that will be best fulfilled by your family there.' I handed Geoffrey a note written in detail at my dictation by my clerk Walter, whose eyebrows had climbed more than once. With it I gave to Young Roger a leather bag of coin. 'This will pay for your travel and for the purchase of the items on this list. Be guided by your French relatives.'

Not averse to the travel abroad, the adventure of it, they departed after a good meal.

'What are you planning?' Lady Marguerite watched them go.

'A lesson in loyalty that Lord Mortimer will be unable to ignore.'

'And they have to go to France?'

'They most certainly do. I have not the time nor the skill to achieve the craftsmanship that I desire.'

'Since you will say no more, I look forward to the return of my grandsons.'

I smiled at her and departed to assess the progress of the building.

Chapter Thirty-Two

Hereford Cathedral and Ludlow Castle in the Welsh
Marches, late May 1328

Our daughters, Catherine and Joan Mortimer, were duly mar-
ried with unsurprising panoply, given that Lord Mortimer had
the controlling guidance in its preparation, in the cathedral in
Hereford, where the ceremony was conducted by the Bishop.
The congregation, a weighty one in number and in power in the
Marches, was given added glory by Dowager Queen Isabella, by
King Edward and Queen Philippa.

I could not help but recall my own marriage in the tiny church
at Pembridge. I might have been a formidable heiress, but the
event bore no comparison with this glittering array of power.
At least Roger stood beside me here when our daughters took
their vows at the cathedral door, the young men presenting their
brides with a book and a cluster of silver coin. He would not
shame me, as he had not when our sons were knighted. It did
not quench my opprobrium of what he had done, but it did not
add to it as my daughters received a ring of marriage and we all
made our way inside to hear the marital Mass.

Both brides and grooms were so young, much of an age as
when Roger and I were wed. Would they find any happiness

together? I prayed that they would, as I recalled the early halcyon days of my own marriage, even when political pressures separated us. Surely we had been happy together before treason had raised its ugly head and Roger had seen other paths by which to retain his power. I prayed that my daughters would not be so wilfully abandoned.

One impression stirred me above all the rest. How powerful my husband had become. The most powerful man in England, so they said; I could not doubt it. There was more than a sprinkling of earls at my daughters' wedding, with royal blood in their veins. They clearly considered it good policy to be seen at this family occurrence and to bow low to Lord Mortimer. Moreover here in our midst to dispense a royal gloss was Dowager Queen Isabella, clad for a celebration. Her beauty, her confidence, her arrogance shone in the shadows of the vast Norman pillars in the cathedral. What man would not worship at her feet. For me it was all wrapped about in a cloud of despair, all cloaked in rich materials and glittering gems. The days of my happiness were over, but all was hidden under outer joy for this celebration for my daughters.

How exhausting it was.

When the Bishop had pronounced his blessing upon all of us, we moved en masse to Ludlow and the anticipated festivities. Who anticipated it most I could not say. There were many who would watch the proceedings, any expected clash between wife and mistress, with malevolent glee.

'How can you tolerate it?' Lady Marguerite shared a litter with me as we so often had in the past. 'At least after bending the knee once in welcome I can pretend that she is not here and enjoy the festivities. You will have to be ever-present as lady of the castle. Unless we both flee to Radnor and leave them to it.'

'It's tempting.' I sighed and dug my fingers into my temples where a permanent ache had centred. The gold filet and crisp-inette bound my hair too tightly. 'I can tolerate it because I must. So must you. There is no escape for either of us.'

'May the Blessed Virgin grant us both strength.'

'It is not strength I need but a magnificent deviousness.'

'And that you have, my dear, as I have seen to my pleasure and astonishment.'

'May God forgive me for it! I fear deviousness is a sin.'

Lady Marguerite's face was expressionless but her tone mischievous.

'On this occasion I am certain He would forgive you. I will offer up a rosary in case there is any doubt. Come to me if you need any help.'

I stood in the centre of my Great Hall and turned slowly on the spot, taking in every detail, every nuance of position and power. If nothing else pleased me, what I saw filled my heart with a delicious species of malice at the success of my venture. I would make this an occasion to be remembered by all. It would keep tongues wagging throughout the summer and into the depths of winter in solar and hall alike. I would indeed employ magnificent deviousness, but at the centre of it, because it was their celebratory time, nothing would be allowed to harm the enjoyment of my daughters and their new husbands. It would be a time to remember.

I had had my own wishes carried out to perfection. There was no shortage of Mortimer and de Geneville power to be seen amidst the impressive chambers of Ludlow Castle, newly created by my husband. I and my women had been busy while the masons and workmen had been building a royal wing for the Dowager Queen. By the time my daughters had been joined in marriage with young men of high blood, all was prepared. Now

I was free to consider the impression that my home would make on our guests. Mortimer banners proclaimed our proud descent on all sides. New rushes had been laid, cushioned stools provided for those of royal blood, the fires aromatic with herbs and apple-wood. The Great Hall was all in readiness for the coming feast. It had taken some effort, but the result was startling.

'By the Rood, my lady. Are you sure about this?' my steward asked.

'I am certain. Are the muscles of my household not capable of constructing an extra dais or two? Of moving stools and trestles? Can we not achieve this? We have built a new tower, a new wing. These additions should not be beyond our capabilities.'

Thus the Great Hall had been created at my demand as a scene from the mythical Avalon of King Arthur. Not with a round table but with three trestles on three separate daises, on three sides of the hall. On one side a trestle table with a fair white cloth at which the King and Queen and the Dowager Queen would sit. Opposite, on the other side, where I had an entrance from my own solar, the table where I and my household would feast. And in the centre, to celebrate these two important unions, a table for the two wedded couples. Not the usual arrangements. Not the usual dignity afforded those who were royal, but I was sure that King Edward would see the humour of it, to give precedence to four young people who were much of an age as himself and his new bride. The rest of the guests were accommodated at trestles in the centre, with a clear view of all the entertainments.

Where would Roger sit? I knew not. An empty chair would be provided at each table. He would choose for himself. I would not make the choice for him.

And the walls? Hung with tapestries of scenes from the Court of King Arthur purchased in France from the finest makers of tapestry and brought here by my two sons. They had not been difficult to discover since they were popular scenes, and would suit my purposes exactly.

The royal party arrived. I curtsied in welcome to the Dowager Queen, as I had said I would.

'My thanks for your accommodations, Lady Mortimer.'

Her smile was brittle in comparison with her self-satisfaction. My words were acerbic and careful.

'You must thank my husband, my lady. The comforts of the new tower are all of his planning.'

'You have gone to much trouble.'

'My daughters are dear to my heart, my lady. They deserve that this day be made memorable. It is their day of celebration.' I summoned our eldest son and heir Edmund. 'If you will show my lady to her solar, where she might rest before the feast. Beware, my lady, of any remaining rubble on the stair. Our stone masons have been hard-worked.'

Isabella could hardly refuse, as I could not say the words that slid into my mind. *You have stolen Lord Mortimer's loyalty from me. I curse you for it. I could wish that you stumble and fall into the ditch.* We all knew our roles here. Lord Mortimer had been quite prepared to change his allegiances. I watched them go; I was warmer towards the King and his young wife, who still showed no sign that she carried a child. Nor did Isabella, for which I was grateful, although her highly embroidered over-gown with its excess of costly material might easily cover the evidence of a moral sin.

The marriage feast was all carried off with precision and a superb display of spiced and roasted dishes from which all ate heartily. The level of sound rose to the roof as pages carried round the ale and wine in chased silver vessels.

'I expect you to be there,' Roger had ordered.

Did he think I would be so lacking in manners that I would absent myself? I think that I had promised to do just that. I was inordinately pleased that I had worried him. At that moment he knew nothing of my seating arrangements, or my tapestries.

'You will preside over the feasting at my side. We will dance together. And if you resist, I will drag you into the dance, my dear Johane. I will not have you make such a scandal that rings through the length and breadth of the country.'

'There will be no breath of scandal from my behaviour at these festivities,' I had replied dulcetly. 'I can answer for no one else.'

Believing full well that he would haul me to the festivities if he had to, of course it would be below my dignity to allow him to do so. A de Geneville knew how to conduct herself. Nor would I draw the attention of the guests from the two young couples. They deserved every pleasure this day, and I had every intention of being present in my own castle.

Remaining in my own solar until the guests were seated to my instructions, clad in the requisite silk and damask, furred and jewelled, my skirts sweeping the floor with understated elegance, I entered the Great Hall through my own solar door, down my own staircase to my own dais. I bowed to the gathering, to the royal party, to my husband who stood, eyes narrowed in suspicion, waiting for me, then took my place where I always sat. It was superbly done. While Roger, always a man of excellent reactions, chose to sit between the two young couples at the centre table. He raised his dark brows in my direction but I could read nothing more in his expression, even when he must have taken note of the new tapestries. If Roger had spared no expense, neither had I.

They were magnificent: three of them, large enough to take the eye, each one with a message all of its own of adultery at the Court of King Arthur. Lancelot the perfect knight; the beautiful but wantonly disloyal Guinevere; the courageous King Arthur who had given his love and friendship only to be betrayed. Three images to tell the tale. Illicit lovers, secretly scheming in flowery groves. Stolen kisses as King Arthur rode out to war. A shared bed of passion while King Arthur knelt in prayer.

I hoped that Lord Mortimer, descendant of Arthur, would appreciate my efforts. Whether Isabella would do so, I could not say.

After the feasting, when the centre trestles were removed, I danced the farandole with Lord Mortimer, its simple steps, its brief joining of hands in a line with other guests, perfect for an occasion when there was no love lost between the lord and his lady. I thought that I danced well in the circumstances. He danced with Isabella, too, as well as with Philippa, while Edward led me in the sinuous lines and circles of the carole dance, the dancers singing the refrain and keeping the tune.

Toasts were drunk, good wishes wished, gifts given, before all drew to a close. I remained until the young people were escorted to their bedchambers where they were blessed and given over into the keeping of Almighty God. Then I retired for the night more weary than I could ever recall, but my mind full of my achievements. Isabella had usurped my husband, over which I had no power, but she had failed to appropriate either my authority or my private chambers in my own castle.

Where Roger might spend the night I had no idea. Not with me. I thought he would have the sense to take one of the chambers in the old Gatehouse Keep despite its damp and draughts. He was not, when required, without moderation and self-denial. If he spent it with the Dowager Queen I hoped that he would enjoy the tapestry over the bed, a final purchase by my sons which I had not requested.

'We thought that you might make use of this,' Geoffrey had

announced with sly enjoyment when he and Young Roger had returned from France, well-laden.

And I had laughed. So had my ladies. It was a scene based on an old French tale of the apocalypse. I could not have chosen better than the many-headed dragon emerging from the sea, vomiting frogs and evil spirits as it appeared. The meadow in which the dragon stood was multi-flowered with the prettiest of bluebells, but the dragon was a fearful creature with vicious teeth and the suggestion of foul breath issuing from its mouth with the frogs, while in the distance approached a knight on a white steed who would dispatch the monster and cast it into a lake of fire.

I prayed that the Dowager Queen would enjoy this scene in her bedchamber.

As for my daughters, they would have memories of this night until their dying day.

Blessed Virgin, may their new husbands be gentle and courteous with them. Amen.

After two days of hunting, feasting and wishing the young people well, the royal party and Lord Mortimer moved on to Worcester. I wished them Godspeed. King Edward was benign and watchful, thanking me for the good hunting of deer and the experience of flying our goshawks after the rabbits in the warren by the river Teme. Queen Philippa was sharply compassionate without having to say a word. For a young woman she knew exactly how to behave, and drew no attention to her own dis-comfiture with her mother-in-law. I even questioned that there was any; Philippa was of a far more placid disposition than I.

'I enjoyed the tapestries,' she said with a smile of some inner amusement.

Isabella continued to preen her power and her success, flamboyantly riding pillion behind Roger through the water meadows, directing where he should look, where he should fly his gyrfalcon. I did not accompany them but, on foot at the river's edge, flew the falcons at the water-birds with my sons and daughters, enjoying their pleasure in the occasion. I could think of nothing more distressing than riding beside my husband and his lover.

Our farewells on their departure were brief, but elegant on both sides. I kissed my daughters and my new sons-in-law. The Dowager Queen inclined her head as I curtsied.

'It has been a memorable experience, Lady Mortimer.'

'It was my pleasure, my lady.'

The royal eyes were sharp on mine.

'I had forgotten the keenness of your wit. I will not forget again.'

'Nor should you, my lady.'

I made an even deeper obeisance, suppressing just a little satisfaction.

'Certainly a memorable occasion,' repeated Roger with an acerbic glint as he prepared to mount as the royal party departed. 'In more ways than one.'

'It was my intent.' I saluted his cheek with grave formality. 'It is not one that I would care to repeat. Was the hunting good with Isabella murmuring in your ear?'

He returned the brief salute. 'It is impossible not to admire you, Johane, even when you are intent on reckless behaviour.'

I could not let him go without making him aware of my struggle to present a dignified mien to the massed Court. Weary to the bone, I curled my hand around his reins to prevent his departure.

'I could have accepted a dalliance with some Westminster whore. Even an affair of sorts with some Court lady. I could have tolerated that. But not this. How could you and your royal paramour hold me up for such public humiliation? You ask more from me than I can endure.'

He released his rein, his expression severe but not hostile.

'I ask no more from you than you can bear, nor will I. You will survive, Johane. You know what is due to your name and your family. You know it well.'

Then I was left alone with my new building, my unfinished garderobes, a set of tapestries proclaiming the joys of adultery and a seething resentment. We had still more daughters to marry. My resilience would be called on yet again.

Chapter Thirty-Three

Ludlow Castle in the Welsh Marches, August 1328

'It's Lord Mortimer, my lady. And the terrible burden he bears. They are returning home.'

My steward had come to fetch me from my solar.

It was in the third week of August, the strains of the wedding celebrations long put aside although the building works were still a nuisance, when a sombre cavalcade wound through the streets of Ludlow. It seemed too benign a day, full of sunshine and bright clouds scudding along on a fair breeze, for such impending grief. The news was brought to me, but I had been expecting this. Drawing my veil over my face I made my way across the inner bailey and up the stairs to the top of the Great Tower Keep, from where I looked down at what would confirm my worst fears. I heard Beatrice and Agnes follow me but I did not acknowledge them. In that moment I could not. My tongue was beyond finding words. If I could I would have howled my grief to the whole castle.

No music. No laughter. No celebration. Roger had returned alone with an escort, but also with an enclosed litter pulled by four horses. A litter that would carry no living passenger. It was draped in black and the Mortimer colours were prominent on

the litter and the horse accoutrements. A dour procession. A
solemnity that spoke its purpose to all who might witness its
passing.

I had been warned of its coming. Roger, in an unexpected
kindness, had not wished me to be shattered with the sudden-
ness of his announcement. Or perhaps on an occasion such as
this his consideration was not unexpected at all. Sometimes he
still had the power to surprise me, to move me. Not all that we
had built together in our early days had been destroyed by his
betrayal. The gates were already open and they rode in to halt
below me. Slowly I made my way down to stand before him as
he dismounted and raised his hand to me in a formal salute.
Perhaps my daughters had followed me. I did not know. All my
attention was on the litter before me.

'Grave news, *mon coeur*. The worst of news.' Such a gentle
name from the past, but it meant nothing to me. It was used
without thought, unless it was indeed compassion. I inclined
my head.

'I know it.'

I knew what he had hoped for, but it could not be.

'Your chapel is still incomplete,' I said brusquely. 'It would not
be seemly to take him there with so much dust and unfinished
stonework. I have made all ready in the Mary Magdalene
Chapel. I thought it was what you would wish.'

His face was severe, the lines of age engraved deep with
nothing to soften them. There was no softness in this day, no
glamour, no flamboyance of the Court. I expect that my expression was equally harsh beneath the veil that I had not raised.
I did not want to reveal any emotion to him. There was no
greeting between us. It was beyond me to show affection or
welcome or even the hatred that sometimes shook me with its
virulence, nor did this occasion demand it.

At a signal the entourage dismounted. Four livery-clad men-at-arms drew back the curtains of the litter and manoeuvred the plain coffin onto their shoulders. His hat and gloves in his hand against his heart, Roger bowed in acknowledgement while I bent my knee into a low curtsey. Then the coffin was carried over the bridge and into the inner bailey. We followed, pacing slowly, into the circular nave of the little chapel where a trestle had already been placed before the altar and our priest awaited us. Incense clouded my wits and my sight. Sunlight painted grim bars across the blue and gold Mortimer banner that was draped over the coffin, highlighting the red de Geneville lion. It was the one that I had stitched for Roger when he went to challenge the King in Shrewsbury. I held back the tears as I witnessed its well-worn state and acknowledged its purpose here today.

'Do you wish to see him?' Roger asked.

'Yes.'

I needed to see and believe. The banner was folded back, the lid of the coffin was removed and there he lay, his body wrapped in leather, spices packed around him, but his face clear to persuade me of the truth.

My son. My second son, Roger. Dead before he had barely lived to a mere twenty-three years. I hardly recognised him. Nothing here of the laughing child or confident young man, the youth dressed as an earl who had been knighted at the coronation of our young King, the young knight who had travelled to France to bring back my tapestries. His features were waxen and austere, and yet he looked so young in death, as if he could wake from this deep sleep if I kissed his brow. He had been so alive at the weddings here at Ludlow. I touched his face with my fingers, struggling hard to curb any outward sign of emotion, even though a mother was allowed to weep and mourn at the death of her child.

My son Roger would never wake to smile at me again.

Queen Isabella was no longer uppermost in my thoughts. Nor Lord Mortimer's perfidy. Suddenly that no longer mattered. I had lost a child. I covered my veiled mouth with my hand. Our children had survived infancy into adulthood. I had no intimations of this until Roger's warning.

'Killed?' I asked. 'Was it a wound? I know of no battles. Do not tell me it was the result of some mindless tournament. The blow of a lance or the wounding of a sword.'

There was no sign of pain in his face but death could wipe away all traces.

'No. A fever. He did not suffer a violent death. I did not know until news came to me that he was gone from us.'

A fever, something a child could withstand but sometimes it swept away the strongest man.

'Thank you. For travelling here with him. For not just sending a courier.'

'I came to grieve with you.'

'Did you?' I felt no emotion. All was drained from me in the shock of seeing my dead son. 'You are kind.'

So much promise. Imprisoned in Windsor when Roger was sent to the Tower, but then released with Roger's return. We had settled our Irish lands on him and his new wife Joan Butler, of impressive Irish heritage. To our sadness, and his, she had died childless, but Roger had arranged a new alliance with the young widow of the Earl of Pembroke. There was still all to hope for, for a young man of much ability. There would be a new Mortimer strain of descendants in Ireland.

Now he was dead.

We stood together, our household behind us, through a Mass for his immortal soul.

Then walked out into the brilliant glitter of sunshine which seemed so much at odds with what we had just witnessed. Rooks called jubilantly from the towers, jackdaws squabbled in the roosting-places, but there was no joy in my heart. I thought that there would never be again. I stood as if I could not make a decision of what to do next. The household drifted away to take up its duties, wrapped in its own memories and grief for a young man lost to us.

'Come with me.'

Roger took my hand in his and led me into the Great Hall, through the shadows that made me tremble with the sudden cold, and from there into my own chambers. In my inconsolable grief I allowed it, watching him as he removed his boots and his cloak. He removed my veil, loosed my hair, and drew me down to my bed where he stretched beside me, holding me in his arms so that I might weep when I could no longer stem the tears. I soaked his apparently new tunic while my heart stilled and I accepted the comfort his arms gave me. We did not speak, merely lay together in mutual grief. If I gave him any comfort, I did not know. If he wept too, I did not know. I hid my face in his shoulder. When I had vowed that I would never touch him again in intimacy, my sorrow demanded the warmth of his arms and I sank into them without question. Within me, the wound of my loss, of both husband and son, was so deep that it screamed for release.

At last my sobs quietened and I wiped my face with my sleeve, although nothing could melt the cage of ice around my heart. This was all wrong. This could not be. I must not allow myself to live in the past. Roger Mortimer was not mine to give me solace.

And yet he tried.

'I am so sorry, Johane.'

'It was not your doing. How could it be? How would we know that he would suffer from a fever? How would we know how to

322

cure it?' I would not be seduced by his kindness. The bitterness was too deep. 'Not unless Queen Isabella, together with all her other attractions, possesses magical talents to pre-empt and cure it.'

I was harsh in my judgement, destroying the intimacy that he had created. I did not care. I sat up, pushing him away, ashamed of so much weakness, and my lack of tolerance after so much kindness. I could do better than this. I swore it would be the last time I allowed him such closeness. I could not afford such fragility. It would be so easy for him to resurrect my love for him. It would do me no good, nor did I think that he meant to do so. How could I have wept on his shoulder as if I needed his comfort? Without a second glance I left the chamber after repinning my veil over my loosened hair and went down to the Great Hall to call for wine and food to be prepared. I did not think that he would stay long. I did not sit with him while he ate but returned to the chapel where I knelt beside the body of my son. I made no response when he joined me there and knelt with me.

He left the next day. He would be going back to Isabella, of course.

'Will you send his body to Wigmore Abbey?' he asked me.

'Yes. I will arrange everything.'

'It is right that he should lie with his ancestors. I will visit. I cannot stay now. There are too many demands on my time.'

'Of course you will visit. I am honoured that you could come today.' How bleak were my replies. 'What will you do with the Irish inheritance? It needs a lord of its own, as we planned when we gave it to Young Roger.'

My voice broke on his name. I turned my back on my husband so that he would not see the despair that engulfed me.

'I will settle it on John. Do you agree?'

'Why not? He has strong Irish connections. He has lived there with us. He was knighted there.'

'So I thought.' He took the reins of his mount from his squire, then turned back to me. 'I would never have wished such grief on you.'

'Of course not. Perhaps it is in the nature of children to bring us grief.'

He bowed and rode away. We had offered up our grief for our son. Now he was returning to his lover and I would curse her until the day of my death. Meanwhile, ever practical, and because there was nothing else I could do other than wallow in self-pity at my loss, I set in train the means to have Young Roger carried to Wigmore Abbey and interred there with all suitable prestige alongside his Mortimer ancestors.

Not that all was a matter of grief after Young Roger's death. It was halfway through November in that same year of loss when my daughter-in-law, Elizabeth de Badlesmere, Edmund's wife, was in residence with me, close to her time. She had grown into a fine young woman, her hair neatly-plaited beneath her coif, and she had carried this new Mortimer offspring with great assurance. Meanwhile Edmund was at Court with Roger, somewhere in England. The promise of a new baby brought us joy as we awaited the start of her pains.

After a day of agony for us all, Elizabeth gave birth to a son whom we named Roger, even though I baulked at it. But it was tradition, Lady Marguerite informed me, to be named Roger.

'Could it not be Edmund?' I asked, a touch peevishly.

'No. The names alternate, to avoid complications.'

Which made sense. I complied with ill grace but some pleasure. Here was the first of a new generation of Mortimers to introduce to the world. I stroked the fuzz of dark hair and kissed the babe's forehead before, late as ever, Edmund arrived in a rush to take his son into his arms after all the pain and anguish of birth was over, and send messages to Elizabeth who was still isolated in her chamber. She would have to be churched before returning to the household to receive her husband's grateful thanks for a robust child with effective lungs.

'You should be proud of him, and of your wife. She had a hard travail,' I said after forgiving him his tardy arrival. 'What kept you? This, by the by, is Roger, your heir.'

'And I am proud of both, Mother. I have gifts to send to Elizabeth to assure her of my appreciation.' He grinned down at the infant who gripped his finger with surprising strength and squinted against the light as if to bring his father's face into focus, but then I remembered that all my children had been tenacious of life. I would not think of Young Roger's death. It was still too painful. 'As for what kept me, I'll tell you in a moment. First let me admire my heir, if he will keep still. Do babies always squirm so?'

He grinned at me as he handed the child back and I prepared to restore him to his mother.

'I should bow low before you,' Edmund said, stopping me in my tracks.

'Why is that? It has not been customary in this household.' I smiled at him, halting at the door, looking back over my shoulder, the babe quieting in my arms. It was good to see my first-born in such high spirits. 'Usually, it is a brief comment in passing, and then not very often.'

'Now it is different. You were never Countess of March before.' I turned foursquare towards him. There was no mockery on Edmund's face. 'That baby who has begun to wail will one day be Earl of March.'

Was it such a great surprise? I thought not. Nothing would any longer surprise me at Lord Mortimer's ambitions.

'Is this your father's doing?' I asked.

'Of course. Parliament has been meeting in London, which is why I was detained. On the last day King Edward created three new earls, at the recommendation of my father. The King's brother, Prince John of Eltham, became Earl of Cornwall. James Butler became Earl of Ormond. And our father became Earl of March.'

I was unsure what I thought about this. It was a great show of distinction, a superb recognition for the Mortimer family, and yet...

'An achievement indeed,' I said dryly, still trying to decide.

'All at the ceremony were impressed.'

'Or worried?'

Edmund frowned a little. 'What is scratching at you, Mother? I thought you would rejoice with the rest of us.'

'Of course I do.'

I handed the child back to its wet-nurse, who had come to discover her charge. Earl of March. Not a town. Not a castle, one of our own, but a whole region of England. An indication perhaps of where he would see his power. I thought about this as I returned to Elizabeth to pass on her husband's good wishes and packets of gifts. It harked back to my own ancestry, the French Counts of La Marche, drawing attention to Roger's connections with ruling houses of Europe. He was now Earl of a vast area, giving him supremacy over Pembroke, Hereford, Gloucester, all the powerful Earls who came within the orbit of the Marches. A magnificent title that King Edward had been prepared to bestow.

How would the Earl of Lancaster, King Edward's cousin, respond to this creation of a power to rival his own? Later, when

I had the leisure to do so, when Edmund and I had shared supper with the girls, I asked him that exact question.

'He was furious. There has already been a clash of will between my father's troops and those of Lancaster at Winchester. Nothing serious, because in the end Lancaster backed down. We must hope it will all come to nothing. There will be arguments and disagreement, but Lancaster cannot dictate my father's policies, or those of King Edward. Which of course is why he is so angry. He sees it as a slight to his own power, but my father holds the whip hand.'

I could not be as hopeful as Edmund.

When I retired to my chamber, leaving the girls to beg details of Court life from Edmund, I was free to look at what had happened. I was Countess of March. Although it would make little difference to me, clearly it would make all the difference in the world to Roger. Once again I was afraid for him, what his ambitions would bring down on his head, and yet the King had seen fit to do this thing. But King Edward would grow and might want to take the power back into his own hands. He might regret making Roger Earl of March.

Did Roger celebrate with Isabella? Did they raise a cup of wine together?

He did not celebrate with me.

I smiled a little wistfully. My grandfather would have rejoiced at this success in the marriage that he had arranged. So would my mother. A pity that I felt so unmoved by it all. In the distance I heard the wail of a new baby. There was the future. I would be happy for my new grandson who would one day, God willing, become Earl of March.

Chapter Thirty-Four

The tournament held at Shrewsbury, autumn 1328

A late autumn tournament had been arranged, and Shrewsbury was in a festive mood. My three still-unwed daughters and I were there to enjoy a clash of arms in which my son John would fight. It pleased me to occupy rooms in the castle built within the great loop of the River Severn, from where we had excellent views of the town and the flat lands to the east. What were we celebrating? Some Saint's Day perhaps, but it was the tournament that attracted Isabella, Beatrice and Agnes, and I was pleased to enjoy the wares of the merchants in the bustling town.

We made our way to the tournament field, no longer expecting the raucous melee, considered to be a thing of the past, but the girls were noisily enthusiastic to see the fields organised for jousting, with pavilions for us to take refreshment and watch the armed combat. John, joining us there, was equally full of enthusiasm. I had seen him ride with a lance and knew him to have become as gifted as his father.

Roger Mortimer was not expected to attend. His new title had roused much enmity, now centred under the banner of the Earl of Lancaster. The new Earl of March would have more on his mind than a Shrewsbury tournament. I was uncertain how I felt about this. A strange mix of relief and regret, although relief would win if Isabella travelled with him. His banners were nowhere to be seen in the gathering of local magnates intent on sharing news, so I settled myself to enjoy a day amongst the festivities.

The jousts began with much energy and we took our seats in one of the pavilions set aside for us. The crowd cheered. So did the girls. Some of the brave knights were unhorsed, limping from the field. Numerous lances were smashed. The shouts from supporters and opponents were loud and often explicitly vulgar. John rode with panache, defeating an adversary, although his mount showed signs of lameness at the end.

'Will he ride again?' Agnes asked.

'I expect so.'

'Does he have another horse?' she persisted.

'Of course. His squire will ensure he is fit to fight.'

I watched my son, a mere eighteen years, proud of his achievements, remembering the past. John had been knighted in Ireland by Roger when he was seven years old. He had travelled with us to Ireland, not yet old enough to be placed in another household, and had been the only son with us in Dublin when Roger had been given the power to create knights. I remembered him, smiling at the sweet memory of him, small and overawed as the sword fell upon his shoulders. In recent months he had been granted castles in Ireland and had received all Young Roger's Irish estates. He was a Mortimer who would do us proud in Ireland. His great-grandfather, Geoffrey de Geneville, would have been proud of him too. I wondered if he still kept the blade I had given him when I had feared for his life in captivity. I was sure that he did.

'They begin again,' Beatrice nudged me. 'And it's John riding first.'

A thunder of hooves, both riders unrecognisable except for their heraldic colours. The strike of lance, but both were unharmed. They turned, preparing to ride again, for the best of three would determine the victory. John curbed his new mount. In that moment he reminded me of Roger with all his verve and flamboyant energy.

They rode hard and fast.

A hit. A powerful blow.

John fell to the ground, his horse continuing riderless, the girls leaping to their feet, while I leaned over the parapet. Perhaps he was stunned. All would be well, I assured myself as I calmed my breathing. He was not the first to be dealt such a blow. I hoped his pride would survive the ignominy of sitting on the floor in the dust. Except that he was not sitting. I would wait, although my heart began to beat erratically, to see him stir, to raise an arm, to sit up.

Nothing. Only his Mortimer tabard fluttering as if alive in the light breeze.

I stood, heart beating hard now as if it would choke me.

Mortimer servants were running up; John's squire removed his helm, and then they lifted him, carrying him off to his pavilion. Injured perhaps, stunned from the fall, or lacking in breath if the lance had struck him in his chest. I told the girls to remain where they were and moved rapidly down the steps from the pavilion. There was no shadow over the sun, but I thought the light deepened around me and I experienced a bolt of sheer fright as I began to run.

By the time I had entered his pavilion, the mail around John's throat had been loosened. I walked forward, pushing his squire aside, intending to issue some pertinent orders for water for him to drink, and some space so that he might breathe. But all my fears were realised. A lance had entered between the mail and his helm. Blood seeped from a massive wound, despite all attempts to staunch it. The physician who had been called raised his shoulders in despair, his hands and robes covered with blood.

'Can you do nothing?'

'No, my lady. No. Forgive me. All is lost.'

'Are you certain?'

I fell to my knees next to my son. My dear son.

'Look, lady. His blood no longer flows.'

John. Another son lost to me, dead before he had barely lived.

'Forgive me.'

'It was not your fault.'

I knelt beside my son, regardless of his blood on my hands and veil as I leaned to kiss his brow. His eyes were closed as if he merely slept, his face pale and unresponsive. What to do? The orders crowded into my mind as duty took over.

Tell the girls. Arrange for his body to be taken to Wigmore Abbey. Send a courier who might discover Lord Mortimer in the depths of some political dealing. And then mourn for this lost son. My second lost son.

I could mourn him for myself.

At that moment I could not accept that he was dead. There were no tears. On whose shoulder would I weep now? I had wept for Young Roger with Lord Mortimer. Now I was alone. And then there was John's squire standing with me.

'My lady. This was packed in Sir John's baggage. He always kept it with him. He said that if aught happened to him or that he needed you, I should return it to you, because you would understand and remember. I believe it was yours.'

On his palm was the little dagger with its plain hilt that I had given John so long ago.

Then I wept without restraint. I could not stop the tears and, loosening the confinement of the circlet, pulled my veil over my face.

Leintwardine and Wigmore Abbey, Christmas 1328

In the days during a doleful Christmas when no one at Ludlow had the heart for any festivities, I decided to ride down through the Marches to Wigmore Abbey in the final week of December to see the completion of Young Roger's tomb. John's memorial still needed a slab bearing his name. I had no notion of whether Lord Mortimer had been to acknowledge his son's interment there. If he had, he had not come to Ludlow.

Approaching the River Teme, which looked to be close to flooding so that I must take care on my return journey, making our way through the village of Leintwardine, I saw that the church there had new scaffolding built along its northern wall. It was a church under the jurisdiction of the Mortimers, yet I had no knowledge of a need for stonework or rebuilding. Ordering my escort to halt I dismounted and walked up the path to the church, trying to step over the puddles and failing. My shoes were soon soaked and so were my hems. I could hear familiar hammering and the voices of workmen from within. I stepped inside to the familiar dust that hung in the air and coated all in grey. Walking slowly down the length of the nave to the small chancel, I was recognised by those working there and the stone mason came towards me and bowed.

'Lady Mortimer.'

'Is there a problem, Master Willem?' I looked up and could

see the sky through the holes in the roof. 'I had no idea that the church had suffered so.'

'No problem at all, my lady, unless it is of my making.' He too looked up at the gaping holes between the wooden structure. 'The Earl has given us instructions to make additions to the church.'

The Earl. It still grated, that this was the result of his power-grabbing. My face was expressionless.

'What is it that you add?'

'A chantry chapel, here on the left of the chancel. As you see, we have the new footings in place, and the outer walls are making good progress despite the constant rain. It's not the best weather for building, but the Earl was in a hurry.'

My ears had pricked up. I knew nothing of this.

'A chantry? To whom?'

I doubted the mason would know but still I asked him. For whom did Lord Mortimer wish to give prayers, that he must add a new chantry chapel to this little church? Why could prayers not be said at Wigmore Abbey? Was it our son John? Would he not have told me?

As expected, Master Willem shook his head. 'It will be a fine space. King Edward himself has agreed, most generously, to send us the lead from the castle at Hanley, to make our roof watertight. We expect it any day. Do you wish for me to show you what we have achieved?'

There was little to see, but indeed it was a good size, with enough windows to let in the light.

'You will not see any of the carving planned, my lady. And the glass has not yet been delivered, but it will be a chantry to enhance the prestige of the Mortimers.'

Master Willem was proud of his work, but still, why would

Roger want a chantry here? I thanked him and rode on to Wigmore Abbey.

My first destination: the graves. Two of them, my two sons lost in so short a time. John and Young Roger. John, who had had so little opportunity to enjoy his Irish inheritance, still had no memorial other than a plain slab on which his name was carved. The carved image of Young Roger was not yet complete but the mail and his shoes were well executed. The dog at his feet, as well as his helm, were still in need of a skilled hand to add a finishing touch. I stroked his shoulder, patted the dog's head, when I had offered up a prayer for the soul of both my sons. Then I went to find the Abbot.

'What is all this rebuilding about at Leintwardine?'

The Abbot looked uncertain, answering with a slight frown.

'So you have seen it. The Earl has ordered it, and paid for its endowment. A chantry chapel.'

'That much I know. For whom is it to be used? Is it for our sons?'

If so, why could he not have established the prayers for their immortal souls in the new chapel of St Peter at Ludlow? The Abbot fixed me with a look of compassion, drawing me into his chamber where he pushed me to sit before a fire and offered me wine.

'It pains me to say it but you must know. The priests who are to be established at Leintwardine, nine of them in all, are to sing Masses daily for the health of Dowager Queen Isabella.'

'Ah...'

'And of course for King Edward and Queen Philippa.'

'Of course.'

'Your name is included too, my lady. And your children.'

'So the state of my soul is of interest to him. As well as Queen Isabella's. I suppose that I should feel grateful.'

'Indeed. Whatever the appearances, you are his much-revered wife.'

'The appearances do not suggest it. I suppose that you can do nothing but approve.'

'Sometimes it is difficult. We live in dangerous times, my lady.'

'Dangerous for whom?'

I should feel grateful for the chantry to offer prayers for me and my children, but I did not. Before leaving the Abbey I returned alone to make a final farewell before the tombs of my two sons. I stood in reverential silence and bowed my head, although my thoughts were awry with all I had learned on this day. Footsteps disturbed me. Footsteps that marched down the nave. Footsteps that I would recognise anywhere. I refused to turn to acknowledge them.

And then of course I did.

I thought he looked unutterably weary, although he walked with typical confidence and authority, even a swagger that had been absent when he last crossed my path, bringing home the body of Young Roger. He bowed, kissed my hand.

'Are you here to mourn your sons?' I asked. 'John's memorial is incomplete as you see. Is this the first time that you have been to pay your respects?'

'Yes. I am more sorry than I can say, Johane.'

He was tight-lipped. Uncommunicative. I thought that he would rather I had not been present.

'You are turning to thoughts of religion again, I see.' I gave him no time to offer a sly and unbelievable explanation.

'Ah, the church at Leintwardine.'

I waited. Then I took pity on him and led him back into the Abbot's chamber where we sat and commandeered the fire and cups of wine. He remained surprisingly contemplative as he sipped from his cup, his legs stretched before him towards the only fire in the Abbey. Now I saw the depth of the shadows on his face. How would a man forced to hold the reins of the kingdom against enemies every day not show signs of hardship?

'I think there might be war,' he announced.

'The Earl of Lancaster?'

'Yes. And the Earls of Norfolk and Kent. Not just over the disastrous Scottish campaign. Who is to say I will not meet my death on a battlefield? The last time I met Lancaster he bawled across the chamber that he would use his army against me, given half a chance. There will be no quarter given if I am taken prisoner. Lancaster will have my head. It would be good to have a chantry pleading for my immortal soul.'

How honest. It surprised me.

'Isabella will plead for you.'

'Isabella will have to fight for her own safety.' He sighed, settling against the cushion as if he had ridden long and hard. 'Don't use your claws against me, Johane. We have lost two sons. I find a need to offer an appeal before God for my remaining sons and their children, our heirs. For our daughters. For grand-children I might never see in my lifetime. It is one way for me to pay my debt to the Mortimers.'

'And to plead for me. I suppose that I should be appreciative. It is certainly an interesting combination of people to be remembered. Husband and wife and paramour and offspring. Perhaps in the fullness of time there will even be a bastard Mortimer child. For the first and only time they will be together and at peace, before God in the prayers of the chaplains. Perhaps you will give the names of the petitioners to different chaplains, so that there will be no muddle.'

He smiled against his will.

'Very apposite! Tell me of yourself. I hear nothing of you.'

'While I hear much of you. Much I would rather not hear.

And an Earl forsooth!' But then I relented. 'I am well. The estates are in good order. Your children thrive. Your grandson, another Roger, Edmund's little son, whom you will see if you deign to visit us, is in good heart. You might even hear him – he has a remarkably loud voice when his will is thwarted. Edmund is very proud of him.'

'You still have not told me about you.'

'What is to tell?' Yet I did, calmly, coldly, as if reciting a list of necessities to be ordered for Ludlow Castle. Oh, I did.

'I resent your betrayal but I will not rant and rail. I am old enough to govern my senses. I despise you for what you have done, now that you flaunt your liaison before the whole country. I am sure that I have become the object of pity and scorn. I resent that too. I loved you. I gave you my loyalty and the support and affections of my youth. I carried twelve children for you. Sometimes I could hate you. And yet you still call to my heart. I will never say so in public, nor will I speak of it again in private. Don't expect my support if affairs go awry. Yet I cannot bury the affection I once felt for you. I wish I could. I despise myself for my failure to hate and hate again. Does that answer your question well enough?'

For a long moment he looked at me, his mind and thoughts unreadable.

'It devastates me.'

'What did you expect? It might devastate you, but not enough that you will leave your paramour and return to me.'

He took a long breath. I watched as he considered his reply.

'Isabella and I need each other.'

'So your adultery is merely a means by which to hold power. Not love. Or even lust.'

'I cannot answer that.'

'I will not ask you to do so. Nor do I believe that I wish you to return. We must draw a line under the past, for love cannot be resurrected after such a grievous blow.' I could feel the pain building within me and changed the subject. 'Why is it suddenly such a danger for you? The King gives you his friendship. Surely you are indestructible.'

Perhaps he heard the sneer in my voice.

'The King gives me his friendship because he must. One day he might decide that he no longer needs my advice or my presence behind his shoulder. The years pass and I see maturity on his brow.'

'And what then?'

His smile was wry. For the first time since his return to England we were engaged in a serious conversation about the state of the country.

'Who is to say? We saw what his father was capable of when he wished to remove those whom he hated or feared.'

As he prepared to leave the Abbey after paying his respects to his two dead sons, because I could not resist, and because the old bitterness had been resurrected by my accusations, I asked the question that had been raised by the chantry that would offer up prayers for the Dowager Queen:

'Are the rumours true?'

'Which rumours?'

'That Isabella carries your child.'

His brows rose, his eyes darkened.

'Not to my knowledge.'

Well, I had ruffled his feathers.

'You must let me know when the birth is expected. I will send a suitable gift.'

'Before God, Johane...'

'He will be half-brother to the King. How important will that make Earl Mortimer? You must be ecstatic.'

338

I smiled with false sweetness and turned away, returning to Ludlow on the following day, surprisingly troubled. King Edward was still very young for the vengeance that Roger feared, but I prayed that Isabella never fell out of love with him. I remembered the tales of the terrible, bloody fate of Hugh Despenser, a man who had earned her undying enmity. I would not wish the same on Roger if she ever came to see him as her foe. King Edward would grow. One day he would refuse to accept any clash of interest in the realm. One day he might well be driven to take his revenge.

Would there be war?

Indeed there was. In the days before the end of the year, on the twenty-ninth day of December, Lord Mortimer declared war on the Earl of Lancaster in the King's name. I could not say that I was surprised, nor was I astonished at the outcome. Lancaster was abandoned by his allies Norfolk and Kent who were afraid of leading their troops against the royal banners. Thus, alone, Lancaster knelt in the mud and begged forgiveness when the royal army arrived before his camp at Bedford. Lord Mortimer had saved England from war, but he had made himself a nest of enemies who would do all in their power to rid themselves of him.

And Isabella's role in all of this? She was present at the deliberate degradation of the Earl of Lancaster, so it was said, eye-catchingly clad in armour and riding a war horse, doubtless enjoying the combative impression she made at the side of her son and her lover. By the Virgin, she could not keep her fingers from dabbling in affairs of state, while Roger had made a cross for his own back. He might have destroyed the power of the Earls, for who could challenge him now, but Norfolk and Kent would find it impossible to forgive Roger for forcing them to change allegiance. As for Lancaster, his humiliation would burn like a scald. He would never forget nor forgive.

I cursed Roger for his short-sightedness, his overweening ambition that would drag us all into the mire again. I should have fallen to my knees to ask forgiveness for my ravaging of the character of the man I had vowed to honour and obey. I did not.

Chapter Thirty-Five

Wigmore Castle in the Welsh Marches, late August 1329

What in the name of the Blessed Virgin was Earl Mortimer planning here? It was the jousting field, the apple of Roger's eye just below the castle walls at Wigmore, that astonished me most. Banners and pennons announced their heraldic associations on all sides. Pavilions had been erected along one side, silk-lined with silken canopies, with seating for any number of spectators. What had this cost him in such lustrous cloth and gold fringing? The jousting course was already laid out.

I had no presentiment of any disaster in this festive scene when I returned to Wigmore for a wedding.

It had not been my intention to go there again, so full as it was with bitter-sweet memories, but my willing attendance was demanded in late August of the year 1329 to ensure all was in order for two more weddings. On hearing that Earl Mortimer and the royal party were in Leominster to the south-east, I had made my own way to Wigmore, envisaging a busy few days. I need not have worried. Roger had taken it in hand in his usual arrogant fashion. I felt ruffled that I should be so unnecessary, but times had changed. Roger's schemes were grandiose. The provision of food and wine as well as ale for the various households descending on us was what I would have expected, except for the vast line of carts and baggage animals bringing supplies to cram every inch of our cellars and storage chambers. It was barely possible to set foot in them. The spices and rare commodities from the East perfumed the air, speaking robustly of the impression that Earl Mortimer intended to make.

Wigmore was bustling with feverish activity and incipient splendour. I hoped the glory of it would not be spoilt by rain, particularly that of the main pavilion in pride of place, taking everyone's eye, sides looped up to make the dais and royal seating visible to all; it was a work of sumptuous skill. Here were the royal colours of King Edward and Queen Philippa, together with those of Dowager Queen Isabella. Would I not expect it? And of course the Mortimer emblems. Two throne-like chairs had been positioned in the centre, draped in cloth of gold, flanked by others of lesser quality. Roger was doing the young King and Queen proud. Earls and barons could already be seen encamped in the valley below the castle, all the way down to the village of Wigmore at the base of the outcrop. It would be a goodly audience for this Mortimer wedding.

Riding with me and my daughters from Ludlow was my son Geoffrey, who was visiting with us from his estates in Picardy.

'How much do you suppose that this has cost him?' he asked, echoing my own thoughts, staring at the evidence of wealth and consequence.

'A royal fortune.'

'So I should say. Did you know? The King has given the Earl a grant of one thousand pounds, as well as all the treasure my father garnered from Despenser on his death.'

I slid a glance in his direction.

'You are remarkably well informed, Geoffrey.'

'I spend time with my father when I am in England. You

342

obviously have not been told that the Earl plans to hold a Round Table tournament here, such as his grandfather did at Kenilworth.'

'So that is it. King Arthur will live again. No, I did not know. I do now.'

It should not surprise me. Discretion? Earl Mortimer did not know the meaning of the word. And yet it seemed all too outrageous. I shrugged and promptly forgot about it.

'Did you know that the Dowager Queen has left land to my father in her will?'

'No. I did not know that either.'

Why would she do that? It was not customary. I wondered fleetingly what role the King would play in all of this, and then they began to arrive, and I thought that I must once again be prepared to make my curtsey to the woman I detested most in England. I joined Lady Marguerite, who was already in residence, and we made our way to welcome those who needed to be welcomed.

Who was it to be wed? Who was it who had spurred Roger to spend so open-handedly, so opulently? Who had brought the royal Court in all its glory once more to the Welsh Marches? There were advantages to be gleaned for the Mortimers in Roger becoming Earl of March, which even I had to appreciate although I might not speak it aloud when I received a visit to Ludlow after months of absence. My emotions were still hostile but I had awarded him a deep curtsey.

'My lord the Earl.'

He bowed low. 'My lady the Countess.'

He took my hand, kissed my cheek.

I made no response, waiting until he released me.

'To what do I owe this visit? Could it not have been dealt with by courier?'

Earl Mortimer grinned, in no manner discommoded. The uncertainties about his future that he had voiced at Wigmore Abbey when weary to the bone were now assuaged under this present grandeur.

'Put down your weapons, put up your lance and sheathe your sword, Johane, and let me in to talk family matters. What brings me is of value to you too.'

I really had no choice. Nor did I wish to continue to air my grievances in the bailey with all and sundry watching us. I had told him that I was old enough to restrain my emotions, and here I was playing the betrayed wife for all to see and hear. I should have more dignity.

'Come then and play the loyal husband. I will feed you without your need to fear any pinch of poison in the repast or the wine.'

I took him to my solar, dispatched my women and waved him to a chair near the fireplace. The summer day was cool. Dissimulation was an art that I was perfecting.

'Why are you here, my lord Earl?' I handed him a cup of my best ale with a false smile. 'Does anyone still call you by the name that your father gave you?'

For a moment he was robbed of an answer.

'Once you did.'

'Once I was your beloved. Now I do not feel inclined. Does Isabella call you Roger? Or is it all the formality of power between you?' I picked up my lute and, seated some little distance from him, began to play, softly at first, experimenting with the plangent tones of a song of despair and love lost. 'Why are you here?'

'To discuss an alliance. Two, in effect, for Agnes and Beatrice. I have arranged their betrothal and subsequent marriages.'

I sat in silence, only my fingers speaking on the chords, while

I let him tell me all the detail. Should we not have planned this together? But now the Earl of March was well used to wielding his own powers. I brought my mind back to his explicit intentions.

'Agnes is to wed Laurence de Hastings, the young Earl of Pembroke, whose right of marriage is in my own hands. Beatrice will become the wife of the son and heir of the Earl of Norfolk, the king's uncle. They are both eminently valuable marriages for our family. I need not tell you that.'

Eminent indeed. I stopped the vibrations of the lute with the slap on the smooth wooden bowl with one hand and sipped from my cup after raising it in an ironical toast. Norfolk was the King's half-brother. Would he allow his heir, fourth in line to the throne of England, to wed one of the younger daughters of a man only recently created earl? A man once imprisoned for treason? I had perhaps not realised the true extent of the power that Roger had accrued in recent months. Thus the authority of the Earl of March. I felt a brush of pleasure along my arms that my daughters would achieve such magnificent marriages and yet, surely, here was danger.

'You are unnervingly silent, Johane. What are you thinking?'

I began to play again with a sweep of my hand over the strings, a lively dance, the bright notes filling the room, music fit for a wedding party.

'That you look high for your daughters.'

'The Earl of March can afford to do so.'

'But this will be an alliance with the royal family.'

'Do I not deserve it?'

'Will the King agree?'

He shrugged a little as if it was a game that he had well in hand and he would play with sharp finesse. As I recalled him in the past. It worried me.

345

'What will Lancaster say?' I asked, well aware that this powerful royal cousin had no love for my husband.

'Everything unpleasant. He is no friend of mine.'

'Then if you know that there will be those who oppose your self-aggrandisement, there is no need for a warning from me.'

I plucked more violently so that the strings complained in a shower of tuneless notes.

'Warning of what?'

'Nothing that you do not already know. The King is growing up. He will not be content with your guiding hand much longer. Is it dangerous to usurp so much power?'

He put his cup down with a click on the nearby coffer top, so that the ale spilt over.

'Do you suppose that I am naive? I live at the centre of Court politics. I hear the rumours, the attacks, the schemes whispered in corners. Do I not know of them, and how to forestall them? There will be no danger for me. I do not fear the King.'

No, he was not naive, but surely he must lie awake during the early hours before dawn and wonder where his future path might lead. There were many who would wish him dead. I stopped playing on a thunderous barrage of musical complaint, then laid my hand over the strings so that all was still and silent again.

'I will pray for you. For your long life as well as for your soul.'

'It is all I can ask of you, my wife. I must be grateful that you have so much generosity in your own soul. Will you help me at Wigmore? Will you give me your support to wed our daughters in style?'

'What do you want me to do?'

'Nothing. All is in hand. Just be there.'

'Of course. But keep Isabella away from me. I presume that she will accompany you.'

'She will be there. I have to say that your lute playing has improved.'

'I have had much time in captivity to spend on it. When I could borrow a lute.'

It crossed my mind to wonder what Roger was planning at Wigmore. He was not going to tell me. It remained, a tiny speck of grit in my shoe, to worry me.

Here I was at Wigmore, as I had promised, where all would be revealed. But what of me during this marriage celebration? I had no role other than a titular one as Countess March. All had been taken out of my hands and I had become an onlooker at whatever it was that Roger had created. Nor could I decide whether to revel in the achievement or watch its unfolding in horror. Oh, the marriages were as smooth as silk, the young people making their vows in such august company before the Bishop of Hereford, who had travelled up the Marches. The girls were fittingly clothed in silks, their bridegrooms looking resplendent in Court attire. Did the Pembroke and Norfolk heirs resent such a marriage with the Mortimers? It was impossible to tell from their smiles as they returned the toasts.

Once the legalities, the ceremony and the wedding feast – and the habitual raucous bedding – were dealt with to the satisfaction of all, the couples were as completely overshadowed as was I. I could return to Ludlow, and I doubted that any would notice the omission of Lady Mortimer, Countess of March.

What he had created for the entertainment of the great and the good was exactly as Geoffrey had warned. Roger had re-created the Court of King Arthur, and for three whole expensive days Wigmore became Avalon. And who was clad as King Arthur, sleek and expensive? Who wore King Arthur's crown, seated on the gold-draped throne? Who wore a jewelled collar and sumptuous robes, antique in style and colour, fit for a mythical ruler? For me the horror outweighed the glory. Not King Edward. It was of course Roger, claiming that it was his right since he was descended from Arthur, the great leader of the past.

Did he care what message he sent out to the lords and barons here gathered?

And who was the beautiful but immoral Guinevere in her flowing robes and gold-edged veils?

Not I. Not Queen Philippa.

Dowager Queen Isabella of course, seated beside her King Arthur, her lover.

From my own seat on an inferior dais, I looked across at King Edward, who sat beside Roger on one of the lesser chairs, admiring his skill at masking his emotions. For the occasion he had been dubbed Sir Lionel, one of the lesser knights of King Arthur's Round Table. Queen Philippa sat beside Isabella, as if one of her handmaids. In an interlude, when Arthur escorted Guinevere to partake of wine and sweetmeats, and Sir Lionel went off to inspect his horse and armour for the coming joust, I went to sit with Philippa who had been left alone. She was not beautiful, nor was she skilled in the arts of flirtatious conversation, but neither was she the rather dull young wife that many thought her. She had a sharp eye and a keen mind, and an ability to keep her own counsel when necessary.

I complimented her on her Arthurian garments.

'Thank you. I do not think that this close head-dress suits me. It gives me a headache.'

'You wear it very well.'

'I must, of course. Do I have a choice as part of this unnerving festivity?'

I returned her smile, and since there was no one to overhear our conversation said: 'You seem to have been overlooked. I am sorry.'

She did not pretend to misunderstand. 'Yes, I am,' she replied briskly. 'And so is my lord the King. Which is even more regrettable.'

'I had no idea this was planned,' I admitted.

'I can imagine. It does not have your imprint on it.' She spoke as if we were of equal age. 'Nor could you have done anything to change what has been done here. We both know who wields the power in this realm and in our households.'

We watched the jousting of some of the young squires for a moment.

'One day my own sons will joust with great success,' Philippa observed, as if she had nothing more to worry her on that inauspicious day.

'I am certain that they will. Perhaps you are carrying a child?' I probed gently.

'Not yet, but I am full of hope.'

The young Queen hesitated.

'I would rather that you say what you are thinking,' I said.

'Then I will!' Her smile became wry with no humour in it. 'My lord the King must remove Mortimer. You know that, don't you.'

'Yes.'

'Will that make us enemies?'

'I hope not,' I replied. 'I have far too much respect for you, my lady, and a woman in my position cannot afford to lose friends.'

'It will cause you pain.'

'Yes. Pain is now part of my life, which I must expect. But with maturity comes the understanding that a woman must absorb the difficulties and trials of life. They will always be there. Happiness is not a gift that comes to us without pain. I must accept what I am given.' I paused, thinking of recent events. 'It has been so for the past years. It has been a lifetime since I could last claim any happiness.'

'You are a courageous woman.'

'I do not think that I am. I have been dropped into this treacherous marriage from a great height when I least expected it after so many years of fidelity. I can either scream in frustration and anger, or live my life as well as I can as a widow in all but name. What I cannot do is change my situation to any degree. I trust that I am strong enough to withstand the weapons used against me.' I turned my gaze on the distant Isabella, enjoying a close tête-à-tête with my husband. 'Such as being forced to entertain the Dowager Queen in my own home as if she were a welcome guest, when I would rather sprinkle belladonna in her dish of spiced plums.'

'I believe that you are quite strong enough to withstand all such trials,' Philippa said. 'We are unfortunate enough to share the same adversary.'

Now we both looked over towards Isabella who was enjoying the moment, her golden veils afire in the sun as she received compliments from the magnates who were prepared to hide any animosity on this occasion. And there was Roger, King Arthur, all gracious power.

'I am sorry that my lord Edward is only Sir Lionel,' Philippa said. 'But to tell the truth I think he likes it, for the moment.'

We laughed a little, but then became serious.

'My lord Edward will not enjoy this situation for long.' Philippa leaned close, lowering her voice, for this was no female chatter. 'Be warned, Lady Mortimer. The Earl of March will be pre-eminent today as King Arthur, but his future is not secure.'

'I know it. One question I would ask and hope that you might reply honestly.' I caught her brown stare with my own. 'Will you advise your husband the King against Earl Mortimer?'

'Most assuredly I will. You could not expect me to do other-wise. I was raised in a spirit of love and affection, but sometimes this must be put aside. The King cannot live at ease with Earl Mortimer beside him, and I will do all in my power to persuade him in such a strategy as will remove him permanently. I will not beg for mercy for Mortimer.' The Queen, seeing my distress, covered my hand with her own, deliberately turning the con-versation. 'Your son John would have relished this tournament. You must miss him.'

I could find no words. Wounds were still tender, and always would be. So many wounds. I turned my face away from the Queen. I would not promote my grief in this gathering. Nor my fears.

And yet there were no outward signs that King Edward had taken offence at his oh-so-casual dismissal. Each day was one of gift-giving. Every day King Edward showered Roger with gifts of great value: jewels and silver-gilt goblets, one noticeably bear-ing the royal arms of France and Navarre, while Roger glowed. If he had hoped to send out the message that he was now a member of the royal family, safe from attack, he had achieved his ends. The King had accepted him. The Dowager Queen sat beside him. The gifts and the company were royal indeed.

With Philippa's warning in mind, I worried, for how could the young King accept this vision of Mortimer ambitions, to rise from a mere baron's son from the Welsh Marches to a nobleman of his own making? And how could Earl Mortimer not read the dangers in what he was doing here, with his vast household and a maintenance of two hundred men-at-arms? There he was, seated in the King's presence, addressing him so carelessly as if he were one of his sons. I trembled for it as the crowd cheered Roger when he rode out to the lists, a gold crown affixed to his helm. He was not royal. How blind he had become: a man so percipient, so aware of his own position, had threatened the King beyond bearing, and I could speak of it to no one. It would all create a rancid boil of resentment; Edward would not be his friend for ever.

And yet for a short time at that flamboyant Wigmore wedding, my fears were laid to rest. King Edward continued with gestures of friendship, Queen Philippa beamed on all present. Earl Mortimer was victorious in the lists and so was Sir Lionel, although it was Guinevere who presented the victory wreaths to the winners.

Chapter Thirty-Six

Wigmore Castle in the Welsh Marches, late August 1329

It was impossible for me to remain distant from Isabella for the whole three days. Our paths crossed of course, when there was no buffer of courtiers and guests between us, when we both knelt in the chapel for Compline, the final Hours of the day, to bring peace through the night. We were alone. The priest gave his uneasy blessing, leaving us so that we must perforce face each other.

For me the memories rushed back. Her arrival in England, unsure, uncertain. Now a woman of determination, of undoubted authority. Once I thought that she looked on me as a friend, but that was many years ago. I assessed her now in my chapel against the sacred images, the windows set with coloured glass, the subtle shadowing of the candle-flames that gilded the edges of her hair beneath her light veil. She was simply clad in an open-sided over-gown, the robes of Guinevere laid aside, now that the festivity was over. How beautiful she still was; but then she was far from her fortieth year. How queenly. How confident as she remained kneeling before the statue of the Blessed Virgin. Here was the body that Lord Mortimer enjoyed in his bed; here was the mind that appealed to his, the beauty to his senses, the

353

sharp tongue that offered him adoration and support and advice. I was entirely eclipsed.

Isabella stood, bowed her head, allowing her rosary to drop from her lovely hands to hang at her waist. I waited, saying nothing, merely waiting. It was not my place to initiate a conversation, much less an accusation. Her gaze, when it turned, was measured, thoughtful. Perhaps she had been considering her words to me. They were innocuous enough.

'Once again I must thank you for your hospitality, as I did at Ludlow, Lady Mortimer.'

'Once again, better to thank my husband, my lady.'

'We leave tomorrow. It has been a superb wedding for your family.'

'It has been a dangerous one.'

'How could it be? Yes, there are lords who envy Mortimer, but he need have no fear of them.'

'And the King?'

'The King does as I advise.'

'I have seen it. One day he will grow beyond your advice, as sons must.'

If such a statement was of any concern to Isabella, she concealed it gracefully.

'Once, when I was little more than a child, I thought there could have been a friendship between us,' she said. 'It is of course impossible now.'

'Adultery destroys many friendships, my lady,' I said. 'God may forgive you for what you have done. I find it impossible.'

'To forgive me or your husband?'

'I see little difference. You are both as culpable. You betrayed me as my Queen. Earl Mortimer betrayed me as my husband. Forgiveness demands a high cost. I do not have the generosity to pay it.'

'We do not require your forgiveness.' Quite deliberately she smoothed the flat of her hand over the silk that fell from her girdle. There it was. The tell-tale curve of a growing child. A pregnancy, far enough gone that I could see the cling of silk before she lifted her hand. I was beyond words.

'He will never return to you,' she said, as glossily self-satisfied as a cat in a sunbeam.

Isabella swept past me, leaving me in the flickering shadows as some of the remaining candles died. Had this been deliberate provocation, maliciously hurtful, or had Isabella advertised her state by chance? I thought that Isabella did nothing by chance.

I said not a word as the silence in the chapel fell around me. Her action had deepened the betrayal. Once I had admired Isabella. Now I despised her for that fatal allure, for that driving ambition, that had drawn Roger to her. In the shadows of the chapel I felt my fingers curl, my nails digging deep into my palms, as a feral cat might sink its claws into its prey.

It had been a wedding of much achievement and much grief for me. If I had ever hoped that there would be a future with Earl Mortimer, it was now destroyed. It would never be possible; he was lost to me. How foolish were women who hoped beyond all sense. This was a denouement that I should have accepted years ago. I deplored what he had done; I loathed Isabella for her careless taunting of me with that unborn child. Yet I feared that I would see his fall from power. Would I enjoy his fall from grace? My emotions remained horribly ambivalent. I feared that there was nothing I could do to prevent it. I was once again a helpless spectator, destined to remain far distant from events, to watch and await the terrible outcome.

I could not let it rest.

The pavilions were packed away, the extravagant clothing placed in coffers to be transported back to Westminster, guests began to depart, my newly wedded daughters travelling with their new households and my good wishes. Should I seek out Roger, offering him advice or warnings that he would find irrelevant? He had not heeded my advice before, and he was now well set in his ways.

I would let him go.

It was he who sought me out, discovering me in the Great Hall, supervising the dismantling of the great arras tapestry, magnificent in its white stitching, all eighteen pieces of it decorated with a myriad of fluttering butterflies, and perfect for a wedding celebration.

'Do we not have servants to do this?' he demanded. He still glowed with the reverberations from his Court of King Arthur. It had indeed been a glorious occasion, worthy of his famous grandfather.

'Yes,' I agreed complacently, in no mind to praise his organisation, 'but these are too fine to be handled carelessly. I doubt that you are going to supervise their taking down and their storage with lavender and rosemary.'

An observation that my husband ignored. 'I doubt you enjoyed it,' he said.

'But you did. Was that not the purpose of this celebration?'

'Without question. It was the culmination of Mortimer power that I have long sought.'

'What have you done?' I challenged, turning away from my task, stepping aside from the servants and their ladders. 'What terrible revenge have you set in motion?'

'I have done nothing to create harm for me and mine. All I did was make a gesture to the nobility who saw fit to honour us with their presence. I am Earl of March. I am not a man to be ignored.'

356

I grasped his wrist, holding tight through the sable fur of his cuff.

'It is a dangerous path that you tread. King Edward is no longer a child. You must see that.'

'He has yet to learn how to manage the power and authority of a king. I am in no danger. Perhaps one day, but not today. Today I will enjoy the power and the spectacle that I created here.'

'You could at least have created for him the role of Sir Lancelot! Not some nameless knight. Sir Lionel, forsooth! It was demeaning.'

'He will not care. He fought and had his victory and presented his victory wreath to Philippa who smiled and reward him with a kiss.'

'While you presented yours to Isabella.'

'She was Guinevere,' he replied simply.

'Surely everyone here would be wagering what your future intent might be. To make yourself King, as Arthur was King? To wear the royal crown on your own brow, perhaps.'

'By the Rood, Johane.' His eyes flashed in sudden anger. 'Do you consider me so foolish that I would usurp Edward and take the crown for myself? Do I not have the measure of Court politics at my fingertips? I know what is possible and what is outside my remit.' He took a breath to calm the ire. 'You should be celebrating the Mortimer achievements, not decrying them.'

'Can you bear a candid reply? I think this Wigmore marriage looked well enough with all the show and the costume, but it has been a disaster. Did anyone enjoy it, other than you and Isabella? Your daughters and their new husbands were eclipsed by Arthur and Guinevere, but were too well-mannered to take issue over it. Our King resented every minute of it, but was too courteous to say so. And don't tell me that you were unaware.

As for any man whom you once could claim as friend, does he any longer exist? I swear that you have no friends. But it is the King whose enmity you have created.'

'I am aware. I saw you talking to the Queen.'

'She detested it as much as I,' I admitted. 'If you are ever in need of royal mercy, Philippa will not fall to her knees to beg for you.' Relative silence had fallen over the castle as the last guests departed. I spoke of what I knew. 'The Queen Dowager carries a child. The rumours were wrong before. Now it is clear to see.'

'Yes.'

'And it is yours.'

'Yes.'

'If that is so, then before God, Roger, your fall from grace is inevitable. The child will be half-brother to the King. The King will not allow the father of his half-brother to direct his steps.'

'If it is a son...'

'If it is a son, yes. King Edward will see you and this child as even more of a threat, that one day you will usurp his power and place your half-royal son on the throne. Does Edward know of this child? Does he seem compliant to you? I see a sleeping dragon that will one day awake. Surely the Dowager Queen should see the dangers too.'

'She believes she is invincible. I will prevail, Johane. Yes I see the dangers but I am in the position to defeat them. I do not fear the future.'

'Then I say that you should!'

'One thing I would ask of you.'

I turned away. Why not hear him? 'Then do it.'

'Speak to no one of the coming child. I want to hear no rumours.'

After which there was nothing more to speak about. Roger

denied any plotting against him, but if he ever truly saw himself under threat, how far would he go to strengthen his position even further? And would it make matters far worse?

My son Geoffrey's opinion of his father's actions left me no doubt in their telling, his dark Mortimer brows forming a bar of disapproval. These days he was busy at Westminster and close to his father. I was delighted to see him when he visited Ludlow in the early autumn. but he was outspoken, uncomfortably so, after the usual exchange of family affairs.

'As for the lords, if my father was a figure of deep suspicion before, after this Wigmore tournament he is become an object of true hatred. Do you know what the King has done?'

'I have no news.'

My senses immediately tightened, the habitual fear whispering around the edges of my mind. In some way I wished not to know. It would merely be another weight on my thoughts to keep me from sleeping.

'King Edward has begun to take significant steps. He has replaced Father's appointed Treasurer, Thomas de Charlton, with Robert Wodehouse, a man close to the King and formerly the Keeper of the King's Wardrobe. Also, the King now has a new personal secretary, appointed by him. Richard de Bury is now Keeper of the Privy Seal.'

'What does your father say?'

'There is not much he can say in the face of such royal intransigence, but he has acquired a dark, saturnine look. King Edward is ridding himself of Mortimer influence. At present it seems to me that the King is attacking the body, inch by inch; one day he will rid himself of the head of the snake.'

I flinched inwardly at so visual a thought. Was it not what I had always expected?

'If my father cannot see it, there is no hope for him. He made of himself a fool, to flout authority so openly. King Arthur and Queen Guinevere? King and Queen of Folly more like!'

'You should not speak so of your father!' I remonstrated, although if it were not so dangerous a situation I might have laughed at his denunciation.

'Someone must tell the truth,' Geoffrey replied, in no manner discomfited.

'I would not dare say it to him,' I suggested.

'Yes, you would. You probably have already done so. And I would too!'

'Then do so. He will take no notice of my advice.'

It would not come amiss for Roger to see that I was not the only member of his family to fear the repercussions. He thought I was seeing the worst scenario, but so was Geoffrey, who had become remarkably sharp-witted during his stay in France and at the Court. The Court gloss did not merely influence his choice of an eye-catching shoulder cape and parti-coloured hose. It did not make me feel any better.

We enjoyed an evening of family discussion. Lady Marguerite fussed over her grandson. Since Edmund too was here with Elizabeth and the baby, it should have been a delightful family gathering. It was not. There were tensions straining at every corner although we avoided discussion of Court affairs. Next day Geoffrey departed on a mission for his father.

'There is still hope.' I attempted to soothe his fears. 'It may not come to the end you envisage.'

'Then why does he not see it? Why does he still parade the Dowager Queen at his side? It only makes matters worse.'

I regarded him, and touched his arm, intending to warn him not to become too embroiled in his father's manipulations, but I did not. He was a grown man and must fend for himself. Grown sons must stand on their own feet, whatever the startling colour of their hose.

'I think that the Earl and the Dowager Queen are tied together, for better or worse,' I said instead. 'They are dependent on each other. It is a bond that will never be broken now.'

'And you would not prefer to have him divided from her? I cannot believe it. You have lived with the humiliation for so long.'

How maturely astute my son had become. He had seen and learned much in his twenty-one years.

'I cannot change what will happen. My wishes are no longer of importance. They have not been for some time.'

He coloured in embarrassment and bent to kiss my cheek. 'Forgive me.'

'There is no need. Why does he still flaunt her, you ask? Or I might say, why does she remain at his beck and call? Love? Or perhaps she is the one who has your father tied to her reins.'

'I have no knowledge of love.'

'One day you will. I pray that you will.'

'But this is lust!'

'Lust is a powerful medium.' And since we were alone together, I broke my promise. 'So is the existence of an unborn child.'

Chapter Thirty-Seven

Ludlow Castle in the Welsh Marches, late March 1330

For the first time in my life I felt the hand of loneliness. My children were married with lives of their own to lead, even Blanche, who had wed a local Herefordshire lord. Of course I was grateful, but I missed them with their bright chatter and dramatic griefs. Lady Marguerite remained full of health and opinion but, despite her advancing years and her complaints about creaking joints, frequently travelled to Radnor for which she had an affection. Only my daughter Isabella remained at home with me. Time hung heavily as I turned my mind from what might be happening at Court to affairs of estate business here in the Marches. Unless it affected the security of Mortimer lands in the west, I wanted no part of it. I no longer questioned travellers or merchants.

And yet it seemed to me that the country held its breath; as if waiting for an event or a disaster. Somebody in my household checked the heavens for falling stars but with nothing to report. The stars continued on their path much as they always did. The belt and sword of Orion the Hunter shone in the night sky, although now beginning to fade. The power in the land continued in the hands of my estranged husband and his lover. Of the secret pregnancy I knew nothing, nor did I wish to know.

With my absent family in mind, and with a sharp attack of guilt, I arranged to travel down the March to the convent where my sisters still lived out their existence as nuns in Aconbury Priory. Had I visited them often? No. The paths of our lives did not cross. As I rode my mare, for I had no wish to undertake a slow journey in a litter, I recalled my last visit so many years ago when I was just wed, when they were shut away there to give me the freedom and power of the vast de Geneville lands and wealth, the freedom to wed Roger Mortimer. All these years they had paid the price for my life of prestige and comfort. Of betrayal.

Lady Marguerite expressed her disapproval when I invited her to accompany me.

'I have no wish to enter a convent, even as a visitor, at my age. I might never come out. What would I have to say to your sisters? What would you have to say to them? It is a visit that will bring you no happiness.' Her face acquired a scowl. 'Don't go!'

'I will. There is nothing to keep me here. Besides, I am suffering from a frequent attack of guilt.'

When I had last made this journey I had been a young bride with the first blossoming of what would become an intense love, carrying my first child. I had seen my sisters as pawns, albeit unwilling ones. I had looked forward to a future still hidden from me, but one in which I would take on the de Geneville mantle and work with my husband to make the Mortimer family a power in the March and in Ireland. Now all I could do was look back. To look forward was far too painful and I was afraid of what I might see. With this visit I would attempt to expiate my sins in neglecting my sisters. I had no idea how they would receive me, with welcome or with hostility. I knew how I would feel if I were in their nun's shoes.

It was a placid journey, where I found it still necessary to be muffled in good-quality wool and fur. There were few travellers on the roads, the merchants waiting for more clement weather. The sight of the Priory settled in the woods and low hills to the south of Hereford was very welcome. When I was bidden to enter and taken inside by a silent nun, it looked no different. I had sent moneys and occasional gifts, but it was still a small foundation with no luxury. I was shown into a parlour where it was indicated that I should wait with a brief explanation. My sisters and the nuns were at prayer. They would come when they were free to do so.

What would I say to them? I did not know. A whim had brought me. A need to meet someone of my own blood. My thoughts turned full circle, so that I regretted this whim and considered leaving, but then there they were. Beatrice and Maud, professed nuns by now of course, clad in black robes with a white wimple, all but their faces obscured. They were so much older, but then so was I. My face too would be lined with age.

They bowed deeply, hands hidden in their sleeves. I returned the gesture. I did not approach or touch them. Their black garments repelled me, but not as much as the closed expressions that had hammered even greater lines into their faces than the years they had spent here. Once again the regret swept over me, that their fate had been for my gain. Of course it was Beatrice who spoke first, in a voice as smooth as whey, but not without a hidden malice.

'We do not see much of you here, Countess. We presume that your husband the Earl is not with you. Doubtless he is busy elsewhere.'

Which made me realise immediately that they were not as

isolated as I might have believed. I wondered how they gained their knowledge of the world outside these walls. The Church had a surprising network of information and gossip, it seemed.

'Yes, he is much occupied. He remains at the centre of affairs at Westminster. He had been with the King at Eltham earlier this year.'

What useless pieces of information. I was uneasy. I knew that they were judging me and Earl Mortimer. Why did their black-robed figures rob me of my usual confidence?

'Do you see nothing of him?' Maud asked, her pale eyes on my face in what might have been thought to be casual interest.

'Sometimes he visits. He has been to Clun, and to Leintwardine, where he has established the chantries to pray for the royal family as well as his own.'

'We know of that.' They exchanged glances. They reminded me of nothing so much as malign crows, plotting together. 'We hear the young Queen has been crowned at Westminster. Did you attend?'

'No.'

'It is said that she was heavily pregnant with her first child, and so much wearied by the ceremony. Perhaps she does not like the Dowager Queen taking precedence over her.'

Where was this leading? I felt my shoulders stiffen. We were still standing facing each other in the small chamber, but the distance between us was spiked with hostility.

'You know far more than I. Did the Dowager Queen take precedence? I doubt King Edward would have allowed it.'

Beatrice smiled, again all gentle spite. 'Perhaps he will banish her to some distant castle, or even a convent, as we were. He will want to rule his own household. But then of course, he does not. He can only do what the Earl of March allows him to do.'

I felt a need to support the young King.

'King Edward has reached his eighteenth year. He will rule his own roost now.'

Although I did not quite believe it. My sisters once again exchanged glances.

Beatrice stated: 'What we do not know, you might tell us. Has the bastard child been born?'

My fingers clenched beneath my cloak that I still wore in this chilly place. This was not generally talked about.

Maud added, her hand clutching her sister's robe as it used to do in the past: 'Or mayhap it died at birth?'

Beatrice smiled, if her baring of teeth could be called a smile. 'Did you know, dear sister, that the Queen Dowager carries your husband's child?'

'I do know it.'

'Did he tell you?'

'Yes.'

'Does it not worry you? Can you accept such flagrant adultery in the man for whom we were sacrificed and locked away here?'

It was like the thrust of a dagger between my ribs, but I kept my reply even and without judgement, either of my sisters or my husband.

'I have no choice but to accept it. What would you have me do? Howl from the battlements of Ludlow Castle? What good would that do except draw attention to the betrayal at the heart of my marriage.'

'Perhaps better than to silently accept.'

My patience fluttered out of my control like a wayward bird. 'Does the Prioress know that you indulge in such gossip?'

'Of course.' But I suspected a sly look in Beatrice's eyes. They did not often get the opportunity to use their knowledge as a weapon. Here was the perfect opportunity to cause distress. What cruel creatures they had become. 'It is not gossip but common knowledge. We learned that the Dowager Queen made a will settling some of her properties on Earl Mortimer late last year, in September, in fact. We doubt she is afraid of death. She is younger than we are, is she not?' Beatrice paused. 'Unless she feared death in childbirth, of course.'

How to turn the conversation into more seemly paths, ones which were not riven with painful holes into which they would push me to see me squirm.

'The Queen Dowager's child, alive or dead, is not my concern. Do you have need of anything?'

'No, sister.' Maud released Beatrice and took a step towards me. 'We are used to this life now. Once we hoped for freedom. Now it is too late. We suffer in winter from aching joints and sometimes difficulty in breathing, but we need nothing from you. Unless you have come here to buy our freedom from the Prioress? But of course you have not.'

Once she had been a gentle girl.

'I have left cloth for new habits,' I said. 'And money.'

Beatrice also smiled. 'We are eternally grateful.' Her smile widened. 'We also hear other rumours.'

I was determined not to ask. I waited, sensing that it was something that I would not enjoy.

'About the old King, the second Edward.'

I was puzzled. 'He is dead.'

'Are you certain, sister?'

'I attended his burial at the Priory Church in Gloucester. I saw his embalmed body. It was a magnificent ceremony.'

'Did you see his face?'

'No.'

They looked at each other.

'It may be that he is not dead. It may be that he is alive and incarcerated somewhere. The body you saw buried was no body at all. It was all a sham.'

I was perplexed. Why would they spread a rumour so outrageous?

'I do not believe it.'

'You may or may not, as you wish. Think of this, sister...' Beatrice's eyes shone with knowledge, looking strangely at odds with her ageing features. 'What if someone rescues him and wishes to restore him to his throne? He has the right to it.'

'Even if this were so – that he is still alive – the old King abdicated in favour of his son.'

'But did he do so willingly? What if there are those who would put him back on the throne with the crown on his head? What will the young King do about that? What will Earl Mortimer do?'

'I know nothing of this.' There was no use in continuing such a line of conversation. How vicious they had become. How bitter. 'I will leave you to your imaginings. I will come again in the summer when the roads are good for travel.'

'To what purpose? You can do nothing for us. We know more than you about what ails this realm. Most of it can be laid at Earl Mortimer's door.'

'And much of what you say is a tissue of scandalous lies and untruths.'

I walked to the door.

'Is it true,' Maud's final question, 'that he demands that all address him as Earl of March? Must you do so too when you meet? Has he grown so vast in self-importance?'

'Farewell, Countess,' Beatrice broke in as I opened the door, horrified at the unbridgeable gulf between me and my sisters. 'We hope that we have been of value to you. We are always pleased to serve the de Genevilles and the Mortimers. And something more for you to consider. If the old King still lives, does his son and heir know about it? I doubt that he will have been kept in ignorance. What does that say about our new King, the third Edward? Would he commit his father to everlasting imprisonment for the sake of his own power?'

'Ask Earl Mortimer about the secret inhabitant of Corfe Castle...' Maud added.

I left, with the briefest of farewells to the Prioress, more unsettled than I had been in months. Was it true? Was there some tale about the fate of the old King that I had missed? I remembered the funeral when I was aware of a tension in the air. But if he was imprisoned somewhere and the interment was all a mockery, who would know of it? It seemed not to be of general knowledge. How my sisters had picked up such a dangerous nugget of information I could not imagine, but the wings of the church were undoubtedly well-practised in carrying gossip. Who was buried in the tomb? Whose body had we venerated in Gloucester? If anyone knew, it would be Earl Mortimer.

The Earl of March would be at the centre of any such happening.

I turned my face homeward, regretful that I had come. Was it better to live in ignorance than in knowledge of such dire circumstances? My sisters had become like ill-wishing creatures. And then there was the child, the poor mite, born into such a disastrous complication of family and power.

The old King? I cast such a tale aside.

But if it were true, Roger must have had his hand in it.

And then that other question: did the young King know about the fate of his father, even as he had knelt to pray by his tomb during High Mass? Did Young Edward know? What a tangled web of deceit. I could see no way out of it that would not bring treachery and bloodshed. I could not see who would emerge from it alive. As for my sisters, I no longer knew them. I did not like what they had become. I had to admit to my own role in this. We all had guilt to bear.

On my return, for some reason, another whim, I stopped at my manor at Pembridge. The buildings were kept in good heart but it was a mistake to come here. I walked through the rooms, finding nothing but heartache. I stayed overnight but used one of the guest chambers rather than the one where Roger and I had shared our bridal night. It seemed a more comfortable thing to do.

When we were within sight of Ludlow, the castle a welcome sight, I pulled my mount to a standstill, simply to breathe and look at the place I called home. I would have to tell Lady Marguerite that she had been right in her denial of my visit. Whether to tell her the rumours, I did not know. Suddenly on my left there was a disturbance in the grass. A buzzard flew up, holding fast to a small rabbit that had fallen easy prey. I watched the lift of its wings, a common enough sight along the Marches. Then with raucous cries, there were two ravens, flying in to dare an attack, to snatch the prey for themselves. The buzzard, far larger, far more powerful, twisted and dipped, holding tight. The ravens persisted, diving, chivvying their adversary, until the buzzard dropped its prey and the ravens fell through the air to pick it up.

I had watched such battles often enough.

Today it had the hint of a dire prediction. The powerful bird of prey, outnumbered, overcome by those weaker but determined and acting together. Birds of ill omen. The buzzard did not die, but it lost the battle. I was unsettled anew.

Chapter Thirty-Eight

Ludlow Castle in the Welsh Marches, late March 1330

I arrived back at Ludlow to be met at the outer gatehouse by my steward, who came to hold my horse's head as I dismounted. I looked across towards an escort in the outer bailey that were still awaiting orders.

'Who is it?' I asked.

'Earl Mortimer. He has just ridden in, my lady.'

Once I might have hurried in immediately to welcome him. Now I did not. He would announce himself to me when he was ready. I walked into the inner bailey and into the living accommodations, where I took refuge before the fire in my solar as the day grew darker towards an early evening. It had been a long, cold journey, and a depressing one at that. This was a homecoming I did not wish for.

'Is the Dowager Queen with him?' I asked my steward when he brought me hot spiced wine and added logs to the fire.

'No, my lady.'

Well, that was a relief.

'Prepare the Earl's chambers, if you will.'

The Earl did not come. Time passed. What was he doing? I

stepped out of my chamber, listening for any conversations and movement. Nothing.

Curious, I strapped a pair of wooden pattens over my shoes, wrapped myself in a thick cloak, pulled up the hood and crossed the inner bailey and climbed the stairs to the top of the Great Tower, overlooking the outer bailey and the distant entrance. The escort had been dispatched to the stables and accommodations long since. All was quiet, all still, except for the guards on the wall-walk who exchanged inconsequential talk and acknowledged my presence with a salute. Where was Roger? Then I saw a flicker of light in the distance, across the width of the outer bailey, in the chapel of St Peter that he had had built to mark his escape from England. There were candles burning behind the windows. What had taken him there? And for so long?

I informed the guard on the gate – I had no wish to be the target of a stray arrow – and, accompanied by a page with a lantern, I crossed the space. My feet sounded crisp on the icy grass; the iron latch on the chapel door was cold to my touch. For some strange reason the whole made me uneasy. Softly I pushed the door ajar. Icy air enfolded me; the chapel was seemingly empty, only the low light burning before the altar. Someone had been putting out the array of candles, leaving only the altar illuminated. There was no priest that I could see. I did not use the chapel, preferring the older chapel in the inner bailey. This might be a place of God, but it was Roger's place too.

If not here, where was he? Clearly he did not wish to see me.

The slightest movement made me halt.

There he knelt, in the shadows, before the altar, alone with head bent, swathed in a dark cloak, his hat and gloves cast onto the floor beside him. I would not disturb him, but nor did I wish to leave. What had brought him here? What had caused his need to pray in this chapel of his own creation? I did not know what I would say to him, but I had no wish to leave him here without some communication. I waited by the door, which I closed very gently. Although there was no noise it caused the remaining altar-candles to flutter, so that he sensed a presence. He turned his head, his hand on his sword hilt. He was in fear, in his own castle. The fear transferred itself to me.

The Earl stood, flexing his shoulders as if they ached from some indiscernible strain, while I stepped forward so that he would see who it was that disturbed him.

'Johane.'

'Who else would it be?'

'A servant.' He shook his head. 'No one, of course, but you. They told me that you were not here.'

'I have been to my sisters in Aconbury. And then to Pembridge.' I would not talk about the sadness there. 'I see that you have been doing some rebuilding at the church where we wed. It seems that everything must be changed and branded with a Mortimer badge.' I walked slowly down the aisle towards him. 'What are you doing here? Asking for guidance? More building to enhance the Mortimer name?'

There was a faint breath of humour in his reply. 'I think I am beyond that.'

I did not think that I had ever heard him so despondent as was presaged in those few words.

'You have many enemies, I think.'

Compassion? No. I was beyond compassion, but still, we had lived so many years together.

'More numerous than the stars.' His voice across the divide between us had descended into harsh cynicism. 'There is nothing new in that to perturb me. When have I not had enemies?' As if he were persuading himself.

'But now they are massing against you.'

'Perhaps.'

'Tell me.'

'So that you can list all my nightmares, and announce them to those who are not my friends?'

He would not speak to me of his fears, even when he had been driven to his knees before God.

'Then keep silent. There is no compunction for you to tell me anything. Anything at all. By the by, it surprises me that you would know the difference between friends or enemies these days. How would you know one from the other?'

Roger laughed in response at my sharp tone.

'Thus speaks my conscience. I think that I will tell you as a punishment. But not in this place.'

And yet we did not move, standing with half the length of the nave between us.

'Where would be better than this?' I asked. 'God will be witness to what we say together. He will not reveal it to any man.'

Collecting a candle he walked slowly towards me so that I could see the grey in his hair, the lines heavily engraved between nose and mouth. I had the sense of fate stalking him. Then, as if it revealed too much, he doused the candle in the folds of his cloak and he was once more wrapped in dark shadows, lit only from behind by the candle remaining on the altar. It was a relief. What would he see in me? We were both growing older and the results were not flattering to either of us. In me he would read bitterness and despair, and a terrible lack of trust.

'Is it obligatory that I must now address you as Earl of March?' I asked. 'Must I curtsey in respect?'

I could sense the invisible curl of his lips. 'Is that what they say of me?'

'According to my sisters in the convent. That you insist on it. They are remarkably well informed. And I would believe them.

374

Your ambitions always knew no bounds, but I would never have believed that they would soar to these heights.'

'I do not feel like soaring at this moment. And you will doubtless call me Roger as you have always done.'

'You do not know what I have called you in the privacy of my solar.' Again I sensed his smile. 'Will you come there now?'

He shook his head.

'Then we remain here. There are questions I need to ask.'

How long ago it was. It came back to me, that I had asked two questions before my marriage. Was this man worthy of me? Was he good to look upon? How naive I had been, with no true idea of what the future would hold for me. Now my questions were far more dangerous ones.

'Then ask them.'

'What of the child? The child that Isabella carried for you?'

He looked down at his hands which were still holding the lightly smoking candle, perhaps so that I could not see his face. I thought that he would not answer.

'I know that you established another chantry at Leintwardine last month, in February, with a chaplain to pray for further members of your family,' I said. 'You named the Earl of Lincoln. There is no Earl of Lincoln, to my knowledge. Was that the new-born child? Did you think I would not know? That no one would find pleasure in telling me?'

I still could not see his face, his expression, even though I took another step forward. If there was grief it was well hidden from me.

'There is no Earl of Lincoln,' I repeated. 'Is this the title of the child?'

He looked up at me, his face ravaged. 'There is no child. It is dead. It died shortly after birth in the last month of last year.'

'Was it a son?'

'Yes. He would have been the Earl of Lincoln.'

'He was not buried at Wigmore Abbey with the rest of the Mortimers.'

That much I knew.

'No. He was not.'

He was not going to tell me where the child was laid to rest. How far apart we had come. How distant we now were. When Young Roger died he had held me in his arms while I mourned. When John had been killed, he had come to Wigmore Abbey to view his son's grave.

'I am sorry.'

'Are you?'

'Of course. For any child that slips from this life without breathing or without fulfilling his promise.'

And it was true, whatever the child's parentage.

'Thank you.'

I took the candle from him, walked to the altar where I relit it, and walked back again. I had had enough of his hiding his emotions. I held the candle so that it fell on his face.

'It will be a relief for King Edward that the child is dead.' How cruel I sounded, but there was honesty needed here between us. 'That he has no half-brother with Mortimer blood in its veins. A brother who might make a bid for the Crown in the fullness of time.'

It was as if I had struck him an open-handed blow. His face became ivory-pale beneath the grime of travel, and for a moment I wished that I had not illuminated him to any degree. Better to leave his feelings swathed in darkness. He took the candle from me but continued to hold it up, as if to make his feelings plain for all to see.

'Yes. You could say that this small death removed one problem.

Yet I regret it. And yes I have been to Leintwardine to change the arrangements there.'

'And does Isabella mourn the death of her child?'

'Of course. As you do. What mother would not?' There was a hint of anger as if he found me insensitive in asking the question. Why would Isabella not mourn her son? 'If that is all between us, Johane, it is time I found a chamber. I must leave early tomorrow. It is urgent that I return to Westminster. If you wish to deliver a litany of what is happening to our children, then it can wait...'

I was not in a mood to allow him to escape me. I had a second question that might just have repercussions for Roger and the whole realm. And for me too. I put out a hand to his sleeve to stop him from walking away.

'My sisters told me another dangerous fact. That the old King is not dead. He is a prisoner under your aegis. And don't just tell me what you wish me to know. Is it true?' He swung round. He had not expected this. This time the blow had been from an edged weapon. Exasperation dug his face into even deeper lines. 'I am waiting to see if you will tell me the truth,' I said.

'You saw him buried at Gloucester.'

'I saw a body interred in the Priory, yes. Is the second Edward still alive, however unrealistic it might seem?'

His chest moved as he inhaled deeply. His fist clenched once again on the hilt of his sword as if against some concealed enemy.

'Yes,' he said harshly. 'It is true, here in this place where there are no witnesses to my confession. How your sisters know, I can only guess at some gossiping cleric. Pray God their voices are not listened to. It is true. Edward is alive and well and locked behind strong walls.'

It took my breath.

'My sisters were indeed full of gossip! Corfe Castle? That is what they say.'

'Yes.'

'Does the King know?'

'Yes. He was told almost immediately after the announcement of his father's death. He knows.'

'Who told him? Was it you?'

'Yes.'

It was a plot then, that became darker and murkier with every admission.

'Does our young King support his father's imprisonment?'

'He does not like it, but yes. His power depends on it. His own crown depends on it.'

My next question must be asked. 'Does he despise you for what you have done?'

'I imagine that he does, but he'll not challenge me. His father's imprisonment is the source of his own authority. If it is made known that his father is still very much alive, what price on Young Edward's crown? He cannot afford to let it be known.'

I thought about this. How complex it had become, and the dangers for those who had constructed the plot if it were ever to be discovered.

'But did the old king not abdicate?'

'Yes, under – how shall I put it – persuasion. There are those who would restore him.'

'Such as the Earl of Lancaster and the Earl of Kent.'

'Particularly Lancaster and Kent. Their royal blood makes them susceptible.'

'What happens if he is released?'

'It is not my intention that he will be.'

'He will die in captivity?'

'Yes.'

It was so cold-blooded, so well constructed.

'Why do I feel that you are not telling me the whole?'

'I cannot afford for it to become public knowledge, Johane.'

'Am I likely to speak of anything you tell me here?'

'You might. Things have changed so much between us.'

'And whose fault is that? I'll take an oath if it pleases you.'

'There is no need.'

'What is it that is on your mind? Apart from keeping your own power intact and pleasing your mistress?'

Roger pushed his fingers through his hair in a gesture of utter frustration.

'It is this, and the whole may very well become known. The Earl of Kent, our present King Edward's uncle, has discovered his brother's existence in Corfe Castle. He is indeed plotting to release him and have him restored. I have seen the letter Kent had his wife write and send to imprisoned Edward. Kent is not without support in this.'

Thus it was told in plain language, cold-bloodedly bleak, in the shadows, light and shade moving across his face as the candle in my hand flickered in the draughts.

'That is what is on my mind,' he added.

'If this becomes known, you face the axe.'

'Yes. Unless I can turn the blame on Kent. He will be put on trial.'

'And you, of course, will prosecute.'

'I will.'

'And he will be found guilty.'

'Indeed.'

'The question is...'

'I know what the question is.'

'The question is, will the King step into this conspiracy with you? Will he agree to the death of his uncle Kent, rather than admit that his father is alive?'

'If he admits that he knows of his father's existence, he condemns himself.'

'If Kent is found guilty you will have him executed.'

'Yes. He will be accused of treason, attempting to bring down the rule of the present King by restoring the old one.'

A silence fell between us, a ripple of concern over my skin. A weight of fear in my chest.

'You are indeed in danger.'

'Thus I was seeking consolation, here in my own chapel.'

He gestured towards the altar where the final candle was guttering, while I was considering even more worrying repercussions. Suddenly a new anxiety had reared its head. Something I had not considered. Something that I should have given thought to.

'You do realise— When the truth of this becomes known at Court— Because is it not inevitable— Your visits here, your conversations with me, however innocent they might be, merely dealing with family matters, they will paint me with the same brush of treason that coats you from nape to heel. King Edward will presume that I am involved as well, that I knew all about the old King's false death. If he chooses to punish you – which we both know he will when he can seize the right opportunity – he will punish me too. You will accuse me of utter selfishness, but do I have to suffer again for your actions? I spent five years incarcerated for my marriage to you. I will not do that again.'

I watched him as he stood silently before me, as I considered my final statement.

'Don't come here to Ludlow again. Don't talk to me. I do not wish to be involved with what you are planning. I do not wish to be suspected of being involved.'

For a moment I thought he looked hurt. That he cared that I had rejected him.

'If that is your wish.' His mouth twisted in wry recognition of my fear.

'It is. Unless it is a family matter which cannot be questioned, stay away. Being your wife has suddenly become far too dangerous again.'

Roger shook his head, once more in control, once more the master of his fate.

'I will assure King Edward that the treason is mine. You and I are not plotting together. You are an innocent party, caught up in events. If Edward decides to instigate any retribution against me, of course.'

'Which he will.'

'Unless I am very clever.'

'Surely you do not think that you can hold the truth back once it is known by even a few? It will be like water rushing over a waterfall to drown all below. You cannot win in this gamble with fate, Roger.'

'I do not see that. But whatever happens, you will not suffer again for my actions, Johane. You lost so many years to imprisonment for me, and suffered the endless fears that you might never be released. If I have any regrets in all this, it is that you have been caught up in my schemes, as you would call them.'

'Thank you. It eases my mind wonderfully. You might also regret that you broke my heart and it can never be mended.'

'Forgive me, Johane. Forgive me if you can.'

Taking a step forward, he took my hand; the touch of his lips tingled with memories of the past, and I let it lie in his grasp. Indeed I returned his clasp in the echo of that simple expression of contrition.

'You go back to Westminster tomorrow, to reshape your destiny,' I said.

'Something like that.' He sought in the breast of his tunic and withdrew a gold chain from which was depended a golden lozenge. 'Once I gave you a heart to express my love. God knows what you have done with it! Beaten it to pieces under your heel, perhaps. But now I would wish to give you this, if you will accept it. It is an amulet to guard against harm.'

'Since when did you believe in such magic?'

I was astonished that he would even consider such a thing.

'Since you are in fear of the future and I owe you so much.' He manipulated it for me with his clever fingers. 'There is a small space in which you might place leaves of St John's Wort for protection. The stone is a sapphire that also has protective powers. Will you take it and wear it in the hope that it will guard against harm from any who might attack you?'

I regarded it, a tiny but beautifully carved gold box set at one apex with a sapphire.

'I trust that Isabella did not have a hand in this,' I said, my reply as chilly as the air around us. 'If so, take it back.'

'No. The decision is mine and I acquired it for you. Will you wear it?' he repeated.

'Your mother would say that silver is a better medium for an amulet, but yes, I will pack it with St John's Wort and I will wear it. Even though you broke my heart past mending.'

He opened my fingers, placed a kiss on my palm, then closed my hand over the little amulet.

'I would ask one boon of you. You are the only one who might fulfil it.'

'Then ask.'

'Whatever the future might hold, there will come a time when I will meet my death, one way or another. Will you bring my body home to Wigmore Abbey so that I might lie with my ancestors?'

A cold hand of some unforeseen destiny curled its fingers around my heart, even though I had lived with this fear for so long now. He foresaw his death. It would be so easy to fold him into my arms and offer solace.

We were both past such intimacy. Instead, I responded to his request as I must.

'I will do it. Come now. You need sustenance before you ride out.'

He did not demur when I led him back to my solar and gave him a cup of ale before the fire. When I returned from sending a servant to prepare his chamber, he had fallen asleep, his head against the chair-back. How weary he looked in the firelight, how strained. Not as much at ease as he would have me think; there were hard shadows beneath his eyes. In the end I woke him, shaking his arm, tempted to smooth his hair that had fallen over his forehead, but I did not.

'You must sleep if you will be fit to ride tomorrow.'

'Then we will say farewell now. I will be gone before you wake.'

Yet I was awake and watched him leave, without further conversation, for what more was there to say between us? I watched him go from the heights of the Great Tower Keep, riding out with his escort, Mortimer banners flying provocatively. He was playing with fire. Around my neck, beneath my under-gown, I wore the gold amulet, yet the little space was still empty of protective herbs.

It was raining heavily, the clouds sweeping away the frost. I stood in the rain and watched, water dripping from my hood, until he and his escort were swallowed up in cloud. There was no lifting of spirits for me, fearing that one day all would indeed be revealed, and Roger would no longer be able to thwart fate's heavy hand. A thundercloud of retribution was approaching fast. All I had of him was an amulet and the impression of his lips against my palm. As for the little brooch that he had given me on our wedding day, I had not destroyed it. I knew where it was kept. I would never wear it again.

Would I ever see him again? Where would all this end for him?

I did not know.

It was Geoffrey, my ever-useful source of Court information, who told me of the outcome of the Kent plot; his frequenting the Court at his father's side would ensure that he knew what was afoot. I allowed him to tell me the details, not revealing that I already knew most of it, and that in so knowing, I was indeed to some extent involved and complicit, although an innocent holder of that knowledge.

'Should I worry?' I asked my son. 'Should you worry?' It would be good to get Geoffrey's view of the turning of Court wheels. Roger was hardly an unbiased source of information. 'Will your father's enemies turn their attentions to his family?'

'I think so. It's dangerous enough, if the old King is still alive and kept under guard in Corfe Castle. My father must be involved.'

He looked at me, to see what my reaction would be. I kept a calm and disbelieving demeanour and shook my head. It could be in my best interests to claim ignorance of all such doings.

'Is this true?'

'So it seems. And there has been a plot by the old King's half-brother Edmund, Earl of Kent, to release the old King and restore him.'

Here was the core of it. 'Will such a plot be successful? I

asked, all innocence. 'And if so, what would happen to your father?'

Geoffrey sat down beside me and puffed out a breath, but whether from relief that I was so unemotional or concern that I might still weep on his shoulder I could not tell.

'We will never know. The Earl has taken it upon himself to ensure that it never happens.'

I noticed that Geoffrey had taken to calling his father the Earl.

'What has he done with Kent?'

'The Earl of Kent is dead.'

Now this I did not know. Roger had taken punitive action to preserve his own safety, and that of the Dowager Queen. I must not forget that. He was protecting Isabella as much as himself. Had I expected Kent to die? I did not think so.

'Executed,' Geoffrey continued. 'On false charges in a trial over which Earl Mortimer presided.'

As I had thought. Playing with fire. Would this not meld his enemies together against him?

'Did King Edward agree to it?'

'Yes. He was not in a position to do much else. I think he is not satisfied, but he agreed to his uncle's execution.' Geoffrey's nose wrinkled in disgust. 'They found it hard to engage a man who was willing to commit the foul deed.'

'The King must hate it.'

'Yes.'

'He must hate your father, too, for putting him in that invidious position.'

It would be interesting to know if Geoffrey was aware of the King's guilt.

'That too. It makes it clear that the young King knew that his father's death and burial was all a mummer's play, that he was willing to take his place in the sham events. Whatever the guilt, Kent is dead, the old King is still a prisoner and the young King Edward is secure.'

'And your father?'

'He still holds the reins of power in his very capable, but many would say immoral, hands.'

All Roger's planning had fallen into line as he had wished, but there was a deep chasm etched between Geoffrey's brows. I stretched out and placed my hand over his where it rested on his knee.

'Tell me what you think.'

'None of the English lords will feel safe. The court that the Earl set up to try Kent was a travesty.'

'And so?'

'I think that ... I think that the Earl's days of power are numbered.'

There it was. Roger's fears, and mine, confirmed by our son.

'Will it happen?'

'Only if King Edward will support my father's overthrow. And of course he will. To silence the Earl, remove his power and also silence his mother, who can be dispatched to a convent. Edward really has nothing to lose if he decides to stir a rebellion against the Earl. There are enough young lords who will support him.'

'Except for his part in the imprisonment and false burial of his father becoming known.'

Geoffrey shrugged. 'It can all be managed, I expect. I have little hope that the Earl will survive this.'

Neither did I.

'Your father is his own man and will pave his own path.' I brought our exchange of views to a close. 'Even if it takes him to the executioner's axe.'

When Geoffrey had departed in lugubrious fashion, I walked

over to the chapel in the outer bailey which held no comfort for me. I remembered Roger kneeling before the altar. He had seen the future, a sickening realisation that struck at me too. Too many enemies, too much fear. To remove Roger would be the priority of many, and I could do nothing to stand in the way of fate. He was guilty of imprisoning the old King, of lying to the country; now he was guilty of the death of the Earl of Kent. How much blame could be heaped upon his head? I too should condemn him for his wilful action. How difficult it was, even through all the pain of his betrayal. He had abandoned me and yet the ties of the past, of duty and of children, were still there and too strong to be denied. It seemed to me to be impossible to cut them loose so that I could turn my back on Roger's doings and announce to the world that I did not care. When I knelt where Roger had knelt, no words came to me other than the obvious ones.

'Blessed Virgin, have mercy. On all of us.'

Chapter Thirty-Nine

Ludlow Castle in the Welsh Marches, late October 1330

Rumours. There were always rumours. Even though I closed my mind to them, they still battered at my hard-won serenity.

The King was dead.

The Earl of March had taken the crown for himself.

The Dowager Queen had given birth to another half-royal son who was fully royal if we now had a King Roger.

I swore that I would ignore them all until I had evidence of any occurrence that would change my life in Ludlow. I gave no credence to any gossip, not even the travellers who claimed personal knowledge. As far as I knew the royal Court was in Nottingham, all alive and well but with no half-royal child to stir the warm pottage into a boiling fury. There was nothing to concern me. Roger doubtless was continuing his vicious onslaught against those who would displace him. King Edward was alive and well and in possession of the crown.

What I did know was that my husband had disinherited the heirs of our old family ally, Roger Mortimer of Chirk, taking the lands for himself. Nothing would stand in his way. Not even kinship. How could he be so blind to the army of enemies that he was creating?

Despite all my good intentions I felt directionless, restless, my mind plagued with faceless fears that any attack on Roger would also encompass me and our children. I had proof enough from the past that I would be an easy target. I arranged a visit to Wigmore Abbey, travelling alone except for my escort, in the comfort of a litter. The graves of my two sons Roger and John were now complete, needing no more attention from me, yet it was in my mind to visit them and remember my sons in my prayers. How ridiculous, I decided, that I received more comfort from the dead than from the living.

Welcomed by the Abbot, who expressed less knowledge than I of what might be occurring in the country, we walked to where the Mortimer graves were ranked and the effigies of the two young men were newly carved, the edges sharp, the features clear. One day they would be as worn and blurred as the old Mortimer warriors who lay beside them, but today they had a likeness to the two children I had carried and loved. I touched their faces, smoothing my hand over cheek and brow of them as young men, then down over the stone folds of the surcoat which covered the armour in which they were clothed.

The Abbot invited me to drink wine with him while we discussed Mortimer matters and I went readily, enjoying the peace of the cloister where some monks sat in silent contemplation, in the warmth before winter set in.

But here was a courier riding hard.

'My lady. My lady.'

He flung himself from his horse at the door, ran around the cloister-walk and dropped to his knees at my feet. How many times in my life had a courier brought news, either good or bad? Momentarily I cast my mind over the past. The dire wounding of Roger's father. Young Roger's death. My hovering imprisonment. There was little that could disturb me now other than an affliction of one of my children. The Abbot helped the man to his feet in kindly fashion in spite of his disturbing the silence of this holy place.

'Tell me it is not one of my children who ails,' I demanded, quelling the faint flutter of fear in my belly.

'I know nothing of your children, my lady. It is my lord the Earl. He is in dire need.'

The flutter acquired sharp teeth, until good sense took hold and I touched his dust-covered arm.

'Why have you come to me? I have no power to do anything to help Earl Mortimer. Why have you not carried your request to the Dowager Queen? Or even the King?' My first thought; my only thought. That Roger had been encouraged to participate in a tournament and been thrown from his horse. 'He is wounded?' I asked. 'What can I do to remedy that?'

I was not motivated to abandon my conversation with the Abbot and the tranquillity of the Abbey. What I could do about it I could not think. If he were injured, a physician would serve the purposes. I had a sudden flash of memory of John's wounds in the tournament in Shrewsbury when there was nothing that could be done by anyone, other than mourn his death as he lay on the floor at my feet, his life-blood draining away. There were well-educated men who would minister to Roger at Court. I did not even know where he might be at this moment. Westminster, I presumed, if his business in Nottingham had come to an end. He would be given all necessary care without my intervention. So far he had led a charmed life.

'Was it a tournament?' A different thought crossed my mind. 'Or the blade of an assassin?'

Roger had made enough enemies in the past three years. It might be that he was already dead.

'Neither, my lady.' The courier had regained his breath and

clutched his felt hat in his hands to the detriment of its shape. I noticed that his knuckles were white. 'He is taken prisoner by the King.'

'Prisoner?'

The talons returned, sharper than before as the words streamed out, a litany of fire and destruction.

'He is like to die as a traitor, my lady. The King accuses the Earl of treason. He demands vengeance for all the sins Earl Mortimer has committed against him.'

The Abbot was forgotten. It had come at last. Had I not warned him? King Edward was now old enough and ambitious enough to rid himself of the man who had controlled his power and his life for too long. Edward was no longer the malleable youth who would enjoy jousting as Sir Lionel. He would wear the crown and seize the power that accompanied it as the mighty King Arthur. To achieve that, Roger Mortimer, the powerful Earl of March, must be removed and dispatched for good. Roger was a prisoner and his life liable to be forfeit. His life was indeed in danger.

Suddenly I was cold, so cold that it was difficult to find words.

'Who sent you here?' I managed. 'Why have you come to tell me?'

The courier exchanged a glance with the Abbot.

'Sir Geoffrey de Mortimer sent me, my lady. He thought that you should know.'

Geoffrey.

'Of course. I recognise you. You are one of Geoffrey's men. You do not wear Mortimer livery.'

'Dangerous to do so, my lady, in this climate!'

'What can I do?' I asked of no one in particular. Never had I felt so helpless. When I had first heard of Roger's adultery, at least then I had been moved by intense fury. Now I could see nothing of the future, feel no emotion other than dread. From Geoffrey's courier there was no reply. He looked at me, willing me to take control. Even the Abbot looked aghast, murmuring the need for prayers.

'Prayers will not keep him from a traitor's death!' I said, with less than my usual courtesy. My mind began to work again. 'Has the Dowager Queen made a plea for his release?'

'So it is said, my lady.'

'Which the King rejected.'

'Aye, he did. It is said that the Queen Dowager is in custody too.'

'So what can I do?' I repeated although I began to breathe easily again, clutching at what seemed a realistic outcome to this disaster. 'I am flattered that you think I would have any influence with the King in this matter. Besides, when his temper has calmed he will forgive and reinstate the Earl. I think my son's fears are not well grounded.' I did not think that Edward was a man of blood, and Philippa would persuade him to have mercy. 'Go back to Sir Geoffrey, and you will find that all has been resolved.'

Roger had many enemies, but likewise, did he not have powerful friends? My heart began to beat steadily again after the first shock.

'No, my lady.'

'No?' I was not used to servants disagreeing with me.

'It is far more serious than that, my lady.'

'Then you must tell me.' I drew him into the Abbot's chamber, the Abbot following as if he expected me to sink senseless to the floor in the face of such dire news. 'You must sit.' I realised for the first time how weary the courier was as I pushed him towards a stool. I was becoming hard-hearted over the years. 'Tell me what you know.'

I was drawn into events in Nottingham as the man forgot his audience and described all he knew in crude detail of Roger's arrest in the castle at Nottingham by those who feared for their own lives and power under Earl Mortimer's hard-fisted regime. He was overpowered, bound and gagged, his associates cut down without mercy. The edifice of power that Earl Mortimer had created was destroyed in that one well-planned attack in which King Edward had at last reclaimed his birthright.

'Dowager Queen Isabella's entreaties are ignored,' he finished. 'She is taken to Leicester where she is kept under restraint. All is uncertain. Sir Geoffrey says I must advise you to come to Leicester. The King considered hanging Lord Mortimer out of hand, but it is thought that he will be put on trial. He has taken Earl Mortimer to Leicester too.'

I looked at the Abbot.

'What do I do? Would my presence in Leicester have any value?'

'You do what your heart tells you, my lady.'

'I have no recognisable heart. It was broken into pieces years ago.'

'We have a duty to the head of the Mortimer family,' he admonished gently.

'Even if they have committed treason?' I turned away. 'What has happened to Sir Geoffrey?' I asked the courier.

'I know not.'

'Will there be a trial for Earl Mortimer?'

'I know not.'

I sighed. 'You know very little of the future, but how can I expect that you should? Thank you for your forbearance. Go and take food and rest.' I turned to the Abbot. 'He is still my husband in the sight of God, so it behoves me to go and discover for myself, and do what I can to save his worthless life, if there is anything within my limited power. I may be powerless, but it feels wrong that I should sit behind my walls at Ludlow and wait to hear the outcome. I will go to Leicester.'

I returned to Ludlow to collect some hastily assembled garments, a lady-in-waiting and an escort without Mortimer colours, deciding that with speed essential I would ride astride. I took Geoffrey's courier with me. We had journeyed east for a very short distance when my path was crossed by a young man instantly recognisable with his heraldic achievements in red and silver. There was no danger for him to travel so ostentatiously. This was the young knight Sir William Montagu who had once taken issue with Roger at King Edward's coronation, warning him of the power of those who would grow to hate him. He stopped and removed his cap in a courteous acknowledgement.

'I see that the news has reached you, my lady.'

'It has. I did not think you to be a friend of Mortimer, to carry such news to me.'

'Nor am I, but King Edward thought that you should be aware. He has sent me to tell you. Not that he has any compassion for your situation, but if you should be travelling to see your husband, it is London for you, my lady. Although I doubt that you will be allowed to see him. You should know. King Edward now has no curbs on his power.'

'My thanks for the warning.' I might despise the show of empty pity, but I would make use of the information. 'What is the King's intent?'

'He was persuaded not to execute Mortimer on the spot when he was taken prisoner in Nottingham. He considered it, and who could blame him, but instead Earl Mortimer will be put on trial.'

'For treason?'

'What else? You must have known the day would come. The

King has drawn up a list of accusations to be made against him, in the presence of the magnates of the realm. You should be warned. It is a list of severe crimes that I think no man could withstand.'

'I still do not see the King as a man of bloody reprisals.'

The young knight was reluctant to dispute the matter with me. 'Better to eat the dog than to be eaten by the dog,' he said.

'I understand what you say.' Then on a thought, dragging my mind from Roger's uncertain future: 'What can you tell me of Sir Geoffrey Mortimer?'

'Arrested too, my lady.'

'And Dowager Queen Isabella?'

'I know not now. Initially her son the King placed her under guard in her chamber.'

I sighed. 'Thank you, Sir William.' He was no older than my sons, but the bearer of the worst of news. 'I fear I can do nothing, but sit helplessly in Ludlow I cannot. Will you ride with me?' Did I read pity in his gaze? I would make use of it. 'I do not ask that you will be an amenable companion, merely a force to ward off Mortimer enemies.'

'And I am not an enemy?'

'That is for you to choose, Sir William.'

I knew well how to be charmingly manipulative. I got my own way.

Chapter Forty

On the road to London, October 1330

He turned and rode with me, a stalwart young man with a stern brow, at odds with his angelically fair hair, or what could be seen of it curling from the brim of his hat. From a powerful magnate family, he was I knew the closest of all King Edward's youthful friends. Whatever it was that I needed to know, Sir William would be able to tell me. If he were willing, of course. I smiled on him, intent on persuading him of my innocence.

'I must be grateful that the King was willing to send you to keep me informed of my husband's delicate position.'

He did not quite smirk. 'I would not have thought it necessary, given your alienation from the Earl. I think his present situation is more than delicate. It is desperate.'

'And yet it would please me, Sir William, and would pass the time, if you told me the accusations against Earl Mortimer.'

A sideways glance was all I thought I was going to get, until he relented.

'There are many.'

'Do what you can, Sir William.'

He took a breath and began to list them, building a creation of treason that surely no man could survive, that would take Earl Mortimer to the scaffold. 'He gave himself the title of Earl of March. He used his power to grant himself, his family and his friends land and castles, after enriching himself with money and jewels from the Treasury. He appropriated the twenty thousand marks paid by the Scots for their sovereignty. Raising money for a Gascon war through a parliamentary grant, he spent it on himself. He appropriated fines and ransoms from knights who did not wish to fight in the Gascon war, a war that never happened anyway.'

And yet... all reprehensible, forsooth. My spirits had lifted slightly.

'Does it sound like treason to you? Does not any man in power make his own wealth? Your accusations have not included one attack on royal power or the person of the King.'

It was bad. Such an accumulation of money and power in Roger's hands, but did it demand his death? Greed yes, but not treason.

'There are worse accusations, my lady.'

'Then you must tell me of those too.'

Sir William's words now began to bite, accusation after accusation as if learned by rote.

'He ignored the King's advisors in the Royal Council and took royal power and government in his own hands. Who was it who had the late King Edward removed from Kenilworth and had him murdered in Berkeley Castle? He forced the present King to march against his royal uncle the Earl of Lancaster. Luring the Earl of Kent into a treasonable plot, he thus ensured his death, removing yet another royal uncle. Is that not treason?'

He paused. I feared that it was.

ANNE O'BRIEN

'Do go on. Is that the sum total?'

'Is it not enough? He is accused of surrounding the King with his own knights and men-at-arms, with the result that the King has been wilfully encircled by men who are his enemies. When they were together at Nottingham, Mortimer ordered that he should be obeyed in all things. Is that not treason, when he has no claim on royal blood? King Edward was thrust to the very periphery of his royal authority. As if he did not exist.'

'Peace. I have heard enough.'

These accusations had become more lethal, filling me with dread. King Edward would now believe that he was fighting for his survival. If this were all true, then he had no intention of allowing Roger to escape justice. The list was all-encompassing. Treason indeed, to attack royal power. Roger had acted as if he were King of England.

'They are a terrible indictment of his life,' Sir William stated. 'He cannot expect Edward's forgiveness. Do not expect it, my lady. It might be better if you returned home now.'

'I understand what you say, but I have a need to continue to Westminster.'

'So you still have a care for his life, my lady? After everything?'

'You are too young and untried to understand my answer to that question, Sir William.'

'All I can say is that he deserves any punishment doled out to him.'

I was reduced to silence. Dowager Queen Isabella had failed in her bid for clemency. Would Edward listen to me? If he would not listen, Roger would die.

The Royal Palace of Westminster, October 1330

Sir William delivered me to Westminster, where it proved to be a heart-rending end to the journey that was as long and wearying as any I had travelled. Nevertheless I made myself known.

'I am Lady Mortimer. I am here to request an interview with the King. If he will grant it, in his mercy.'

It was my decision not to announce myself as Countess of March.

I had already been refused access to my husband, once more locked in the Tower, but then I had not expected any less than an outright refusal. Nor did I have much in the way of hope that Edward would be open to my request to appeal directly to him. Yet I must try, or why was I here? I might as well be far to the west in the Marches, awaiting the news of an agonising death. Now I waited in an empty and draughty antechamber in the Palace of Westminster, deciding that I must find accommodation. I could be here for some days, unless an intemperate King refused me out of hand, and banished me back to the Marches.

I had all but given up hope – how ignominious if my request were simply ignored – when a page in royal livery emerged from the direction of the royal chambers.

'Lady Mortimer.' He bowed neatly, and I recognised the early lessons in chivalric behaviour such as had been delivered to my own sons. He was very young and stiffly courteous but he would learn. 'My lord the King will see you. You are to come with me.'

I was shown into a small private chamber, the walls glowing with what I imagined were the King's favourite tapestries rioting with fanciful birds and flowers and chivalric knights about to engage in conflict. With a love of outward show and luxury, today he was clad in garments more fit for a day at ease, in sharp

399

contrast with when I had seen him last at Wigmore when he was full of his victory in the tournament, clothed in his flowing Arthurian surcoat as Sir Lionel. Since then a line had grown between his brows, and his lips were stern with no hint of a softness in welcome. Much water had passed under the bridge for this young King since Sir Lionel had ridden in the lists. Would I fail before I had even opened my mouth? I thought so but I would do what I could.

I braced my knees, swallowed against the dryness in my throat, and managed a formal curtsey.

'I did not expect to see you here, Lady Mortimer.'

'You were kind enough to send William Montagu as your courier, my lord, to deliver the bad news. How could I not respond?'

He frowned at me, but it was an expression of astonishment rather than disapproval.

'What do you hope to achieve? Do you believe that you owe Mortimer any debt? He betrayed you, lady. I would say that you owed him nothing.'

And there was the crux of it. My reply was clear, worked out through the long journey.

'I owe him all my children, who have brought me joy. I owe him years of contentment before his initial arrest and exile by your father. He bestowed on me care and happiness and, for many years, a depth of love that I could not doubt. Many women cannot experience even half as many blessings in their marriage as I have, my lord.'

'Which he then destroyed through lust and weakness. And an overwhelming desire for power which drove him to take what was not his, to seize and hold.'

I gave neither assent nor denial. It was true. Instead:

'What do I hope to achieve? Mercy, my lord. I am here to beg for clemency.'

'What a worthless word that is,' Edward replied without hesitation. 'I am in no mood to dispense clemency. I am in no mood to be generous to a man who stole my birthright and waged war against members of my own family.'

I took a breath and tried again. This was a risk.

'Do you not have the power, my lord? Do you not have the power to withstand the demands of Earl Mortimer's enemies who will clamour for his death?' I hesitated then risked another plea. 'In the name of your new-born son, can you not find it in your heart to grant freedom? Dispossess Earl Mortimer, banish him, but do not bring him to his death. In your son's eyes, as he grows, he will mould himself on your example, as a man of the noblest character.'

Now the frown spoke of disapproval of my reasoning.

'I have the power. It may be that my voice in the demand for Mortimer's death is the loudest in the clamouring. Have you considered that?'

'I have considered it. Do I not understand the sins that were committed against you? But do you not have the potential greatness to hold out the hand of mercy? Once Lord Mortimer was the most loyal of subjects. It was only the attacks by Despenser against his lands that drove him into rebellion. If you were prepared to win him over, he would be loyal again.'

It was the weakest of arguments as I well knew. So did the King.

'I find that impossible to believe. Those days are long gone, when Mortimer would be content with mere loyalty to a King. Why would I pardon the man with so heavy a hand in the death of my father?'

I would say it. I would risk all and break this spell of fulsome blame. I looked up to where the King stood on a shallow dais with his hand gripping the carved back of his chair, and I held his furious stare.

'Do we not both know, my lord, that your father is not dead? Have you not been complicit in the hiding of such a critical act? Your uncle of Kent knew of it. So did Earl Mortimer. Whose was the blame in consigning the second Edward to Corfe Castle and creating a mockery of an interment in Gloucester Cathedral, to which we all came and bowed the knee? We talk of blame here today. Are you not as complicit as Earl Mortimer?'

There was a terrible shattering of the rich ambience in that beautiful room. Even the expertly stitched knights seemed to wait for the reply, while I continued to hold the royal gaze even as my limbs trembled at my daring to speak such words.

'I knew nothing of it! I knew nothing until it was done!'

'But you did nothing to put it right, in your living father's name, my lord. You were willing to leave him there at Corfe for the sake of the crown on your own head. We are not all blameless, my lord, in this world of political manoeuvring and power-grabbing. Earl Mortimer is not the only culprit.' I took a breath. 'You would be remembered as a King of wisdom and greatness if you held out your hand to him. Of valour in the face of your enemies.'

The King shook his head. 'You cannot expect me to accept any blame in my father's fate. It was not done by my consent.' He held up his hand to silence me. 'I have many years in which to earn that accolade of greatness, and I will strive to do so. You have made your plea, Lady Mortimer, and I admire you for it, but I must reject it.'

'Is there no hope?'

'No. Mortimer will face trial.'

'May I see him?'

'No. It would not be appropriate.'

'What of my son Geoffrey? You have imprisoned him too. What is his crime?'

Edward allowed himself a faint smile.

'He has none, except as his father's son. I cannot afford to allow him freedom to rescue Mortimer. You may see him. He is in the Tower. I have no objection to your visit.'

'Is he on trial too?'

'It is not my intent. Or not so far.'

It was a threat. A minor one, but still a threat. The King turned his back on me, walking towards the window so that the light gilded his fair hair right royally as with a holy corona. When he turned back, I could no longer see his expression, but I heard the edge in his voice. I had not expected it.

'I should warn you, Lady Mortimer. I am not entirely convinced of your own innocence.'

'I have never been anything but a loyal subject, my lord. You are unjust.'

'We will see. You now have my leave to retire.'

Which I did with a silent inclination of my head. He was young enough to be my son, but how much fatal power he wielded. How barricaded he was against any of my arguments. What hope was there? None that I could see.

Taking the only path open to me I cast myself on the mercy of Philippa, who was beaming over the cradle of her new son, another Edward, now a good four months old. I had no difficulty in gaining access to her private chambers, where she smiled a welcome which eased my heart a little and invited me to sit at her side, where I sank onto the cushioned stool, aware of how content Philippa looked in her adoration of her new son. I stretched out my hand to touch the child's fingers, smiling in spite of everything when he opened his eyes and curled his hand around my thumb.

'I am here, my lady...'

'I know why you are here,' Philippa broke in. 'I admire that you would travel so far for the man who rejected you so recklessly, without thought for your feelings.'

'My conscience says that I must. Those I most dearly love in this world are my children. You will understand that. You feel the same intense love for this little one. Earl Mortimer is their father. I owe him something.'

Her smile had become strained.

'I understand. Children are a great comfort. But sometimes the actions of their father is beyond the realms of human forgiveness, whatever the Church might preach. I cannot forgive your husband. I cannot help you.'

'No. I don't suppose that you can.' Had I not known it from the start? 'You were my last hope, my lady.'

How young she was, but how clear-sighted.

'He cannot be allowed to live. He is too dangerous. He cannot be trusted. I must give all my support to the King, my husband.'

'What of exile?' I asked. 'Is that not possible?'

'You know the answer to that. He has family abroad who could be persuaded to support him to raise another insurrection.'

Of course I knew that.

'He returned once with great success. Would he not try again if he could raise an army from our enemies in Europe? Imprisonment is equally fragile for a man who can still hold men's loyalties. The King cannot be forever looking over his shoulder because Mortimer is alive.'

I wondered if Philippa was aware of the second Edward's existence. I thought that she would be. The King would keep nothing from her, but then he was the recipient of all her loyalty.

'What of Dowager Queen Isabella?' I asked.

Philippa's brief laugh was harsh. 'Well, there's the contrary argument, Lady Mortimer. She cannot be allowed to die. She is Edward's mother and thus has earned a place in the realm.'

'What will you do with her?'

Would she be honest with me?

'She will be stripped of all power. She will live comfortably, not as a prisoner. She will be allowed to come to Court and visit us and her grandchildren, but perhaps not as frequently as she might wish. I will not have her treading on my heels. She has caused enough damage to the security of this realm. My lord Edward also deserves a little peace from his mother's dabblings.'

It seemed unfair that Isabella should be treated so leniently, but I accepted the reasoning and recognised the shine of malice in the Queen's lambent gaze. A silence fell between us, except for a cry of frustration from the baby in the crib. Philippa immediately put out her hand to rock the babe into quietness.

'The King does not trust me,' I said. 'I do not deserve that.'

'I know. When time passes, he will come to accept that a wife does not always share the sins of her husband. Until then you will have to accept that he will give you no redress. And I cannot speak for you.'

A chilling thought.

'What do I do now?' Although I knew the answer.

'Go back to Ludlow and let events play out here. That is what you *should* do. But I know you won't. Neither would I in your shoes. You will remain here until all is at an end for your husband.'

'Yes.' I returned her gaze. 'I would ask one boon.'

'I know what it is. That you might see him. I will try. Edward will refuse but I might find a way.'

'Thank you.'

'It will do no good, you know. It will not give Earl Mortimer hope, and you will suffer more.'

'Yet I feel that I owe it to him. The last thing I do for him.' I tried a smile but it was only a sad twist of the lips. 'I will not help him to escape, I assure you. I know that this is the end.'

'We will give you accommodation here, until that end is accomplished.'

Accomplished. It sounded like a creation rather than a destruction of a life.

Chapter Forty-One

The Tower of London, October 1330

I was fetched after dark from the chamber with which I had been provided close to the royal apartments, luxuriously appointed, a terrible contrast with the cell inhabited by my husband. A man whose allegiance could not be detected in his dark clothes and close-fitting hood stood at the door. He addressed me without name or title.

'Wear a cloak with a hood and wooden pattens. Silence is of the essence. Do not speak but follow closely. Wear nothing of value. You do not need your maid.'

I knew where I was going and silently blessed Philippa for her intervention, one wife to another. Whether Edward knew what had been done in his name I knew not. It did not matter. What had it taken for her to arrange this for me, when she would privately wish Earl Mortimer to hell with the speediest dispatch? Yet she had done it.

I was led through dark corridors, down steps until we reached the river where a boat awaited me. The tide was with us although I had never realised how unnerving it was to be rowed in the black of night along the Thames. There was no moon, the clouds heavy, blotting out all light even from the stars. There was no lantern on the boat, the rower finding his way by instinct and experience. Eventually the bulk of the Tower loomed on our left and I was taken to the quay where my escort helped me out.

More steps, more corridors, until a door was unlocked and I was allowed to enter. There were no windows, the room dark and damp with the stench of imprisonment, and almost as black as the night on the river. There would be no opportunity to escape from this confinement, as had once been achieved. The King was determined that the prisoner would stand trial and face justice. But then, who would help to rescue Roger Mortimer now? I could not name one friend who would come to his aid. If I ever hoped for some mercy in the end, this cell destroyed it. I could barely see him, only aware of a shuffle of movement in the far corner where there would be a bed. The rattle of a manacle, quickly muffled as the figure stilled. So he was chained to the wall. No, King Edward had no intention of allowing another escape.

I hammered on the door that had been closed behind me. My escort, who had been standing outside, opened it a fraction.

'What now? Time passes.'

'I need a candle.'

'There were no orders for that, my lady.'

'I was given permission to see him. I cannot see him without a candle. Fetch one now. Indeed, fetch two for my own safety. I cannot see my hand before my face.'

Only one arrived. Should I have been grateful for it? The horrors it illuminated were not what I would have wished to remember when I carried the flickering light closer so that I might see more than the bend of his knee, the flex of his arm behind his head. He sat up, showing me that he had been wilfully manhandled. There were the bruises that bloomed on his face, flesh swollen around one eye, hair filthy and dishevelled.

His clothes were torn and rank. Beside him there was a pot of water and a plate that might indicate that at least they were feeding him. And yes, he was chained by his ankle and wrist to the wall.

'What are you doing here?'

Not the welcome I might have expected, but in the circumstances understandable; his voice was gruff, as if ill-used over many hours. Once I would have stepped into his arms. Once I would not have questioned his loyalty and his love for me. It was all too far in my past to bother to recall. In that moment I asked myself the same question. Why had I come, since it would achieve nothing for either of us? What was I doing here? The answer came into my head. It had to be done. To make an end between us before the axe made it final, to give any final solace that it was possible for me to give. It would be cruelty for me to abandon him to this appalling isolation. And yet what solace could I offer? There was none.

I kept my distance, the candle in my hand as I governed my face and any emotions that threatened to weaken me. The room was thick with fear, with suffering, with pain. My reply was harsh because I dared not allow it to be otherwise.

'I am come to see you, because it has been allowed, but not to give you hope. I tried to plead for mercy. I have seen the King and the Queen. There will be none.'

Again the harsh croak of a response. 'I expected none. It will be better for Edward if I am dead.'

I thought he might retreat from the idea of his approaching death. I had been wrong. He accepted it. Roger continued, his voice rough with reality.

'Death is my destiny now. If I could see you plainly, I think I would see astonishment writ on your face.' He pushed himself to sit up with some difficulty and a clink of metal against

409

metal. 'Think about this, Johane. Would I wish to live out my life
incarcerated in the Tower or some distant fortress? Would I wish
to be aware, every day, that some fell hand had been sent with
a knife to end my existence and hide my body in an unmarked
grave? I would rather be dead. But you know that as well as I. If
you have been in conversation with those around you, you will
also know that the charge of treason has been carefully drawn
up. It is outrageous, but there is enough truth in it to proclaim
me guilty. I should thank you, but you should not have travelled
all this way in a lost cause. Why did you come?' And now I
heard a note of real emotion. 'I have no demands on you. I have
destroyed any claim on your loyalty to me as your husband.'

'We are still tied by law and duty. And by memories of what
we shared in the past.'

He shook his head as if to deny such ties. 'I have nothing that
I can say to you to make your visit worth its doing.' And then
after the briefest of pauses, 'Last time we talked, in the chapel
at Ludlow, you made me a promise. Will you do that one thing
for me? Only you can achieve it. That my remains be taken back
to Wigmore. That I can lie with my Mortimer ancestors in the
Abbey.'

'Yes. I remember.'

Of course it was what he would want. I had made the promise,
not seeing the end like this, or so rapidly. But I had made it.

'Will you promise me? It will give me some ease in my final
hours on this earth.'

'I will do what I can. I will speak with the King. But I cannot
promise I will have any success.'

'Thank you.'

The silence drew out between us while the candle wax fell
onto my uncovered hand. What more could be said? He had
destroyed all that held us together. In that cold, dark place I

suddenly found it difficult to draw breath. It was Roger who broke the vicious silence.

'Soon you will be free of me. You might even enjoy another marriage to a man who stays at home.' My eyes must have widened. 'Had you never thought of that? You are too valuable an heiress for the King to allow you to remain unwed. King Edward will already be looking about the Court to discover a suitable mate for you. He will want the Mortimer and de Geneville lands under his power.'

My self-control was firmly back in place.

'I must attempt to persuade the King not to honour me in such a fashion,' I said more briskly than I had intended. 'Besides, of what value would it be to him? Our estates will of a certainty be confiscated and held in the King's hands, for him to dispose of as he wishes. My fate will be irrelevant. Perhaps he has in mind a convent for me. I swear I will fight against it.'

'I doubt he will leave you landless for long.'

I would not tell him that I too was suspect. The Mortimer-de Geneville inheritance might just be lost for ever from our children.

'There is no more to say between us. Go home, Johane. I cannot regret what I did. Ambition ruled and I would not change that, nor the role that the Queen played in it. I can regret that you were hurt in the process. How many men of authority wound their wives in the doing of it? I wish it could have been better for you. We had good years and fine children.'

'You were blinded by power. Power that could never have been yours as soon as Edward grew to maturity.'

'As I knew. It was merely holding back the tidal flow of the young King's authority, and enjoying it while I could. As for the Dowager Queen ...'

I prayed that he would not speak her name. I did not need

411

her image in this cell with us. But he did. Perhaps it had to be spoken this last time.

'I needed Isabella and she needed me. And there was desire between us, I'll not deny it. It is all gone and past now.'

I stood rigidly silent and unmoving, the candle burning down, as his voice croaked into silence again. Then:

'Give me your hand.'

I did, the one that was free of the candle, as if I too were still under his command, when I was not, while he struggled to his feet. Movement was difficult for him. He kissed my fingers and then my palm, as he had at Ludlow, before releasing me and stepping back.

'Do you wear the amulet?'

'I do.' It lay, now redolent of St John's Wort, between my breasts, beneath my shift. 'It would have been better if you had kept its magical powers for your own preservation.'

He laughed softly, little more than a rusty croak. 'I fear that its efficacy would be wasted on me. Not all the magic in the world can save me now.' The laughter stopped abruptly. 'One other request...'

'There are more?'

'One more, and one that it will be easy for you to obey. Do not come to the execution, when the time comes. I do not want you there. I forbid it. If you were ever obedient to my desires, this is the time. Nor will it do you any good. Go home. Remember the good days when we rode in the hills with the hawks and the wolfhounds. When our children were small and learning to ride. Remember them. Remember the sharp griefs of our partings, and the delight in our reconciliations.'

'What will you remember on your way to your execution?' I asked with a hardness of heart that astonished me, even as I spoke the words.

How dare he wish me good memories when it all ended like this. Anger swelled within me when I thought all emotion had been wrung from me. What would he remember? Would it be the glory of the power, the delight of Isabella's body? I swore it would not be memories of me.

But Roger did not hesitate, and his answer should not have surprised me.

'I will remember the land of the Marches. When I was young. Standing on the wall-walk of Wigmore Castle with my father, dreaming of what was to come in my life, when I too was Lord Mortimer. And I will remember when you stood with me and we dreamed together.'

The candle guttered. His words had moved me unbearably.

'Then I too will remember. I will pray for you.'

'Pray that the King might yet be lenient.'

'I will.'

We still hoped for a good outcome. Or were we just playing with words, blind to the truth, to cover up the agony here between us? The candle flickered a final time and went out, plunging us both back into darkness.

His final words: 'Don't come to the execution, Johane!'

But then, as the door was opened to let me out, I heard his voice, soft from the shadows.

'I am so sorry, Johane. But my regrets make no difference, do they?'

'No. No, they do not.'

Yet at that moment I would gladly have taken away his pain and made it my own, but I could not. He must bear it himself, as he had always done.

Using sense rather than sight I stepped forward to touch his hair with my fingers, to run them down over his cheek. It reminded me of our farewells in the dark of night when he went into exile, but then there had been every chance that he would return. This was a far more desperate parting, knowing that it would be the last intimacy that we shared and I would remember it for all time.

'God be with you, Roger, to strengthen you at the end.'

My return journey by river, difficult and choppy since the tide had not turned, was one of black despair even though the moon had shredded some of the cloud. A last resort perhaps. Did I consider going to see Isabella? Did I wish to? No, and no. she had been sent under guard to Berkhamsted Castle a good score of miles outside London. She would be of no value to me in this battle for Roger's life, or his death. Indeed, she would be nothing but a hindrance.

The trial of Earl Mortimer before the lords began on the twenty-sixth day of November, a Monday. To my relief I was allowed to sit with Geoffrey in the Tower where he was kept in some comfort that had not been permitted to his father. At least he was not chained to the wall.

'I fear it will not be long,' he said when we had nothing more to say about his own health and prospect of release. That took us no time at all.

'No. It will not be long.'

The outcome could not be doubted with Lancaster and the Earls ranged against him. Geoffrey and I stood together when the news was delivered to us. Bound and gagged, so that he was unable to speak in his defence, half-blind through the hours without light, his face drawn and cruelly-lined from the interminable days without good sustenance, Earl Mortimer listened to the list of charges with no reaction. He was found guilty of all crimes given against him by the earls, barons and peers. There had never been any hope of his release. He was sentenced as a traitor and enemy of the King and of the realm, to be hanged, drawn and quartered.

Throughout the whole of it, he was not allowed to speak to defend himself.

'As if a common criminal!' I half whispered.

Not even executed. No sword or axe to put an end to his life, as any well-born traitor could expect. Roger Mortimer was to be degraded in death as punishment for his sins in life. I left Geoffrey and shut myself in my chamber at Westminster. No one disturbed me. I presume that it was the Queen who saw that I was provided with all I needed. I did not leave my chamber. I could speak to no one. It had all been expected but I was numb with shock and outrage.

It was three days, as I was told, before Earl Mortimer was taken to Tyburn, the site where criminals met their end. He was clad in the velvet glory of the same black over-tunic with embroidered hem and sleeves that he had worn at the false funeral of the second King Edward. Not that its glory remained intact for long. He was dragged through the streets, tied to an oxhide between two horses. Two miles of it across cobbles and ruts to reduce him to a mass of agony, of scrapes and bleeding and perhaps even broken bones as he was hauled over the unforgiving surface of the streets. Earl Mortimer was damaged, wounded and bruised.

I was told. I asked that Sir William Montagu be allowed to visit me and tell me what I had to know even though nausea rose in me. I would not watch, but it would be so wrong of me to let him go to his death with no acknowledgement. I knew that I could trust Sir William to give me an honest account, without pity since he had none, but perhaps with the clarity that I needed. He told me as if he were reporting on the outcome of a minor skirmish which would have no real bearing on my life.

I listened in the same manner. I suspected that he did not tell me the worst of it.

Unlike the trial, Earl Mortimer was allowed to speak, and did so. What strength of will enabled him to make his voice heard above the crowd drawn to witness his dispatch? He admitted that the execution of the Earl of Kent had been part of a conspiracy. But what of the murder of the second King Edward? He refused to speak of that.

No, I would not watch his ultimate humiliation which was not befitting a man of high blood when he was stripped naked at the last and hanged by the neck where common thieves were put to death. I could not watch, and despaired as Sir William told me of the end. I would not remember it, the terrible wanton destruction. And yet I knew that it would live with me until the day of my own death.

Instead I would remember him as he was in Ireland, setting out to wage war against the Irish rebels with the Mortimer colours spreading bravely over his head. Or riding the Marches, the wind tousling his hair and reddening his cheeks, his delight in the wolfhounds and the hawks. His love of show and fine garments. His pleasure in his rebuilding at Wigmore to make of it a palace. I remembered his voice. I remembered his love for me and the touch of his hands when he proved that love. I would remember all of that as an offering to him.

I would remember him as he had asked me to remember, when he was young and free and uncontaminated by that terrible ambition as a descendant of the mythical King Arthur. I wished he had never been told those tales of chivalric power.

I would not remember Sir William's description that I had insisted that he give, for in the end Earl Mortimer was hanged like a common law-breaker, unclothed, his body disfigured. I would not remember the agony of his death throes, nor that his body was left hanging in that ultimate humiliation for two whole days. Who would cut him down? Who would take his body to a fittingly holy place for some semblance of rest? I did not know, and I had no power to change it. King Edward's vengeance was complete. My emotions seemed of no value in the face of such suffering. Suddenly, without him breathing the same air, my life seemed empty.

I returned to Ludlow, where Lady Marguerite awaited me in my solar.

'He is dead,' she said, her face grey and drawn. A statement, not a question. She would have known in her heart, as I knew in mine.

'He is dead.'

She took me in her arms and at last I wept.

'All is over, finished. He broke my heart,' I repeated my final words to him, 'but I wish it had not been like this.'

But it was not finished. It was far from finished.

Chapter Forty-Two

Ludlow Castle in the Welsh Marches, 1331

It was not over and finished with, not by any means. All I had feared was enacted on the Mortimer family as King Edward sought his ultimate revenge, as if death were not enough. And why would Edward not demand redress? My husband had usurped his power and his authority, if not his actual crown. Had he not heaped humiliation on the young King? Thus royal retribution was played out before my eyes. The document was delivered to Ludlow, for me to see and witness. Lady Marguerite sat beside me as I read.

I was stripped of my lands and those inherited by Roger from his father. All the proud Mortimer inheritance was destroyed in a line or two of clerkish writing. All the titles, either inherited from our ancestors or acquired by one means or another during Roger's lifetime, all were gone. There was nothing for my sons and grandsons to inherit. No lands, no titles, no authority; their Mortimer inheritance was destroyed except for the name, which in many households was one of disgrace.

I dropped the document with its royal seals onto my lap and stared out of the window at the walls and the circular nave of the chapel that no longer belonged to us.

'What has he done with the body of my son?' his mother demanded of me.

The years and the strain had taken their toll on her of late, her hair severely hidden beneath her veil completely white, but the fire was back in her eyes and her voice.

What indeed.

Roger's body lay unmourned and unmarked in the Greyfriars church in Coventry. Why Coventry? Why taken there from London? We had nothing to do with such a place, which was no doubt Edward's intention. Out of sight, out of mind. There would be no significant tomb to draw attention from those who had once been Mortimer friends. The despicable Earl Mortimer would be forgotten, wiped out in history as the years marked their time. King Edward's vengeance was complete. I could have wept for my powerlessness.

To be fair to the King, he did not drive me out of Ludlow. I was to be allowed to stay, due to his grace, but it was no longer mine. The King could dispose of it as he wished. I waited for the announcement that I was dispossessed of it, and I must wed again. And who would it be? Meanwhile what of my daughters? They were not punished unduly, wed to men whom Edward had decided that he could trust. It was a relief to me that they did not suffer for Roger's sins. My son Edmund, once the Mortimer heir, could still claim his freedom. But not Geoffrey, who had been so close to Roger in those final months. He still languished, a prisoner in the Tower.

Behind and above it all, looming whenever I allowed my thoughts to stray in that direction, lurked the memory of Roger's death, as recounted to me. I had insisted that I be told. Better to know than to imagine the cruelty of it, the horror of it. Yes, the death of a traitor, but it coloured my whole life, as it was the death of someone once dearer to me than life itself. Once

419

I had loved him. With this image of a traitor's death taking precedence, I discovered a remnant of that love still remained, albeit well buried under my reluctance to admit to it. My conscience troubled me, knowing what his wishes were after his death. Did treachery and betrayal destroy any right to have final wishes fulfilled? Probably yes, but I could not accept what King Edward had done.

Thus I was driven once more to take the road to London. To Westminster. To petition the King. I might not have any true hope of success, but to do nothing was not what I could accept. At least it would lay my conscience to rest.

'You waste your time, Johane.' Lady Marguerite was nothing if not frank in her assessment of my plan. 'A long journey with no reward.'

'And if I do not try? Can I live with that? I have a promise to fulfil.'

I stood in the middle of an array of coffers and folded garments.

'What promise?'

'Between me and your son.'

'Is such a promise binding, given his betrayal of you?'

'I have asked myself the same question.'

'And what reply did you get?'

'None that makes any sense. You are still hard on your son in death.'

She turned her face away. 'He has destroyed the Mortimer family.'

'Then it is my task to resurrect it. We have enough young Mortimers who would be loyal to the King given the opportunity.'

Lady Marguerite thought about this, refolding a linen shift, although it was perfectly well folded already. She scattered a handful of dried lavender flowers between the folds.

'I will come with you,' she announced. 'You cannot suffer alone. I gave birth to him, so is not some of the blame mine? I will accompany you.'

'Indeed you will not.' I smiled at her with all the affection I would have given my own mother. 'Days in a litter will do your bones no good at all. I will go alone, morbidly in sorrow, clad in black once again. The King might have pity on a solitary widow who weeps over his feet and who looks incapable of treason.'

'The King would be a fool if he thinks you incapable of anything to which you put your mind!'

She enfolded me in her arms and pressed a kiss to my temple.

'Go with God. I will pray for you and for the success of your venture.'

There it was. One final task, to fulfil my promise to Roger. I would beg on my knees if I had to. If the Queen could do so, to petition the King for mercy, then so could Johane de Geneville, Johane de Mortimer, once Countess of March.

The Royal Palace of Westminster, Spring 1331

I was granted an audience without too much ingratiation or humiliation on my part, being kept waiting no more than a quarter-turn of the hour in an antechamber that was as cold and draughty as when I had last visited the palace. Had he expected me? Our young King had a mummer's gift for hiding his feelings and enacting a role, so I would not know.

I stood before the King, burdened as he was with more cares, although at least he now had the power to determine how they should be dealt with. He was as fair and handsomely featured as his father, but there the similarity ended. His features were stern with authority. He did not smile at me, welcome me or show any pleasure, but then I did not expect it. I did not think that he would act towards me with malice.

'Lady Mortimer. Again.'

Just the hint of wariness. At least he gave me the courtesy of the title of which he had stripped me.

'Are you here alone?' he asked. 'It is a long distance to travel.'

'I am, my lord, with an escort, of course. The roads can be dangerous for any with the Mortimer name.' I could not resist the bite of my reply. 'My son who might have accompanied me is still imprisoned by you in the Tower.'

'I presume that you did not flaunt your banners.'

'No, my lord. I was not going into battle. I am here to plead a cause in the name of peace.'

He paused, meeting my eyes, but seeing no antagonism there, he merely nodded. I curtsied, pausing before kneeling. Perhaps I would not have to do so. I would if I must.

'I suppose that I should have expected you to return,' Edward said.

Plain speaking was all I could bring to this meeting, I had decided in the days of discomfort in my litter. No pretence necessary here.

'You must indeed have expected me. There is unfinished business between us, my lord.'

'Not to my mind.'

'There is much in mine.'

'Then speak it.'

I sensed the sigh.

'The matter of my husband's trial. I understand that he was allowed no voice to answer those who tried him. He was given no legal defence. How could he conduct a defence, bound and gagged as he was? Is this legal, to condemn a man who is rendered deliberately voiceless, unable to answer the accusations made against him?'

The King's reply was brusque.

'I know all of this. What do you wish me to do? He is dead. I cannot turn back the events of the past year, even if I wished it. There was enough evidence to hang the whole Mortimer family.'

'You are unjust, my lord.'

'Then say what it is that you have come here to say.'

I sank to my knees, deciding that now would be good policy. I bowed my head.

'I plead for restitution of what rightly belongs to my family.'

All said in so few words. The King stood motionless, his hands clasped on the gold-chased buckle of his belt. He had listened to me, then kept me waiting for his reply. When he gave it, it was damning.

'This is all water under the Mortimer bridge, my lady. What value in discussing it again? Tell me what you want in plain words, but I think the answer will be no. Do stand up!'

Young Edward was short of temper this morning, but I could not wait for a more benign attitude. I did not yet stand.

'I am here to petition to have our Mortimer lands, and my de Geneville inheritance, restored to us,' I repeated. 'Mortimer titles and Mortimer lands, and my own de Geneville inheritance that I brought to that marriage. My two living sons are innocent of any treason.'

'Your sons must answer for their father's sins.'

'At least Earl Mortimer did not have your father murdered,' I announced, dangerously revealing the events of the past that King Edward would rather have masked in silence. 'That accusation was false. Imprisoned, yes, but not murdered. And as we both know, when you were told of the truth of it, that your father was still alive, you were quick to live with his apparent death and go through the mockery of his burial, because it kept your crown in your own hands.'

King Edward walked around me, almost stalking, a terrible silence loud in my ears.

'You walk on very uncertain ground, Lady Mortimer.'

'I have nothing to lose, my lord. You have made sure of that.'

'I will not restore your lands or your titles. Is that all, Lady Mortimer? Now, I have ambassadors waiting from Flanders...'

This was it at last. I had known that he would refuse, there was never any hope of his compliance, but in his refusal he might just grant me my final petition.

'No, my lord. It is not all that is on my mind, and on my heart. If you will put off the noble ambassadors for a few more moments. I have come all the way from Ludlow to request that you give me leave to take my husband's body back to Wigmore, so that he might lie at the Abbey with his ancestors. It was his wish.'

'So that he might attract those who would set him up as a martyr?' the King snapped back. 'Those who might be attracted by his power in taking control of my kingdom? I want the Marches to settle in peace, without a Mortimer allure restored to their midst.'

'Yet still I beg, my lord.'

'I cannot do it.'

'Why not? What damage would it do to you? Do you not have the power to re-inter an enemy and still keep the peace in an unsettled land? I had thought you a man of compassion. Can you not find it in your heart to treat a subject done to death by your orders with respect?'

I had asked that question once before. I would ask it again.

'I will not. I do not wish to show my enemies that I am willing to forgive and forget. I will relieve you of any further need to beg, my lady. Mortimer will remain buried in Coventry at the Greyfriars. You may go.' Yet he stepped across the divide and with a hand to my arm lifted me to my feet. 'You are a brave woman and a persistent one. I wish you a safe return, Lady Mortimer. And there is no value in petitioning my wife to speak with me. My decision is made and will stand for all time.'

'I am sorry you have no generosity towards your enemies.'

'I have none.'

'What of my son Geoffrey who still languishes in the Tower, without trial?'

'He will remain there. Until I choose otherwise.'

My final petition. All I had left.

'Then do you have any compassion towards me? I am already bereft of my lands and my titles. My younger son is in the Tower. Are you satisfied, or do you demand more from me?'

His eyes narrowed.

'To what purpose?'

'Do not, I beg of you, push me into another marriage.' I saw the shadow cross his face as if he had already considered it. 'I have had my fill of marriage. I am no traitor. I do not need a husband to keep me under surveillance.'

He turned his back on me. When he spoke it was as if it were a mere conversation.

'When Mortimer took my power and used me as a pawn in his power-games, when he lived openly with my mother in spite of the marriage vows he had made to you, yet you still met with him. What did you discuss together? Did he ask your advice? Did you give him your opinion of how he might tighten his hold on this realm? You say that you are no traitor. How do I know that? My father saw fit to imprison you when Mortimer first fled the country. Perhaps even he doubted your loyalty. It may

425

be that your remarriage would ease my mind. You are as capable of stirring up Mortimer emotions as your sons.'

The accusation took my breath but my reply came swiftly enough.

'Your father did imprison me, and my younger daughters, those he did not send to convents. It was completely unjustifiable and without any evidence. I have never worked against you. Earl Mortimer and I have children in common. It was necessary to see to their futures. We arranged their marriages, as you are well aware. When my sons died, he mourned with me. Would you expect less of a man with some degree of honour and integrity?'

'Honour? Integrity?' He swung back to face me, his face iron-hard with anger. 'I saw none of it.'

'I saw much in the early years of our marriage.'

'And what of the later years? He broke your holy marriage vows.'

'He held me when my son died. He was capable of much compassion.'

'I have said all I have to say. Good day, Lady Mortimer.'

I stopped at the door but did not turn to look at him.

'I beg of you to release my son who has never worked against you.'

Without waiting for a reply I left the room. Left London. The decisions were in Edward's hands. The remnants of the Roger I knew had all been obliterated. Perhaps something could be saved. I had planted a handful of seeds and could only hope that at least one of them would sprout a blossom.

I stared west with unseeing eyes. Perhaps it had indeed all been a waste of my time.

Chapter Forty-Three

The Church of the Greyfriars in Coventry, Spring 1332

May the Blessed Virgin be praised.

The sun had not yet risen. All was dark with darker shadows where the meagre candlelight did not quite reach between the pillars. I raised my hands in thanks to the Blessed Virgin as I stood in the Church of the Greyfriars in Coventry and watched the proceedings through the haze of my black veil. Lady Marguerite was wiping tears from her cheeks, but I would not draw attention to myself, or to what was being done here.

I had not expected it. I did not know what had changed his mind.

What was it that I watched with such a churn of emotions?

It was an exhumation. Without Mass, without prayers, without a chanted accompaniment from the friars, all was conducted in silence. The stone slabs lifted, the body below lifted out, back into the world. I held Lady Marguerite's arm to give her strength. She should not have come but had insisted despite the drag of years on her flesh and bones.

The King, regardless of all his hard words, had relented to one of my petitions. The result had brought Lady Marguerite and me to the Church of the Greyfriars in Coventry.

What had persuaded him? Was it Queen Philippa who had called on his sense of rightness, whispering in his marital ear? Was it Edward himself, accepting that Roger's trial had seen no justice in it, such a farce of a trial as it was? Not that the outcome would have been any different had he been able to speak and argue his case, but at least justice would have been seen to be done. Had the King been shamed into making one small gesture towards my pleas? Perhaps our young King had now taken on the heavy mantle of governance, accepting that the wounds of the past must be healed and much forgiven if he was to create a new kingdom, paved with gold and peace. I had always thought him to be a young man of considerable talent and much intelligence. He was beginning to make friends and smooth over the cracks of his father's reign. Forgiving Earl Mortimer was, after all, merely one tiny step in that plan. The death to which King Edward had condemned Roger had been a despicable one, as he well knew.

Of one thing I was certain. Dowager Queen Isabella had no part in this. I doubted that she would care. What a selfish love that had been. He was no longer of any value to her, alive or dead.

The King had agreed to Roger's reburial. Not in Wigmore as I wished, as Roger had wished, but to be reburied in the Greyfriars church in Shrewsbury. At least it was within hailing distance of the Marches, or the shot of a bow from an experienced archer. I had been granted permission to accompany the body, as discreetly as possible and with the smallest of escorts, and be present at the re-interment. The King wanted no attention drawn to his mercy or the re-emergence of his enemy's body. And yet he had been generous.

The body, disguised and totally anonymous in its leather wrappings, was placed in a plain wooden coffin, the rough work of some local carpenter. From there it was carried by four of the friars and placed on the bed of an even more rustic wagon which awaited us. It was barely dawn when there was no audience unless it was a man leading a pair of oxen and an elderly woman arriving to pray before the work of the day.

With the briefest of exchanges between the friars and myself and an exchange of a letter bearing the royal seal, we travelled slowly towards the west, not attracting any undue attention. I had thought of travelling by litter but horseback was a more practical mode, clad as any travelling women in cloaks and hoods on pilgrimage, riding pillion behind their grooms. We might have been any merchant's household, bent on business, except for the weapons concealed about my escort. Roger had made too many enemies in his final years to take our security for granted. What we did not do was exhibit any Mortimer colours. King Edward had forbidden it, and on this journey to Shrewsbury I was not in the mood to defy him. No one took any notice of us, not even when we put up at a common inn overnight; the covered wagon might have carried barrels of wine, except for the night-watch posted around it.

On the third day the familiar outer reaches of Shrewsbury came into sight. We crossed the bridge over the loop in the River Severn, before turning to follow its banks to where the fraternity of Grey Friars had built their church. We were expected. I was escorted into the chamber of Friar Godfrey with whom I was acquainted, while the coffin was carried to lie before the altar in the sanctuary. Our conversation was long and became somewhat heated, but not so much that Lady Marguerite and I were denied the privilege of remaining in one of their guest chambers overnight.

Next morning at dawn the friars sang Mass and the Office of the Dead, which I thought they had not done when Roger was buried in Coventry. We attended, standing just within the door. The atmosphere was heavy, the remains of Roger Mortimer an unwelcome guest. A purse of gold exchanged hands between myself and Friar Godfrey which did something to ameliorate his sour expression. He would not disobey me. I was still Lady Mortimer, Lady of Ludlow, in this part of the world. Lady Marguerite, standing beside me with sharp eyes on Friar Godfrey, merely added to the weight of the decision we had forced upon him.

Walking down the length of the church I came to a halt beside the coffin. I bent my head as if in prayer, laying my hand flat against the wood.

'I have done all in my power to keep the promise that I once made to you.'

Then I turned and walked to the door.

There was a brief hiatus but as the sky brightened, after a cup of ale in the friars' lodging, Lady Marguerite and I left with my escort and the covered wagon to continue our journey towards all the places I would call home. Friar Godfrey continued to frown as I helped Lady Marguerite into the saddle behind her groom, and I inclined my head towards him. I ignored his disapproval. He had not the power, nor in the end the desire, to stand in the way of my wishes. There was no one on the streets of the town to see or note our presence or our later absence.

Lady Marguerite put back her hood and dark veil as we left the town.

'Have we done the right thing, Johane?'

I looked across at her. She did not appear to be unduly worried.

'Assuredly we have.'

There were no doubts in my mind. I nodded across at her attendant groom. The Mortimer loyalty of our escort was without question; they were deaf and blind to any events that others might query.

'What will the King say?'

'The King will not know. And what the King does not know he will not worry over.'

Lady Marguerite smiled her compliance. We were of the same mind.

Chapter Forty-Four

Ludlow Castle in the Welsh Marches, autumn 1354

A visitor to Ludlow, causing my heart to pick up its beat. I received few visitors these days, but here today was my grandson, another Young Roger, Sir Roger as he now held claim to that title. I was sixty-eight years old, suffering the pains of old age in the winter months when the winds blew cold and frost made the rushes sparkle along the River Teme. I might be less sprightly but I was still clear in thought and relished this visit with its news from the outside world.

The years had moved on since Lady Marguerite and I had journeyed to Coventry and then to Shrewsbury together. Years of peace at home and military successes for England abroad. And some at home for me. Suddenly without warning, two years after the remains of Earl Mortimer were given into my care to be interred at Shrewsbury, King Edward had seen the error of his ways and sent me a document granting me a full pardon for the treason that I had never committed. Strangely it meant nothing to me. My conscience was clear.

What had arrived with the pardon mattered much more. It was what amounted to a letter of apology. All my property was restored to me, all the content of my dower, together with remuneration for my loss of income since the day when all had been sequestered.

I ask your forgiveness, Lady Mortimer, and trust that you can now live in comfort and peace.

It was hardly an effusive apology from the King, and there was no mention of the reinstatement of the Mortimer properties or the titles for Roger's heir, my grandson, this Young Roger who was about to cross my threshold. To my relief there had been no discussion of a remarriage for me. I could set my mind at ease and settle to live comfortably in Ludlow.

Thus, in spite of the constant scratch of our Mortimer losses, I had achieved a level of contentment in these later years although the deaths of those closest to me had brought me to my knees more than once before the altar at Wigmore Abbey. I had outlived so many of my children that grieving became a part of my life. So many lost of the twelve children to whom I gave birth: of my four sons I had outlived three; four of my eight daughters no longer lived to give me company in these later years of my own life. I would mourn them to the day of my death; Edmund my eldest son dead of a fever when visiting our manor at Stanton Lacy; Margaret my eldest daughter dead in childbirth. Young Roger of course, in the days when my Roger had come to break the news; and John, dead in the tournament in Shrewsbury. But also Joan and Isabella, and my youngest daughter Blanche, succumbing to nameless ailments and fevers for which no cure had been found.

I must give thanks for those who survived, I reminded myself daily when I knelt in prayer. Geoffrey, released quietly by King Edward, was enjoying his French inheritance, preferring not to risk another dose of captivity if King Edward ever changed his mind. My daughters Catherine, Agnes, Beatrice and Maud, all fulfilled and safe in their own families. And their children, my grandchildren, who brought me such joy.'

I had also lost the acerbic wit and comment of Lady Marguerite, a woman whose courage I had admired and whose company I valued far more than I had my own mother's. Sometimes I had to admit to loneliness, but I had something to fight for and would continue to do so, sending off an alarming number of petitions until I achieved what I had set myself to achieve. Or until death took me by the hand and led me from this life of travail.

Now I remembered the birth of this young Roger here at Ludlow as if it were yesterday, and here he was demanding admittance. I was overjoyed to see him. He looked so like his father, Edmund, the Mortimer heir who had died such a few months after that terrible death at Tyburn. When Young Roger smiled at me in welcome I saw not Edmund but Roger, Earl of March. My Roger, when he was young and we were content together. The deep brown of his eyes, like the fur of a summer bee. The glint of Irish red in his hair when the sun caught it as he dismounted. He was now twenty-seven years old, a young man in full strength and confidence as he swung down from his horse. I loved him dearly.

I waited in my solar. My days of rushing to meet guests had long gone; they must come to me, but I stood without noticeable effort and embraced him, which he accepted well enough. He had been making a name for himself in King Edward's wars in France, which he saw as the best means of re-establishing the Mortimer name.

'You look in good spirits, Grandmother.'

'My spirits are in excellent state. It is my joints that complain. I am old and creak in my bones.'

'I dare not ask your age! Would you tell me if I did?'

He grinned; he was as winsome as his grandfather.

'Certainly not. What brings you to my door?'

'Some news from Westminster.'

As my family was well aware, I had been petitioning King Edward with praiseworthy frequency, so that I was in all honesty forced to accept that the King probably wished me to perdition. It seemed wrong that the Mortimer estates should still be in royal hands and my grandson unable to inherit as was his right. I and my descendants were not daubed with the same treacherous brush as my husband had been, as Edward must know, even though I was not beyond blurring the truth of events after Roger's death.

'Good news?' I was cynical to the last. 'Has he rejected my petitions once more? I sent two last month.'

'No, Grandmother. You must have been very persuasive.'

'Are you going to tell me the news or keep me waiting until I truly die of old age?'

A warmth had begun to wrap itself around my cold heart. I knew immediately what it must be. There was only one piece of news that would bring me joy.

'Here it is. I must now address you as Dowager Countess of March.' Sir Roger bowed with flamboyant flourish and gentle malice, his hand on his heart in deepest respect. 'And I am now the Earl of March. The King has reversed the judgement on my grandfather. The estates and the titles are once more ours. The Mortimers are Lords of the Marches.'

Abruptly I sat, surprisingly emotional now that it had happened, my eyes staring unseeing once again into the savage events of the past, my hand lying loose in my lap. At last. I had achieved all that I had hoped to achieve before my own death. My grandchildren would no longer be punished for Roger's misdemeanours. All was reversed. We were forgiven, reinstated, recognised as a family of great magnates in the Welsh Marches.

'Does it please you, Countess?'

'Not before time.' I would not admit to the pleasure. 'So what persuaded him? Don't tell me that you have promised him money that you do not have, for his French wars.'

'No, it was your argument. In the end he had to see the honesty in it. Our King is a man of honour and generosity.'

'He denied me.'

'But now he sees the rightness in it.'

And I recalled the argument I had placed at his feet. Roger had been refused the freedom to speak in his own defence, rendering his trial a travesty, his guilt decided before the lords had even met. How could a man bound and gagged argue his own cause, even if that cause was suspect? It was a distortion of justice, a mockery, and should not sit well on the shoulders of a righteous King. Only on the scaffold had Roger's voice been restored to him, and then it was too late. Not that it would have made any difference, but now the King has seen the flaw in his justice. Thus the humiliating, degrading judgement given against Earl Mortimer had been finally declared void.

'Thank you.' It was all I could say.

'It was all your doing, Countess.'

I recalled my argument to a very young King almost twenty-five years before, when I had also demanded that I should not be forced into another marriage. Twenty-five years. So long ago, but now it was done. I was free to remain at Ludlow, Lady Mortimer, Dowager Countess of March. Would another marriage have given me happiness? Perhaps so, but I had had no desire for one. Nor did I seek a convent. I enjoyed keeping a close eye on the management of the estates far too much.

'I think that it has more to do with your service for the King,'

I remarked to Sir Roger after he had provided us both with a cup of wine and we had toasted our newly restored pre-eminence. I would give praise where it was due. I sat and studied him as he walked around the room. What a distinguished soldier he had become, fighting at Crecy, rewarded when made a Knight of the Order of the Garter. He had been knighted by Edward of Woodstock, the Black Prince himself. Yes, Young Roger had done far more than I to re-establish the Mortimers in royal circles. My pride in him knew no bounds. He was married to Philippa de Montagu, daughter of Sir William who had been such a hostile companion as he rode with me to Westminster when Roger's life was still hanging in the balance. They had children of their own, ensuring that the Mortimer line was safe. There would be Mortimer Earls of March far into the future.

I smiled at the thought of Young Roger's marriage with a de Montagu. There had been much rebuilding of bridges; the passage of years had helped to heal so many wounds.

'And how is Dowager Queen Isabella?' I asked with what Sir Roger would realise was not a smile, merely a twist of the lips. 'Does she remain in good health? Does she dabble in royal affairs still?'

Sir Roger lifted a shoulder in a slight shrug.

'I think not. She does not frequent Court over-much, although she is free to do so and occasionally comes to see her grandchildren. Queen Philippa makes her welcome.'

'Is she still at Hertford Castle?'

'Yes.'

She had been treated leniently, far more than she deserved to my mind. No treason. No adultery. No complicity in the imprisonment or the supposed death of her husband, the second King Edward. I wondered if she was still beautiful. She had kept her wits, it seemed.

'Do you think of her at all?'

My grandson had come to a halt in front of me to ask a question that might have elicited a painful reply from me. Did I think about her? Did I despise and detest her for what she and Roger had done to my marriage? Time might not heal completely after all, but it drew the sting.

'No. She robbed me of much happiness but the blame was not all hers.'

'It was not yours!'

'No, it was not. Your grandfather was born with ambition running like wild-fire through his blood. It drove him to decisions that had disastrous repercussions. He must bear his own blame, but I can no longer dwell on his sins, or those of Isabella.' I lifted my cup again for a second toast. 'If it were not for him, you would not be Earl of March. Let us be grateful.'

After much exchange of family gossip I had made my decision so that I stood, walked to the door, summoned my steward and began to make arrangements for horses and escort to be arranged for a short journey. Silently Sir Roger watched and listened.

'Where do you go?' he asked.

'Wigmore Abbey.'

'Is it necessary?'

'Yes.'

'The weather is not clement.'

I patted his arm. 'At my age I cannot wait for the clemency of the weather.'

'I see that you are as wilful as ever.'

'And you are impertinent.'

'Do you wish me to accompany you?'

'Yes. I think you should, now that you are Earl of March. In fact, I think that it is imperative.'

He slid a look in my direction but asked no more questions.

Wigmore Abbey: a short journey and well within my capabilities, even if I had to persuade Sir Roger that I did not need a
litter. The familiar wooded country was beginning to take on
its autumn tints and the air smelt of wood-smoke. We were
welcomed by the Abbot, as calm and gracious as ever, although
there had been changes in the clerics who served us and God
over the years. After expressing his satisfaction at our reinstatement, he left us to our own devices.

'Why are we here?' Sir Roger asked.

'To pay our respects to your Mortimer ancestors who lie at
rest here in the church.'

'I have paid my respects before. So have you. What is so
urgent now?'

'No urgency. Or perhaps there is. Come with me.'

My grandson escorted me round the tombs, along the nave
and in the chapels of the Abbey. There were more than a handful
of them, with the space for many more Mortimers. This would
be our mausoleum stretching forward into the future, whatever
happened at Court. Some were engraved slabs on the floor, some
had an effigy. Where would I lie when my time came? I could
think of worse places. I would come here with a suitable effigy,
as fine as the carved figure of my lovely daughter Blanche which
now rested in her dower church at Much Marcle.

'It is not right that my grandfather does not lie amongst them,'
Sir Roger observed, bending to inspect a long-dead Mortimer in
mailed armour and helm of at least a hundred years ago.

'True. It was his wish.'

And I promised it.

Now Sir Roger stood beside the tomb of his father Edmund,
dropping to one knee to place his hand on the cold stone effigy.
And then his uncle, another Roger Mortimer, my son who had

been brought home by my husband after his untimely death. Mortimer of Chirk was here, his combative features smoothed by the stone mason into an amiable expression that I had never seen in life. Finally his great-grandmother, Lady Marguerite, who lay serenely, carved in marble, more at ease in death than she had ever been in life, with an incised amulet carved into her clasped hands.

'I know that you petitioned that my grandfather be removed from Coventry since we had no connection with the place,' Young Roger said. 'But what happened then? I was three years old. My father died and I don't recall that it was talked of, after my mother married again. If he was moved, he was buried in Greyfriars in Shrewsbury. Is that so?'

'Yes.'

'Why would he not be brought back here?'

'You know why not, if you have any knowledge of power-play. The King was not in a forgiving spirit. He had no intention of returning your grandfather to the Mortimer heartlands, stirring up too many memories of broken promises. Better that he remain anonymous elsewhere. King Edward wanted no visits to Earl Mortimer's grave, to rouse old hostilities, or old loyalties. There would be no cult of Earl Mortimer to fire men's ambitions in the March. The King was quite adamant. It must not happen.'

We inspected the older tombs, some of them with clear names and dates, some of them not. Some small Mortimers were marked by simple slabs. I knew them well even though they were not of my own blood. They were as much mine as any de Geneville.

'Now here was a true Mortimer hero!'

Roger stood at the foot of the glorious effigy of Roger Mortimer, my Roger's grandfather whom he had admired above all men, the man who had instilled in my Roger the Arthurian legends. He still wore his mail and helm and held his sword as if he would wake with the dawn and use it in combat. His mailed feet rested on a snarling lion.

I walked on.

There was no Mortimer son of Roger and Isabella laid to rest here. I did not know where he had been buried. Perhaps it no longer mattered. Perhaps I should not have come here today. All it did was rouse old griefs. And yet I had a purpose.

Sir Roger rambled away, perhaps losing interest in the past, crouching to run his hand over his father's sword, stroking the head of another more amenable lion at his feet. I remained where I was.

'Roger,' I called.

He stood, turned his head. 'Have we finished in this place of the dead, Countess?'

I could tell that he wished himself on the move.

'Come here.'

He came back to my side. 'Are you weary? Do you wish to go home?'

I shook my head, gripping his sleeve to keep him still.

'Hear me. When I die, I wish to be buried here.'

'You will live for ever, Countess.'

'No I will not. Now listen. Do you hear me? Do you heed me? I wish my remains to be brought from Ludlow and laid here, in this place.' I pointed at the bare slab beneath my feet. 'You are the only one I can burden with this task. Will you promise me?'

'Yes. You wish to be buried here.' I could tell that he was humouring me. 'Why here?'

'It is my wish.'

'Why not next to my father, Edmund? Or even Lady Marguerite, to keep you company?'

'Here, Roger. It must be here.'

441

'Very well.' He looked down at the plain slab, next to the one on which I was standing. There was no effigy here, no decoration. 'Whose is this?'

There was one word on the slab, in deeply incised letters.

MORTIMER

I stepped to stand at its foot. 'A Mortimer. Some poor unknown from years past. We shall never know.'

'And you would be interred here, beside some unknown Mortimer, probably a man of little connection.' He knelt, his attention suddenly caught up. 'It looks newer than some, and better-quality stone, too. The name is still sharply carved.' He traced it with his hand, his fingers discovering the hard-chiselled edges. 'I don't recall it from my visits here as a child.'

'Why would you? You were very young.'

'Not so young. Was I not lectured on my family history and those who lay here in honour of the past...?' He looked up at me, brows angling a question that he did not care to ask. 'Should I know who is buried here?'

When I did not reply he unfolded the banner that had been laid across the foot of the slab. It had seen better days, the colours ravaged by weather and battle, the gilded fringing tangled and tarnished, but it was still recognisably a Mortimer device with the gold and blue. He lifted it with care, as his grandfather had once done, running his gloved fingers over the stitching. There were the blue and gold of the Mortimers together with the red lion of the de Genevilles in rampant display. It was the best work I had ever completed, the fine stitching shining through the depredations of age.

'I do not remember this either.'

'You would not. It was stitched for your father just before he went into exile. Before you were born.'

He slid a glance in my direction. 'Did you sew it?'

'I did.'

It had remained in my keeping since Roger had returned it to me with Young Roger's body. I might have burned the tapestry I created, but I would never destroy this symbol of the Mortimer-de Geneville alliance, or the sharp memory of its coming once again into my possession. My grandson stared at it. It was as if this new Young Roger was fitting together all the separate pieces of a puzzle. Then he smiled.

'I suspect that you have had more than a meddling hand in what appears to me to be a dangerous and possibly outrageous deception,' he stated.

'And you are a disrespectful grandson to speak to me in such a manner.'

But I returned the smile, holding out my hand as he rose to his feet.

'Does my uncle Geoffrey know? Do my aunts know?' he asked as he tucked my hand within his arm.

'No. Better that they do not know. Better that they believe there to be an unmarked grave in the keeping of the Greyfriars in Coventry or Shrewsbury. Better that the taint of Mortimer treason dies with Roger.' I held his gaze with mine, with all the authority I could muster. 'And with me. Roger and I will bear the blight of treason together, until we are both beyond retribution.'

It gave my grandson food for thought, his eyes dropping before mine. 'Then I pretend ignorance,' he said.

'It will be of value to all of us if you do.' Reaching up to kiss his cheek, I took from my purse on my girdle a small package wrapped in leather. 'You might like to give this to your wife.'

Unwrapped, it revealed a familiar silver brooch with its tender message: *I am a love token. Do not give me away.*

'Are you sure?'

'I am certain. It needs a good home where it will be appreciated.'

The gold amulet with its attendant sapphire I kept for myself. Who knew when I might still need it against an attack of malicious magic?

'Take this too,' I said. 'I will have no more need of it.'

I handed to him a slim damascened blade, an undecorated dagger, which he took from me, running his thumb over the blade that had not been sharpened for many a year.

'Where did you come by it?'

I shook my head, having no wish to remember it as Roger's gift when he abandoned me to go into exile, or it being returned to me over John's dead body at Shrewsbury. Some items were just too painful.

'Give it to one of your sons,' I said. 'When they are old enough to understand the value of such a weapon.'

Before we left, I replaced the old banner on the plain slab, first pressing my hand, palm down, on the cold stone. It was right. It was justice. I would control the body of the man who lay here in death even if I could not in life. He had been brought here, under my aegis, whatever the King might say. It had taken a purse of coin to persuade Friar Godfrey at Shrewsbury to agree and keep his thoughts and mixed loyalties to himself. Why would he care whether Roger lay at Coventry, at Shrewsbury or at Wigmore? Roger Mortimer, first Earl of March, was restored. He was home. And I had fulfilled my ultimate promise.

'Bury me here,' I repeated to my grandson who was named after him.

Next to him. Better there than any place else. So it would be for all eternity.

'Why did you do it?' Young Roger asked. 'Why did you defy the King so outrageously?'

When I shook my head, refusing to give him the reply he desired, he bowed in respect and left to arrange that the horses be made ready.

'Why did I do it? Why did I defy the King and bring my Lord Mortimer home?' I asked, my words dropping into the silence. 'For justice,' I told the ghosts that surrounded me. 'For justice. For memories that could not be erased by betrayal, and will live with me as long as I draw breath.'

It seemed as if the Mortimer ghosts leaned in to hear more, so I told them what they wished to hear.

'And for love.'

Acknowledgements

I have so many acknowledgements to make, and so many thanks to give:

To all at Orion Publishing who continue to make me feel so welcome.

To Charlotte Mursell, my editor, for her enthusiastic support, for her words of wisdom and endless patience when encouraging me to place emotions before the complex politics of *A Court of Betrayal*. She is right of course!

My thanks to the whole Orion Publishing Team; they have given me splendid support in the launching of the notorious Roger Mortimer and his intrepid wife Johane de Geneville.

As always, my thanks to Jane Judd, my agent, who continues to offer me her friendship and her advice through all the intricacies of the publishing world, as well as giving me the first review of my new book. She is always only a phone call or an email away. I am very appreciative.

To all at Orphans Press who maintain my website and my newsletter, and come to my aid with all the technical knowledge that I do not have.

And finally, all my thanks to the medieval Mortimers from the Welsh Marches. They are the true heroes and heroines behind *A Court of Betrayal*.

Credits

Anne O'Brien and Orion Fiction would like to thank everyone at Orion who worked on the publication of *A Court of Betrayal* in the UK.

Editorial
Charlotte Mursell
Snigdha Koirala

Copy editor
Francine Brody

Proofreader
Jenny Page

Audio
Paul Stark
Jake Alderson

Editorial Management
Charlie Panayiotou
Jane Hughes
Bartley Shaw

Contracts
Dan Herron
Ellie Bowker

Design
Tomás Almeida
Joanna Ridley
Helen Ewing
Rose Cooper

Finance
Jasdip Nandra
Nick Gibson
Sue Baker

Marketing
Ellie Nightingale

449

Sales
Jen Wilson
Esther Waters
Victoria Laws
Toluwalope Ayo-Ajala
Rachael Hum
Ellie Kyrke-Smith
Sinead White
Georgina Cutler

Production
Ruth Sharvell

Publicity
Sian Baldwin

Operations
Jo Jacobs
Dan Stevens

If you enjoyed *A Court of Betrayal*, then don't miss
Anne O'Brien's *A Marriage of Fortune!*

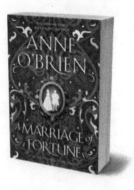

England. 1469.

A fortunate marriage will change history.
A scandal could destroy everything...

Margaret Paston, matriarch of the Paston family, knows
that a favourable match for one of her unruly daughters is
the only way to survive the loss of their recently acquired
Caister Castle. But as the War of the Roses rages on,
dangerous enemies will threaten even her best laid plans.

Margery Paston, her eldest daughter, has always strived
to uphold the Paston name and do her mother proud.
But when she loses her heart to a man below her station,
she must make a terrible choice: will she betray her
family and risk everything for a chance at true love?

Anne Haute, first cousin to the Queen, is embroiled in a
longstanding betrothal to Sir John Paston, the eldest son and heir
to the Paston seat. But despite his promises, Anne can't help but
doubt that he will ever keep his word and make her his wife...

In the midst of civil war, each of these women must decide:
Head or heart? Love or duty? Reputation – or scandal?

AVAILABLE NOW.